Outstanding [illegible]
Stephanie Barron's Jane Austen mysteries

JANE AND THE GHOSTS OF NETLEY

"One of the season's twistiest, tautest, most tantalizing tales of sleuthery!" —*Time*

"Charming!" —*Kirkus Reviews*

"Intrigue, treachery, and murder with a rousing conclusion!" —*Booklist*

"Series and historical fans are in for a treat!"
—*Library Journal*

"A wonderfully intricate plot full of espionage and intrigue. . . The Austen voice, both humorous and fanciful, with shades of *Northanger Abbey,* rings true as always. Once again Barron shows why she leads the pack of neo–Jane Austens."
—*Publishers Weekly* (starred review)

"*Jane and the Ghosts of Netley* is the best of the series— and its ending is most memorable. A fine mystery."
—*The Denver Post*

"The latest installment in Stephanie Barron's charming series is a first-rate historical mystery. Barron writes a lively adventure that puts warm flesh on historical bones. The nice thing is she does so in a literary style that would not put Jane Austen's nose out of joint."
—*The New York Times Book Review*

"With elements of an espionage thriller and a Regency romance, [this] is a book Barron fans have been awaiting. The suspense is superb. . . . Barron brings historical mysteries to a new level."
—Romantic Times Bookclub Magazine

"Barron remains true to Austen's real character . . . [and] is equally skillful in depicting the daily life of impoverished gentility during the Regency era. . . . Well worth reading." *—Deadly Pleasures*

"Stephanie Barron's series wittily blends Austen's life and her novels into satisfying mysteries and what could have been. Readers unfamiliar with the series can read this installment and enjoy it as a stand-alone story. Just be prepared to search out the other books—both Barron's and Austen's—and settle in for a long session of pleasurable reading." *—Mystery News*

"An exciting cerebral mystery thriller."
—The Midwest Book Review

JANE AND THE PRISONER OF WOOL HOUSE

"There's plenty to enjoy in the crime-solving side of Jane. . . . [She] is as worthy a detective as Columbo." *—USA Today*

"Jane Austen aficionados once again have cause to rejoice, as Barron maintains her usual high standards in this latest literary historical." *—Publishers Weekly*

"An ideal vehicle for the classic cozy murder mystery. Who knew?" *—The New York Times Book Review*

"A murder mystery for everyone . . . Barron has penned a clever mystery and a diabolical plot."
—*Old Book Barn Gazette*

"A carefully written, thoroughly researched novel . . . An enjoyable, authentic portrayal of this classic author, a strong setting and a thoroughly enjoyable plot will convert new readers to the series as well as satisfy longtime fans." —*The Mystery Reader*

"If you appreciate the literary acumen of Jane Austen the author, you might be surprised to discover you are even more entranced by Jane Austen the detective!" —*Aptos Times*

"An appealing mystery that amply repays the reader."
—*Mystery News*

"The narrative is true both to what's known about Jane's activities at the time and to her own private journalistic voice." —*The Denver Post*

"The mores and manners of Jane Austen's 19th-century world are brought skillfully to life in *Jane and the Prisoner of Wool House.* A skillfully told tale with a surprise ending." —*Romantic Times*

"[A] skillful re-creation of Austen's ethos and prose."
—*Library Journal*

JANE AND THE STILLROOM MAID

"Another first-rate addition to the series."
—*The Christian Science Monitor*

"Barron does a wonderful job of evoking the great British estates and the woes of spinsters living in that era . . . often echoing the rhythms of the Austen novels with uncanny ease."
—*Entertainment Weekly*

"Details of early 19th-century country life in all cases ring true, while the story line is clear, yet full of surprises." —*Publishers Weekly*

"Very appealing . . . As in Austen's novels, the relationships are complex and full of suppressed passion." —*Booklist*

"Barron writes with greater assurance than ever, and her heroine's sleuthing is more confident and accomplished." —*Kirkus Reviews*

"This work bears all the wonderful trademarks of the earlier titles, including period detail, measured but often sardonic wit, and authenticity."
—*Library Journal*

"Stephanie Barron does an excellent job of creating Jane Austen's world. . . . A chilling mystery with a solution that will leave you spellbound."
—*Romantic Times*

"*Jane and the Stillroom Maid* has a marvelous cast of characters. The dialogue is lively and sharp and Ms. Barron beautifully depicts the English estates and countryside." —*Rendezvous*

"Barron keeps the mystery alive until the end."
—*Murder Past Tense*

JANE AND THE GENIUS OF THE PLACE

"This is perhaps the best 'Jane' yet. The plot moves smoothly and quickly to its denouement. Barron's mysteries also educate the reader, in a painless fashion, about the political, social and cultural concerns of Austen's time. Jane [is] a subtle but determined sleuth."
—*Chicago Tribune*

"Barron artfully replicates Austen's voice, sketches several delightful portraits . . . and dazzles her audience with period details." —*Publishers Weekly*

"Barron has succeeded in emulating the writing style of Austen's period without mocking it."
—*The Indianapolis Star*

"A gem of a novel." —*Romantic Times*

"Barron tells the tale in Jane's leisurely voice, skillfully recreating the tone and temper of the time without a hint of an anachronism."
—*The Plain Dealer*

"Cleverly blends scholarship with mystery and wit, weaving Jane Austen's correspondence and works of literature into a tale of death and deceit."
—*Rocky Mountain News*

"Faithfully and eloquently recreates a time and place as well as the diary voice of one of the most accomplished women of the early 19th century."
—*The Purloined Letter*

"The skill and expertise with which Stephanie Barron creates her series featuring Jane Austen seem to get better and better with each succeeding entry. The author has attained new heights in her portrayal, with Miss Austen as observer, of a fascinating period of English history."
—*Booknews* from The Poisoned Pen

JANE AND THE WANDERING EYE

"Barron seamlessly weaves . . . a delightful and lively tale. . . . Period details bring immediacy to a neatly choreographed dance through Bath society."
—*Publishers Weekly*

"Barron's high level of invention testifies to an easy acquaintance with upper-class life and culture in Regency England and a fine grasp of Jane Austen's own literary style—not to mention a mischievous sense of fun."
—*The New York Times Book Review*

"For this diverting mystery of manners, the third entry in a genteelly jolly series by Stephanie Barron, the game heroine goes to elegant parties, frequents the theater and visits fashionable gathering spots—all in the discreet service of solving a murder."
—*The New York Times Book Review*

"Charming period authenticity." —*Library Journal*

"Stylish . . . This one will . . . prove diverting for hard-core Austen fans." —*Booklist*

"No betrayal of our interest here: *Jane and the Wandering Eye* is an erudite diversion."
—*The Drood Review of Mystery*

"A lively plot accented with fascinating history . . . Barron's voice grows better and better."
—*Booknews* from The Poisoned Pen

"A pleasant romp . . . [Barron] maintains her ability to mimic Austen's style effectively if not so closely as to ruin the fun." —*The Boston Globe*

"Stephanie Barron continues her uncanny recreation of the 'real' Jane Austen. . . . Barron seamlessly unites historical details of Austen's life with fictional mysteries, all in a close approximation of Austen's own lively, gossipy style."
—*Feminist Bookstore News*

JANE AND THE MAN OF THE CLOTH

"Nearly as wry as Jane Austen herself, Barron delivers pleasure and amusement in her second delicious Jane Austen mystery. . . . Worthy of its origins, this book is a delight." —*Publishers Weekly*

"If Jane Austen really did have the 'nameless and dateless' romance with a clergyman that some scholars claim, she couldn't have met her swain under more heart-throbbing circumstances than those described by Stephanie Barron."
—*The New York Times Book Review*

"Prettily narrated, in true Austen style . . . a boon for Austen lovers." —*Kirkus Reviews*

"Historical fiction at its best." —*Library Journal*

"The words, characters and references are so real that it is a shock to find that the author is not Austen herself." —*The Arizona Republic*

"Stephanie Barron's second Jane Austen mystery . . . is even better than her first. . . . A classic period mystery." —*The News & Observer,* Raleigh, NC

"Delightful . . . captures the style and wit of Austen." —*San Francisco Examiner*

"Loaded with charm, these books will appeal whether you are a fan of Jane Austen or not." —*Mystery Lovers Bookshop News*

JANE AND THE UNPLEASANTNESS AT SCARGRAVE MANOR

"Splendid fun!" —*Star Tribune,* Minneapolis

"Happily succeeds on all levels: a robust tale of manners and mayhem that faithfully reproduces the Austen style—and engrosses to the finish." —*Kirkus Reviews*

"Jane is unmistakably here with us through the work of Stephanie Barron—sleuthing, entertaining, and making us want to devour the next Austen adventure as soon as possible!" —Diane Mott Davidson

"Well-conceived, stylishly written, plotted with a nice twist . . . and brought off with a voice that works both for its time and our own."
—*Booknews* from The Poisoned Pen

"People who lament Jane Austen's minimal lifetime output . . . now have cause to rejoice."
—*The Drood Review of Mystery*

"A light-hearted mystery . . . The most fun is that 'Jane Austen' is in the middle of it, witty and logical, a foil to some of the ladies who primp, faint and swoon."
—*The Denver Post*

"A fascinating ride through the England of the hackney carriage . . . a definite occasion for pride rather than prejudice." —Edward Marston

"A thoroughly enjoyable tale. Fans of the much darker Anne Perry . . . should relish this somewhat lighter look at the society of fifty years earlier."
—*Mostly Murder*

"Jane sorts it all out with the wit and intelligence Jane Austen would display. ★★★ (four if you really love Jane Austen)." —*Detroit Free Press*

"Carries a rich Regency tone. The atmosphere, characters, and varying dialects come to life in unforgettable style. The mystery plot is woven with historical facts and impressive twists and turns."
—*Murder Past Tense*

Also by Stephanie Barron

Jane and the Unpleasantness at Scargrave Manor

Jane and the Man of the Cloth

Jane and the Wandering Eye

Jane and the Genius of the Place

Jane and the Stillroom Maid

Jane and the Prisoner of Wool House

And coming soon in hardcover from Bantam Books

Jane and His Lordship's Legacy

Jane and the Ghosts of Netley

~ Being a Jane Austen Mystery ~

by Stephanie Barron

BANTAM BOOKS

NEW YORK • TORONTO • LONDON • SIDNEY • AUCKLAND

JANE AND THE GHOSTS OF NETLEY
A Bantam Book

PUBLISHING HISTORY
Bantam hardcover edition published June 2003
Bantam mass market edition / May 2004

Published by
Bantam Dell
A Division of Random House, Inc.
New York, New York

ISBN 0-553-58406-5

Manufactured in the United States of America
Published simultaneously in Canada

OPM 10 9 8 7 6 5 4

For Phil and Linda
and
for my uncle Frank J. MacEntee, S.J.

Thanks for all the pilfered stories.

Jane and the Ghosts of Netley

Chapter 1

Bare Ruin'd Choirs

Tuesday, 25 October 1808
Castle Square, Southampton

~

THERE ARE FEW PROSPECTS SO REPLETE WITH ROMANTIC possibility—so entirely suited to a soul trembling in morbid awe—as the ruins of an English abbey. Picture, if you will, the tumbled stones where once a tonsured friar muttered matins; the echoing coruscation of the cloister, now opened to the sky; the soaring architraves of Gothick stone that oppress one's soul as with the weight of tombs. Vanished incense curling at the nostril—the haunting memory of chanted prayer, sonorous and unintelligible to an ear untrained in Latin—the ghostly tolling of a bell whose clapper is muted now forever! Oh, to walk in such a place under the chill of moonlight, of a summer evening, when the air off the Solent might stir the dead to speak! In such an hour I could imagine myself a heroine straight from Mrs. Radcliffe's pen: the white train of my gown sweeping over the ancient stones, my shadow but a wraith before me, and all the world suspended in silence between the storied past and the prosaic present.

Engaging as such visions must be, I have never ventured to Netley Abbey—for it is of Netley I would speak, it being the closest object to a romantic ruin we possess in Southampton—in anything but the broadest day. I am far too sensible a lady to linger in such a deserted place, with the darkling wood at my back and the sea to the fore, when the comfort of a home fire beckons. Thus we find the abyss that falls between the fancies of horrid novels, and the habits of those who read them.

"Aunt Jane!"

"Yes, George?" I glanced towards the bow, where my two nephews, George and Edward, surveyed the massive face of Netley Castle as it rose on the port side of the small skiff.

"Why do they call that place a castle, Aunt? It looks nothing like."

" 'Tis a Solent fort, you young nubbins," grunted Mr. Hawkins, our seafaring guide. "Built in King Henry's time, when the Abbey lands were taken. In a prime position for defending the Water, it is; they ought never to have spiked those guns."

"But we have Portsmouth at the Solent mouth, Mr. Hawkins," Edward observed, "and must trust to the entire force of the Navy to preserve us against the threat from France." The elder of the two boys—fourteen to George's thirteen—Edward prided himself on his cool intelligence. As my brother's heir, he was wont to assume the attitudes of a young man of fortune.

My nephews had come to me lately from Steventon, after a brief visit to my brother James—a visit that I am certain will live forever in their youthful memories as the most mournful of their experience. I say this without intending a slight upon the benevolence of my eldest brother, nor of his insipid and cheeseparing wife; for the tragedy that overtook our Edward and George was entirely due to Providence.

Nearly a fortnight has passed since a messenger out of Kent conveyed the dreadful intelligence: how Elizabeth Austen, the boys' mother and mistress of my brother Edward's fine estate at Godmersham, had retired after dinner only to fall dead of a sudden fit. Elizabeth! So elegant and charming, despite her numerous progeny; Elizabeth, unbowed as it seemed by the birth of her eleventh child in the last days of September. The surgeon could make nothing of the case; he declared it to be improbable; but dead our Lizzy was, despite the surgeon's protestations, and buried she has been a week since, in the small Norman church of St. Lawrence's where I attended her so often to Sunday service.

I suspect that too much breeding is at the heart of the trouble—but too much breeding is the lot of all women who marry young, particularly when they are so fortunate as to make a love-match. Elizabeth Bridges, third daughter of a baronet, was but eighteen when she wed, and only five-and-thirty when she passed from this life. With her strength of character, she ought to have lived to be eighty.

It remains, now, for the rest of us to comfort her bereaved family as best we may. My sister Cassandra, who went into Kent for Elizabeth's lying-in, shall remain at Godmersham throughout the winter. Dear Neddie bears the affliction with a mixture of Christian resignation and wild despair. My niece Fanny, who at fifteen is grown so much in form and substance as to seem almost another sister, must shoulder the burden of managing the younger children, for the household is without a governess. There is some talk of sending the little girls away to school, that they might not brood upon the loss of their mamma—but I cannot like the scheme, having nearly died when banished as a child to a young ladies' seminary. The elder boys, Edward and George, endured their visit to brother James at Steventon and appeared—chilled to the bone with riding next to Mr. Wise, the coachman—on Saturday. They are bound for their school in Winchester on the morrow.

Their happiness has been entirely in my keeping during this short sojourn in Southampton. I have embraced the duty with a will, for they are such taking lads, and the blight of grief sits heavily upon them. They forget their cares for a time in playing at spillikins, or fashioning paper boats to bombard with horse chestnuts. The evening hours, when dark descends and memory returns, are harder to sustain. George has proved a restless sleeper, crying aloud in a manner more suited to a child half his age. He will be roundly abused for weakness upon his return to school, if he does not take care.

My mother, I own, finds the boys' spirits to have a shattering effect upon her nerves, which invariably fail her in moments of family crisis. No matter how diligently Edward might twist himself about in our reading chairs, engrossed in *The Lake of Killarney,* or George lose a morning in attempting to sketch a ship of the line, their exuberance will drive my mother to her bedchamber well before the dinner hour, to take her evening meal upon a tray.

Yesterday, I carried the boys up the River Itchen in Mr. Hawkins's skiff, and stopped to examine a seventy-four that is presently building in the dockyard there.[1] The place was a bustle of activity—scaffolding and labourers vied for place in a chaos of scrap wood and iron tools—and left to myself, I should not have dreamt of disturbing them. But under the chaperonage of Mr. Hawkins, a notorious tar known to all in Southampton as the Bosun's Mate, we received a ready welcome from the shipwright. Mr. Dixon is a hearty fellow of mature years and bright blue eyes who takes great pride in his work.

"Miss Austen, d'ye say?" he enquired sharply over our introduction. "Not any relation to Captain Francis Austen?"

"I am his sister, sir."

"Excellent fellow! A true fighting captain, or I miss my mark! And no blubberhead neither. You won't find Frank Austen playing cat-and-mouse with Boney; goes straight at 'em, in the manner of dear old Nelson."

"That is certainly my brother's philosophy. You are acquainted with him, I collect?"

"Supplied the Cap'n with carronades last summer, as he could not secure them in Portsmouth," Mr. Dixon replied. "He should certainly have need of them, once the *St. Alban's* reached the Peninsula. A great hand for gunnery, your brother. Now! What shall we find to engage the interest of these young scrubs, eh?"

[1]A third-rate ship carrying 74 guns, this was the most common line-of-battle vessel and a considerable number were built during the Napoleonic Wars; by 1816, the Royal Navy possessed 137 of them. They weighed about 1,700 tons and required 57 acres of oak forest to build.—*Editor's note.*

He scrutinized my nephews' faces, well aware that nothing more was required to command their full attention than the spectacle of the seventy-four.

The great third-rate towered above our heads, her keel a massive construction of elm to which great ribs of oak were fixed. She was nearly complete, the decks having been laid and the hull partitioned into bulkheads, powder magazines, storerooms, and cabins, with ladders running up and down. The Itchen yard is ideally suited for such a ship, for the river water flows in through a lock, and the finished vessel may float down to Southampton Water in time.

"Jupiter!" Edward exclaimed. "Isn't she a beauty, though! How long have you been a-building?"

The shipwright gazed at his work with ill-concealed affection. "Nearly three years she's been under our hands, and you shall not find a sweeter ship in all the Kingdom. No rot in her timbers, no crank in her design; and we shan't hear of this lady falling to pieces in a storm!"

"Are such things so common?" I murmured to Mr. Hawkins.

The Bosun's Mate glowered. "Have ye not heard of the Forty Thieves, ma'am? All ships o' the line, built in rotten yards? Floating coffins, they were—though I served in no less than five of 'em."

"Good Lord."

"When is she to sail, Mr. Dixon?" George enquired.

"We expect to launch her at Spithead in the spring. Perhaps your naval uncle will have the command of her! Should you like to look in?"

"*Should* we!" the boy replied. "Above all things!"

"Jeremiah!" Dixon called. "Yo, there—Jeremiah! Now, where is that Lascar?"

A dark-skinned, lanky fellow with jet-black hair ran up and salaamed, in the manner of the East Indies. A Lascar! The boys, I am certain, had never encountered a true exotic of the naval world—one of the renowned sailors of the Seven Seas. I smiled to see Edward's expression of interest, and George's of apprehension.

"Jeremiah at your service," he said, with another low bow. "You wish to see the boat, yes?"

Mr. Dixon slapped my nephews on the back so firmly George winced. "Get along with ye, now. The Lascar won't bite. Refuses even to touch good English beef, if you'll credit it; but he's a dab hand with a plane and a saw."

Nearly an hour later we bid Mr. Dixon goodbye, and Mr. Hawkins turned his skiff towards home. Yesterday's water party proved so delightful, however—so exactly suited to my nephews' temperaments and interests—that on this morning, their last day of liberty, I was determined to get them once more out-of-doors.

THE ABBEY RUINS, AND THE SCATTERED HABITATION that surrounds them, lie southeast of Southampton proper, just beyond the River Itchen. In fine weather, of a summer's afternoon, one might walk the three miles without fatigue; but with two boys on my hands, and the weather uncertain, I had thought it wiser to make a naval expedition of our scheme. As the diminutive craft bobbed and swayed under the boys' restless weight, I feared I had chosen with better hope than wisdom.

"Sit ye down, young master, and have a care, or ye'll pitch us all over t'a gunnels!" Mr. Hawkins growled at George. Mr. Hawkins is not unkind, but exacting in matters nautical. I grasped the seat of George's pantaloons firmly; they were his second-best, a dark grey intended for school in Winchester, and not the fresh black set of mourning he had received of our seamstress.

The Bosun's Mate maneuvered the skiff into a small channel that knifed through the strand, and sent the vessel skimming towards shore. Above us rose Netley Cliff, and the path that climbed towards the Abbey.

"That'll be Netley Lodge." Hawkins thrust a gnarled thumb over his shoulder as he rowed, in the direction of a well-tended, comfortable affair of stone that hugged the cliff's edge. "Grand place in the old days, so they say, but nobody's lived there for years."

"And yet," I countered as the boat came to rest on the shingle, "there is a thread of smoke from two of the four chimneys."

The Bosun's Mate whistled under his breath. "Right you are, miss! Somebody has opened up the great house—but who?"

"Perhaps a wandering ruffian has taken up residence," George suggested hopefully.

Mr. Hawkins shipped his oars. "Beyond is the village of Hound—nobbut a few cottages thrown up, and scarce of folk at that, what with the war. They'll know in Hound who've lit the fires at t'a Lodge."

A freshening wind lifted Edward's hat from his head, and tossed it into the shallows; he scrambled from the boat in outraged pursuit.

The Bosun's Mate sniffed the salt air. "Weather's changing. 'Twon't do to linger long, Miss Austen, among those bits o' rubble. I'll bide with a friend in

Hound while ye amuse yerselves at t'Abbey." He tossed a silver whistle—the emblem of his life's ambition—into George's ready hands. "Just ye blow on that, young master, when ye've a mind to head home. Jeb Hawkins'll be waiting."

THEY RAN AHEAD OF ME, STRAIGHT UP THE PATH, IN A game of hunt and chase that involved a good deal of shrieking. I very nearly called after them to conduct themselves as gentlemen—my mother, I am sure, would have done so—but I reflected that the path was deserted enough, and the boys in want of exercise. In such a season the visitors to Netley must be fewer than in the summer months, when all of Hampshire finds a reason to sail down the Water in search of amusement. The summer months! Even so! I had visited Netley last June in the company of the vanished Elizabeth—charming as ever in a gown of sprigged muslin, with a matching parasol. Elizabeth, who would never again walk with her arm through mine—

I breasted the hill, and caught my breath at the sight of the Abbey ruins: the church standing open-roofed under the sky; the slender shafts of the chancel house and the broken ribs of the clerestories; the grass-choked pavement of the north transept; and the cloister court, where wandering travellers once knocked at the wicket gate. A tree grows now in place of an altar. Ivy twines thick and green about the arched windows, as though to knit once more what the ages have unravelled. A futile hope: for all that time destroys cannot be made new again, as my poor George and Edward have early discovered.

The boys plunged into the ruined church, and

continued their game of pursuit; I proceeded at a more measured pace. I have come to Netley often enough during my residence in Southampton, but familiarity cannot breed contempt. This place was built by the good monks of Beaulieu in 1239, and throve for more than three hundred years as only the Cistercian abbeys could: wealthy in timber, and in the fat of the land; a center of learning and of prayer. There are those who will assert that by the reign of King Henry the Eighth, prayer was much in abeyance; that but a single volume was found in the library at the Abbey's dissolution; and that the monks were more eager to ride to hounds—hence the name of the neighbouring hamlet—than to offer masses for their benefactors. King Henry dissolved the monasteries of England in 1537, and with them, Netley; and the yearly income from all the property thus seized was in excess of a million pounds. Henry used his booty to political effect, rewarding his supporters with rich grants of land; and Netley Abbey was turned into a nobleman's manor.

There is an ancient legend in these parts that one wellborn lady, forced into the veil, was walled up alive in the Abbey walls; but though many have searched for the lady's tomb, no one has ever found it. There are stories, too, of scavengers among the Abbey's stones, struck dumb and blind in attempting to lift what was not theirs. Whether haunted or no, the manor did not prosper, and ended, with time, as a blasted testament to King Henry's ambition.

I have long been partial to the Roman Catholic faith, as the object of devotion of no less a family than the Stuarts: maligned, neglected, and betrayed by all who knew them. I must admit, even still, that Henry's seizure of monastic property, and its eventual decay, has proved an invaluable contribution to the beauties of the English landscape.[2]

Do spirits walk among the fallen timbers of this house? Do they mourn and whisper in the moonlight? I have an idea of a shade, poised upon the turret stair, her white habit trailing.

Absurd, to feel such a prickling at the neck in the middle of the day—to pace insouciantly down what had once been a sacred aisle, as though under the gaze of a multitude; to listen attentively to birdsong, aware that the slightest alteration of sound might herald an unwelcome intruder. Ladies have often called upon the ghosts of Netley—there is nothing strange in this. . . .

In the distance, I heard young Edward's shout of triumph and George's, of despair. The birds continued to sing; a shaft of sunlight pierced the ruined window frame, and a breath of wind stirred the ivy. I traversed the south transept and turned for the turret stair, which winds upwards into the sky—the turret itself having crumbled—and gives out onto the Abbey's walls. Here one may walk the perimeter of the ruin, with a fine view of the surrounding landscape. My head into the wind, I paced a while and allowed myself to consider of Elizabeth.

I am not the sort to indulge in grief; I have known it too often and too well. The older I become—and I shall be three-and-thirty this December—the more I take Death in my stride. I have not yet learned, however, to accept the caprice of its whims—nay, the absurdity of its choice, that would

[2] The opinion given here is a rough paraphrase of sentiments Jane first expressed at the age of sixteen in her *History of England, by a Partial, Prejudiced, and Ignorant Historian.—Editor's note.*

seize a young woman of health, beauty, prospects, and fortune, a young woman beloved by all who knew her—and yet leave *Jane*: who am possessed of neither fortune nor beauty nor a hopeful family. I live as but a charge upon my relations.

Would I, in a spirit of sacrifice, exchange my ardent pulse for Lizzy's silent tomb? If a bargain could be made with God—a bargain for the sake of young Edward and George, or the little girls so soon to be shut up at school—a bargain for dear Neddie, crushed in the ruin of his hopes—would I have the courage to strike it?

I cast my eyes upon the flat grey sheen of Southampton Water—on the smoking chimneys of Hound, tumbling towards the sea; on the distant roofs of Southampton town, glinting within its walls. Dear to my sight, who am selfish in my grasp at life. *Forgive me, Lizzy. Though I loved you well, I cannot wish our lots exchanged.*

The boys' voices had grown faint. Thunder pealed afar off, from the easterly direction; the unsteady day had dimmed. I descended the turret stair, grasping with my gloved hands at outcrops of broken stone, and sought my charges in the ruined refectory.

This was a groined chamber seventy feet long, lit by windows on the eastern side. For nearly three hundred years the Cistercians had dined here in silence, with their abbot at their head. The remains of a fresco adorned one wall, but the fragile pigments had worn to nothing, and the saints stared sightless, their palms outstretched. The refectory was empty.

Or was it?

Just beyond the range of vision, a shadow moved. Light as air and bodiless it seemed, like a wood dove fluttering. My heart in my mouth, I swiftly turned; and saw nothing where a shade had been.

The sound of a footfall behind me—did a weightless spirit mark its passage in the dust?

"Have I the honour of addressing Miss Austen?"

I whirled, my heart throbbing. And saw—

Not a ghost or envoy of the grave; no monk concealed by ghoulish cowl. A man, rather: diminutive of frame, lithe of limb, with a look of merriment on his face. A sprite, indeed, in his bottle-green cloak; a very wood elf conjured from the trees at the Abbey's back, and bowing to the floor as he surveyed me.

"Good God, sir! From whence did you spring?"

"The stones at your feet, ma'am. You *are* Miss Austen? Miss *Jane* Austen?"

"You have the advantage of me."

"That must be preferable to the alternative. I am charged with a commission I dare not ignore, but must require certain proofs—*bona fides,* as the Latin would say—before I may fulfill it."

"Are you mad?"

He grinned. "I am often asked that question. Would you be so kind as to reveal the date of your honoured father's death?"

Surprise loosed my tongue. "The twenty-first of January, 1805. Pray explain your impudence."

"Assuredly, ma'am—but first I crave the intimate name of Lady Harriot Cavendish."

"If you would mean Hary-O, I imagine half the fashionable world is acquainted with it. Are you quite satisfied?"

"I should be happy to accept a lady's word." He bowed again. "But my superiors demand absolute surety. Could you impart the title of the novel you sold to Messrs. Crosby and Co., of Stationers Hall Court, London, in the spring of 1803?"

I stared at him, astonished. "How come you to be so well-acquainted with my private affairs?"

"The title, madam."

"—Is *Susan*. The book is not yet published."[3]

"Just so." He reached into his coat and withdrew a letter, sealed with a great splotch of black wax. "I hope you will forgive me when you have read *that*."

I turned over the parchment and studied the seal. It was nondescript, of a sort one might discover in a common inn's writing desk. No direction was inscribed on the envelope. I glanced at the sprite, but his raffish looks betrayed nothing more than a mild amusement.

"I have answered your questions," I said slowly. "Now answer mine. What is your name?"

"I am called Orlando, ma'am."

A name for heroes of ancient verse, or lovers doomed to wander the greenwood. Either meaning might serve.

"And will you divulge the identity of these... *superiors*... for whom you act?"

"There is but one. He is everywhere known as the Gentleman Rogue."

Lord Harold Trowbridge. Suddenly light-headed, I broke the letter's seal. There was no date, no salutation—indeed, no hint of either sender's or recipient's name—but I should never mistake this hand for any other's on earth.

[3] Austen wrote the manuscript entitled *Susan* in 1798 and sold it to Crosby & Co. for ten pounds in the spring of 1803. The firm never published it, and Austen was forced to buy back the manuscript in 1816. It was eventually published posthumously in 1818 as *Northanger Abbey*. —*Editor's note.*

From the curious presentation of this missive, you will apprehend that my man has been instructed to preserve discretion at the expense of dignity. I write to you under the gravest spur, and need not underline that I should not presume to solicit your interest were other means open to me. Pray attend to the bearer, and if your amiable nature will consent to undertake the duty with which he is charged, know that you shall be the object of my gratitude.

God bless you.

I lifted my gaze to meet Orlando's. "Your master is sorely pressed."

"When is he not? Come, let us mount the walls."

Without another word, he led me back to the turret stair, and up into the heights.

"There," he said, his arm flung out towards Southampton Water. "A storm gathers, and a small ship beats hard up the Solent."

I narrowed my weak eyes, followed the line of his hand, and discovered the trim brig as it came about into the wind.

"Captain Strong commands His Majesty's brig *Windlass.* My master is belowdecks. He asks that you wait upon him in his cabin. He has not much time; but if we summon your bosun and the two young gentlemen, and make haste with the skiff, we may meet his lordship even as the *Windlass* sets anchor."

"You know a great deal more of my movements, Orlando, than I should like."

"That is my office, ma'am. He who would serve as valet to Lord Harold Trowbridge, must also undertake the duties of dogsbody, defender—and spy." He threw me a twisted smile; bitter truth underlay the flippant words.

"His lordship does not disembark in Southampton?"

"He is bound for Gravesend, and London, with the tide. You will have read of the family's loss?"

I reflected an instant. "The Dowager Duchess?"

Lord Harold's mother, Eugenie de la Falaise, formerly of the Paris stage and wife to the late Duke of Wilborough, had passed from this life but a few days ago. I had admired Her Grace; I mourned her passing; but I could not have read the *Morning Gazette*'s black-bordered death notice without thinking of her second son. It had been more than two years since I had last enjoyed the pleasure of Lord Harold's notice; and though I detected his presence from time to time in the publicity of the newspapers, I have known little of his course since parting from him in Derbyshire.

"Had the dowager's death not intervened, his lordship should have come in search of you himself. But Fate—"

"Fate has determined that instead of Lord Harold, I am treated to an interview with his man," I concluded. "Pray tell me, Orlando, what it is that I must do."

Chapter 2

Beauty's Mask

25 October 1808, cont.

~

I CANNOT SAY HOW ORLANDO HAD ACHIEVED NETLEY Abbey, for I espied no stranger's dory hidden along the shingle as we hurried in the direction of Mr. Hawkins. The falling dark and spitting rain hastened our footsteps, but still the old seaman was there before us, in attendance upon his sturdy craft—George having blown his whistle manfully for the better part of our descent. The Bosun's Mate's surprise at finding a fourth among our party was very great. He glowered at the green-cloaked sprite, and said by way of greeting: "I'd a thought you had more sense, miss, than to take up with strangers."

"Mr. . . . Smythe . . . is a very old acquaintance—fortuitously met on our road to the Abbey."

Orlando bowed; the Bosun's Mate scowled.

"We have suffered an alteration in our plans, Mr. Hawkins," I said. "Would you be so good as to intercept that naval vessel presently dropping anchor in Southampton Water? I should like to be swung aboard."

"Swung aboard!" George cried. "Oh, Aunt—may we bear you company? I should dearly love to set foot in a fighting ship!"

"It is not to be thought of," I replied briskly. "Your grandmamma will be every moment expecting you."

"But—*Aunt*!"

"The young gentlemen, Mr. Hawkins, should be conveyed at once to the Water Gate Quay, and thence to Castle Square."

Edward and George groaned with disappointment; the Bosun's Mate stared keenly across the Solent. "That brig is never the *Windlass*? She didn't ought to be in home waters; ordered to the Peninsula in July, she was, and not expected back 'til Christmas."

"You know the better part of the Captain's orders," Orlando observed quietly, "but not, I think, the whole of them."

Mr. Hawkins cleared his throat and spat. "It's a rum business, all the same. Get into the boat wi' ye, Mr. Smythe—and haul an oar if ye've a mind to reach that brig by nightfall."

IT WAS NEARLY DARK AS THE SKIFF PULLED ALONGSIDE the *Windlass*, and though a brig will never equal a ship of the line, the sides of the vessel soared above our tiny craft. Edward stared; George's mouth was agape; and at a blast of Mr. Hawkins's whistle, a lanthorn appeared at the rail. The bosun's chair was let down. From the speed and efficiency of these movements, I judged that we were expected—nay, that we had long been observed in our passage up the Solent, and the chair readied against my arrival.[1]

"Shall you be quite safe, Aunt?" George's voice quavered.

"Safe as the Houses of Parliament, my dear."

Edward frowned. "What must we tell Grandmamma?"

"That an acquaintance of your Uncle Frank—an officer of the Royal Navy—had news of him that could not wait."

"You're bamming," George scoffed.

"I shan't be above an hour; but you are *not* to put off dinner."

I had suffered the bosun's chair before, in being swung aboard my brother's commands; but never had I attempted the exercise in darkness. Orlando hastened to assist me.

"I'll see the young gentlemen safe at home," Hawkins said, "but I'll return, miss, to ferry you to shore. Friends or no friends, I'm loath to leave you with this crew. Lord knows what they might get up to."

A jeering laugh from above put paid to his sentiments; at a word from Orlando, I was borne aloft. I gripped the chair's rope in one gloved hand, and with the other, waved gaily to my nephews; but in truth, I was wild for them all to be gone. I could think

[1] The bosun's chair was formed of a simple board, rather like the seat of a swing. Sailors used it when repairs aloft were necessary; but it was frequently employed to assist ladies up the side of a ship, as they could not be expected to mount rope ladders while wearing skirts. —*Editor's note.*

only of the man who waited within, by the light of a ship's lanthorn.

"MY DEAR MISS AUSTEN."

He received me quite alone, in Captain Strong's quarters, where a handsome Turkey carpet vied for pride of place with a folding desk. He had been absorbed in composing a letter, but rose as though he had long been in the habit of meeting me thus, and not a stranger these two years. His grey eyes were piercing as ever, his silver hair as full and shining, his looks more engaging than I had seen them last—and his whole figure such a blend of elegance and arrogance, that I felt I had never been truly admiring him before with justice.

He grasped my gloved hand and raised it to his lips. "How fortunate that Orlando should have chanced to find you."

"I suspect that Orlando does nothing by chance."

"But for a lady to answer such a summons so swiftly must be extraordinary. I am in your debt, Jane. Are you well?"

"As you see. I need not enquire after *your* health, my lord. The Peninsula clearly agrees with you."

His eyes glinted. "The Peninsula? Have you busied yourself with researches? What else have you learned?"

"Nothing to the purpose. I was as astonished at your man's appearance as anyone could be."

"And yet you hastened aboard—to my infinite relief." He lifted my chin and studied my countenance. "You are a trifle peaked, Jane, even by lamplight. I cannot approve the shadows under your eyes."

"I have had a good deal on my mind of late."

"So have we all. You should not wear black, my dear—you are far too sallow to support the shade. Willow green, I think, or Bishop's blue." His gaze roved over my figure. "Bombazine! But surely you are not in mourning?"

"My brother Edward has been so unfortunate as to lose his wife."

"Not Mrs. Elizabeth Austen? Of Godmersham Park?"

I inclined my head. Lord Harold had been privileged to meet Lizzy once, during a flying visit to Kent in the summer of 1805; she had bewitched him, of course, as she had everyone who knew her.

"Such a pretty woman! And hardly out of her youth! It does not bear thinking of. Childbirth, I suppose?"

My countenance must have turned, for he said abruptly, "Forgive me. I ought not to have pried. But I was never very delicate where *you* were concerned."

"I understand that you have lately suffered a similar bereavement. I was most unhappy to learn of Her Grace's passing."

"It was not unexpected, Jane—but it could not have occurred at a more troubled season."

"My lord, why are you come to Southampton?"

"In pursuit of a woman," he replied thoughtfully. "A beautiful and cunning creature I should not trust with a newborn kitten. I am hard on her heels—and but for this matter of death rites, should have subdued her long since."

Whatever I might have feared—whatever I might have expected—it was hardly this. I was overcome, of a sudden, by foolish anger; hot tears started to my eyes.

"You asked that I dance attendance—cut short

my nephews' pleasure party, confound my friends, and be swung aboard your ship—so that you might boast of your conquests? Good God, sir! Have you no decency?"

"What a question for *Jane* to pose," he replied brusquely. "You must know that I abandoned decency for necessity long ago. My every thought is bent upon Sophia. When you have seen her, you will comprehend why. She is magnificent—she is perilous—and I shall not rest until I have her in my grasp."

I turned for the cabin door. "It is no longer in my power to remain, sir. Be so good as to summon a party of seamen to convey me to the Quay."

"Have you heard of the Treaty of Tilsit, Jane?"

My hand on the latch, I stopped short.

"—the document forged last year between the Tsar of All The Russias, and the Emperor Napoleon? The treaty sets out, in no uncertain terms, the division of Europe between the two powers. It describes the destruction of England."

"I have heard the name."

"It is for Tilsit I was sent to Portugal. It is for Tilsit that good men have died—nay, shall yet die in droves—on the Iberian Peninsula. Are you not curious to learn more of such a potent subject?"

"My brother convoyed the English wounded from Vimeiro," I said faintly. "He delivered French prisoners to Spithead as recently as September."[2]

"It shall not be the last time." Lord Harold's voice was sharp with weariness. "Come away from the door, Jane. We have much to discuss."

[2] The British army engaged the French at Vimeiro, Portugal, on August 21, 1808. It was the first British conflict on the Peninsula, and a decisive victory.—*Editor's note.*

• • •

It is now nearly a twelvemonth since Napoleon Buonaparte placed his brother Joseph upon the throne of a unified Iberia—a move occasioned by the sudden descent of French soldiers on their trusted allies' soil. At the close of last year, the Spanish king fled to Paris; and though the Portuguese crown declared war on England, Buonaparte pronounced the kingdom null and void regardless. The Portuguese royal family chose exile in Brazil, their fleet escorted by Britain's Royal Navy—which did not care to see good ships fall into the Monster's hands.

The Chief Secretary for Ireland, Lieutenant General Sir Arthur Wellesley, urged our current government to challenge the French on behalf of the Iberians.[3] The decision to invade was seconded by the Navy, which yearned to deny Buonaparte use of Lisbon's deep-water harbour. Thirdly, the lives of British subjects were at issue, for the town of Oporto is overrun with Englishmen engaged in the Port wine trade. The idea that purveyors of domestic comfort—so vital, now that the wine from French vineyards is denied us—should be abandoned to the Enemy, aroused indignation in every breast.

Public sentiment on behalf of ports, Port, and the Portuguese ran so high that Sir Arthur sailed from Cork in July and touched first at Corunna and Oporto, where the British and natives alike regarded him as a liberator. I know this not merely from official accounts forwarded to London newspapers, but

[3] Wellesley was thirty-eight years old in 1808, and would make his career in the Peninsular War. He was eventually created the Duke of Wellington, and confronted Bonaparte for the last time at Waterloo in 1815.—*Editor's note.*

from my brother Frank, who escorted Sir Arthur's troopships to the Portuguese coast.

By the first week in August, however, Wellesley's fortunes were in decline. He found himself at the head of some thirteen thousand men, but short of cavalry mounts and supply waggons—and on the very eve of Vimeiro, superseded in his command by the arrival of no less than *six* superior generals, despatched by a nervous Crown.

Frank's ship, the *St. Alban's,* stood out to sea off the heights of Merceira, and witnessed the French attack on the twenty-first of August. In the event, Sir Arthur proved too clever for Marshal Junot, who was thoroughly routed; but Generals Burrard and Dalrymple, Wellesley's superiors, declined to pursue the retreating Enemy. As the *St. Alban's* carried off the wounded English and the French prisoners, the British commanders signed a document of armistice, allowing the defeated Junot to send his men, artillery, mounts, and baggage back to France—*in British ships.*

Public reaction to this infamy was so violent, that Dalrymple, Burrard, and Wellesley were called before a Court of Enquiry in September. King George censured Dalrymple; Parliament denounced the armistice. My brother fulminated for weeks against the stupidity of landsmen. Sir Arthur Wellesley, though protesting that he deplored the armistice, had signed the document—and thus shared his superiors' disgrace.

Nothing would answer the public outcry so thoroughly as a re-engagement on the Peninsula, with the Honourable General Sir John Moore, a celebrated soldier, at the head of a stout army. The General is presently encamped with twenty-three thousand men somewhere near Corunna; and we live in daily expectation of victory.

"Buonaparte has quit Paris," Lord Harold told me, "and is on the road for Madrid. He intends to join Soult, wherever the Marshal is encamped."

"I should not like to be in Sir John Moore's shoes."

"Of course not—your own half-boots are far more cunning, Jane, though they *are* black. But do not pity General Moore. There has not been such a command for a British officer since the days of Marlborough."

"You believe, then, that we shall drive the French out of Portugal and Spain?"

"On the contrary: I hope that we are mired in the Peninsula's muck for years to come. Only by forcing the Emperor to engage us on land, can we divert him from his mortal purpose—the destruction of England's Navy, and with it, England herself."

I laughed at him. "Do not make yourself anxious, my lord. The Royal Navy should never accept defeat."

"Fine words, Jane. But you laugh at your peril. Buonaparte knows that he cannot prevail so long as England has her Navy; we know that England cannot survive so long as France possesses Buonaparte, and his Grand Armée. To defeat us, the Monster must seize or build more ships than we command: he cannot hope to destroy the Royal Navy with less than two vessels for every one of ours."

"But Buonaparte thinks like a grenadier, not a sailor. Consider Trafalgar! French ships—aye, and Spanish, too!—routed, captured, or sunk!"

"Buonaparte has learned Nelson's lesson. He will build more ships. Tilsit provides him with all that he requires: the timber of Europe—the labourers of a continent—and the command of every dockyard from Trieste to Cuxhaven. It is merely a matter of time before we fall to the French."

I was silent an instant in horror. "But what is to be done?"

"Only the impossible. We must draw off the Monster—we must throw bodies into the Peninsula, into the maw of Napoleon's cannon—to buy time for the Crown. We must bend all our energy towards outwitting the Enemy's spies, by land or by sea. That is why I sailed to Portugal a year since—and why I am come tonight in haste to Southampton, in pursuit of a dangerous woman."

THE SHIP'S BELLS TOLLED THE WATCH; A CAVALCADE of pounding feet outside the cabin door heralded the end of one crew's vigil above decks, and the commencement of another's. The brig rolled gently beneath my feet, a movement as mesmerising and soporific as Lord Harold's voice. I had lost reckoning of time as surely as I had lost the will to leave him. My mother, Castle Square, the bereaved boys... all had vanished, insubstantial as a whiff of smoke.

Lord Harold moved to the cabin's stern gallery, his gaze fixed on the lights of Southampton that twinkled now across the Water. When he spoke, it was as though to himself alone—or to some shadow present only in memory.

"Did I understand what she was, that first night I saw her? Did I recognise the cunning behind Beauty's mask? August 1807, the Governor-General's ball, Oporto. Well before the fall of the Portuguese crown, or the siege of the English colony. She wore *capucine* silk, and a demi-turban of the same hue.[4] Ravishing, that heated colour entwined in her dark hair, suggestive of the seraglio. One could hardly glimpse her countenance for the sea of gentlemen pressing their suit."

I had an idea of the scene: a vivid swarm of English and Portuguese, the warmth of August, the mingled scents of sandalwood and tuberose in the humid air. Her cheeks would be flushed with heat and admiration; her gaze, despite the press of other men, would find Lord Harold's. Were they worthy of each other? Both strong-willed, calculating, careless of opinion? The attachment must be immediate. Did he dance with her that night, under the Iberian moon?

"We were introduced by the Governor-General himself—Sophia simpering at her old friend, allowing her hand to linger a trifle too long in the roué's paw. *He knew my late husband,* she told me a little later, *in the days when I was happy.*"

"She is widowed, then?"

"Three years now, and left with considerable wealth, if the French do not strip her of it. I should judge her at present to be not much older than yourself, Jane—but she has ambitions the like of which should never stir in your quiet breast."

What would you know, my lord, of a lady's ambitions? What can you perceive of Jane? I thought. But I said only: "You mistrust her—and yet, there is admiration in your voice."

"Does the hussar respect his opponent, as the sabre whirls overhead?" he demanded impatiently. "Of course I admire her. Sophia Challoner possesses

[4] Burnt orange.—*Editor's note.*

the wit and courage of a man, honed by a woman's subtlety."

"And is it the subtlety you cannot forgive—or the wit, my lord?"

"That is ungenerous." A spark from those cold grey eyes, disconcertingly akin to anger. He deserted the stern gallery and threw himself into a chair.

"She came to me the morning after the ball, and invited me to tour the Port factory in her phaeton. The late Mr. Challoner, you will comprehend, was a considerable merchant in the trade. His two nephews manage the business on Sophia's account—"

"She has no children?"

"Challoner was an elderly man when she beguiled him, Sophia no more than seventeen; an early trial of her powers. The nephews, prosperous young men, are divided between admiration of her charms and distrust of her motives. Challoner left all his property—including his business concerns—to Sophia alone. The nephews, naturally, had lived in expectation of the inheritance."

"I perfectly comprehend the circumstances."

"She was utterly charming that morning: entertaining me with good jokes and stories of the Oporto worthies; driving her pair with a competent hand; leading me with authority through the warehouses and the aging casks. I did not perceive it at the time—but she acted by design. She hoped to gain my confidence and, with a little effort, my heart."

"She had tired of playing the widow?"

"Sophia never plays at anything, Jane—except, perhaps, at love. In all else, she moves with deadly earnest. No, it was not marriage she desired—but intimacy."

"And is this the full measure of her guilt, my

lord? That she presumed to trifle with Lord Harold's heart?"

"She is guilty of *treason,* Jane," he returned harshly. "Nothing more or less than the absolute betrayal of all our trust and hope."

"That is a perilous charge to level at any Englishwoman."

"Well do I know it! But I have my proofs. The French instructed Sophia Challoner as to my true purpose in descending upon Oporto. She understood that I was sent to observe the weakening of Portuguese resolve—the betrayal of the Crown's trust—and the purpose in French guile. She knew that I was in daily communication with the British Government. Her object, in mounting a flirtation, was to pry loose my secrets—and sell them to the Monster."

"But why, my lord? Why should any child of Britain so betray her duty to the King?"

His gaze darkened. "I do not know. Out of love, perhaps, for a ruthless Frenchman? Or is it mere jealousy that drives me to suspect that the Enemy owns her heart? Does she move me still, though I apprehend what she is? Hell's teeth, Jane, but I have been a fool!"

He looked so miserable—nay, so shaken in his own confidence—that I grasped his hand tightly in my own. "What have you done, my lord?"

"I have talked when I should not. I have trusted too easily. I have allowed myself to be flattered and deceived."

"Then you have been a man."

He lashed me with his eyes. "When I quitted your side in September of 1806, I was in considerable torment."

I knew that he spoke the truth; I had witnessed his attempt to win the heart of an extraordinary young woman—Lady Harriot Cavendish, second daughter of the Duke of Devonshire. He had failed, and for a time, had disdained Society.

"Sophia, with her considerable arts, perceived how I might be worked upon." His voice was raw with bitterness. "I was too susceptible; I gradually fell into her thrall. She was—she *is*—beautiful, possessed of superior understanding, and careless of the world's opinion. She is also brutal, calculating, and governed solely by interest. If she possesses a heart, I have not found it."

"And yet—the affair did not endure. Your eyes were opened to her true character?"

"Vimeiro opened them, Jane."

"Our victory over the French? Was Mrs. Challoner cast into despair?"

"Not at all. Vimeiro was her finest hour! All of England wonders at the easy terms of the armistice: that the French were allowed to depart the field with their lives and goods intact, escorted home in British ships. What the public cannot know is that the dishonourable document, that has proved the ruin of Generals Dalrymple and Burrard, was forged at the insistence—the wiles—the subtle *persuasion* of Sophia Challoner, who seduced Dalrymple even as she dallied with me!"

"Then it is Dalrymple, my lord, and not yourself who must be called the fool."

He released my hand and rose restlessly from his chair. "Jane, when I encountered them together, I behaved as a jealous lover. I very nearly called Dalrymple out—nearly killed the man in a duel!—when I should have divined immediately how much the wretch had betrayed."

"The armistice is over and done these two months at least," I cried. "Do not goad yourself with painful memories!"

"Do you think that one battle makes a war? Even now, Sir John Moore and the thousands of men under his command await the brutal blow that Marshal Soult must deliver. Moore does not know where Soult is encamped; he must outmaneuver and outmarch a chimera. Intelligence of the Enemy is absolutely vital—as is complete disguise of Moore's intentions. Can you guess, Jane, what should be the result if our General's plans were delivered to the French?"

"Is that likely?"

"I live in dread of its occurrence. That is why I have come to Southampton."

"Leagues upon leagues divide the Channel from the Peninsula, my lord."

"But the Peninsula's most potent weapon—Sophia Challoner—is *here,* Jane," he said softly. "She quit Oporto in a Royal Navy convoy this September, and has taken up residence in her late husband's house."

I revolved the intelligence an instant in silence. "Can even such a woman do harm from so great a distance?"

He took my face between his hands and stared into my eyes. "That, Jane, is what I intend for you to discover."

Chapter 3

Voices in the Wind

25 October 1808, cont.

~

"...WET THROUGH TO THEIR UNDERGARMENTS, AND what the Master of Winchester will say when we return them in such a state—ague or worse, if I'm not mistaken—I cannot think. Two boys, exposed to the dangerous night air and the perils of Southampton Water after dark—! What if one of them should suffer an inflammation of the lungs? How shall I face my dear Edward? *His heir,* perhaps, taken off by a chill, only weeks after the death of his poor, poor wife! It does not bear considering, Jane!"

"Yes, Mamma," I replied steadily, "but the boys enjoyed their adventure, and Mr. Hawkins pressed his oilskins upon them during the journey home. We are likely to find that *he,* unfortunate man, suffers an inflammation of the lungs."

I had achieved Castle Square at the disreputable hour of eight o'clock, to discover dinner consumed, the boys in their bath, and my mother in high dudgeon. My dear friend Martha Lloyd, who forms a vital part of our household, ordered tea at my arrival and set about heating a brick in the embers of the fire. I was grateful for her presence. Although she took no part in the present dispute, her efficient bustle must serve as relief.

"What has Mr. Hawkins to do with it?" Mamma's looks suggested apoplexy. "Mark my words, Miss Jane, you shall come to no good end! To follow the whims of a stranger—to board an unknown ship—is what I cannot like! You might have suffered all manner of abuse—been carried off without a word of warning—and ended a captive in a sultan's harem! You are far too trusting and too independent of convention for your own good. People will talk. At your age, and with your unfortunate history, you cannot be too nice in your habits."

My history, as my mother would term it, has been characterised by a penchant for stumbling over corpses that even I have begun to regard as a morbid hoax of Fate. It is true that my study of murder commenced with the refusal of the most respectable offer of marriage I had ever received—in December of 1802—and my mother might be forgiven for drawing the obvious conclusion: that my taste for Scandal has driven away all my suitors. Several years had lately intervened without the presentation of a body, however; and I dared hope that I was quite free of the blight.

"Captain Strong was anxious that news of Frank should be conveyed to poor Mary," I observed mildly, "and his First Lieutenant, Mr. Smythe, was most pressing in his invitation to come aboard. Perhaps I ought not to have accepted the invitation—"

"No lady of delicacy should have done so."

"—but I understood that the Captain must sail with the tide. Imagine my suspense! I was every moment believing that Fly had been wounded—or taken ill—or even, God forbid . . ."

"But as your brother is merely three days out from Portsmouth, Captain Strong excited your worst fears to no purpose," my mother rejoined crossly. "You have lost your heart to that Lieutenant, I'll be bound. What is his name?"

"Smythe. He is perfectly respectable, Mamma, and by this hour, is safely at sea."

"You were always a girl to set your cap at the most disreputable sort of person—first Tom Lefroy, an *Irishman,* by my lights; and then that abominable smuggler who went by the name of Sidmouth—"

"How I detest that phrase, Mamma! *Setting one's cap.* It is so decidedly vulgar."

"Not to mention the *gentleman* whose name I vowed should never more be suffered to pass my lips."

She referred, of course, to Lord Harold Trowbridge—whose attentions she had long misapprehended as a seducer's. My mother's hopes warred with her disapproval of Lord Harold in this; for like any sensible widow left with two spinsters on her hands, she longed to see the family's fortunes made through a brilliant and unexpected alliance. However dreadful his reputation, Lord Harold was yet a duke's son.

How shall I learn anything of Mrs. Challoner? I had asked him as he stood by the brig's rail, preparing to bid me farewell.

She lives in a place called Netley Lodge, he replied. *A grand old manor near the Abbey ruins. You must have observed it. . . .*

I had, indeed—but a few hours before. And wondered at the smoke curling from the disused chimneys. Martha reached now for my untouched tea and replaced it with a glass of Port. "For medicinal purposes, Jane. I should not like you to catch cold. Your spencer is wringing with wet, my dear."

"As are your nephews' heads!" my mother snapped.

"I shall undertake to write a letter to the Master of Winchester"—I sighed—"informing him that Edward and George may prove a trifle delicate in coming days. Dr. Mayhew must be aware of Elizabeth's passing, and his sympathies will be already excited on the boys' behalf. They may be spared the worst of Winchester for at least a week."

Martha snorted. "I should judge them hearty enough. They were spraying the scullery with hot bathwater when I left them, exuberant as two whales."

LATE THIS EVENING, ALONE AT LAST IN MY OWN BEDchamber, I built up the fire to a good blaze, drew off my stained gown, and laid my damp spencer by the hearth to dry. It was impossible not to think of him: at Gravesend, perhaps, or sailing past Greenwich. If the brig had made good time, he might even now be arrived at Wilborough House. The great limestone façade would be draped in black, the lanthorns shuttered.

"My mother is to be interred on the morrow," he had said, "and by Thursday or Friday at the latest I shall be returned to Southampton. Orlando stays behind—I shall put him off with Mr. Hawkins this very hour. He is to engage a suite of rooms at the Dolphin Inn against my return."

"Why cannot Orlando watch Mrs. Challoner in my stead?"

"Because he is known to her as my manservant," Lord Harold said quietly. "I do not want her to apprehend, at present, that she moves under my eye. Do you dabble in watercolours, Jane? Or sketch a little, perhaps?"

"A very little—but I am no proficient, sir. It is my sister who possesses that art."

"Then you might borrow her paintbox and easel, and set up in the ruins. Be seized by a fine passion for ancient habitation and lost sacerdotal faith. Spend hours—fortified by a suitable nuncheon—in the environs of Netley Abbey. Contrive to keep a weather eye on all activity at that house."

"So that I might learn . . . what, my lord?"

"How Sophia Challoner intends to despatch her intelligence to France."

"And if it rains?" I enquired with asperity.

He threw back his head and laughed. "You might beg shelter from the dragon. She will entertain you charmingly, I am sure."

I had written only the previous day to my sister Cassandra at Godmersham, but the habit of communication is strong, and I could not douse my candle without conveying a little of the boys' adventures at the Abbey. No word should pass my lips, however, of my encounter with Lord Harold; Cassandra required diversion amidst her painful duties, not a further increase of anxiety. She never heard news of the Gentleman Rogue with equanimity.

. . . the scheme met with such success that I fear young George might run off to sea, if his taste for Winchester does not increase. Mr. Hawkins allowed them to take the oars on the voyage home, and both are now possessed of sizeable blisters on their palms. Our nephews should not part with them for the world, and shall probably earn the esteem of their fellows, when once they are returned to school. . . .

A boy cried out in his sleep, tortured by nightmares. I raised my head from my letter and felt the stillness of the house. It must be George. Did he dream of his mother? And did she walk tonight among the ruins of an abbey?

"Aunt Jane!"

The voice was deep and fluting by turns, the voice of a boy on the verge of manhood. I turned towards the doorway, and discovered Edward standing there—his taper, lit from the lamp left burning in the hall, trembling in the draughts. He looked ghostly and forlorn in his long striped nightshirt, his grey eyes shadowed. Edward, whom I had considered too stoic for nightmares.

"What is it, my love? You should not be awake."

"Might I have a drink of water? The pitcher in our room is bone dry."

I laid down my pen and reached for the earthen jug that sat on the dressing table. "Then pray avail yourself of mine. You do not suffer from fever, I hope, as a result of your drenching at the Abbey?"

He shook his head, and took the proffered cup.

"Was that you I heard, calling out in your sleep?"

"The wind howls so—it woke me, Aunt. I hear voices crying."

I searched his countenance. He was not a youth to bare his soul. Even when his father's letter from Godmersham arrived, with an account of his mother's funeral service, Edward had read over the whole without flinching. It was George who had sobbed aloud.

"There are voices in the wind, I tell you." The grey eyes slid up to my own. "I heard a woman cry. And the wail of a baby. Aunt Jane—is my brother well? My youngest brother?"

The child whose birth had somehow killed his mother.

I brushed back the tumble of hair at his forehead. His skin was clammy with nightmare. "Your Aunt Cassandra wrote that Brook-John is thriving. It was not his voice you heard, Edward, nor was it your mother who wailed. You must imagine her free of all care and pain, my dearest. You must imagine her—*happy*."

He drained the last of my water and silently returned the cup. I could not believe my words had convinced him. His mother's first joy had always been her family. How now, divided from all she held dear, could Lizzy find solace in the Lord?

"It seems a chilly sort of faith," Edward said.

Chapter 4

Cat and Mouse

Wednesday, 26 October 1808

~

LORD HAROLD'S FEAR—THE SPUR THAT HAD DRIVEN him to Southampton despite the claims of family duty—urged the most serious consideration. I had meant to be up at dawn, in preparation for a morning's work of sketching among the ruins—though what argument I should offer my mother on behalf of such a scheme, I could not think. I was prevented this essay in prevarication, however, by the combined application of Fate and Habit: the former being the tendency of public conveyances to break down, and the latter, my excellent parent's inclination to fancy herself ill.

She kept to her room before breakfast, but as there was nothing surprising in this, I saw no cause for alarm. It was Martha's office to disabuse me.

"Your mother, Jane, believes she has taken an inflammation of the lungs," she said as we settled ourselves at the table. "She ascribes it to the quantity of moisture introduced into the atmosphere of the house last evening, and her exposure to Mr. Hawkins. The Bosun's Mate, I am persuaded, resides in a *most* unhealthful part of town."

"He never does!" George cried in outrage. "He is a famous fellow, and cleaner than Grandmamma by a mile!"

"That will do," I told him sternly. "Apply yourself to your toast. I should judge your Grandmamma to be merely tired." Privately, I recognised a tendency to believe herself ill-used, and a determination to cause as much trouble as possible for everybody, but saw no occasion to abuse the lady before her relations.

"She has a decided cold in the head," Martha supplied, "and I have begged Cook to provide her with a hot lemon cordial—though where we are to find lemons in such a season, I am sure I do not know. You might carry the boys to the docks this morning, Jane, and discover whether there is an Indiaman at anchor; they are sure to have preserved lemons aboard, against the scurvy."

The boys whooped; my heart sank. Much as I loved them, I felt a more pressing claim upon my attentions this morning. I had meant to ask Martha to take them in charge—but could hardly do so *now*. Martha was always my mother's favourite nurse; she had learned the art at the bedside of her own dying parent, and would be much in demand for the rest of the day.

We had settled it among ourselves that the boys should be sent back to school after an early dinner, so as to enjoy to the full their final hours of liberty. But as we carried the teacups into the scullery, amidst much scolding from Cook, a messenger arrived from Roger's Coachyard requiring us to present our charges early, as the conveyance intended for the four o'clock stage had suffered a split in its axle-tree.

"Places for the noon stage are sure to be hotly contested," I observed as I herded my nephews up the stairs. "We must set about packing."

A quantity of goods flew into the boys' trunks—mourning clothes fresh from the tailor, academic robes, stray books and spillikins, horse chestnuts and toy boats, along with a tidy box of confections prepared by Martha's hands in the Castle Square kitchen, against the scanty commons likely to be afforded them hereafter. Half-past eleven found us hurrying through town to Roger's, hallooing for Mr. Wise to secure the young gentlemen's seats beside him on the box. It is George's greatest ambition to someday win admittance to the Whip Club, and he is zealous in observing what masters of the art fall in his way—though Mr. Wise is *quite* elderly, and must disappoint with his care and steadiness.[1]

We were in good time to witness the arrival of the London mail, and with it, a quantity of disembarking strangers. It was unlikely I should discover any acquaintance among their ranks—the mail being the lowest, and least preferred, form of transport available—but my eye wandered over them all the same.

[1] The Whip Club was known after 1809 as the Four-in-Hand Club, and was comprised of a fashionable set of gentlemen who emulated the skill of public coachmen by handling the reins of four horses driven as a team. They met quarterly for group driving expeditions and wore white drab driving coats with numerous capes, over a blue coat and a striped kerseymere waistcoat in yellow and blue. Membership was based upon the skill of the driver and was thus highly exclusive. —*Editor's note.*

A few women I judged to be superior domestics, or the wives of shopkeepers; a middle-aged clerk; a common seaman returned from leave; and a young man—a young man so extraordinarily handsome, and genteel in his looks, that I all but gasped aloud to see him emerge from such a conveyance.

He was fair-haired and blue-eyed, his countenance fresh and open; and there was an air of easy competence in his figure as he gazed about the bustling coachyard. His clothes were good, though hardly fashionable. I judged him not much above twenty, and country-bred—the younger son of a gentleman, perhaps, intended for the Church.

"Is it rooms yer wanting, sir?" enquired Mr. Roger in his brisk and friendly way, as the gentleman's trunks were let down from the coach. "Or perhaps a hack?"

"An inn, I guess."

The drawling voice fell strangely on my ears; the elegant young man was an *American.* They washed ashore in Southampton on occasion, but such as I had observed were merchant seamen who haunted the quayside. This man was gently-bred, accustomed to ease, and nice in his manners. Distinctly an oddity; and all my assumptions regarding him must be false. Being an American, he might be anything—it was impossible to judge.

"There's the George," Mr. Roger ticked off rapidly, "the Star, the Vine, the Dolphin, and the Coach & Horses. Shouldn't think you'd be comfortable at the last, but any of the others'd do. The Dolphin's a bit dear," he added doubtfully.

"Let's say the Vine, then," returned the stranger.

"What name shall I give the trunk-boy?"

"Mr. Ord."

At that moment, the horn blew for the Winchester stage. I had just time enough to press my nephews to my breast, button Edward's cloak more firmly under his chin, adjust the angle of George's hat, and give them each a gold guinea forwarded by their father—when they scrambled up to the box.

"Farewell, Aunt!" Edward cried, "and a thousand thanks for your kindness!"

Something of last evening's nightmare trembled for a moment in his youthful voice. Then the coachman cracked his whip; the horses surged forward; and the stage bore north, towards the toll road.

I watched them out of sight. George grinned and waved to the last.

When I looked about the yard once more, the American was gone.

LORD HAROLD MIGHT AIRILY SUGGEST THAT I KEEP Mrs. Challoner under my eye, but he can have known little of the surrounding landscape, or the distance to be bridged between Castle Square and Netley Lodge. Several choices were presented me: to walk the three miles to the Abbey—a fine course in good weather, and of an early morning, but not at the hour of one o'clock, with the resumption of last night's rain ever threatening; to hire a hackney chaise, and arrive at the Abbey in style; or to avail myself once more of Mr. Hawkins. My purse being, as always, quite slim, I chose the Bosun's Mate rather than the more costly hired chaise. Approaching the Abbey by water had an added advantage: I should land below the ruins, and walk directly past Netley Lodge on my way up the hill.

"Miss Lloyd did ought to boil these lemons in a

quantity of gin, and dose the old lady—your honoured mother, beggin' yer pardon, miss—every second hour," Hawkins declared as he heaved at his oars. He had procured the fruit from a moored Indiaman as readily as I might pluck daisies from the back garden. " 'Tis a remedy no seaman would be without, when the catarrh and the megrims strike. If the lemons don't do for her, the gin surely will; there's nothing equal to Blue Lightning for clearing the head."

The tide was with us today, and carried us swiftly down the Water. As we neared the landing thrust out into the shingle, I stole a glance at Netley Lodge, where it rose like a snug bastion from the cliff above. The leaded windowpanes, staring south, gleamed in the watery sunlight. I had an idea of flurried housemaids unleashed upon a suite of rooms.

"And so the Lodge is opened up," Mr. Hawkins observed, "after more'n ten year of dust and desolation. My crony in Hound told me the whole of it yesterday. The gentleman as owned it made a fortune in the Peninsula, and died before he saw his home again. Merchant, he was, in the Port trade, and his lady were carried out of Oporto after the siege. Right thankful she is to be back on English soil."

"Indeed? Is she a comfortable matron, with a hopeful family?"

"Neither chick nor child, and her a Diamond o' the First Water. So Ned Bastable says—he being rated Able thirty years or more, and a rare one for intelligence now he's turned on shore.[2] His granddaughter

[2] Seamen in the Royal Navy were designated Ordinary or Able, depending upon their level of skill and experience. Able Seamen were paid slightly more than Ordinary.—*Editor's note.*

Flora is parlour maid at the Lodge. She were snapped up ten days ago by Mrs. Challoner's steward, a great chuckle-headed lump with a black beard and a name Flora can't pronounce. The lady's maid is French, Flora says, and speaks not a word of the King's English; but quite superior, and knows how to keep her place. Three large trunks it took, to stow Mrs. Challoner's gowns; the maid spent the better part of two days putting 'em to rights. They're a queer lot at the Lodge, and no mistake."

"And is Mrs. Challoner quite alone in that great house?"

"She wishes to live retired, after all the crush and noise of the Oporto colony. She's a widow, after all—though she don't dress in black."

The gates to the sweep were thrown open, and the gravel newly raked; lights were kindled within the rooms; and a pair of under-gardeners toiled at scything the withered lawn. I dared not linger before the prospect of Netley Lodge, however intriguing, for I could not tell how many pairs of eyes might be directed at the Abbey path. I grasped my easel in gloved fingers and strolled steadily past, the poke of my bonnet eclipsing any view of the rooms. Where should I position myself? At the breast of the hill, so that I might observe both the Abbey ruins and the house below? I should be unlikely to overlook the sweep and carriage court from that vantage, but no other should serve—

The sound of hoofbeats, thudding dully on the damp turf under my feet: a horse was galloping from the direction of West Wood, the dense growth of trees at the Abbey's back. In another moment the rider came into view, bent over the reins with an expression of wild elation on his countenance. The hair under his black top hat was fair as the sun, his body was taut and controlled in the saddle; every feature proclaimed nobility. He must have come from the Itchen ferry, along the path I should have walked, had time and the weather permitted.

He swept towards me, a figure of surprising power. In the grip of the horse's punishing stride, he was as different from the modest young man I had seen in Roger's Coachyard as man could be—but it was the American stranger, just the same: the gentleman called Ord.

He slowed as he passed, and raised his hat with civil grace; but I heard the breath tearing in his lungs. His countenance was flushed, his blue eyes alight. He had ridden hard for the sheer joy of freedom after the cramped journey in the London mail, I thought; he had hired a mount at the Vine Inn and coursed out towards the Abbey, it being the principal beauty in these parts.

Or was his direction spurred by more than a young man's high spirits? Was he driven by fear and peril—by the wicked goad of statecraft? As I watched, he pulled up before the gates of Netley Lodge and jumped down from the saddle. Without a backwards glance, he led his mount up Mrs. Challoner's new-raked sweep.

Curious, indeed, that within an hour of alighting in Southampton, the fresh-faced stranger had sought first to meet with one woman: Lord Harold's dangerous spy.

Chapter 5

Flames in the Night

26 October 1808, cont.

~

"THERE IS A LETTER FROM GODMERSHAM," MARTHA informed me in a lowered voice as I entered the house this evening, "that has your mother in an uproar. Only think: Your brother Edward has offered her a freehold—a cottage, to be sure, but a freehold all the same—on one of his estates. She has merely to name her choice. Wye, in Kent, or Chawton Cottage, near Chawton Great House. It is something to think upon, is it not?"

"A freehold!" The easel and paintbox slipped from my hands onto the Pembroke table. It was nearly four o'clock, and my mother should be awaiting her dinner; I had found it necessary to appear in good time this evening, as recompense for past sins. But my thoughts were all of Netley, and the interesting meeting I had witnessed there; Martha's present communication came to me as from the moon.

"Rents in Southampton are only increasing, and now that Frank and Mary have settled on the Isle of Wight—"

"Indeed." My brother Fly and his young family had quitted the Castle Square house nearly a month before, to establish an independence in rented lodgings on the Island, as naval officers will refer to the turtle-shaped bit of land opposite Portsmouth Harbour. My mother was ill reconciled to the change; and though Frank professed himself determined to meet his portion of the Castle Square rent, as well as that of his new home, we would not hear of burdening him. I knew, however, that we should be hard-pressed to scrape together the yearly rent.

"But another removal of the household!" I sighed. "Shall we ever be at peace, Martha?"

"If you accept your excellent brother's offer—perhaps." She looked at me seriously. "And, Jane: if either establishment proves too cramped for the addition of a fourth, pray do not hesitate on my account. I shall shift for myself. I am quite equal to it."

"Out of the question, my dear. We cannot do without you."

Martha smiled—though tremblingly—and went in search of Edward's letter while I divested myself of spencer and bonnet. To leave Southampton, a mere eighteen months after achieving Castle Square! But a freehold—what that should mean to my mother, and to our general comfort! I might live once more in a country village, and watch the seasons change without the glare and tumult of a city. Either position would prove to our advantage, for Wye has all the charm of proximity to Godmersham, and Edward's dear little children; while Chawton Cottage should be close to our steady acquaintance in Hampshire. And Henry, my beloved elder brother, had lately opened a branch of his bank in the town of Alton, but a mile from Chawton Great House—

"Poor Edward!" I mused as I rewound a bit of black ribbon through my hair, "to think of *us,* in the depth of all your misery. Amiable soul, to work for our welfare when your own is so thoroughly destroyed!"

"MARTHA TELLS ME THAT YOU HAVE BEEN *SKETCHING,* Jane, at Netley Abbey! That is a queer start for one of your age," my mother exclaimed. She had thrown off the threat of pulmonary inflammation on the strength of Edward's communication, and had consented to rise for dinner. "You are missing Cassandra, perhaps, and intend to conjure her in memory!"

"I am quite accustomed to missing Cassandra—she is more often in other people's houses than her own. I merely observed, in walking through the ruins yesterday, a picturesque that cried out to be seized on paper."

"Your love for that old Abbey certainly increases! Or was it the hope of meeting a certain Lieutenant, and captivating him with your skill in paint, that drew you there?"

"Are you much improved in health, Mamma?" I enquired.

"Let me see what you have done, my girl. Fetch your work!"

Surprised, I rose to retrieve my sketchbook from the hall table. I had managed to establish myself on the promontory above the footpath, and had remained there nearly two hours, despite a chilling wind. I was anxious to learn whether Mr. Ord should remain at Netley Lodge but a half-hour—as befitted a slight acquaintance—or an entire afternoon. His great black horse had not yet reappeared when the lateness of the hour urged me to collect my paints and summon Mr. Hawkins.

"There is only a very little . . . I merely attempted to capture a likeness . . ." I faltered, as she turned over the two poor watercolours I had achieved.

"You will never exhibit Cassandra's talent, I fear—but we cannot all be everything, Jane. Cassandra is a beauty, and you are a wit; she paints, as Beauty must, while you sharpen your pen and commit the world to paper." She patted my cheek with sudden fondness. "I hope you are not entertaining morbid thoughts of conversion to Rome—of walling yourself up in the living grave of a French convent!"

"Indeed I am not, ma'am."

"Jane?" Martha gasped in incredulity. "The good sisters should all revolt within a twelvemonth!"

"You wrong me, Martha. I do crave a bit of solitude and peace—a walled garden, perhaps, if not a cell—in which I might revolve the simple tales my mother pretends to praise."

For want of a kerchief, my parent pressed her napkin to her eyes. "You may be forced all too soon, Jane, to give up this cunning town and bury yourself in the country. Martha has told you of your brother's letter?"

"A freehold! Dear Edward! That he should think of *us*!"

"Pity he did not choose to do so long since—that we might have been spared the pain of so many removals! First Bath—then Southampton—and now—God knows where."

"Chawton or Wye, Mamma. Edward is very plain."

"Well he should be! His generous impulse has been long enough in coming. But so it always is with your great men." She glared at me darkly. "Edward may command more wealth than the rest of the family put together, Jane. Three years I have been a widow—and he only considers now of his family, when he is deprived of the chief delight of his life? Death has leveled his humours, you may depend upon it. He means to value such relations as he still claims, while life and breath remain to him."

"Perhaps you are right, Mamma." I knew better than to challenge such caprices and whims. "Do you fancy Wye, or Chawton?"

"It hardly matters," she said doubtfully. "They are equally troublesome, in being such a great way off, and neither replete with acquaintance."

I raised my brow expressively at Martha; we both could expect considerable agitation from Mrs. Austen in the coming days. She should rather remain in an unhappy situation, and avoid the trouble necessitated by change, than to exert herself towards an improvement of her prospects.

"I am a little acquainted with Wye," Martha mused over her glass of orange wine. "It is pretty enough, and I should judge but two miles from Mr. Edward Austen's estate. Chawton, however, has all the advantage of being in northern Hampshire, where so many of our old friends are established—and the accommodation appears excellent."

" 'A bailiff's cottage,' " I recited from my brother's letter, " 'in the Great House village.' " We had all been conducted on a visit through Chawton Great House, Edward's secondary estate, the previous summer when dear Elizabeth was yet alive. It had lately been quitted by its tenants, and was in a period of refurbishment; silent, echoing, august, and chill. Young Fanny had delighted in losing herself among the numerous twisting passages, the hidden doors and secret chambers; the little children had run like puppies through the extensive park. But I could not recall the bailiff, or his habitation.

"Edward writes that the cottage has no less than six bedrooms—several garrets for storage—a garden—and a few outhouses," my mother lamented.

"Such riches!" Martha exclaimed. "And in a country village, we might have a pony cart, by and by!"

At that moment, the peace of the dinner hour was riven by the clangourous tolling of St. Michael's bells, not a quarter mile distant from Castle Square. The tumult of sound—for each of the great bells in the tower must have loosed its tongue—shattered the night air in rolling waves, so that the very walls of the house commenced to shake.

"Good God!" my mother cried, and rose with her hand at her heart. "Are we invaded? Has the Monster crossed the Channel?"

I sped from the table to the front hall, followed by Martha. We threw open the door and saw a crowd of common folk—sailors, carters, tradesmen—at a run through Castle Square. They were bound, to a man, for Samuel Street, and thence, down Bugle in the direction of the wharves. Most were shouting unintelligibly. As I stared at them in consternation, I glimpsed a familiar figure slipping through the crowd like a hound on its scent: Orlando, the green-cloaked sprite. Had he taken his suite of rooms at the Dolphin, in expectation of his master's return? I nearly called out his name, but was forestalled by Martha.

"What has happened?" she cried to a passing lad.

"Fire! The wharves are alight!"

"Lord, Jane—that part of town is not far off. Should we consider of the house? Ought we to begin packing?"

I shook my head. "Where can such a blaze go, between the Water and the walls? They are not eight feet thick for nothing. Let us return to my mother, however. She will be in need of smelling salts."

In this I misjudged the good lady; she was, in fact, on tenterhooks to learn the news—and was only prevented from gaining the street by the condition of her dressing gown. "What if sparks are blown by the wind?" she demanded. "What if the roof catches alight? I do not place my confidence in your *walls,* Jane. Recollect the affair in Lyme, when your father was yet alive. We were very nearly burnt in our beds."

"But in the event, were saved by means of numerous buckets of water, briskly applied," I observed, "which are bound to be employed in the present case. Fires are common enough in port towns, Mamma. We cannot escape them, with so much tar and wood about."

She was determined to sit up in the parlour, however, in expectation of flight; and spent the next several hours established over her needlework in a rigid attitude, with frequent ejaculations of fright. At last I could bear it no longer, and put on my cloak.

"You are never going out into that crowd, Jane!" my mother cried indignantly. "You shall be crushed. I am sure of it."

"I shall not sleep until I know the worst," I informed her firmly, and stepped into the night.

I STOOD IN SAMUEL STREET, GAZING THE LENGTH OF Bugle. The lurid glow of flames threw the wharves in sharp relief, as though they were stages erected for this sole performance, and the darting black figures that bent and swung over their water casks, a representation of the Inferno. I had not progressed much past West Gate Street when the heat struck my face like a blow. The smells of charred timbers and acrid resin tingled in my nostrils. And then, with a sound akin to cannon, some part of the wharf exploded.

I cowered involuntarily, my hands pressed against my bonnet. Splinters of wood rocketed into the air. Men screamed aloud. The flames shot skywards in a hellish arc, under a roiling cloud of smoke black against the vivid scene; a vat of tar, perhaps, had flared in the heat, or a cask of gunpowder.

"Out of the way, damn 'ee!"

I turned—gazed full into the eyes of a pair of frightened dray horses—and stumbled backwards onto the paving. I had been standing open-mouthed in the very middle of Bugle Street, directly in the path of a waggoneer intent upon hauling water to the wharves. He sawed at the reins, glared at me in contempt, and clattered onwards over the stones.

As I recovered myself, the rapid pulse at my throat receding, a distant *boom!* brought my head around. A second explosion—and a third—but from a completely different direction than the wharves. I hastened to my right, down West Gate Street, and mounted the steps to the town walls.

I was not alone. A crowd of onlookers, most of

them women, stood with their silent faces turned towards the dockyard on the River Itchen. A flare of red blazed on the horizon; it branched and twined and climbed like a monstrous spider over the skeletal form that rested there.

"It's the seventy-four," I breathed, remembering the lovely ship of the line, half-built in the Itchen yard. I had walked through its ribs with Edward and George but two days ago. "The seventy-four is burning."

"They'll never save her," a woman beside me declared. "Not with the wharves aflame, and most of the men hard at work here in town. *Two* fires in one night—and that after a bit of rain? It's Devil's work, I'll be bound."

"Devil's work," I said thoughtfully. "Or the Monster's?"

Chapter 6

Beauty's Face

Thursday, 27 October 1808

~

I AM NO HORSEWOMAN, BUT LAST NIGHT'S FIRE DEmanded expediency; and so I walked this morning before breakfast to Colridge's hack stable, where for the price of a few shillings I was swiftly accommodated with a skittish dun mare. Her name was Duchess, and she turned her nose willingly enough in the direction of Porter's Mead, the broad gallop east of the town. As she trotted through the green meadow, I attempted to recall the few riding lessons I had endured at Edward's Kentish estate. My seat was indifferent, I wore an outmoded riding habit of Elizabeth's, made over for my use, and the reins felt awkward in my grasp; but Duchess must have been served with far worse mistresses in her life of hire, and offered no snort of contempt.

From Porter's Mead it required but a few moments to achieve Nightingale Lane and proceed thence along the strand to the Itchen Dockyard. We had nosed up the yard's river channel only three days before, with Mr. Hawkins; but being land-bound this morning I sawed hesitantly at the reins, turning the mare's nose to the north. She tossed her head, drawn by the sharp scent of the sea, and would have contested the point—but that I forced her around and skirted the dockyard at its rear. From the slight promontory above, I could rest a bit in the saddle and survey the scene of devastation below.

The dockyard's wooden enclosure was scarred by fire and broken in places, so that I might gaze through what had once been a solid perimeter. In an effort to combat the fire, the lock gates had been opened to permit the surging river to douse the flames. Now a welter of mud and charred wood lay stinking in the watery sun. The seventy-four's ribs had fallen in a heap of refuse all about the scaffolding, which was similarly burnt to non-description. A dense odour hung heavy in the air; I knew its acrid weight should cling to my garments for days to come. I held a gloved hand over my nose, eyes narrowed against the smoke that still spiralled from the wreck. Three years Mr. Dixon's pride had been a-building in his yard—a thing of beauty and promise; the blasting of hope felt as brutal as the ruin of iron and oak.

A party of men, some wearing the canvas trousers of shipyard tars and others the rough nankeen of labourers, heaved purposefully at the spars. I discerned Jeremiah the Lascar, his face grim and his air morose, but of the genial Mr. Dixon there was no sign. I touched my heels to the mare's sides, and obediently, she rocked her way down the grassy slope.

The sound of hooves ringing on gravel brought the men's heads up to stare at me in surprise. One spat derisively in the ashes and returned immediately to his labours; the others studied my countenance warily. After an instant, recognition lit the Lascar's face. He stepped forward, his hand raised to his dark brow.

"Good morning, Mem-Sahib. Where be the young masters today?"

"Safely returned to school. My condolences, Jeremiah—I saw the flames last night from the town's walls. You have a deal of work before you."

He laid his hand on the mare's bridle and ran long fingers over her soft nose. Duchess snorted and thrust her head into his chest.

"That lovely ship," I mourned. "Was it an accident? An oil lamp overturned in a pile of sailcloth?"

The Lascar bowed his head. "Do not believe it, Mem-Sahib. There was evil at work in this yard last night."

"The smell of tar is very strong. You think the fire deliberately set?"

"Pitch was spread over the ship before the fire was lit. Pitch is still hot on the spars. We have shifted them with our hands, and we know."

I touched my heels to Duchess's flanks, as if to approach the smoking embers, but the Lascar stood firm, his hand at the mare's head.

"You go now. It is not safe."

"I heard no alarum last night, before the explosion. How came Mr. Dixon to desert his post?"

Jeremiah's countenance hardened. "Do not say such things, I beg. Dixon Sahib has gone to his rest."

"Poor man, I can well believe it. He loved that ship so, he must be ill with exhaustion and despair."

The Lascar stepped backwards and glanced significantly towards the ruined timber walls, and the vestige of what had been the shipwright's offices. I followed his gaze, and saw a pallet lying on the ground, with a loose covering of dirty canvas. Under it lay something that must—that could only—be the shape of a man.

"Mr. Dixon?" I whispered in horror. "How dreadful! Was he overcome by the heat of the flames?"

"Fire did not kill him." The Lascar's voice was sombre. "We found him there last night when the smoke first rose into the sky, and the men came running to open the lock. Dixon Sahib's throat was cut from ear to ear. Murder, Mem-Sahib! And when I find the one who did it—"

His fists clenched on the mare's reins.

I CROSSED AT THE ITCHEN FERRY AND RODE ON, through the gentle fields and coppices of Weston, the ground rising and falling as if formed by the Channel tides. Duchess stretched out her nose in the sharp October morning and seemed ready to gallop, but I could not trust myself so far in the saddle, and held in her head. It was as much as I could do to manage the horse, for my mind was full of the bitter intelligence lately imparted. Mr. Dixon, murdered! His throat cut and the seventy-four destroyed! No mere vandals, then, had torched the ship—but an enemy who moved with deadly purpose. The fires on Southampton's wharves must have served as diversion, intended to draw the townsfolk away from the River Itchen. With the men already fighting the flames near the quay, response to the second fire must be slow; too slow to save the seventy-four, as the event indeed had proved. It was a calculated evil—a plot well-sprung. A marshal in the field could not have done better.

And all this, but a few days after Mrs. Challoner opened Netley Lodge.

I could not like the coincidence. What had Lord Harold called her? *The Peninsula's most potent weapon.* I longed for him suddenly: the steady look, the careless strength. For suddenly, I was afraid.

The day was yet young, the hour being not much past ten and most of the world still at breakfast. My sketchbook and paints were secured in a saddlebag, and I had every intention of o'erlooking Netley Lodge for much of the morning. I could not stomach a third full day among the ruins, nor did I believe my outraged parent would condone such a scheme, did she know of it. The word *murder* would run through Southampton swift as fire along a ropewalk, and my days of rambling the country alone were at an end. I must make the most of the hours remaining to me.

My road was the same as Mr. Ord's had been the previous day. There are advantages in approaching the Abbey by land, as one reaches the ruins from the west. In arriving by sea as I had twice done, I approached from the east—passing Netley Lodge on my way. Today I might establish myself high in the Abbey walls without exciting the notice of anybody at the house, and gaze down upon its activity for the whole of the morning.

But I was forestalled—routed—and thoroughly undone before I had even so much as dismounted at the Abbey's wicket gate. As I emerged from West Woods, I discerned the rattle of a tidy equipage, and in another instant it appeared: a phaeton and pair, driven by a lady at breakneck pace. The grey geldings were perfectly matched, and their action admirable. I must have started in the saddle, or perhaps the prospect of a race was too much for the mettlesome Duchess, for she stretched out her neck, seized the bit in her teeth, and careened down the road at a gallop.

Never had I been subjected to such a pace! I abandoned the reins and clung desperately to Duchess's neck, all but unseated in the wretched sidesaddle. Too terrified to emit a syllable, I divided my attention between the heaving ground and the approaching phaeton, certain that one of us must give way or endure a fatal crash.

The lady's gaze never faltered. She neither pulled up nor slowed her reckless course; she merely shifted her equipage with deft hands to the far side of the road, and scarcely glanced at my figure as I hurtled past. Duchess, intent upon a race, made a sharp turn in the phaeton's wake, and redoubled her gait to catch up to the pair.

This final maneuver was too much for me. As the dun mare came around and gathered herself to spring, my grasp on her neck faltered. With a cry of dismay, I was flung wide and landed hard on the verge of the road, knocking the breath from my body and the sense from my head. I was aware of a great pain, and of the sound of the mare's hoofbeats receding; and then I knew nothing more.

"WOULD YOU LOOK AT THE RENT IN THIS BONNET? It's a wonder she wasn't killed." A gentleman's voice, with something odd in its tone... something familiar...

"The little fool has not the least notion of how to

manage a horse. Such poor creatures ought to be strangled in their cradles, before they ruin a perfectly good mount from ignorance and caprice." His companion spoke briskly, as though she would save her pity for the wretched Duchess.

"Pshaw! You don't mean it!"

"I never mean anything I say. I merely love to hear myself speak. You ought to know that, thus far in our acquaintance. Pass me the basin, pray."

A cool square of cloth was pressed delicately against my brow. Light as the pressure was, it caused me pain, and I groaned and turned my head into the cushion.

"There's no card in her reticule—nothing to betray her name or direction. A sketching book and paints in the saddlebag."

"She probably aspired to Genius among the ruins," the lady observed caustically. "I am surprised, however, that a gentlewoman—even one so shabbily dressed—should go jaunting about the countryside alone. Has she affixed her signature to her work?" Again, the cool cloth bathed my forehead; the odour of vinegar assailed my nostrils. I winced, but did not open my eyes; I felt sure the light should split my head in twain.

"No. From the quality of these, she hesitated to claim maternity."

A rich chuckle. "You are *too* bad. What about the horse?"

"Hired of a livery stable. Name's on the saddlecloth."

"—a private mount being rather above her touch. Then if she does not rouse by nightfall, we must send José Luis to enquire at the stables. They must be wanting their mare."

Nightfall? What hour of the day could it be? And where in God's name was I?

I opened my eyes and attempted to rise.

"Steady," the lady advised, and her firm hands thrust me gently back. I was lying on a broad bed in a room with a peaked ceiling and dormer windows; my spencer and bonnet were set on a chair. She was seated nearby: masses of auburn curls, a gown of garnet silk, and the basin of vinegar in her lap. Her dark eyes, heavily-lashed, gazed at me coolly. It was quite the most elegant countenance I had seen in years.

"Steady," she repeated, and laid her free hand on my arm. "You have had a fall, madam. You are quite safe, and among friends, and the doctor shall be with us presently."

"But—"

Despite her words and the pain in my head, I sat up and gazed in bewilderment about me. A fair-haired young man in a correct suit of black cloth stood by the leaded window, and beyond him was the sea. I knew that view of the Dibden shore; I had gazed upon it a thousand times. But then I must be—I could *only* be—

"You are at Netley Lodge," she explained, "not far from where you were thrown. Can you perhaps recall your name?"

"Jane Austen." My voice was a whisper; I knew now what name I should put to Beauty's face.

"That gentleman is Mr. James Ord. And I am Sophia Challoner."

Chapter 7

The Horrors of War

27 October 1808, cont.

~

DR. JARVEY—A PHYSICIAN SUMMONED FROM SOUTHampton, and not a mere surgeon or apothecary of Hound—ran his fingers over my skull and shook his head gravely at a large lump that had swelled above my left ear. Upon learning that I had lost consciousness for the period of a half-hour, he looked dour and prescribed absolute quiet for the rest of the day.

"She must not be moved, and she must be subject to the closest scrutiny. If nausea ensues, keep her awake at all cost, even if you play duets until dawn to effect it. There is danger of a fracture to the cranium, and in such cases, derangement of the senses is likely. To fall asleep in that eventuality should be fatal. However, if she is *not* retching by the dinner hour, give her this"—proffering a draught against the pain—"and send your servants to bed."

With which dubious advice, he quitted the room, leaving me in some suspense as to whether I should die or no.

"We must send word to your people," Mrs. Challoner observed after he had gone. "Where do they reside?"

"Southampton. My mother is resident in Castle Square."

"The mare must be fixed to her stable in any case, and her hire discharged. I shall send my manservant José Luis"—she pronounced the name heavily: *Show-zay Lew-eesh*—"to town with the horse, and your note of explanation. Shall I pen it for you?"

As my head distinctly ached, and Sophia Challoner appeared far better suited to decision, I agreed. What my mother's anxieties should be, upon discovering that I had hired a horse—much less fallen from it—I could not think. But there was a cup of tea at my elbow and the prospect of an entire day's *tête-à-tête* with the Peninsula's most potent weapon. If I could but keep my composure, I might learn much.

She fetched ink and paper, and settled herself once more in the chair by my bed. As she bent over her task, I studied her perfect countenance. A skin like alabaster, dusted with rose; the dark hair a brilliant counterpoint. A single thread of blue vein pulsed at her temple. She held her pen in elegant fingers. One of them sported a great jewel, polished and cut, that was the exact hue of her gown. Did she possess a similar ransom for every costume she owned?

"*Dear Mamma*—that is how one always commences, I understand, though I lost my own maternal parent well before I could write," she drawled.

"*Do not be alarmed at receiving this from a stranger's hand, for I am quite well.* One always lies to one's mother, I believe?"

"From about the age of six. Although in this, as in everything, I confess to a marked precocity."

She raised her eyes to mine, and I observed a look of vast humour in them. "Well done, Miss Austen! We shall deal famously with one another! *I have suffered a fall from my horse, and am very kindly bidden to remain at the home of a gentlewoman, Mrs. Challoner of Netley Lodge, who happened upon me as I lay unconscious in the road.* That should terrify her suitably. She will pause at this juncture, and exclaim aloud, and one of your domestics shall be enjoined to fetch hartshorn and sal volatile."

As this was palpably true, I could not suppress a smile. "Pray include a sentence to the effect that the horse has been returned to Colridge's, as she will be in some amazement at the idea of my riding, and must divide her anxiety between myself and the mare."

"I am shocked to hear it. Have you been very much mounted?"

"Not above a few times in my life."

She frowned slightly. "What possessed you to take a gallop?"

"The horse possessed me, I am afraid."

"How very unfortunate. *Dr. Jarvey has been called, and declares that nothing is amiss, save a considerable bruise to my head. I shall expect to be returned to you tomorrow in Mrs. Challoner's phaeton—*"

"Indeed, that is very kind of you, but hardly necessary. I am perfectly able to walk—"

"*—in Mrs. Challoner's phaeton. Your loving daughter*—should you like to affix your signature?"

I scrawled my name at the foot of the billet, and lay back upon my pillows. The scene of such a note's reception was one I was thankful to avoid.

I never saw José Luis, but when the manservant and the mare had been despatched to Southampton, Mrs. Challoner ordered a tray of cold meat and bread to be sent up to my room. The young girl who brought it—with a fresh face and a diffident look that suggested she was little in the habit of service—I guessed to be Flora, granddaughter of Mr. Hawkins's crony from Hound. When the maid had set the tray on a table and curtseyed in her mistress's direction, Mrs. Challoner closed the door behind her and offered to read aloud, if it should amuse me.

I had recovered strength enough to capitalize upon her willingness, though I suggested lassitude, and made a very poor picture of health.

"What of your guest, Mr. Ord?" I enquired feebly. "I should not like to occupy all your attention."

"Oh—as to that, the gentleman may come and go as he pleases," she replied indifferently. "He is not actually staying in the house, but merely called a few moments after we returned from the accident, and was immensely helpful in carrying you abovestairs."

"Was he?" The idea of myself, insensible in the arms of young Adonis, was riveting. "I am deeply grateful."

"He is probably immersed in a great volume of sermons, or some such, in the library. Mr. Ord is a student of theology, you will observe, though he *is* an American. My late husband possessed an admirable collection of books, but I have hardly had occasion to look into them since my arrival at Netley."

"My condolences, Mrs. Challoner. I should never have believed you a widow."

"Because I do not go in black?" She surveyed me satirically. "My husband was an excellent man, Miss Austen, but a good deal older than myself. He died three years since; and though I may yet regret him, I have learned to survive him. And only consider of the library he left me! Perhaps when the cold sets in, I may establish myself by the fire and read the whole winter long. There shall be no occasion for driving out in the phaeton *then.* I cannot abide the cold."

"Are you so recently come to this house?"

"I am but five days in residence." The novel she might have read to me lay unopened in her lap; her dark eyes assumed a thoughtful expression. "I fled the Peninsula in the first week of September, when the siege of Oporto was entirely lifted and the British troops were carried off from Vimeiro."

"Did you?" I exclaimed, as though the intelligence were news. "But that is extraordinary! My brother—Captain Frank Austen, of the *St. Alban's*—was engaged in that very endeavour! Did you perhaps chance to meet him?"

"I was denied the pleasure," she replied with a faint smile. "My family in Oporto were so good as to secure me a cabin in the *Dartmoor,* a fourth-rate intended for the conveyance of French prisoners. I was of infinite use, in serving as interpreter for the Captain, and thus could flatter myself I proved less of a burden than he had anticipated."

"I am sure you were invaluable," I told her earnestly. "French prisoners! How uncomfortable you must have found it—dealing with the Enemy!"

"Not at all. Any number were quite handsome."

"And did you remain aboard the *Dartmoor* until the Lodge was ready to receive you?" I enquired innocently. A considerable period fell between the first week of September, and the last week of October. Did Lord Harold know of her whereabouts in the interval?

"I was several weeks with friends," she said vaguely, "who are situated not far from London. Now—should you like to hear a little of this book?"

"I should rather hear of your experiences in Oporto—if you are not unwilling to share them."

"But of course!" she cried, her eyes alight, and commenced to regale me with tales of the English colony.

She was an excellent narrator, and could bring to vivid life the smallest detail of an Oporto morning: the plumage of an exotic bird, glimpsed through an open window; the rattle of carriage wheels in a stone courtyard; the clash of steel as two *partis* duelled in the moonlight for the hand of a ravishing maiden. I walked with her beneath scented trees, and ate blood-red oranges fresh off the boats from Tangier; I smelled the musky odour of sherry casks drying in the dim light of warehouses, and sipped the velvet Port on my tongue. I listened with aching heart to the siren sound of a guitar, and swirled in mantilla'd company for several nights in succession—only to rise in the early sunlight, and tear like the wind along the cliffs above the sea.

"How much of the world you have seen," I murmured, "while I have lived out my span in a series of cold English towns! We know a good deal of rain, and the occasional blooming rose in England; but nothing like your healing sun. You must feel a great longing for all that you have left!"

"There is a word in Portuguese that exactly suits my sentiments," Sophia Challoner said slowly. "It is *saudades*. I have *saudades* for Oporto—nostalgia, homesickness, a mournful feeling of loss. No single word in English may encompass it. But even *saudades* may pass in time."

"You do not intend to return?"

She glanced away from me through the leaded window to the sea. It lay like a silver belt between the Dibden shore and Netley Cliff. "I do not think the Peninsula will be habitable for years. This battle at Vimeiro was but the first toss of English dice." She turned back from the window, her eyes smoldering. "Have you ever witnessed the killing of men, Miss Austen?"

What a penetrating question! I had seen enough of the dead, to be sure; but I doubted that it was *this* she intended. "If you would mean, am I intimate with war—then I must confess that I am not. My two dear brothers are daily thrust into the worst kind of danger, in serving His Majesty's Navy; and for them, I feel an active anxiety. But it cannot be akin to viewing the effects of battle at close hand. I collect that you have done so, Mrs. Challoner?"

"I drove out in my carriage at the height of the French advance," she said dreamily. "I was in the company of a friend—a Frenchman long resident in Oporto—and thus able to pass through Marshal Junot's lines. A cannonball exploded not five feet from the carriage wheels, startling the horses, and had there not been a mass of waggons directly in front of us, and a brave coachman at the reins, I am sure we should have bolted. As it was, I observed a young lieutenant of hussars decapitated where he sat his horse. The head fell almost at my feet."

I shuddered. That she could speak of such things with such dispassion—

"I hate this war," she muttered viciously. "The

flower of youth—sons of noble families, or of humble ones; Portuguese, French, Spanish grandees—their horses, their bright folly of uniform dress—their glittering swords as violent in the downward arc as a guillotine—all blasted to ruin, dismembered and left in torn shreds upon the ground, and the dark birds circling. To look upon such a scene as Vimeiro, Miss Austen, is to look for a while at the face of Hell."

We were silent an instant, I from deepest sensibility, she from the horror of her recollections. Her hand gripped the spine of her book so tautly that all color drained from the skin, and the great stone on her finger glowed like blood in the candlelight.

"But what is one to do?" I asked quietly. "Men like the Monster will go to war, in a tilt at power beyond imagining; and men like my brothers will swear to prevent it. You cannot stop them coming to blows."

"But I may at least *try*." She sat erect in her chair, her gaze fixed implacably on my own. "War is vainglory and ruin, Miss Austen. It brings waste upon the countryside and desolation into the bosom of every family. I shall do all within my power to thwart this folly, and the men who would further it. No other course is open to those of us who are fated to live in such times."

"On the contrary, madam. War is hateful, as is all wanton loss of life—but when the battle is thrust upon us, we have one course at least: to meet it honourably, and defend what we love. I should not like to see England in the hands of Buonaparte; and I am certain my brothers would say the same."

"You think the Emperor so different from your King, then?"

"*Our* King, Mrs. Challoner."

She smiled at me then. "I forget. So easily I

forget! I was but five years old when I left my home in England, and have spent all my life since in the Peninsula. It is hard to feel allegiance to much beyond the few friends I have long known and loved. But I have wearied you with stories and harangues long enough. Rest now, and perhaps you will be well enough to descend for dinner."

She touched my hand lightly, rose in a swirl of scented silk, and was gone: leaving me in some bewilderment of sensation regarding her.

Did I understand what she was, that first night I saw her? a voice whispered in my ear. *Did I recognise the cunning behind Beauty's mask?*

Had Lord Harold judged this woman wrongly? Was she a lady of subtle purpose—or one of deep feeling? Did she intend that I should be taken in by her tale of dead soldiers? Or had she loved a man who died at Vimeiro? What possible motive could she find for deceiving *me*—who was but a stranger?

She is guilty of treason, *Jane.*

I could not begin to judge Sophia Challoner. I only knew that I honoured her fierce conviction—and could not find it in my heart, yet, to condemn her.

PERHAPS AN HOUR LATER, I AWOKE FROM A LIGHT sleep. The house was utterly silent and my mouth was dry. I rang the bell for the housemaid, then rose and walked unsteadily to the leaded windows. The bedchamber was set into the corner of the house, with views looking both south and west. From one window, I might survey the traffic of Southampton Water: a few fishing boats bobbing at anchor, and an Indiaman making its heavy way towards the quay.

From the other, I could just glimpse the brow of the hill that led to Netley Abbey, half a mile distant.

Two figures were toiling up the footpath: a man with yellow hair and a lady in garnet-coloured silk. She was a little ahead of the gentleman, as though she were familiar with the direction, and intent upon leading the way. I could not conceive of Sophia Challoner following in any man's footsteps.

"Are you quite well, miss?" enquired the maid from the doorway.

I whirled around. Flora, the granddaughter of Mr. Hawkins's crony, Ned Bastable. She could not be much above fifteen. "I am merely thirsty," I replied. "Could I have a jug of water?"

She bobbed a curtsey, and went off to the kitchen. I glanced once more out the window, and saw that in the interval required for conversation, a third figure had appeared on the Abbey path: hooded and cloaked in black, and standing as though in wait for the two who approached. I narrowed my eyes, the better to study the scene: the motionless form, august and slightly sinister, and the toiling pair below. What could it mean?

I followed the walkers' course until they breasted the hill, and stood an instant in greeting; I observed Sophia Challoner bow her head and curtsey low. Then all three began the descent into the ruins and vanished from view. I wished, in that instant, that I might be a bird on the wing: hovering over the ramparts of the walls in observation of the party. Did they pick their way to the south transept, and mount the chancel steps? Was it mere idleness that drew them hence—the love of a good walk, and a picturesque landscape—or did they flee the house to talk of deadly policy?

And who was the third, garbed in black?

"Your water, miss."

Mouse-brown hair under a white cap; gentian-blue eyes. I accepted the glass. Flora was lacking in both age and experience, and might be encouraged to share her confidences. "Your mistress has gone out?"

"She will have her exercise," the maid said.

"And may command Mr. Ord to bear her company. Is he often useful in that way?"

Flora smiled. "The young gentleman haunts the house, miss. He is but two days arrived in town, and has spent the whole of it with my mistress! Do you think that he is in love with her?"

"Does he behave as though he were?"

"I cannot rightly say," Flora replied doubtfully, "him being an American, and one of the Quality. He keeps a room in Southampton, as is proper, but appears after breakfast and does not quit my mistress's side until past supper!"

"They must be very old acquaintances."

She shook her head. "He brought a letter of introduction, on his great black horse. It's my belief they'd never laid eyes on one another before yesterday. And yet he behaves as though he were her cousin."

"That is indeed strange," I said thoughtfully. "But perhaps, after all—he *is*. One might possess any number of colonial relations one has never met."

The maid curtseyed and left. I stood a while longer by the leaded windows, the glass of water in my hand, but the walkers did not reappear. It was vital that I gather my strength, for I had no intention of dining on a tray in my room this evening. If Mr. Ord hoped to stay for dinner, then I should break bread with him. Lord Harold would desire no less.

Chapter 8

The Recusant

Friday, 28 October 1808

~

"AND SO WE MAY HAVE AN END TO ALL SCHEMES OF watercolour painting, I devoutly hope!" my mother cried when I appeared like a prodigal in the breakfast parlour this morning. "Pray impress upon her, Mrs. Challoner, how very improper it must be for a young woman to wander about the countryside entirely alone! And on horseback, too—when you have never acquitted yourself well in the saddle, Jane."

"I am afraid her mishap must be laid to my charge, Mrs. Austen," Sophia Challoner said evenly. "Had I not breasted Netley hill in my phaeton when I did, the mare should not have started, and Miss Austen must have been spared an ugly ordeal."

"Every sentiment revolts! When I consider my daughter, rambling among the hedgerows like a gipsy, and falling off of horses she has no business riding—when I consider of you lying insensible, Jane, in the road—I am thankful you were not murdered before Mrs. Challoner discovered you!"

"You exaggerate, Mamma. What has murder to do with it?"

"Everything, miss! You cannot be aware of the horrors we have endured in your absence; but it is in my power to inform you that the shipwright of Itchen, one Mr. Dixon, was done away with two nights ago—his throat cut, if you will credit it—and the magistrates none the wiser!"

"The shipwright?" Mrs. Challoner enquired. "Why should anyone serve such a fellow with violence?"

"In order to reach his seventy-four," I replied. "A handsome ship, and nearly complete when it was destroyed by fire Wednesday evening."

"But I saw the flames! I could not help but observe them, from the Lodge—the blaze illumined the entire waterfront! How very extraordinary! Is it the work of vandals? Or a rival shipyard?"

"Very likely both," my mother asserted, "for every sort of miscreant will wash ashore in Southampton. It is always so with your port towns."

"I wish I had known as much when I determined to remove here." Mrs. Challoner preserved an admirable command of countenance for one whom, I must suspect, knew more than was healthy of the Itchen fire.

"We are vastly obliged to you for doing so. Only think what might have befallen Jane else! Her head should never have been put to rights." My mother threw me a quelling look. "Pray sit down, Mrs. Challoner, and let us supply you with coffee and muffin—for you cannot have breakfasted properly, in quitting the house so early."

The lady inclined her head, but professed herself bound for her dressmaker on an errand that could not wait; and with many wishes for my continued good health, and promises of future visits, she gracefully mounted the steps of her perch phaeton and took up the reins.

"What a very daring young woman," my mother observed from the parlour window, a note of awe in her voice. "Driving herself, with only a manservant behind! That is what comes of living in foreign parts!"

The manservant was the very José Luis—or, as Mrs. Challoner preferred to call him, Zé—and he had proved a taciturn, powerfully built Portuguese fellow. He was as careful of Sophia Challoner as a hawk should be of its young, but he had spared me hardly a glance as we rolled briskly down the road from Netley this morning.

"Her Hindu coat, I vow and declare, is beyond anything I have seen this twelvemonth," my parent continued. She was correct in this; for the dove-grey sarcenet was trimmed with tassels and silver fox. "What *can* she find to discuss with a milliner? She must hardly want for a pin."

"Except, perhaps, gowns of a suitable weight for the English winter. She has surely never required them before, being almost a native of the Peninsula—and will dress in silk, though complaining all the while of the cold. I supplied her with Madame Clarisse's direction."

Madame Clarisse, though born Louisa Gibbon, maintained a *modiste*'s establishment of the first stare in Bugle Street. All the ladies of fashion waited upon her there, in the pretty pink and white dressing room, and were supplied with finery at breathless expence.

"Very proper, I am sure. Mrs. Challoner looks the great lady."

By this imprecation, my mother meant to imply that her new acquaintance appeared to be in easy circumstances—far easier than our own.

"She is a widow, and her fortune acquired by the Port wine trade," I said distantly.

"Trade! I should not have detected it in her vowels, Jane. But then I recollect—the Challoners of Hampshire have long been Recusants, and one is never certain what Papists will get up to.[1] They must earn their living as best they can, poor things."

"The Challoners, disciples of Rome?" I could not imagine the mistress of Netley Lodge educated by nuns in a French cloister. "But Mrs. Challoner merely took that name at her marriage. It is possible that her husband alone was a Recusant—and that she does not adhere to the faith."

"Possible," my mother admitted doubtfully, "but I cannot think it at all *probable,* Jane. The Papists are very careful whom they marry—and recollect: Mrs. Challoner has spent nearly the whole of her life in Portugal. With such a husband, and priests and churches at every side, who should blame her if she

[1] Recusant was the label applied to those British subjects who refused to swear an oath of allegiance to the Church of England, and thus to its secular head, the Crown. Included in this group were a variety of sects, but the term was generally taken to denote Roman Catholics, whose allegiance was accorded to the pope. As a result of refusing to swear the oath, English Catholics of Austen's era were barred from taking degrees at either Oxford or Cambridge, holding cabinet positions or seats in Parliament, serving as commissioned officers in either the army or the navy, or entering the professions as physicians, lawyers, or clergy. They were thus consigned to the roles of leisured gentry or merchants in trade. They were forbidden, moreover, to educate their children in their chosen faith—and thus frequently sent school-age progeny to France for instruction.—*Editor's note.*

fell into disreputable habits? Indeed, I must say that she acquits herself very well, considering. I should not object to your knowing more of her."

With which gesture of magnanimity, my mother left me to nurse myself in peace.

"THE PAPERS SPEAK OF NOTHING BUT THE PENINSULA," Martha Lloyd noted with a sigh some hours later, "and the tone of comment is unrelieved by optimism. Poor General Sir Arthur is covered in disgrace—I am certain his career is at an end."

Martha being of the opinion that I should remain quietly at home so soon after an injury to the head, we had settled down by the parlour fire and given ourselves over to perusing the recent numbers of the London papers. We had been forced to forgo them of late, in deference to my nephews' amusement and my sudden passion for watercolours.

"Do not pity Sir Arthur," I advised. "He is a Wellesley, and as a family they have a genius for self-preservation. He has been routed for the nonce, but shall regroup and advance the stronger for it."

"I did not know you were a student of military strategy," said a voice from the hallway, "much less of politics. I ought to have guessed it. Pray continue, Miss Austen."

I glanced up from my paper to find our maidservant, Phebe, hovering in the doorway; at her back was a gentleman, an expression of languid amusement on his countenance.[2]

[2] From this reference to a housemaid named Phebe, it would seem that the Austens' faithful servant Jenny, who had been with them since 1803, had left their service.—*Editor's note.*

"Lord Harold Trowbridge!" I observed. "I had not looked for you in Castle Square today—but you are very welcome."

Martha thrust herself hurriedly to her feet, her countenance flaming, as the Rogue strode into our parlour. She had learned enough of Lord Harold—from my mother's veiled hints and my own obscure remarks—to comprehend that no meeting with such a man could ever be easy.

"May I present my friend, Miss Lloyd, to your acquaintance? Lord Harold Trowbridge."

"A pleasure," he said, bowing correctly in Martha's direction.

"Pray accept my sincere condolences on the loss of the Dowager Duchess."

"You are exceedingly good, Miss Lloyd. I attended Her Grace's funeral rites only yesterday, and I may say they were exactly as she might have wished. Mr. John Kemble, the tragedian, broke off his London engagement in order to declaim the death scene of Ophelia; and very prettily he spoke it, too. It was my mother's greatest ambition to play at tragedy, you know, but she had a fatal talent for the comic."

"Indeed, sir?" Martha's countenance struggled to suppress the outraged sentiments of Christian virtue, as well as the indecision battling in her soul. Ought she to support me in the presence of my dangerous acquaintance? Or did true friendship dictate a flight from the room as swiftly as possible?

I pitied her, but could not hesitate.

"Martha, be so good as to consult with Cook on the preparation of the pullet. No one has your genius for receipts—and I should hate to see a good bird spoilt." Her lips twitched, from mirth and relief; she nodded once to Lord Harold, and sailed out of the room like a black ship of the line.

"I did not know you were entertaining guests," he observed, as the door closed behind Martha. "Forgive me, Jane, for having lately commanded so much of your time, when others had far more vital claims upon it."

"Miss Lloyd forms a part of our household, my lord. She has been in the nature of a sister to me since childhood; and being now quite alone in the world, she elected to throw in her lot with ours."

"Ah." In that single syllable, I detected a world of understanding. A household of four women: one elderly, and the others, spinsters long since left upon the shelf. *A cattery,* we should be called in the fashionable world of gentlemen's clubs; or worse yet, *a party of ape-leaders.* I had never surprised an expression of pity in Lord Harold's eyes, and I hoped I should not discover one now.

"How does your head, my dear?" he asked abruptly.

"It is repairing apace. You knew of my injury?"

He took up a position by the fire, his hand gripping the mantel. "I was informed of it last night by Orlando. Though he was forbidden to shadow Mrs. Challoner, he was expressly charged with observing *you,* and was ravaged with suspense when he saw you taken up in the dragon's equipage. Nothing would do but he must despatch an express, urging me to make all possible haste south, as you were clearly subject to torture in the fiend's clutches."

He spoke lightly, but the words were in earnest. Of a sudden, I recalled the green-cloaked sprite slipping through the crowd of townsfolk on the night of the fires. Had Orlando been lurking in Castle

Square, in closest watch of my door, when the alarum first went up?

"Your solicitude—and Orlando's care—is a considerable comfort. I collect that you have heard of Wednesday night's conflagration?"

"Arson, throat-cutting, and the destruction of a sweetly-built vessel," he replied. "The report was intriguing enough to be taken up by the London papers."

"I looked into the ship with my nephews on Monday, at the invitation of Mr. Dixon, the shipwright."

"Who lost his life but two days later! Did he appear uneasy, Jane? As though he feared disaster?"

"He seemed as complacent as any man who took pride in his work, and believed the world to do the same. Now the Itchen yard is a veritable ruin, my lord, and Dixon's men amazed."

"You have seen the place since the blaze?" he demanded.

"But yesterday morning. It stank of the pitch that was spread over the ship's timbers."

"Such work might be intended to suggest mischief among the lower orders—but Whitehall is not so sanguine. The Admiralty is afraid, Jane, that Wednesday's murder is but the first assault in a wider campaign."

I raised my brows. "The Peninsula's *most potent weapon*?"

"I doubt that Sophia torched the seventy-four."

"She has courage enough," I mused, "but might abhor the blood and pitch such work should leave upon her clothes."

Lord Harold's eyes gleamed. "Jane, what is your opinion of the lady?"

"I quite liked her. She is all that is charming," I

replied frankly. "In Mrs. Challoner we may see the union of beauty, understanding, and good breeding; a creature of captivating manners, wide experience, and unfailing taste. Had you said nothing in her dispraise, I should have taken her straight to my heart. When she spoke so passionately of her beliefs—when she declared that this war must be stopped at any cost—I felt myself prey to a dangerous sympathy. She should find it easy to win hearts to her cause: she might persuade the Lord Himself against consigning her to Hell."

"Well put. Having heard so much, I am thankful you spent no more than twenty-four hours in the lady's company. But I should never suggest that Sophia was turned a murderer. I have an idea of her in the role of Cleopatra."

"Reclined upon a couch, and toying flagrantly with the fate of nations?"

"You demonstrate a head for strategy, Jane—if *you* commanded the direction of Enemy forces, and could regard the affair at Itchen as but a trial of your strength, where next should you aim your Satanic imps?"

"At Portsmouth," I told him steadily. It was the greatest naval dockyard along the Solent: the first port of call for every ship returning from the Channel station and our blockade of the French. Opposite Portsmouth Harbour lay Spithead, the deep-water anchorage where any number of His Majesty's vessels awaited the Admiralty's orders. Both should be an open invitation to the marauding French.

"But of course," Lord Harold agreed. "You should aspire to ruin Portsmouth, and Deptford, and Woolwich and Chatham and Plymouth—His Majesty's most trafficked yards. You might even strike at private shipwrights, such as Mr. Dixon, did you possess time and agents enough."

"Is the English coast so riddled with traitors?"

"Possibly." He regarded me intently. "In September, we carried off our victorious troops and some French prisoners from Vimeiro, as you know. By disposing our ships in convoys, we offered a tantalising form of safe passage through our own Channel blockade. It is possible, Jane, that we ferried enemy agents home in our own vessels: men who crept aboard under cover of night, and now await their orders in every Channel port."

I rose and took a pensive turn about the room. "And you believe it is Mrs. Challoner's duty to despatch these agents on errands of mayhem?"

"I confess I do not know. How does she conduct herself?"

"Quietly. In the six days she has been in residence, she has devoted more time to her wardrobe than to affairs of state."

"Have you observed her to communicate with anyone?"

I glanced at him then. "An American. He arrived by the London mail on Wednesday morning, and is putting up at the Vine. He rides a splendid black hack, and spends the better part of each day at Netley Lodge."

"An American!" he repeated, in tones of astonishment. "Now *that* is an alliance I should not have anticipated. And yet—why not? Americans have long enjoyed the confidence of the French. They bear England little affection. Any attempt to wrest control of the seas from the Royal Navy should meet with American approval, as providing greater scope for their own vessels and commerce. By Jove, Jane—what you say must interest me greatly. An *American*!"

"He is very young, my lord—not above twenty. He is exceedingly handsome—"

"He would be," muttered Lord Harold.

"—possesses good manners, appears to be of good family, and goes by the name of James Ord. The housemaid informed me that he was totally unknown to her mistress before Wednesday, when he appeared with a letter of introduction in hand."

Lord Harold snapped his fingers, as though bidding Sophia Challoner to the Devil. "I must learn what I can of the fellow. The Admiralty may know something—"

I saw Mr. Ord now in memory, as he had appeared only last evening: the correct black coat, neither behind nor before the fashion; the delicate cut of feature in the laughing countenance; the warmth of the blue eyes as he gazed at Mrs. Challoner. He looked to be little more than a boy as he sat in her dining parlour, exclaiming over the excellence of his capon. *And have you lived the whole of your life in England, Miss Austen? Then you are indeed fortunate. It is a comfort to know that not all of us are born to be wanderers.*

Lord Harold broke in upon my thoughts. "Have you any notion what part of the Colonies—I beg your pardon, the United States—Mr. Ord hails from?"

"Baltimore. He has been making the grand tour, and arrived in London last week from a period at Liège."

"Liège? Not Paris?"

"He may have travelled through the capital, my lord."

"Liège is a town of unfrocked Jesuits and perpetual scholars—there can be little to interest a youth in such a place."

"Mr. Ord is a student of philosophy."

"Is he, by God?" Lord Harold's eyes had narrowed; he commenced to pace feverishly about the room. "Philosophy—or revolution? What does he find to do at Netley Lodge?"

"During the brief period in which I observed him, he read a great deal—played at whist—composed a letter to home—sang Italian airs with Mrs. Challoner—accompanied the lady in her exercise—"

"They walk out together?" Lord Harold interrupted.

"I was in the house but a day, my lord. You cannot expect me to speak with authority."

"But on the occasion you observed her?"

"—She walked with Mr. Ord to Netley Abbey." Of a sudden a black-cloaked figure rose in my mind: motionless, vaguely forbidding, impossible to dismiss. "They encountered a third person among the ruins—it seemed as though by design. I surveyed them from too great a distance to make much of the figure."

"Did they, by Jove?" His lordship seemed much struck. "Pray describe the fellow."

"He was cloaked and cowled in black—a monk returned from old."

"The Cistercians wore white, my dear," he corrected absently. "Still—what you say intrigues me. The man made an effort at disguise, and that must always be suspicious. You saw him meet Mrs. Challoner?"

"She curtseyed to him."

"The Abbey ruins. Though excessively public in

certain seasons, they must be quite deserted as autumn advances, and offer certain advantages as well: from that elevated position, one might observe the whole of the Solent. As the good monks divined so many years ago."

"One might observe the Solent from nearly every window in Mrs. Challoner's house," I objected drily.

"But if one intends to signal a confederate on the opposite shore—or perhaps a ship—Are there ramparts among the ruins?"

"The walls are achieved by a turret stair. Orlando and I espied the *Windlass* from that height."

"Excellent Jane! You have done better than I might have dreamt. Come, fetch your cloak."

"Why, sir? Am I going out?"

"We have much to do, and little time in which to effect it. Pray do not stumble over your mother in the passage," he added as I made for the door. "She has been listening at the keyhole this quarter-hour at least."

Chapter 9

On Heroines

28 October 1808, cont.

~

MY MOTHER STOOD BEFORE THE MIRROR IN THE hall, arranging withered leaves and raspberry canes in a Staffordshire vase. Although she had not elected to make a cake of herself in crouching before the parlour latch, I recognised the diffident look of guilt on her reflected countenance.

"Jane!" she hissed. "*That man* is closeted within! I learned the whole from Martha. What is he about? How can he conceive of showing his face in Southampton, after the shabby treatment he served you in Derbyshire?"

As the shabby treatment had consisted of several intimate visits to the ducal house of Chatsworth, I could not share her indignation.

"If you would mean Lord Harold, Mamma, he

has very kindly paid a call of condolence, having learned of our dear Elizabeth's passing. His lordship is likewise in mourning. He recently lost Her Grace the Dowager Duchess."

"Naturally—I saw the notice a few days ago. Poor woman; she was but three years older than myself, though hardly as respectable. An actress, you know, and French. That must account for the strangeness of the son—for I cannot find out that his brother Wilborough is so very odd. *He* must take after the paternal line." She gave up her efforts with the vase and surveyed me critically. "Lord Harold might as easily have written you a note regarding Elizabeth, as any trifling acquaintance should do. What does he mean by descending on Castle Square in all the state of a blazoned carriage?"

I shrugged indifferently. "No doubt he has business in Southampton, Mamma, and merely offered us the civility of a morning call. As for the chaise—I have an idea it is on loan from Wilborough House. His lordship is but this moment arrived from London."

"Is he, indeed?" She looked much struck, and began to fidget with the pair of garden shears she held in her hands. "And what does he prefer by way of a cold collation, Jane? For I have not a mite of meat in the house—not so much as a partridge! We might send to the tavern for brandy, I suppose—"

"Pray do not disturb yourself," I begged her. "Lord Harold has kindly invited me to take an airing in his equipage. He declares that I am looking peaked."

"And so you are!" my mother cried. Two spots of colour flamed suddenly in her cheeks. "An airing in his equipage! And he is only this moment arrived in town! But, Jane—my dear, dear girl! Now his mother is gone, I suppose there can be no objection to his marrying where he likes! Not that she was so very high in the instep—and foreign besides—yet she may have had her scruples as to connexion. There can be no question of prohibition now, for I am sure His Grace the Duke doesn't trouble himself about his lordship's affairs. Only think of it, Jane! How grand you shall be!"

"Mamma," I interposed desperately lest Lord Harold should overhear, "I believe Martha is in want of you in the kitchen."

"Fiddlesticks!"

"Indeed, madam, Martha is calling. You should not like your dinner spoilt."

Nothing but food is so near my mother's heart as marriage. She turned hastily for the passage. "Enjoy yourself, my dear! And when you have accepted his lordship, pray apologise for my having disliked him so excessively in the past. I am certain we shall deal famously together, once he has given up his opera dancers. Take care to wrap up warmly! You never appear to advantage with a reddened nose!"

IN THE EVENT, THE CARRIAGE WAS A CLOSED ONE, with the Wilborough arms emblazoned on the door—as I had suspected, an equipage of his brother's, pressed into service. The squabs were of pale gold silk; a brazier glowed at our feet. The coachman had been walking the horses this quarter-hour in expectation of his master's summons.

Orlando was mounted behind. He was magnificent today in a round hat with a broad brim, and a dark blue livery; the woodland sprite was fled. I smiled into his dark eyes and received an answering twinkle; but he was on his dignity, and offered no word.

"The Itchen Dockyard's fate is uncertain, with the shipwright murdered; but it is possible we may find Mr. Dixon's workers there, labouring to reverse disaster's effects," Lord Harold said.

"They cannot cause the ship to spring, phoenix-like, from the ashes."

"Absent the shipwright, to whom should I speak, Jane? Is there a yard foreman?"

"I do not know whether he bears that title—but there is a Lascar, one Jeremiah by name, in whom Mr. Dixon appeared to repose his trust."

"We may achieve the place, I think, from the road above Porter's Mead?"

His lordship informed his coachman of the direction, and settled himself on the seat opposite. The door was closed, and all the bustle of town abruptly shut out; and for an instant, consigned to that sheltered orb of quiet, I was struck dumb with shyness. When I had last driven out in Lord Harold's company, it had been August in Derbyshire, and the equipage an open curricle. Then he had taken the reins himself, the better part of his attention claimed by the road. Now we surveyed each other across an expanse of satin-lined cushions. The interior of the chaise was finer by far than the condition of my dress; I felt that I ought to be arrayed in a ball gown, with shoe-roses on my slippers.

"I have treated my mother to a falsehood," I said in an effort to break the silence, "for I assured her you desired to give me an airing. That must be impossible in a closed carriage."

"We shall not be confined for long." The

keenness of his glance was disconcerting; was it possible the Rogue felt as awkward as I? "I am so accustomed to your company, my dear, that I forget what is due to propriety. Your excellent parent is even now surveying our departure from behind her parlour curtain, and considering whether I have compromised your reputation. Have I ruined you, Jane, a thousand times in our long acquaintance?"

The question was so direct—and so unexpected—that I failed to contrive a suitable answer. "Naturally. Having been seen even *once* in your company, I have not a shred of respectability left."

"Shall I offer for you, then?" he demanded abruptly.

The rampant colour rose in my cheeks. Oh, that I could believe he had heard nothing of my mother's speculations!

"Pray do not say such things even in jest, my lord. You must know that I aspire to a career as an authoress, and such ladies never marry. Domestic cares will eat up one's time, and leave no room for the employment of a pen."

"If you insist upon trifling with a gentleman's heart—then tell me of this novel of yours. This *Susan.*"

I remembered how Orlando had enquired about my book's publication, as he stood in the Abbey ruins; naturally his intelligence derived from his master's. "I never speak of my writing to anyone."

"But your brother Henry *does.* He possesses not the slightest instinct for discretion, you know. It shall be his undoing one day."

Henry and his fashionable wife, Eliza, Comtesse de Feuillide, had long formed a part of the London *ton,* though their circle was less lofty than Lord

Harold's own. The Rogue enjoyed my brother's company whenever they met—and how often that might occur, in the *mêlée* of London routs, I could not say. It had been some time since Eliza had mentioned Lord Harold in her correspondence.

"I wrote *Susan* so long ago, I declare I hardly recall her outline. She was the first of a long succession of works to fall from my pen."

"There are other novels? All dedicated to a different lady?"

"No less than four books are entombed in my wardrobe, sir, and none of them fit to be read beyond the fireside circle, I assure you."[1]

"I wonder." He studied me thoughtfully. "You are not unintelligent, and possess, moreover, an acute understanding of the human heart."

I found I could not meet his gaze.

"The novel portrays, one imagines, the veritable apogee of all Susans?"

"She is a young girl, for there can never be so much interest in a woman once she has passed the age of five-and-twenty. It is better, indeed, for the novelist's fortunes if her heroine should expire before that point."

"I am entirely of your opinion. Does Susan suffer a painful end?"

"Hardly as swift as she might wish, and not within the compass of the novel. I fancy she dies in childbirth, like all the best women of my acquaintance—but for the purposes of this story, I have merely sent her to an abbey."

[1] Jane probably refers, here, to the manuscript versions of *Northanger Abbey (Susan), Pride and Prejudice (First Impressions), Sense and Sensibility (Elinor and Marianne),* and *Lady Susan.* She had also begun, and abandoned, a novel entitled *The Watsons* by 1807.—*Editor's note.*

"Excellent decision, given the environs to which you are subjected. Does she moon among the ruins, intent upon discovering a swain?"

How to describe my poor neglected darling, languishing these many years in the dust of Stationers Hall Court?

"Let us assume, for the sake of argument, that my purpose falls beyond the mere entertaining power of the best novels," I attempted. "Let us assume, in fact, that my object is to satirize such works—in the very act of mastering the form."

"Subtle Jane! But how is such an ambition to be satisfied?"

"By portraying a creature so enslaved to the practice of novel-reading, that she ceases to discern the difference between the stuff of books, and the stuff of life."

"A victim of literature!" Lord Harold crowed aloud. "Very well—and so, among the ruins, does she mistake past for present, and imagine herself a nun?"

"Nay, my lord. She is sent on a visit to an ancient abbey, where she hopes to encounter mysterious decay—only to suffer the disappointment of a modern establishment, thrown up over the bones of the old, where all is just as it should be! The master of the house has *not* murdered his wife; his daughter is *not* a prisoner in the tower; and the handsome young suitor is anything but a foundling prince. In short, he is a clergyman."

"How very provoking! I did not think you could be so cruel to children of your own invention." He leaned towards me, his face alight. "What is it about novels that engages your interest—nay, that commands your powers?"

Torn between the duty of turning his scrutiny

with an arch remark—and the desire to unburden myself to one who might actually comprehend—I gave way, as is generally the case, to Desire.

"All of life, my lord, is found among the workings of three or four families in a country village. You may laugh if you dare"—for his sardonic mouth had turned up at the corners—"but what I say is true. In the hopes and sacred dreams of a young girl on the verge of womanhood, one may see as much of courage and destiny as in the most valorous deeds of the Ancients, with far better scope for conversation."

"All of Fate, encompassed in a Susan! I do not like your ambitions so circumscribed, my dear. You had better call her Clorasinda, or some other name of four syllables, and exchange this respectable watering-hole for London, where the full panoply of human folly is on daily parade."

"I cannot bear the thrust and noise of a town; and besides—people themselves alter so much, with the passage of time, that there is infinite material for a patient observer. In the relations between men and women alone, one might detect endless subtlety and variation."

"Just so. I wonder, Jane, when I shall meet myself in your prose?"

"Never, my lord. You should defy my attempts at subjugation."

He drew down his brows at this. "At last you have said what may be understood. It is a delicious power, is it not, to subject the unwitting to the lash of your pen? *This* is what truly beguiles you, Jane. You have found your weapon in words. You set out your creatures as examples of the human type—you anatomise them with a few deft strokes—and there is the character of Man exposed: in all its weakness, foible, arrogance, and careless cruelty."

"And its goodness," I amended. "I may laugh at what is absurd, but I hope I may never meet true worth with derision."

"I cannot regard the world with the indulgence and affection you do," he returned. "My greatest fault is a propensity to despise my fellows, when I do not condemn them."

"Perhaps," I suggested hesitantly, "that is because a man is more often taught to exploit another's weakness—to use what is vulnerable for his own ends—than to respect what is admirable and good?"

He glanced at me swiftly. "Tell me, Jane—have I ever attempted to exert that kind of power over *you*?"

"No, my lord."

"—Though I may often have been tempted?"

I knew, then, that I had played at cat's paw with a lion. Lord Harold apprehended my vulnerability—my brutal weakness: how I longed to be at his side at any hour, the merest observer of an intellect and a decision so acute as to leave me breathless—how I longed for his regard, and strove to merit it. How I led a parched existence in his absence—though that absence might endure for years—aware that true life occurred wherever *he* might be. The knowledge of all Lord Harold understood fell upon me there, in the intimacy of his closed carriage; and I gasped, as though I wanted for air.

"Do not look so alarmed, Jane," he said briskly. "We were speaking, I think, of novels. You ought to demand the return of your *Susan* from Messrs. Crosby and Co.; they seem disinclined to publish, and the sacrifice of so much talent upon the altar of male stupidity is not to be borne. Once you have succeeded in retrieving the copyright, you must entrust the manuscript to me."

I swallowed hard on my emotions. "You are very good, my lord."

"I am a scoundrel," he rejoined gently, "but as we both apprehend that much, there is nothing more to be said."

IN THE INTERVAL OF A DAY, THE YARD'S MUD HAD dried somewhat, though the smell of pitch and timber was just as strong as I had found it the previous morning. I understood the cause once Lord Harold handed me down from the carriage: Mr. Dixon's men had cleared a space at the centre of the yard, and piled the remains of the seventy-four near the sea wall. Vast charred timbers of elm and oak rose into the sky like a devil's scaffold, and flames licked at the base. The ship was become a pyre, with all Mr. Dixon's hopes freighted upon it.

"The Lascar?" Lord Harold shouted.

The cloud of smoke was heavy enough that I could distinguish none of the men who tended the bonfire. My eyes smarted and my nose burned. I shook my head helplessly. Lord Harold, perceiving my streaming looks, motioned me back to the carriage. The coachman and Orlando both were at the horses' bridles, for the great beasts had no love of fire.

"Take Miss Austen to Porter's Mead," his lordship cried to his coachman above the crackle of burning wood. "I shall join you there in a quarter of an hour."

Amble handed me within, and I collapsed on the elegant cushions in a paroxysm of coughing. We were under way in an instant, the horses wheeling towards the sea. I found, when I recovered myself, that

Orlando was seated opposite, and that in his hand he extended a clean linen handkerchief marked with a great scrolling monogram: *H.L.J.* Lord Harold's own.

In his other hand was a silver flask.

"May I suggest a drop of brandy, ma'am, to clear your throat? I need not attest to the quality."

I took both the linen and the flask without a murmur. In managing women, the valet, it seemed, was as adept as his master. "Orlando, how did you happen to join Lord Harold's service?"

"Out of gratitude," he said gently. "His lordship saved my life."

"And are you able to describe the circumstances?"

An expression of pain—or was it hatred?—flickered across his countenance. But he neither hesitated nor demurred. "I was sentenced by the French governors of Oporto to hang, ma'am, on a charge of thievery. His lordship . . . persuaded . . . the men who held me in keeping to let me go. You will forgive me if I say no more."

"You need not. I have an idea of the scene. Are you Portuguese, Orlando? For you betray not the slightest hint of accent in your speech; from your manners, I might believe you born to luxury in an Earl's household."

"I never knew my mother," he replied, "but was named in the Italian at her insistence, before she died. My father was English, an army infantryman. He was carried off by a fever when I was but sixteen. From that moment to this, I have made to shift for myself. I wandered the world for some years, until I was so fortunate as to earn his lordship's notice."

"You have no other family?"

He smiled faintly. "None of which I am aware."

"And you are how old?"

"Seven-and-twenty, ma'am."

"What did the French believe you stole, Orlando, during your sojourn in Oporto?"

"Bread." His gaze remained steady. "We had been subject to blockade, you understand, some months. Food was exceedingly scarce. I was hungry; the French plundered what little we had, and kept their stores under guard in a warehouse. It had once been a shed for aging sherry. I noticed an aperture for drains—I am a slight fellow, and adept at worming my way into every sort of hole."

"Lord Harold must find such talents useful," I observed under my breath, and returned the flask to Orlando's keeping.

"THE LASCAR IS A CAPITAL FELLOW," HIS LORDSHIP declared as he joined me on the Mead some twenty minutes later.

I had quitted the carriage and commenced walking the length of the meadow, out of a desire for exercise and a compulsion to feel the wind on my face; Lord Harold came up with me quickly, covering the ground in long, easy strides that must always appear graceful.

"He means to urge the Company of Shipwrights to put their silver behind retrieving the Itchen yard, and asked that I help him to do it.[2] I shall certainly intercede—indeed, I may invest funds of my own—for with such a dedicated fellow among the ranks, the yard is likely to prosper."

[2] The Company of Shipwrights incorporated in 1605.—*Editor's note.*

"Provided you may protect it against purposeful arson. Jeremiah is a shipwright, then?"

"The Lascar? Lord, no! I should not think the Company would allow a foreigner to set up in business, when good English shipwrights are in want of places—but he is certain to find employment if the yard remains open, and is canny enough to comprehend that greater influence than his is required to secure his future. He has agreed to serve as my spy, moreover, within the ruined yard. But I digress: I meant to learn from him what I could of the night the seventy-four was fired."

"And?"

Lord Harold offered me his arm, and turned towards the carriage. His excellent black coat of superfine bore a distinct odour of charcoal.

"Jeremiah lodges off the Rope Walk, with several of his kind—Able Seamen who take ship for a year or two, then spend their earnings in a single week ashore. The Lascar had taken his dinner and turned his attention to his favourite pastime—the carving of a model ship—when a cry arose in the street outside. One or two of his fellows had been sitting on the lodging-house roof, drinking rum together and wagering as to the names of ships presently anchored in Southampton Water, when the flames first lit the Itchen yard. Jeremiah climbed immediately to the rooftop, astounded at what he saw. From that height it was clear the blaze had already reached the third-rate's masts. The speed of the conflagration seemed at the time remarkable, but we apprehend now that pitch, in being liberally spread upon the timbers, effected it. Unlike his mates, however, who were agog at the fire, Jeremiah searched with his gaze among the surrounding streets. From his lofty perch he hoped to espy Mr. Dixon raising the alarum. The Lascar, you must understand, has spent years at sea and is accustomed to standing watch in the crow's nest. His eyes are very keen, even in the falling dusk."

We reached the blazoned chaise, Orlando standing at attention. He swept open the carriage door and bowed low, managing the air of the loyal retainer so well that he might have affected it on the stage. Play-acting, I decided, must be the valet's true calling: he ought to be put in the way of an introduction to his lordship's old friend, the tragedian John Kemble. Then he might spend his days in adopting strange masks, and throwing his voice—child's play for one of his experience.

"Tho' a crowd of folk commenced to run *towards* the yard," Lord Harold continued as we paused by the open carriage door, "Jeremiah espied a single figure running *away* from it. The man was cloaked in black from neck to boots, and wore a hood over his head. He carried no lanthorn, though the streets were growing dark; and to the Lascar's mind, he seemed at pains to avoid the most trafficked road. Jeremiah watched him course through the alleys that join the yard with the Rope Walk, and disappear from view somewhere in the vicinity of Orchard Lane—at which point the crisis at the yard could no longer be ignored. The Lascar recognised the utility of opening the sea wall in order to douse the flames, and summoning his mates, raced to accomplish the purpose. It was then he discovered the body of Mr. Dixon."

"The cloaked figure he espied was responsible for firing the ship?" I enquired as Orlando handed me within.

"And possibly for slitting the shipwright's throat."

Lord Harold pulled closed the door. "The man may have worked alone, or in the company of another whom the Lascar could not see."

"Mrs. Challoner?"

"Recollect, Jane, the evidence of your own eyes. You saw her curtsey to a cloaked figure in the Abbey ruins only yesterday. Perhaps she intended to thank the fellow for a job well-done."

Chapter 10

The Secret Passage

28 October 1808, cont.

~

THREE-QUARTERS OF AN HOUR LATER, I HUDDLED IN the middle of Jeb Hawkins's skiff with my cloak wrapped tightly around me, convinced that I had quitted the living world entirely. A curtain of fog drifted towards Southampton from the mouth of the Channel, and hung dully over the landscape. My fingers were knotted in my lap against the chill off the sea, which penetrated the thin kid of my gloves; the airing, I decided dispiritedly, would certainly redden my nose.

From the Itchen yard, his lordship had turned to the Water Gate Quay, and there discovered the Bosun's Mate engaged in mending nets. The hale old fellow was seated on the eastern side of the Quay, his gnarled hands twisting and unfurling his sea-worn rope; but he readily agreed to take us out to Netley Cliff. If he wondered what fascination the place must hold, he forbore to enquire; it was enough for Jeb Hawkins that a duke's son had need of his services.

The duke's son was poised now in the bow, his gaze roaming the dim outline of Netley Cliff. Mr. Hawkins, his scowl in abeyance, bent and strained at the oars; at his lordship's insistence, the locks were muffled with strips of leather. Silent and barely visible, we moved as wraiths over the surface of the Water.

Suddenly, Lord Harold raised one hand in a gesture for silence, and pointed with the other towards the cliff.

"There," he whispered. "Perhaps four feet above the shingle, to the left of the barnacled rock. Observe."

I narrowed my weak eyes to search the looming cliff face, half-obscured by the hanging mist. I could discern nothing out of the ordinary.

"Cor!" muttered Jeb Hawkins. "Fifty year an' more I been sailing this coast, and never did I discover the same. A cut in the cliff, broad enough for a man, with an iron grill to close it. It'll have been hidden by seagrass, maybe, as is presently disarranged."

"Well done," Lord Harold said softly. "That is the mouth of a drain once employed by the monks of Netley Abbey. Some five hundred yards it runs, straight through the hillside from the Abbey kitchen to Southampton Water. Tales have it that the Cistercians disposed of their refuse by such means; others, that the passage was a swift escape to the boats, when the monks were under attack. A second branch of the passage is more prosaic: it runs to the fish ponds, and served the monks with supper."[1]

"Did you merely suspect the existence of such a passage, from a general knowledge of the ways of monks?" I demanded. "I should have thought that everything to do with a cloister must be foreign to *your* experience."

"You neglect to mention, Miss Austen, that among my other sins I may count a country boyhood," he rejoined. "One of the lesser Wilborough estates—in Cornwall, I confess—is built on the ruin of just such an abbey. I explored its cunning features thoroughly in my youth, particularly when I desired a spot of fishing, or to escape the wrath of an outraged tutor. The Cistercians were masters of the hidden back door: they lived in mortal fear of plunderers, particularly when they settled along the coast. Do you recall, Jane, that Mr.... *Smythe*... seemed to materialise from the very stones at your feet, when you met him in the Abbey on Tuesday?"

I had thought Orlando a ghost; and had remarked, moreover, that he had left no boat near the cliff landing.

"Were you perhaps in the vicinity of the Abbey kitchens at the time?" Lord Harold persisted.

"I believe I was in the refectory. Are you suggesting that Orlan—that Mr. Smythe—employed this self-same passage?"

Lord Harold smiled. "Let us say that it appealed to his habits of stealth."

"Have your agents bolt-holes all over England?"

[1] The passage Lord Harold describes still exists at Netley Abbey today. —*Editor's note.*

"In every seaport accessible to the Channel, at least. Mr. Hawkins—I should like to land."

"Land it is, guv'nor."

The Bosun's Mate thrust hard to port with his oar, and found purchase on the shallow bottom; in another instant the skiff scraped over gravel. Through the wisps of fog I could discern, now, the iron grill set into the limestone cliff, at about the height of a man's waist; a narrow strip of shingle ten feet wide divided it from the sea.

Lord Harold stepped into the water, careless of top boots and pantaloons; but I had no wish to soil my fresh new bombazine. I began to gather my skirts about my knees, in an effort to spare as much of the cloth as possible. He turned back as though I had summoned him, and without a word of deference lifted me easily into his arms.

"Good God," I gasped. "Put me down, sir!"

"In two feet of water? None of your missish airs, Jane, I beg." He strode implacably towards the shore, and set me on my feet. "Mr. Hawkins, have you a lanthorn in that boat?"

"I have, my lord."

"We require it."

"Very good, my lord."

The Bosun's Mate was fairly falling over himself to do the gentleman's bidding, I thought sourly. Was it the courtesy title that inspired such alacrity? Or the weight of his lordship's purse? I ran my hands over my skirts, as though fearful of some permanent injury, but the performance was wasted on Lord Harold, who was already working at the drain's mouth.

"Mr. Smythe, as usual, may be trusted to admiration. The stonework is free of dirt, and the grill has been recently oiled."

Mr. Hawkins appeared with a glowing lanthorn. Lord Harold swung open the tunnel's grate, and gestured inwards with infinite politesse. *"Après-vous, mademoiselle."*

I peered into the passage. Beyond the narrow opening, it widened considerably. Mindful of my gown, I collected myself into as small a figure as possible, and found Lord Harold's hand at my elbow. He hoisted me upwards to the tunnel's sill. The glow of the lanthorn followed.

"There is room to walk abreast," he observed in a whisper. "Thank heaven you are not a weighty woman, Jane."

"In wit alone, my lord."

"Hah."

The pool of light eddied at my feet; I could feel him near me in the dark. The tunnel was utterly silent and somehow oppressive, as though we stood in a sealed chamber that no time or hope could ever liberate. Here was an adventure worthy of an abbey—or the romantic heroine of *Susan*! She should have detected immediately a fluttering ghost, receding down the passage, and must have followed with pounding heart and fainting sensibilities!

My pulse throbbed loudly in my ears; I shared a little of my heroine's trepidation. Had I been able to reach for Lord Harold's hand—but I refused to exhibit weakness. Instead I stepped forward into the passage. It was lined in smooth, rounded cobblestones—the sort that served as ballast in seafaring ships—with sand in the crevices between.

The lowness of the ceiling forced us to walk as aged crones, our backs bent. The lanthorn light and my companion's self-possession soon relieved me of uneasiness, but I could find no purpose in his researches: had he made this journey merely to exhibit the method by which his henchman had discovered me on Tuesday?

He stopped short and held the lanthorn close to the passage floor. "Footprints. You observe them? There, and there, in the sand."

"Orlando's?"

He shook his head. "A man's boot, certainly, but too large for his. Someone else has been here."

I felt a chill along my spine. What if the creature awaited us even now, hidden by the unplumbed dark? I recollected the cloaked figure that had attended Mrs. Challoner and her American yesterday, at the head of the Abbey footpath. Then, I had thought his air sinister; in the isolation of the underground passage, the memory inspired mortal fear.

"Jane," Lord Harold whispered, "lift your eyes from the ground and tell me what you see ahead."

The shadows welled like living things, dancing away from my sight. I strained to pierce them. "Nothing but a division in the tunnel, my lord—a secondary passage, descending to the left."

"The way to the fish ponds, I suspect. We shall continue to the right, until we achieve the passage mouth. There should be stairs debouching in the kitchen."

"You are unfamiliar with this passage?"

"Entirely—but I apprehend its utility." He laid a finger to my lips—a touch as glancing as a feather. "Silence, Jane. We must endeavour not to disturb the Abbey's ghosts."

He stepped forward, and though I wished I might turn and flee back along the way we had come, I forced myself to put one foot before the other. My breathing was overly loud in my ears; the rustle of bombazine as clattering as grapeshot. Every movement must reverberate among the stones. Of a sudden the toe of my half-boot struck the edge of a cobble, and I stumbled forward, throwing out my hands to ward off a fall. I landed heavily on the passage floor.

Lord Harold turned at the noise, his lanthorn making a wide arc; and as the light flared in the passage ahead of him, I glimpsed something—a spark of gold. I reached out and grasped it: an object the size of a door key, fashioned of metal.

"A cross," I said as I held it to the light. "It looks to be made of gold."

"A crucifix," Lord Harold corrected. He assisted me to rise and took the thing when I offered it—turning the gold under the lanthorn. "You found this even now, on the passage floor?"

"Perhaps a long-dead monk let it fall, centuries ago."

"It is too well-polished, too delicately chased. Curious." He looked at me thoughtfully. "Will you keep it, Jane?"

"Should I not leave it here, in expectation that the owner might return?"

"It could prove useful. Place it in your reticule for safekeeping."

I did as he bade me, feeling like a thief.

"You are not injured, I hope?" his lordship enquired.

"My gown will be soiled, if it is not already torn; but I am entirely out of temper with women's apparel, and cannot lament the cost. You will be leaving me at home in future, and placing your trust in the stealthy Orlando."

He grasped my hand by way of answer, and led me forward.

• • •

"IT BREAKS MY HEART TO SEE THE OLD STONES THUS, despoiled of their marble. Only think what this place once was, in the days before King Henry worked his change on the land!"

The words filtered down through the rotting wood of the tunnel hatch, set into the stone a mere foot above our heads. We stood poised in the middle of the ascending stairs that led from passage to kitchen, and in another moment I am sure that Lord Harold should have thrust open the hatch-door, and we must have been discovered, but for the woman's voice starting up in the midst of conversation.

Heat and chill washed over me in waves, from a suspense at our situation; for the voice, I readily discerned, was Sophia Challoner's.

"The mantelpiece, I imagine, now forms the center of some gentleman's household?"

It could only be Mr. Ord who spoke; but the American's tone was far more serious than the one he had adopted at his lady's dining table.

"Everything that could be scavenged has been stripped from the place. The same is true throughout England—for Henry was accustomed to highway robbery, and liked to call it politics."

The heels of her half-boots rang on the paving above my left shoulder; involuntarily, I ducked, and felt Lord Harold's hand in warning at my waist.

"That accounts, I suppose, for the air of sadness," Ord said. "It is far more oppressive within the Abbey than in standing upon the walls. There one might have an idea of the old days, when the abbot commanded one of the finest views of the Solent, and welcomed visitors from every part of the world."

"Oh, *why* does *mon seigneur* not come?" Sophia Challoner demanded tautly, as though she had heard nothing of his wistful speech. "We have been waiting here full half an hour—and still he does not appear."

"There might be a thousand causes for delay. Do not make yourself anxious, I beg."

"I am always anxious," she muttered, low. "I eat and sleep and breathe anxiety. It has become my habit, since Raoul was killed."

Lord Harold's hand tightened on my waist.

"You merely take the grief from these old stones," Mr. Ord replied gently. "Let us go out and look for *mon seigneur* on the path. I am persuaded you will benefit from the air."

She said nothing by way of reply; but the rapping heels made their way across the room, and faded out of earshot. With stealthy grace, Lord Harold drew me back down the stone passage. Although we moved with haste, I did not stumble, and neither of us spoke until we stood once more at the tunnel's mouth. Then Lord Harold smiled faintly.

"How close we came to discovery, Jane! And what, then, should I have said to Sophia?"

"That you share her opinion of King Henry as a thief and a vandal, and should be charmed to make her companion's acquaintance."

"He speaks with a pronounced American accent. Mr. Ord, I presume?"

"But who is this *mon seigneur* they expected? A man in a long black cloak, perhaps?"

"Mon seigneur," Lord Harold repeated. "*My lord,* in the French. A nobleman of the present regime—one of the Monster's able minions? And does he serve as Sophia's agent—or her master? I pity the fellow. Tho' he command the greatest of temporal

powers, he will yet shudder to encounter Sophia's wrath. She is more terrible even than Napoleon when she suffers a disappointment."

"You are very hard upon the lady, sir."

"It is my habit, Jane, with regard to all the fair sex—excepting yourself."

"She betrays a marked preference for lost Papist glory."

"In this, as in everything, she is squarely at odds with England. I believe I shall position the long-suffering Orlando in this tunnel, for the nonce, and charge him with listening well at trapdoors. We might learn much of the Enemy's plans, from a pair of ears well-placed."

I recollected the footprints on the tunnel floor—the prints *not* of Orlando's making—and my heart misgave me. "What if the French lord uses this passage as his method of approach? The evidence of Mr. Hawkins's boat on the strand may have warned him of our presence today, and turned him back from his appointment—but what if he were to happen upon Orlando?"

Lord Harold thrust open the grilled door. "So much the better," he answered grimly. "Orlando might slit the villain's throat, and save us all a world of pain."

Chapter 11

Stowaway

Saturday, 29 October 1808

~

. . . Mamma is hourly torn between raptures over the pretty little village of Wye, and the contemplation of what it should mean to possess full six bedchambers without the necessity of filling them all. For my own part, I should like to see us settled in Hampshire—near enough to our friends and relations for the sake of society, but without feeling too great a dependence, as we might in such proximity to Godmersham as Wye offers. Kentish folk in general are so very rich, and we are so very poor, that I fear the temptation to comparison would improve the opinions of neither.

I raised my pen and stared in dissatisfaction at the letter to my sister. I had come to a full stop from an inability to convey what was chiefly in my mind: Lord Harold Trowbridge, and the business that had brought him to Southampton; Lord Harold, and the veil that had been torn from my eyes in the confines of his carriage. I could say nothing to Cassandra of the interesting Mrs. Challoner, or her assignations among ruined stones—nothing of the young American on his lathered black mount, or of cloaked and sinister strangers. I ought not even to mention his lordship's name, in fact; Cassandra feared his influence over my heart.

You are most unlike yourself, Jane, when that man is near, she had chided me once in Derbyshire. *When admitted to his sphere, you grow discontented with your lot—and he is the very last gentleman on earth to improve it. By such attentions, he exposes you to the ridicule of the world for disappointed hopes, and himself to charges of caprice and instability.*

Cassandra is so thoroughly good—so determined to greet each day with an equal propriety of demeanour and ambition—that she invariably puts me to shame.

And yet, I cannot see Lord Harold again without my whole heart opening—to him, and to the prospect of a far wider life than I have ever dreamt of enjoying.

I drew forth a second sheet of foolscap and scrawled, for my own eyes alone:

—If I am a wild beast I cannot help it—

Then I threw both sheets of paper into the fire, and hurried downstairs to breakfast.

"*Four hours* in a closed carriage with a gentleman of Lord Harold's reputation—and you *still* have not received an offer of marriage?" my mother demanded as she sipped her tea from a saucer. "He should never have served you so ill, Jane, had your father been alive! Mr. George Austen, Fellow of St. John's College and Rector of Steventon, should have made his lordship understand his duty quick enough! I ought to forbid Lord High-and-Mighty the house."

"Recollect, Mamma, that Lord Harold cannot be thinking of marriage at present. He is in mourning."

"As are you, my dear—as are we all! But one cannot bury oneself in the grave with the deceased! One must, after all, cling to life!"

"More toast, ma'am?" Martha suggested.

My mother selected a slice of beautifully browned bread from the plate that was offered. "I *cannot* think what the two of you find to talk about. Men are never much interested in the opinion of ladies—and his lordship, in the opinion of anyone but himself. It is not as though he calls for the sheer pleasure of gazing at your countenance—which you will admit, my dear, has grown rather coarse of late. You *will* not take my advice, and make use of Gowland's Lotion, though Martha has found it infinitely beneficial. Do you not, Martha?"

"Oh—certainly, ma'am. There is nothing to equal Gowland's."

"Even our Mrs. Frank said, before she went off, 'Only think, Mother Austen, how thankful I am for your recommendation of Gowland's Lotion! See how it has entirely carried away my freckles!' "

"Rubbish," said a brusque voice from the breakfast room doorway, "Mary has never sported a freckle in her life—so do not be telling such shocking great fibs, Mamma, purely for the sake of bubble reputation."

My brother Frank strode cheerfully into the breakfast parlour amid exclamations of surprise.

"Fly!" I cried, "my intelligence was correct! I was informed on Tuesday that you were not three days out of Portsmouth—and here you are in Southampton, the very day after!"

"Who could possibly know so much of my business?"

"Captain Strong, of the *Windlass,*" I replied.

"Excellent fellow, Strong! But I made better time than he guessed, and put in at the Island yesterday morning. It was then I heard the sad news from Godmersham. I could not be passing so near your door, Mamma, without stopping to condole."

He looked very grave as he said this. Frank had spent a good deal of time in Edward's company in recent years—indeed, he had passed the whole of his honeymoon at Godmersham—and must feel for his brother, and mourn the passing of Elizabeth, who was always so generous. But I knew that some part of his gravity was reserved wholly for his wife, and the trials of childbirth she must inevitably undergo. Little Mary, so fresh and pink and fair-haired in the first flush of marriage, had very nearly been carried off by the birth of her first child last April; and Frank was in no haste to repeat the experience.

"You are wearing black gloves," I observed. They looked oddly with his white pantaloons and second-best naval coat.

"It was partly to obtain them that I journeyed up the Solent. Nothing so well-made is to be had in Portsmouth; they are all for economy there. Indeed,

I carry a commission for Mary's dressmaker at present—a woman lodged below in Bugle Street."

"Madame Clarisse?" Martha suggested.

"Just so!"

"It is a great comfort to see you once more at home, Frank," my mother said plaintively, "for I do not count those dreadful lodgings you *would* take, as being a home. It seems a very great while since you went away."

As my brother had quitted Castle Square but a few weeks before, it was to be expected that Mrs. Austen should be made unhappy.

"Mary is well, I suppose?" she added. "For my part, I should be very low, indeed, if left entirely without friends in the midst of an island, my husband at sea. But not all of us are possessed of congenial spirits—or a taste for society."

Frank's brow darkened. Before he could hurl a biting retort, I said quickly, "What foresight you have shown, dear Fly, in making your removal—for you should have been forced to it in any case, by the flight of your mother and sisters! We have had a deal of news from Godmersham! In the midst of all his trouble—in the very depths of despair—our excellent brother has thought only of his family. Edward offers us a freehold, Frank, to be taken up this summer! He offers us *two* situations, in fact—and my mother has only to choose that which suits her."

"It is such a comfort to possess *one* child who understands his duty," the lady murmured.

"We were just canvassing the merits and weaknesses of our choice," Martha threw in. "Perhaps you could offer an opinion, Captain? One cottage is in Kent, at a place called Wye; the other, in the village of Chawton."

"Go anyplace you like—provided you remain in Hampshire," he declared warmly. "Chawton must be the preferred situation."

Martha blushed pink.

"A complete removal of the household, at my advanced age, is painful to contemplate," my mother mourned. "But beggars cannot be choosers. When I consider how happy we all were, only a month since! And now, so much has changed—"

She rose with an air of oppression at this final remark, and swept towards the door.

"I suppose you will wish your best love conveyed to Mary?" Frank called after her.

"Whatever you think best, dear boy," she returned in a failing accent, "—for you *shall* do as you please."

IT WAS AGREED THAT MARTHA AND I SHOULD WALK out with Frank into Bugle Street, she to complete some shopping, and I to consult with Madame Clarisse. We have all of us been forced to take some pains with our mourning—for though we intend to honour Lizzy's loss, we are likely to be out of black clothes by the turn of the year.[1] I have two gowns of bombazine and crepe, according to the fashion, but my clothes shall not impoverish me—for by having my black velvet pelisse fresh-lined with the turnings

[1] The custom of going into black clothes at the death of a relative increased during the Victorian era, which made an elaborate ceremony of mourning; but in Austen's day, it was customary to honor only the closest relations with prolonged adoption of black. A spouse might adopt mourning clothes for half a year or longer, but more distant relations would shorten the period and the degree of black clothing, wearing merely black gloves or hair ribbons in respect of the most distant family members.—*Editor's note.*

of my cloak, I shall avoid the expence of bespeaking a new one. I shall require nothing further than a pair of black gloves and some hair ribbons. It is pitiful to economise in the matter of Elizabeth's observance—she who was always exquisitely dressed—but I so abhor the necessity of mourning, and the somber reflections to which black clothes invariably lead with each morning's toilette, that I cannot bear to throw my money after the privilege of obtaining them. I feel certain that Elizabeth would not only understand, but applaud, my sentiments.

"You know of the firing of Itchen Dockyard, and the destruction of the seventy-four?" I enquired of my brother as we quitted the house.

"Naturally. I had the news as soon as I touched at the Island—your naval set can talk of nothing else."

"And do you credit the idea," Martha asked, "that the act was deliberate? For my part, I cannot conceive of such wickedness! I am sure that we shall discover it was all an accident, in a very little while."

"The shipwright—old Dixon—did not cut his throat by accident." Frank's tone was caustic. "A finer fellow never lived—he would do anything to aid a fighting captain! And his sweet ship, too—as neat a third-rate as one could wish. Dixon took me through her in July, before I set out for the Peninsula. Pressed his carronades on me, too, having learned that I could not beg or steal the same from Portsmouth yard."

"I met Mr. Dixon so recently as Monday," I said. "He was all that was amiable, and asked to be remembered to yourself before he sent young Edward and George to look into the ship. They were quite taken with the naval life."

"Pshaw, Jane—those boys are cut to a gentleman's

jib. Too old to put to sea, besides; our brother ought to have tossed one of 'em into my hold long since. Henry or William, now, might serve," he added thoughtfully, with respect to my younger nephews. "I could take both of 'em on the *St. Alban's* without the slightest trouble. I shall endeavour to write to Godmersham with the offer."

"You are very good," Martha told him. "It may serve as some recompense for all we owe your brother."

"But tell me, Frank," I interrupted, "does the Navy have no idea who might wish to destroy the shipwright and his seventy-four?"

My brother eyed me dubiously. "You take a rare interest, Jane. Is it because of having met old Dixon? Or is Mamma cutting up nasty—talking of the streets being unsafe, and no self-respecting woman likely to walk alone about town? How glad Mary shall be to have escaped such a coil!"

"Is she not frightened at being alone?" Martha queried faintly.

"There is nowhere safer for a lady than the Island! After Wednesday's fires, all of Portsmouth is on the watch for mischief."

"And thus the blow shall probably come elsewhere," I murmured.

"I may say that the Admiralty has long feared such a cowardly turn," Frank asserted. "It is said that the Emperor's agents have gone to ground in the Channel ports, and await the proper moment to destroy our peace. When I landed my French prisoners at Spithead last month, and saw them conveyed into the hulks at anchor there—I heard talk of others, who formed no part of the surrendered troops, put ashore by night and intent upon all kinds of devilry."

Martha gave an involuntary squeak, and came to an abrupt halt on the paving. "I believe I shall just look into the poulterer's, Jane. Captain Austen—I shall pray for your continued safety. Be so good as to send my compliments to your dear wife and child—"

And without a backward glance, she made for the comparative safety of the shop's interior.

"If you are not careful," I told my brother, "you will be inspiring nightmare in that dear creature's mind! Is it possible that you carried off one of these foreign agents in the *St. Alban's*?"

"Not a stowaway," he replied doubtfully, "but a rum cove enough. He came aboard at the request of General Dalrymple, and was ensured free passage on my ship—a great, tall fellow in a black cloak and cowl."

"How sinister you make him sound! Was he an Englishman, bound for home from Oporto?"

Frank shook his head. "That was the very devil of it, Jane. I was assured the man was a Portugee—a friend and ally of our forces, who thought it best to put the Peninsula at his back. He may have spoke the tongue right enough, but I'll swear the fellow was no Iberian."

"Did you learn his name?"

"It was Silva, or some such—I cannot entirely recollect. A common enough handle, by all accounts, in that part of the world. I asked him to dine in my cabin one night, as should be only proper—and believe me when I tell you, Jane: the man spoke nothing but French!"

Was it possible that the man Frank described was the very one I had observed Mrs. Challoner to meet in the Abbey ruins? To think that my own brother had given the Frenchman passage—an agent of the

Monster's, perhaps, who intended our ruin! But a black cloak was decidedly common. Perhaps I made a significance out of nothing—

I glanced at Fly distractedly. "Where did this curious stranger of yours, the dubious Portugee, disembark from the *St. Alban's*?"

"Portsmouth—but I have an idea that he was bound for Brighton."

"Indeed? A curious destination. What attraction may a watering place hold, on the threshold of November?"

"Only one." Frank paused before Madame Clarisse's door. "Our Senhor Silva bore a letter of introduction to no less a personage than Mrs. Fitzherbert."

"Mrs. *Fitzherbert*?"

There could not be *two* ladies who bore that name. My brother's mysterious passenger had intended to visit one of the most powerful women in the Kingdom: the beautiful and notorious Maria Fitzherbert, scion of a great and influential Catholic family, twice-widowed before she was thirty, stalwart of the Recusant Ascendancy—and mistress to the Prince of Wales.[2] Some claimed that the Prince had actually married her in 1786, one of the many heedless acts of his youth—though such a union must be illegal. The heir to the throne of England should be barred from holding the crown, did he ally himself to a Catholic. In view of the animosity the rebellious

[2] Maria Fitzherbert was born Maria Anne Smythe on 26 July 1756 in Jane Austen's own county of Hampshire. Her mother was the half-sister of the Earl of Sefton; her paternal grandfather, a baronet created by Charles II in gratitude for loyal Catholic support during the Civil War. She thus belonged firmly among the Recusant Ascendancy, as noble Catholics were called.—*Editor's note.*

Prince bore his father, King George III, this might be regarded as one of the union's chief attractions.

Mrs. Fitzherbert had spent the better part of her thirties as unofficial consort—but the Prince was notoriously free with both his affections and his purse, and want of funds drove him to seek an official union that might meet with public approval, and encourage Parliament to put paid to his enormous debts. He broke off his relations with his Catholic wife, and hurriedly wed his cousin, Caroline of Brunswick, in 1796—though some called it bigamy. This sanctioned union never thrived, and the royal spouses separated for good a mere three weeks after their wedding night. Mrs. Fitzherbert, meanwhile, retired to her establishment in Brighton—purchased by the Prince at public expence—and saw no more of the man she persisted in regarding as her lawful husband.

Barely three years after his public union with Caroline of Brunswick, the Prince was once more hot in pursuit of the Catholic beauty, threatening that he should commit suicide, or waste into a decline, if she did not consent to a reunion. Entreated to return by no less a personage than the Queen herself, who hated the Princess of Wales and was consumed with anxiety for her son's health, Mrs. Fitzherbert at last relented. *The Times* announced the reconciliation in July 1799, and though the lady continued to maintain a separate establishment, she has been generally inseparable from the Prince for the past nine years. The two spend the majority of their time in Brighton—which has become a centre of Fashion: the Prince at his Pavilion, and Mrs. Fitzherbert in her Egyptian-style house on the Steine.

"Mrs. Fitzherbert, indeed," I murmured. "I

wonder—did she receive your Senhor Silva? And what could they find to talk about?"

"What do you care?" Fly demanded impatiently. "The wind is deuced chill, Jane, and we are standing about on the pavement, when we might be comfortable with the *modiste*!"

"I am merely surprised at the turn your story took. From your description of the cloaked devil, I expected to learn that he made straight for Southampton, in order to fire Mr. Dixon's yard."

Frank threw back his head and laughed. "Your flights of fancy are beyond everything, Jane! Trust a woman to make a horrid novel of the slightest commonplace!"

Chapter 12

Pin Money

29 October 1808, cont.

~

MY BROTHER DID NOT STAY ABOVE TEN MINUTES with Madame Clarisse, for his wife's commissions were of a trifling nature. I required a fitting of the second black gown I had bespoken, and the seamstress being occupied in the accommodation of another lady, who appeared so heavily with child that she might be confined at any moment, I was forced to bide my time. When Frank had concluded his business, and held me unaffectedly to his bosom, I charged him with carrying my best love to his hopeful family.

"Shall we see you again in Castle Square before the *St. Alban's* puts to sea?"

"I cannot tell, Jane—I am at the disposal of the Admiralty, and must go where they will. But I shall make a push to bring Mary to you, if the trip can be managed."

He was about to open the *modiste*'s door when the office was performed by an elegantly-attired woman standing on the pavement outside the shop.

Her gaze swept my brother's figure from head to toe, and with an expression half of amusement, half of contempt, she stepped back to permit her mistress's entrance.

The creature sailed into the room without so much as a glance at my poor brother, who hastened to doff his tricornered hat. She wore a *manteline à la Castilliane*—a short cape of orange and purple velvet trimmed in spotted leopard, and fastened with a jeweled brooch at the right shoulder; her matching velvet hat was *à la Diane.* The broad brim of the latter swooped low over her eyes, and her dark auburn hair was knotted tightly at the nape of her neck—but I should never mistake the vision for anyone but Sophia Challoner.

"Ah, ma'am—always a pleasure to see you!" cried Madame Clarisse, abandoning her burdened client and dropping fervently into a low curtsey. "What a picture you do make, to be sure! Silk velvet, I'll be bound, and the plain white muslin train, as must be proper. Straight from *La Belle Assemblée,* or I miss my mark!"[1]

"But, unfortunately, from last April's number," Mrs. Challoner replied tranquilly. "I am sadly behind

[1] *La Belle Assemblée,* despite its title, was not a French ladies' periodical but a British one, subtitled *Bell's Court and Fashionable Magazine.* It was printed in London and contained numerous fashion plates with descriptions of materials, trims, and appropriate accessories, for both men and women. It was common to carry such engravings to one's *modiste* when ordering a gown.—*Editor's note.*

the fashions in England, as you see—and must endeavour to make amends. I expect a party of guests at the Lodge in a few days, and should blush to appear in such disarray. I wonder, Madame Clarisse, if you might spare me an hour this morning?"

"Oh—but of course—indeed, I can spare you any amount of time, Mrs. Challoner, for I am sure Mrs. Phillips"—with a careless wave at the expectant mother—"and Miss Austen will prove no very great charge upon my labours."

Sophia glanced sharply about the room. "Miss Austen, did you say? But where is she?"

I stepped forward and offered the apparition a courtesy. "Good morning, Mrs. Challoner! I must count myself fortunate that we meet again! May I have the honour of introducing my brother to your acquaintance?"

Frank, though a trifle awed by the lady's fashionable looks, managed a neat leg.

"Captain Austen, of the Royal Navy: Mrs. Challoner, of Netley Lodge. Mrs. Challoner was lately taken off of Oporto, Frank, by His Majesty's forces."

"Good Lord!" my brother exclaimed. "I was in Oporto myself, you know! What vessel was so happy as to bear you home to England, ma'am?"

"The *Dartmoor*, commanded by Captain Felbank."

"Then I may declare that you were in excellent hands. You enjoyed a safe passage, I hope?"

"Not a moment of sickness, though the weather was abominable. Are you presently on shore-leave?"

"I may wish for such blessings at every hour, ma'am—far oftener than I enjoy them. I am returned to port but a day, and may expect to quit it on the instant. Such is the nature of war. My dear Jane—time wastes, and I must leave you—"

"Pray urge your dear wife to call in Castle Square."

Frank kissed my hand, bowed again to Mrs. Challoner, and completely ignored her elegant dresser in passing through the door.

THE BURDENED MRS. PHILLIPS TOOK HERSELF OFF, with an air of oppression and ill-usage on her countenance. I could not blame her, for the contrast between Mrs. Challoner's blooming looks, and every other person in the room, was almost too much to be borne. I am sure that Madame Clarisse would have given me several broad hints to be gone, with the promise of a fitting at another time, should my discomfiture prove more convenient to the mistress of Netley; but in this the charming Sophia would take no part. She insisted upon seeing me fitted out in my dreadful black bombazine, and though I blushed to be critically surveyed, while Madame Clarisse knelt at my feet with a quantity of pins in her mouth, I could not demur. I might have pled fatigue, and departed in the direction of my home—but that I abhorred the loss of such a prime opportunity of furthering my acquaintance with the *Peninsula's most potent weapon.*

"What do you think, Eglantine?" she enquired of her dresser as the two gazed at my reflection.

"I cannot like the style," the Frenchwoman replied in her native tongue; "it is too plain about the neck for prettiness, and taken together with the dull black of the fabric, must make the lady appear a penitent."

I understood this frank opinion well enough to

flush an unfortunate red; but if Mrs. Challoner observed the change, she did not regard it.

"I wonder if Madame Clarisse is familiar with the demi-ruff à la Queen Elizabeth, pleated in Vandyke?"

"To be sure I am familiar with it!" the *modiste* cried. "Mrs. Penworthy has been wearing the same these five weeks and more, with an olive-green walking dress in Circassian cloth. Buttoned down the front it is, and formed high in back, with open lapels at the bosom. The sash is salmon pink, and tied in small bows on the right side. Over her left arm, Mrs. Penworthy affects a shawl of pale salmon figured in dark blue—quite elegant, I'm sure, when worn with straw-coloured gloves and shoes."

"But I am in mourning," I reminded them gently, "and must make do with black."

Madame Clarisse rose to her feet, and surveyed me with a practiced eye. "She has the bosom for it—the sash should go high under the arms, to frame her décolleté. I suppose we might cut the middle anew, and set in the buttons on the bodice with a white chemisette behind the open lapels. Forgive me for speaking as I find, Miss Austen, but you've rather a short neck—and the white demi-ruff, Vandyke-stile, should lengthen its appearance to admiration."

"But is so much attention to fashion, at such a time, entirely proper . . . ?" I suggested feebly.

"There's no harm in setting off the black with a touch of linen," rejoined the *modiste* stoutly, "and no dishonour intended to the Dear Departed, neither."

With the French dresser urging her support in flurried accents, and Sophia Challoner draping a pleated collar high about my neck, and prescribing a change in coiffure—parted down the middle, with curls on either side—I found myself suddenly transported to giddy heights: to an admiration of my countenance and figure I had long since abandoned, and a conviction that with a trifling expence, I might achieve an accommodation with the hated black I had never before envisioned.

"You must never wear such a dismal cap on your hair again," Mrs. Challoner enjoined, "for it makes you look a good deal older than I'll warrant you are. What would you suggest, Eglantine, by way of head-gear? An Incognita, trimmed Trafalgar style? A Polish Cap, bordered in sable? Or an Equestrian Hat of black, ornamented with leaves?"

All three modes were assayed, and I professed myself most partial to the Equestrian, as being the more suitable for a Bereaved.

How proud my dear Lizzy should have been! How ardently she must have urged me to adopt the new mode in deference to herself—who was always so elegantly attired! How vital it suddenly appeared, that I should purchase these paltry additions to a costume infinitely worthy of them—and refashion my old gowns, too, under the instruction and ingenuity of Mrs. Challoner!

"Do not be fretting the cost, Miss Austen," declared Madame Clarisse, "for the work on the gown is a matter of a few days, and the fribbles and frills amount to no more than . . . let us say, forty-eight guineas complete."

"Forty-eight guineas!" I cried, aghast.

"Including the hat. And for such a paltry sum, you shall be the admiration of all Southampton!" Madame declared in triumph.

A wave of heat washed over me, followed sickly by a flood of chill. *Forty-eight guineas!* When I lived on a mere fifty pounds per annum—and the year was nearly out![2] At present I could command no more than seven pounds in my private funds, and the idea of petitioning a loan of my mother—or poor Martha, for that matter—must be entirely out of the question. Pride forbade it; pride, and the necessity of adopting economy, when one lives as I do in the most straitened circumstances.

Mortification overcame me. I glanced at the *modiste*—saw the incomprehension in her looks—and then at Sophia Challoner.

She placed her arm about my shoulders and spoke in the gayest accent. "My dear Madame Clarisse, you have exhausted Miss Austen with your efforts, and I am certain that you have exhausted *me.* I think it best if we repair to a nearby pastry shop, and indulge in a restorative cup of tea. I am longing for a bit of shortbread, and I have heard that Mrs. Lacey's is *nonpareil.* Will you accompany me, Miss Austen? Or do I impose upon your morning?"

"Not at all," I replied. "I have no fixed engagements. But I thought you intended to commission a gown . . . ?"

"Expect me in an hour, Madame, when Miss Austen is recovered," she told the *modiste.* "She will know then whether she likes the result of our officious interference, or should prefer to have her gown cut to her own cloth. Good day."

• • •

[2] The guinea was a unit of currency that was often used for the cost of expensive items, such as horses, carriages, and certain items of clothing. A guinea connoted twenty-one shillings—one shilling more than a pound. Thus, the cost of Jane's costume—though hardly exorbitant by the standards of the day—amounted to eight shillings more than her yearly income. By contrast, a good hunter could command seven hundred guineas at Tattersall's Auction Room.—*Editor's note.*

Mrs. Lacey's pastry shop was three doors farther down Bugle Street, on the opposite paving. The dresser, Eglantine, was consigned to wait with the phaeton and pair, which José Luis was leading along the stretch of Bugle that fronted the *modiste*'s shop. He stared at me balefully as I passed.

"How menacing he looks," I observed faintly, "in that long black cloak he chooses to wear! I do not recall having seen it before!"

"It is the national habit of Portugal, Miss Austen," my companion replied indifferently, "and suits him admirably. The poor man should not know where to look, did I subject him to a white-powdered wig and the livery of a major-domo! José Luis should leave my service at once—and that I cannot allow. He was taken on by my late husband, and has been with me a decade or more."

I considered the cloak as I followed Mrs. Challoner's brisk footsteps in a fog of gratitude at my escape, and misery, and disappointment—for, in truth, the amendments made to my sad gown of mourning had been immeasurably cheering. I saw, like an abyss yawning at my feet, the gulf that lay between those of means, and those without. On the far side of the cavern sat the comfortable and the happy, in cheerful looks and easy circumstances; and on this side stood I: arrayed as a penitent for the sin of spinsterhood, counting over my sparse competence with a haggard air. The idea was maudlin—it was ridiculously indulgent—but I could not outpace it, and must link arms with Oppression, and step side-by-side into Mrs. Lacey's room.

"Shortbread, a pot of tea, and—what will you take, Miss Austen? A bit of marzipan, perhaps?"

"Thank you. I *am* partial to marzipan."

I sank down in a chair near the shop window, while Mrs. Challoner drew off her gloves. "I owe you an apology. It is despicable to lead a friend into a compromising position, whether the error is done through spite—or merely ignorance. I cannot plead spite; but ignorance may be just as painful in its effects. Forgive me, Miss Austen."

I summoned my dignity. "I confess myself surprised, Mrs. Challoner, that you consider an apology either necessary or within your power. You have been all kindness. It is I who must consider myself the obliged."

"Do you imagine," she demanded as she seated herself beside me, "that I have always gone in leopard spot and velvet capes? Do you imagine the jewels I wear"—with a negligent shrug of the brooch at her shoulder—"came to me at my birth? I was forced to flee England as a child—my father a desperate character with a price upon his head!"

"Good lord!" I exclaimed. "I had not an idea of it! What can your parent have done?"

"He killed a man in the heat of passion," she said soberly. "From a desire to be revenged. It was the height of the Gordon Riots, you understand—and my family was the object of a mob."[3]

"The Gordon Riots? Then—are you an adherent of the Catholic faith, Mrs. Challoner?"

Her lip curled. "If I may profess any faith at all.

[3] The Gordon Riots occurred in 1780 when Lord George Gordon moved that a petition protesting Roman Catholic influence on public life be taken into immediate consideration by Parliament. In response, Protestant mobs burned Catholic chapels and looted Catholic property over a period of a week; Newgate Prison was stormed and its prisoners liberated; the killed and wounded number 458. Lord George was tried and acquitted of High Treason as a result.—*Editor's note.*

There have been times when I have questioned the existence of Providence—Catholic or otherwise. My family's history is not a happy one."

I reached for her hand. "Can you bear to speak of it?"

"There is comfort to be found in confession," she returned, "as we Catholics know. Where should I begin? With the Riots themselves, I suppose. On the third night of that dreadful week, my mother was pulled from her carriage and beaten to death—and my father's warehouses destroyed at the hands of a Protestant rabble. In the depths of his despair and rage, my father killed a man. Perhaps he was drunk—perhaps he was quite out of his mind—I do not know. I know only that at the age of five, I was carried by night to a ship that rode at anchor in the Downs—and transported in stealth to the coast of Portugal. My father thought to make a second fortune there. But how we lived, I know not! Those were desperate years, Jane. Those were moments when I might have taken my own life from blackest despair!"

"Do not say so!" I whispered. "It is no wonder—with such a history—that you bear these shores scant affection."

Or that you might, if well worked upon, consider a campaign of terror against its interests?

"Fortunately, I had my beauty," she declared with a gallant smile, "and tho' I had not two farthings to rub together—at the age of seventeen, my hand was sought in marriage by Mr. Challoner. I may admit to you now that it was solely from penury that I was forced to such a step!"

"You did not love your husband?"

"I valued him. I held him in affection. At the hour of his death—and we had then been married more than ten years—I infinitely esteemed him. But love? Of a romantic kind? For a man of phlegmatic temperament, nearly thirty years my senior, and twice widowed when we met? Do not make me *weep*, Miss Austen."

The tea was brought, and she drank deeply of her cup.

"I have often wondered whether it is better to live for the idea of love," I said slowly, "and grow old in expectation of a man who never appears—or to grasp at the chances thrown in one's way, and accept a certain . . . moderation of experience."

"I take it that you have spurned several offers in the past?"

"If by several, you would mean *two* . . . I have not repined in my refusals—and I cannot declare that I regret them even now. The prospect of a lifetime's tedium, in the company of a gentleman one abhors, has always sunk every possible merit attached to the situation."

She threw back her head and laughed. "Tedium! When one might possess all the power of freedom?— For no one is so free, I assure you, as a married lady of position, wealth, and liberal instincts, well-launched and established in her chosen society. Love, my dear Miss Austen, can be nothing compared to *freedom*. And freedom is only possible when one may command the means to purchase it."

"Have you never felt the tenderer emotions, then?" I asked her curiously.

A shadow passed across her face. She set down her cup. "Everyone loves. It is merely the foolish who submit to love's whims."

"That is a speech that smacks of bitterness, Mrs. Challoner."

"If you would instruct me, Miss Austen," she said sharply, "pray call me Sophia. I shall feel the sting of your words less keenly, if they are offered by a friend."

I smiled. "I could never intend to wound you—you, who are all kindness. It is I who must beg pardon, Sophia."

"Let us declare ourselves mutually absolved," she returned, with a spark in her deep brown eyes, "and blot out our indiscretions in the exchange of confidences. *You* shall inform Madame Clarisse that you want none of her Vandyke collars, and retire in a cloud of solvent virtue; and I—I shall impart the dreadful truth: I loved a gentleman once, but he was killed; and my heart has suffered a blight from which it shall never recover."

"You have my deepest sympathy."

Those words of hers, overheard in the Abbey ruins, recurred now in memory. *I eat and sleep and breathe anxiety. It has become my habit, since Raoul was killed.* The name was French; had he died at Vimeiro? Was it *this* that had hardened her hatred of the English cause?

"It should have been something, to unite the freedom of wealth with the delights of passion," she continued, with an effort at lightness, "but we cannot all expect such relentless good luck. And my situation is hardly so mournful. I am left with the means to trick myself out in the most current fashions—and excite the despair of every hopeful fortune-hunter in the Kingdom! *There!*" She snapped her fingers. "I give you *that* for love!"

"A pity," murmured a voice at my back, "when you appear capable of so much more."

I turned—and looked straight into the eyes of

Lord Harold Trowbridge. His sardonic gaze passed over my countenance without the slightest hint of recognition.

"Mrs. Challoner," he said with a graceful bow. "And in Southampton, of all places! I rejoice to find you once more established on your native shore."

Chapter 13

The Cut Direct

29 October 1808, cont.

~

"I AM AFRAID, SIR," SAID MRS. CHALLONER COLDLY, "that you have the advantage of me. I do not recollect that we have ever met."

She picked up her gloves and rose from her chair, as though desirous of quitting the pastry shop on the instant.

Lord Harold did not give way; but neither did he importune her to recognise him. He merely stood square in her path to the door, with a faint smile of amusement on his lips.

"Now, now, Sophia," he said softly. "Your cruelty is unwise. It goads me to indiscretion. My sense of honour must urge the revelation of *exactly* how well you knew me in Oporto—and I should not like to put this unknown lady"—with a polite nod in my direction—"to the blush."

Her lips parted as though to hurl every kind of abuse at his head, and in an effort to play my part, I rose and murmured, "Perhaps I should leave you now, Mrs. Challoner. The *modiste* will be every moment wanting you, and I—"

"Stay," she commanded, her black gaze fixed upon Lord Harold's visage. "I recollect, now, the... *gentleman's*... name. You are Lord Harold Trowbridge, are you not? Second son of the Fifth Duke of Wilborough? You spent a good deal of time in Portugal once, but ran off before the French could engage your fire. Allow me to introduce my friend, Miss Austen, to your acquaintance; and then pray have nothing more to do with her."

"Charmed." He bowed low, a twisted smile on his lips. "You are in excellent looks, Mrs. Challoner. The air of Hampshire agrees with you."

"I have never felt better." There was a challenge in the words, as though she tempted him to defy her; but whatever fierce emotion seethed behind the mask of her countenance, his lordship did not deign to notice it.

"And so you are set up in Netley Lodge?" he enquired genially. "Vastly pleasant, I'm sure, to possess a house on the seacoast. That part of the country is rather lonely, however; you will be sadly wanting for visitors. Perhaps I shall look in one day, just to see how you do, now that my business has brought me to Southampton."

"Business?" She spat the word as though it were a curse. "What business has ever engaged your notice—except that which does not concern you?"

"We second sons are driven to trade," he

observed drily. "Our habits of expence—our want of fortune—we must all make our way in the world as best we can. Some marry advantageously; some game themselves into Newgate. I choose to invest my funds in the most profitable ventures I may find—and thus am concerned in the fate of a neat little Indiaman fresh out of Bombay. The *Rose of Hindoostan* put into port two days ago. I have descended upon the South in order to consult with her captain. It is a happy chance, is it not, that throws us together?"

"And like all such chances, swiftly fled." She held out her hand with a brilliant smile. "Pray enjoy your interval in Southampton, my lord—but do not look to find me again in town. I expect a large party of friends within the week, and cannot hope to venture forth while they remain a charge on my time."

"Indeed?" His lordship's grey eyes glinted. He bent over her palm, then turned with deference to me. "Miss Austen—a distinct pleasure. You are not, by any chance, related to Mr. Henry Austen, of the Henrietta Street banking concern?"

"Why," I said in apparent astonishment, "he is my brother, sir!"

"I am a little acquainted with him. An excellent fellow; and his wife is all that is charming. Good day to you!"

He left Mrs. Lacey's establishment directly, and I observed that my companion's eyes followed his figure as he made his brisk way down the street.

"Only fancy," I observed, "that such a lofty-looking gentleman should be acquainted with my brother!"

"I should not be surprised to learn that Mr. Austen refuses even to acknowledge his lordship, when they happen to meet in the street," she retorted bitterly. "Lord Harold Trowbridge is everywhere known as the Gentleman Rogue—and no self-respecting member of the *ton* would deign to receive him. If it were not for his brother, the Duke of Wilborough, he should long since have been dropped by Society; but as it is—"

"What has he done, to earn such disapprobation?"

"What has he *not* done, you should better ask! Lord Harold has committed every conceivable kind of intrigue—seductions, duels, entanglements—the ruin of young women throughout the Continent; the destruction of happy families; the delusion of gamesters. Lord Harold is a rakehell of the worst order—and as to the men he chooses to keep about him! He has, in his employ, a valet who is criminal enough to have been hanged, had his lordship not bought off the Oporto justice."

"But that is scandalous!" I cried in horror. "And you know this to be true?"

"I have met the valet in question, and am acquainted with his history from a source I should consider unimpeachable: the French officer charged with bringing the fellow to justice. The valet is a thief and an intriguer; a man as familiar with picklocks as he is with blackmail. He should steal a lady's jewels one night, and pilfer her *billets-doux* the next—demanding the balance of her fortune, if not the gift of her favours, as the price of his silence. The number of my friends in Oporto who have been brought to the edge of despair by that cur's salacious lies! I cannot begin to number the tales one might tell, of Orlando and his master!"

"You believe, then, that the valet is goaded on by Lord Harold?" I enquired, in tones of shock.

"I am certain of it. My lord may cant and prattle of Bombay traders—but his fortune is ill-got, Miss Austen. The two of them collude in every sort of thievery, if one may credit the stories from the Peninsula. But I care nothing for the injuries of others—I have suffered too much myself at Lord Harold's hands."

I trained my voice to the deepest sympathy. "He is certainly a handsome gentleman, and might cause any amount of suffering. Did he toy with your affections?"

"From the first moment I saw him, I hated him," she muttered, low. "He is the sort of man who will never be happy until he has the world entire in his thrall. Earlier I vowed that freedom is a lady's greatest prize—but I tell you now, Miss Austen, that with such as Lord Harold, no woman could ever be at liberty. He should demand subjection to his will—and take absolute mastery to himself. A woman's soul should never be her own, within that man's orbit. His brand of dominance is of a sort I cannot endure."

I had never considered Lord Harold in this light; to me, he was the paragon of understanding. He offered my intelligence the respect it demanded, and my feelings a wordless empathy. But perhaps, in the thrall of passion, he might behave as any man: with the cruel desire to exert his influence. I remembered, of a sudden, his words of yesterday: *Have I ever attempted to exert that kind of power over* you? —*Though I may often have been tempted?*

Her voice broke through my thoughts. "But you will understand the reason for my violence of feeling when I say that he has destroyed every hope of happiness I once held in the world."

"That is a heavy charge, indeed!"

"There was a gentleman in Oporto—Raoul,

Comte de Trevigne—whom I might have consented to marry. He was killed not long before I quit the Peninsula forever. Indeed, his death is the chief reason I could no longer remain."

"Was he killed at Vimeiro?"

She shook her head. "He was found in his bed, with a ball in his temple. Suicide, they called it. But I believe—I am virtually certain—that it was Lord Harold's hand that took Raoul's life."

"Good God!" I ejaculated. "But what reason could his lordship find for outright murder?"

"Jealousy—rivalry—the hatred of another too good to comprehend his lordship's evil."

"But have you proofs?"

"None that might stand in a court of law. I only know that Lord Harold challenged my love to a duel of honour. And when the Comte would not accept—he was forced to kill him by subterfuge and intrigue."

"How dreadful," I breathed.

She pressed her fingers to her brow. "To think that I should encounter that man, all unlooked-for, in Southampton!"

"You certainly were not happy in the meeting," I faltered. "I felt all the awkwardness of it! And admired your forbearance."

"Forbearance? Is that what you call it?" She laughed harshly. "When I attempted the cut direct—and could hardly keep a civil tongue in my head thereafter? I believe, my dear Miss Austen, that you must be an angel."

"Pray, Sophia," I returned with feeling, "if you would praise my sensibility—do not hesitate to call me Jane."

• • •

I QUIT THE PASTRY SHOP WITH MY HEAD FULL OF what I had just learned. The more I saw of Sophia Challoner, the more perplexed I became—for if she played a subtle part, and merely affected the emotions she paraded for my benefit, then she did so with an artistry that defied detection. I found that I could not consider Lord Harold—or his theories regarding the lady—with my usual equanimity. I valued him too well, and had been acquainted too long with his ways, to credit the degree of malevolence and calculation Sophia Challoner accorded him. But what if my lord was blinded?

What if his former passion for the lady—unrequited, or indeed spurned in deference to the love she gave her French count—had swayed his opinions? What if he saw treason where mere rage and sorrow warred for dominance?

What if Sophia Challoner was innocent?

"You are very serious today, Miss Austen."

I stopped short at the head of Samuel Street. He was on the point of exiting a tobacconist's shop, with a paper parcel under his arm; if I closed my eyes, I might breathe in the subtle scent of the pipe he sometimes indulged, though never in my company. An odour of shaved wood and cherries clung on occasion to his clothing; I had caught the ghost of it once, and missed, sharply, my departed father.

"I merely seem pensive and distracted, from the ugliness of my apparel," I replied.

"And I had thought it the effects of the company you keep."

Such penetration! I could not immediately answer him.

"May I have the honour of escorting you to Castle Square?"

"Thank you. That would be most kind."

He fell into step at my side. We passed a stationer's, a poulterer's, and a linen draper's shop, without exchanging a word even as to the encroaching coldness of late autumn. An unaccustomed awkwardness grew between us; but I determined not to be the first to break the silence. I could not be entirely sure of my tongue.

"You did very well at Mrs. Lacey's," he observed at last. "I hoped that you might avoid exclamation—a too-ready notice of me, that might betray our acquaintance. It is vital that Mrs. Challoner believe us strangers to one another. I should not like her to comprehend our degree of intimacy."

And what exactly is that, my lord? Am I as much in thrall to your whims as Mrs. Challoner is to her French masters?

"—But in the event, you were the soul of deceit. You bid fair to make an admirable spy, Jane."

"I suppose I must bend to the spirit of such compliments, since you *will* bestow them."

"Mrs. Challoner's reception of me bordered on the uncivil."

"On the contrary, sir—she had long since overstepped the *border* of that country, and stood firm in its very heart. She blames you, I gather, for the death of a Frenchman in Oporto; and she is not the sort of woman to embrace forgiveness."

"The Comte de Trevigne." He pronounced the name as an epithet. "The man was a scoundrel—and wholly worthy of her."

"She claims that you shot him dead, my lord."

"Then she deludes herself! I may have charged the fellow with cheating at cards—an assertion that twenty or so others might easily support—but the Comte refused, point-blank, to defend his honour."

"You did not..." I hesitated. "You did not despatch him in cold blood?"

"Do you believe I would lie about such a thing?" Lord Harold glanced sidelong. "Can it be that *Jane* has begun to doubt my word?"

"Not your word," I said hastily. "If you were to give me your word as to events—then naturally I should accept it. But it is not solely the course of events, in Oporto and elsewhere, that we must consider. There is the *construction* you place upon that history, as opposed to Mrs. Challoner's. I find that I am quite torn, my lord, between you both. You each of you bring such conviction—and passion—to your accounts."

"Torn, between truth and deceit?" he demanded indignantly. "Was it but four nights ago, Jane, that I unburdened myself to you aboard the *Windlass*? Have you forgot a tenth part of what I then said? Nay—have you forgot the deadly peril in which the fate of this war hangs? In which the fate of your *brothers* may be decided? Good God, woman! Are you so lost to sense?"

"I merely hesitate to condemn another on such slight evidence as you have offered regarding Mrs. Challoner."

"Very well," he said bitterly, "then you must await the issue of events. Await the burning of ships and the murder of good men and the destruction of all our hopes. Take the burden of guilt upon your own head—for I confess I am weary of bearing it."

"My lord," I said determinedly, "you are over-hasty. I must enquire whether a sense of injury, inspired by Mrs. Challoner's attachment to another, has . . . clouded . . . your interpretation of events."

His footsteps slowed as we approached Castle Square. "—Whether, in fact, I have wronged Sophia Challoner, out of a hatred born of thwarted love?"

"Exactly so."

"My dear Jane," he answered wearily, "if you have not understood, by this time, that I love but one woman in the world—then we have nothing further to say."

With that awful remark, he bowed—and departed in the direction of the High.

Chapter 14

Domestic Arrangements

Sunday, 30 October 1808

~

"Well, girls, I have determined to accept my dear Edward's offer of a freehold, and shall write to him this very hour to convey my gratitude," said Mrs. Austen as we removed our wraps in the front entry.

The chill weather of the previous week had abated, and the walk from St. Michael's Churchyard was positively spring-like. I regarded my reflection in the glass with disfavour, however, for it showed none of the good effects of a hopeful morning. My eyes were heavy-lidded and smudged with black; I had slept but little the previous night, being haunted by the implications of Lord Harold's parting remark. Was it possible—did I delude myself in thinking—that I was somehow dear to him? Or when he spoke of loving but one woman in the world—did he refer to Lady Harriot Cavendish, who had spurned his advances two years since?

"Jane," my mother said sharply, "you are not attending. Martha kindly asked *which* freehold of your brother's I intended to accept. Are you so devoid of interest regarding your future abode? Or do you hope to form no part in the establishment, being bound for the grandeur of London on that reprobate's arm?"

It must be impossible for a Lord Harold to love a mere *Jane*—she whom others had left on the shelf, a spinster of insignificant connexion and little beauty, whose purse did not extend even so far as the purchase of an Equestrian Hat. Consider the infinite charms of a Lady Harriot: daughter of a Duke, and child of his oldest friends; a member of the Whig set from birth; a girl of trenchant wit, no little beauty, and a comfortable independence. Even did I hold Lord Harold in my power, he should be filled with repugnance at my present disloyalty—my persistence in questioning his judgement—the swiftness with which I had championed Sophia Challoner, and on so trifling an acquaintance as three days.

"I mean to settle in Chawton," my parent persisted. Her gaze, fixed perplexedly on my face, shifted to Martha's. "Can it be possible that the child is ill?"

I shall never see him again, I thought. *I shall learn presently that he is gone away, and that will be an end to all speculation—and sleepless nights.*

"Chawton shall suit us very well, Mamma. I am exceedingly happy in the choice."

"Fiddlesticks!" she exclaimed, and went off to write her letter.

• • •

MARTHA AND I MIGHT HAVE SETTLED OVER A BOOK, or taken up our embroidery, or written letters ourselves to a numerous correspondence—but an unaccustomed restlessness had me in its grip. I paged listlessly through the latest newspapers, my eyes straying from reports out of the Peninsula, which were all cavalry regiments and quantities of cannon. The King had refused once more to consider the question of Catholic Emancipation; red waistcoats for gentlemen were very much worn; and the Prince of Wales had attended a rout at the London residence of Lord and Lady Hertford.[1] If Mrs. Fitzherbert was also among the company, the fact was suppressed, from notions of delicacy.

"It is such a lovely day, Jane, and the weather shall soon be dreadful—should you not like to take a ramble about the countryside?" Martha enquired wistfully.

I looked up from my paper. My dear friend's face was pale and sallow, her air as restless as my own. "That is an excellent thought! You have been too much confined of late. You want exercise, Martha—a good, long walk within scent of the sea."

"But can your mother spare us?"

"We should only be a plague upon her time,

[1] Catholic Emancipation, or the Irish Question, as it was sometimes called, erupted throughout the final years of George III's reign as a result of the inclusion of Irish representatives among the members of the unified Westminster Parliament from 1801. Those Irish members who were also Catholic were "debarred" from taking their seats under the provisions of the British constitution. The Whig opposition, and even some Tories such as William Pitt the Younger, raised the necessity of "emancipating" Catholics, or according them the full rights of all British subjects, but George III refused even to consider the question, because as king he had sworn to uphold the Church of England. Catholic Emancipation was finally passed by the Duke of Wellington's administration in 1829.—*Editor's note.*

otherwise. She is all plans and lists, sums and stratagems, in deference to the Chawton scheme."

"That is partly why I wish to go, Jane. We may not have occasion for such jaunts in future; and if we *are* to quit this place by spring, I must make my farewells."

"Shall you miss Southampton?"

"What I know of the place," she said with a faint laugh. "I have never once attended the Assembly at the Dolphin. I have barely set foot inside the theatre in French Street. And I have never ridden out in a chaise to view the villas of the surrounding country—"

It was true: from a habit of self-denial, or deference to my aged parent, Martha had seen very little of the town during the year and a half she had been resident in Southampton. Once buried in the country, where every kind of society must be limited, her opportunities for enjoyment should be fewer still. I felt a great pity and gratitude towards my friend: for I realised that my own adventures had sometimes been bought at Martha's cost.

"Where should you like to go today?"

"Netley Abbey," she replied promptly.

Of all directions, it must be the least favoured! I could not hear the name without conjuring the face of Mrs. Challoner—the cloaked stranger who waited in the ruins—or my knowledge of the curious tunnel, and the gold cross I had discovered there. Something of my surprise must have shown in my face, for Martha said, "I know you must be tired of it, Jane; but your enumeration of its beauties has made me long to see it again. And the day is so very fine—only think of crossing by the Itchen ferry! How the wind shall sweep our faces, scented with the spice of every Bombay trader sailing up the Solent!"

"Of course we shall go," I told her briskly. "I stay only to fetch my cloak."

We walked arm and arm along Southampton's walls, the least trafficked resort for quitting the town. From the steps at the foot of our back garden we might ascend the ancient fortification, and circumvent the streets entirely, arriving with ease at the road for the Itchen ferry. I left the idea of Lord Harold behind, with the crumpled newspapers, in the stuffy Castle Square parlour; a little of vigour and happiness had returned. But my peace was short-lived.

"I cannot help feeling that this offer of your brother Edward's is highly propitious," Martha ventured.

"You refer to the cottage? How shall you like living there?"

"Oh! Above all things! One is never so happy in town as in the country!"

"A pretty little place set into a garden must have everything to recommend it—particularly when it costs nothing each year."

"And it comes at such an *interesting* time in your own affairs," she persisted. "I am persuaded that you must feel yourself relieved of a considerable burden. You need not consider the fate of your mother and sister—or even my own situation, which is, I am happy to say, extremely comfortable, and should merely be improved by the hope of fulfilling a greater function, in attempting to supply your absence."

"Absence?"

She came to a halt near one of the ramparts and leaned over it to gaze at the New Forest. "You cannot expect me to believe that you are so silent, Jane, from debating the merits of Wye over Chawton. You cannot be thinking that I have failed to see what is in your heart. You neither hope nor expect to remove from Southampton to live in your brother's freehold. You have greater things in view."

"Indeed, Martha, you wrong me."

"*Wrong* you?" She gazed at me in limpid astonishment. "I can think of no one more deserving than my beloved Jane. You cannot ignore your heart's desire! You have played the dutiful daughter long enough. Do not throw away a chance at joy, my dear, from fearing to live too well. You will be three-and-thirty next month; and the world is so uncertain! For all of us, as well as the men we love—"

She broke off, and turned her head resolutely towards the sea. It had been many years since I had suspected Martha of an attachment for my brother Fly—her junior by nine years, and the husband of a charming girl half her age. That she took an abiding interest in his welfare—that she feared for his safety whenever he should put to sea—could not be surprising in one who lived almost as another sister among his family; but I knew a deeper motive sharpened her anxiety.

"I like your Lord Harold, Jane," she said resolutely. "He is exceedingly solicitous for your welfare, and he appears to respect the liveliness of your mind—without which, any man should be intolerable. I hope—nay, I *know*—that you will be very happy."

"You presume too much, Martha! Indeed—you presume far more than I!"

"Since his lordship arrived in Southampton, I have not spent above five minutes in your company." Her tone and air were rallying. "I cannot account for the fact that you are at liberty this morning—but am happy to make use of what intervals of enjoyment fall in my way."

She could know nothing, of course, of my past errands at Netley Abbey—nothing of the intrigue that lurked among those tumbled stones. She should visit it this morning with the same delight as any small girl embarked on a pleasure party, little suspecting that if Lord Harold's suspicions were correct, the fate of the war might be determined there. Though she valued my understanding, she must see in Lord Harold's attentions nothing greater—and nothing less—than the most ardent courtship.

I blushed from awkwardness, and would have disabused her if I could. Truth seemed the chief kindness I could offer my own wounded heart, as well as hers—but being sworn to a brutal silence, I merely kissed her cheek instead.

We achieved the Itchen ferry in silence.

Chapter 15

The Ghost in the Abbey

30 October 1808, cont.

~

THE CHAISE WAS VISIBLE FROM THE TURRET STAIR: A sleek, black equipage emblazoned with the Trowbridge arms, coursing at a leisurely pace past the Abbey ruins in the direction of Netley Lodge. Orlando was not in evidence today—both his correct round hat and his elfin cloak were absent from the footman's step. I stood among the ruins in the chill sunlight and watched the horses' progress, never doubting that Lord Harold should turn into the gates, and pull up before the door, and force his notice upon a lady loath to receive him.

Was Mr. Ord likewise dancing attendance? Should the three principals compare notes on their various travels—or theories of war?

And if Martha and I had tarried a little on the

road, and been overtaken by his lordship's carriage as we toiled through West Woods, should he have halted the team and taken us up? Or would Jane have proved an impediment to the object of his morning?

I beat the rough stone of the parapet with one gloved hand and turned away from the dazzling prospect. I disliked nothing so much as jealous, catlike women; and I was fast becoming the very picture of one. But I was too aware what Mrs. Challoner's reception of Lord Harold should be to discern nothing singular in such a visit; and I knew, moreover, that if he truly suspected her of treason, his lordship's best policy should be watchful silence, not pushing sociability.

I must ask myself—and ask again: What irresistible force drew Lord Harold to Sophia Challoner?

It could not, as he claimed, be hatred.

Was it possible that my words of yesterday had jarred him to comprehend the truth? Had he lain awake long into the night, considering the justice of my sentiments—and apprehended that he had wronged the lady from an excess of bitter love? Perhaps he had come, even now, to throw himself at her feet and beg forgiveness.

How did Mrs. Challoner appear this morning? What ravishing costume, complete with jewels, had she donned in respect of the Sabbath?

I could not bear to contemplate two such figures contained in a single drawing-room—with or without the ingenuous Mr. Ord. Furious at my degree of sensibility, I set foot on the topmost stair, vowing never to think of the teazing man again.

"Martha! Martha! The hour grows late, and we have three miles yet to walk!"

A faint cry from below was my only answer. She

must have ventured far into the Abbey. I eased my half-boots down the worn stone treads, one hand gripping the shattered supports, and thought fleetingly that a woman might fall to a bruising death in attempting this stair in haste. I had no more conceived the unpleasant notion than I achieved firm ground; but as I turned into the relative darkness of the south transept, a hand clutched at my elbow.

"Good God!"

My cry was met with an answering shriek. The voice was quite young—a mere girl's, in fact—and when I peered through the dimness of the chancel ruins at the youthful face before me, I saw that it was not entirely unfamiliar.

"Is that Flora?" I enquired. "Housemaid to Mrs. Challoner?"

"Miss Austen?" She bobbed a curtsey. "Begging yer pardon, miss, but I never thought to find a living soul in this part of the ruin—thought you was a ghost, I did, when I laid my hand on yours—"

"The discovery of a ghost, though unpleasant in fact, must form the substance of every young girl's romantic sensibility; but I regret to say that I am very much alive. Are you well, Flora?"

"Yes, miss—thank you, miss, and hoping your head is quite set to rights?"

"Never better. I find that a knock or two, once in a great while, succeeds in ridding the brain of a good deal of nonsense. Have you happened to meet with another lady in these ruins? I am in search of my friend, Miss Lloyd."

The housemaid's gaze fell to the stone floor. "I've seen no one, miss. I should not have come if I thought to find visitors."

"Are you absent from your work without Mrs. Challoner's leave?" I enquired mildly.

She glanced over her shoulder, and began to wring her hands in her apron. "She told me I might have an hour or two for my own, so that I might recover my senses after a fit of strong hysterics; tho' indeed, I'd have said she wished to be rid of me!"

This was so nearly incomprehensible a speech that I was determined to decipher it. "Has your mistress taken you in dislike, Flora? Or is the case otherwise 'round?"

To my surprise, her great eyes of gentian blue swam with sudden tears, and she threw her apron over her face and sank down onto the stones, weeping.

"There, there," I murmured as I perched beside her. "It cannot be so very bad, I hope?"

"You don't know, miss, what it's like," she sobbed. "Living in that great moody house with the gusts blowing off the sea. Not like it is in 'ound, where I was raised, and the cottages all hunker companionable-like into the hillside—the Lodge is right out on the edge of the cliff, and the wind batters it like it means to have the house into the Solent, one o' these days. The weather sets a body to thinking. It's no wonder I've had nightmares. I've hardly slept a wink since I left my home."

"What sort of nightmares sent you running to the Abbey, Flora?"

"The kind that come by day," she replied darkly. "There's evil work afoot at the Lodge, as I may attest—and my mistress is in the thick of it."

This so nearly approximated Lord Harold's view of things that I did not know whether to furl my brow in consternation, or cry *huzzah!* in relief.

"What possible evil may Mrs. Challoner do? You saw how kindly she treated me."

"Aye—but that was merely by way of throwing dust in a body's eyes," Flora declared. "You will understand the truth of it when I tell you, miss, that she is a witch."

This conclusion was so unexpected that I nearly laughed aloud.

"Incubus or succubus, Mrs. Challoner's the one or t'other—except that I can never rightly recollect what the words mean."

"What can your mistress possibly have done, to inspire such terror?" I exclaimed. "You must know that witches are no very great moment in England. They were cast out years ago with all popish things, and went to live in Italy."

"It's what comes of biding so hard by the Abbey," the maid said with a wild look around the blasted chancel. "Ghosts do walk the cloister by night, miss, and I've seen their lanthorns bobbing in the darkness."

"Does a spirit require a taper to light its way?" I enquired in amusement. "Surely you mistake. You have glimpsed a pleasure party overtaken by nightfall, and given way to dire imaginings."

"I know the difference between a ghost and a pleasure-party," Flora insisted stubbornly, "same's I know the difference between dusk and midnight. It were past the witching hour and turning towards dawn when the lanthorn were raised Tuesday night."

Tuesday night. The maid had observed a light on the ramparts only hours after I had first met Orlando, and learned of Sophia Challoner aboard the *Windlass.* Coincidence?

"I remember the day," Flora persisted, "on

account of Wednesday's fire, and that poor Mr. Dixon with his throat cut. 'It's the Devil's work,' I says to myself, making the sign against the Evil One as my grandfer taught me, 'and the mistress is to blame.' "

"Why should you think Mrs. Challoner has aught to do with lights at the Abbey? Surely she is asleep in her bed at such an hour?"

"The mistress fairly haunts this place," the maid insisted. "Rambles about the ruins at all times. And she's a close one, she is—never tells a body nothing about her doings, or who to expect at the door. This very morning, I went to answer the bell and nearly stumbled over the mistress. Held out her hand, she did, as though to fend off a dog—and said, 'Very well, Flora, I shall attend to it myself.' Wouldn't open the door before me, and stayed to watch that I was safely gone in the servants' wing. But later, I saw who had come."

Lord Harold? But no. There had not been time enough since the chaise's arrival for a fit of strong hysterics.

"A great, tall man wrapped up in the black cloak," Flora informed me impressively. "Nose as sharp as a blade, and eyes that glittered dark like a serpent's. Not that I saw him to speak to—this was just a glimpse, like, through the pantry door. But the mistress was a perfect lamb when he was near—treated him like a prince, she did, with her head bowed and her voice low; and that Mr. Ord—he fair fell over himself with deference!"

"Mr. Ord? He was present, too, at the Lodge this morning?"

Flora nodded. "They all closeted themselves in the drawing-room, and that's when the black arts was raised."

"Black arts?"

"Mumbling in a foreign tongue, like spells—and the burning of some stuff, sweetly-sick and unnatural."

"But Mrs. Challoner is accustomed to speak Portuguese," I said slowly, "and several of her servants, I believe, can speak nothing else. Can this be what you heard?"

"This waren't no Portugee," Flora returned stoutly. "I've come to know the sound o' that talk when I hear it—I know the French, too, as Eglantine uses. Not but what all foreign speech sounds the same—except this sort: the kind she and Mr. Ord and that man in the black cloak were muttering this morning. Sent chills down my spine, it did; and when I considered, miss, that I was all alone in the house—a respectable young maiden, such as might serve for a sacrifice if they found they were in need of one—"

"You were alone in the house?" I interrupted.

"Mrs. Challoner sent that Eglantine, and the housekeeper Mrs. Thripps, off to church with Zé the manservant—and it's the scullery maid's day off—and when I considered of my position, miss, and the prospect of maiden sacrifice—why, naturally I had strong hysterics!"

"Naturally."

A cloaked figure, waiting in the Abbey ruins. I had observed Mr. Ord and Mrs. Challoner bow to him only a few days ago. But why conduct conspiracy in the Lodge itself? What caution—or abandonment of the same—had led to the shift in their meeting? And what in Heaven's name was this gibberish about witchcraft?

". . . boxed my ears and told me that I was a stupid girl, and if I did not mean to set the whole of Hound on our backs, I must regain control of myself this instant! So I cried all the harder, and she declares as she can do nothing with me. Turned me out of the house to collect my wits—and now I find myself shrieking at you, miss! I expect I'll learn I've lost my place, when I get back to the lodge," she concluded mournfully.

"Flora," I said gently, "you must try to remember. Did you overhear the gentleman's name—the man in the long black cloak?"

She shook her head. "The mistress called 'im by his title. A French handle, it were—not like those spells they was parsing."

"What did Mrs. Challoner call him?"

"Mon seigneur."

My lord. The very words I had heard Sophia utter in the ruined refectory, as I stood below the tunnel hatch. It was something to tell him, I thought—that his spy was engaged in witchcraft. But perhaps the idea should not be news to Lord Harold. He had long been subject to her spell.

I SUGGESTED THAT FLORA MIGHT DO WELL TO VISIT her mother's cottage in Hound, and take a tonic from exposure to her little brothers and sisters, before returning to her post in the servants' wing. She was seized with the idea, and acted upon it immediately, being uncertain how much of liberty might remain to her.

"I may never go back," she told me defiantly; "but perhaps, when the mistress considers of the stories I might tell, she'll make it worth my while to remain in her service. 'Twouldn't do to have a tale of witchcraft whispered about the country, would it?"

"Have a care, my dear. You would be well advised

to make your apologies to Mrs. Challoner. I am certain you have allowed your young mind to run entirely away with you."

She smiled at that, but did not look convinced; and took herself off in the direction of Hound with a pretty air of unconcern. She had learned, at the very least, the endless utility of a fit of strong hysterics; but perhaps she had long employed that particular weapon in her arsenal.

"What *did* she witness this morning, I wonder?"

"Nothing she will not turn to advantage," rejoined a wry voice at my back. "Pray God her mistress does not wring the girl's neck on the strength of her hints."

"Orlando!" I swept round and detected his figure—woodland green from head to foot—taking its ease against the wall of the south transept. "You have the most uncanny method of materialising from thin air! How long have you overlistened my conversation?"

"Long enough. The maid Flora is full young to possess so canny a brain—but such an one shall never suffer abuse in silence."

He knew her name, her business, and something of her character—all in the space of a few moments' conversation. I remembered, of a sudden, Sophia Challoner's description of the sprite: *The valet is a thief and an intriguer; a man as familiar with picklocks as he is with blackmail.* Could such an elf be so malign?

He swept off his hat—a black tricorn with a single white feather—and bowed low. "Miss Austen. I hope I find you in good health?"

"Thank you. I am very well."

"That is excellent news—because your walking companion, alas, is not. She has stumbled upon my bolt-hole in the refectory floor—and stumbled, I fear, to her injury. Her right foot will not bear weight; and in attempting to walk in search of you, she fell into a swoon."

"Oh, Lord," I breathed. "*Martha!* And I have been nattering with a housemaid, when she was every moment in agony—"

"Not agony," corrected Orlando as I hurried past him towards the refectory. "One is never in much pain, you know, when one is insensible. It was when I heard her fall so heavily to the stone floor that I deemed it safe to emerge from the tunnel hatch. I first made certain the lady was in no danger, and then went in search of her companions. Imagine my surprise in discovering her companion to be *you,* Miss Austen!"

I paid scant heed to this chatter as he followed me through refectory, buttery, and kitchen itself, to find Martha propped with her back against a block of tumbled stone, and a blank expression of pain on her countenance.

"My dear!" I cried, and sank down beside her. "I owe you an apology! I cannot think how we came to be separated. And you have turned an ankle!"

"The right one," she feebly replied. "I cannot stand, Jane. I do not know how we are to return to Southampton on foot. I have been sitting here considering of the problem—and I have decided that you shall have to fetch assistance. Much as I blush to require it—"

"Orlando," I said with decision, "pray go in search of your master. I must beg his indulgence for the use of his chaise—and his coachman, of course."

"His lordship himself being of not the slightest use in the world," Orlando observed. "But I must observe, Miss Austen, that my appearance at Netley Lodge will cause considerable talk. I did not arrive with his lordship in the chaise."

Out of deference for Martha's ignorance, he said nothing further; but I readily took the point. Orlando had been deputed to spend the morning—or the latest of several mornings—in attendance upon the tunnel hatch, in the vain hope that the cloaked *mon seigneur* might mutter sedition above it, and encompass Mrs. Challoner in his ruin. If Orlando were to petition at the Lodge for Lord Harold's aid—or that of his coach—at Netley Abbey, Mrs. Challoner should immediately understand that his lordship's valet had been despatched to the ruins while his master idled in her drawing-room. Our secrecy should be at an end. Martha's injury, and my pressing need for assistance, should succeed in placing the French spies on the watch.

"I comprehend, Orlando. Would you be so good, then, to go in search of a fellow named"—what *was* the name of Flora's grandfather, Jeb Hawkins's old friend?—"Ned Bastable, a retired seaman of Hound, and enquire whether he should be able to assist us? He might have a cart, or even a boat that should succeed in conveying us with a minimum of discomfort to Southampton."

"An admirable suggestion, madam," Orlando returned gravely. "I possess a boat myself, however, lying at this moment on the shingle below the passage. Allow me to assist your companion below stairs, and thence to the Solent. Between us both, we might have her home in a trice."

I stared at him, for what he proposed argued the inclusion of Martha in our company's narrow confidence. But a glance at the injured ankle—already swelling beyond the strictures of my friend's boot—argued the swiftest accommodation available.

"Martha," I said firmly as I placed an arm under her shoulders, "you must forget entirely what you are about to see. No word of its existence must ever pass your lips."

"Do you know, Jane," she murmured faintly, "I think I may promise you that—"

And as, with my help, Orlando lifted her—she fainted dead away.

Chapter 16

The Oddities of Mr. Ord

Monday, 31 October 1808

~

WE SUCCEEDED IN GETTING MARTHA HOME BETWEEN us, although I confess that the weight of an insensible, middle-aged woman, clothed in voluminous black silk and a wool pelisse, nearly staggered the goodwill of myself and Orlando both. We half-supported, half-dragged her the length of the subterranean passage, and had the good luck to see her revived in the brisk air of the shingle. As we attempted to shift her into the valet's small dory, however, she very nearly had us over by screaming aloud that she could not swim, and clutching at the gunwales in a manner I found hard to bear, being up to my knees in cold saltwater at that very moment. I knew for a certainty that Martha had never set foot in a boat before; she was much given to reading lurid stories aloud from the newspapers, in which bright young ladies with limitless prospects were dashed to their deaths in one water-party or another. But once settled amidships she clung to her seat like a limpet, jaw clenched, and failed to utter so much as a syllable. Orlando gamely bent his weight to the oars, and had us returned to Southampton in little more than twenty minutes; and on the Water Gate Quay he secured a party of midshipmen to escort the mortified Martha to a hack chaise, which conveyed us expeditiously to Castle Square. The valet refused so much as a groat in recompense for his labours; and I thought, as I watched his slight figure turn back to his dory, and once more ship the oars, that he had managed our rescue quite as efficiently as his master should have done.

We were received with such a clamour of exclamation and lament that my friend might as well have been set upon by thieves at Netley Abbey; and my mother grimly pronounced the belief that no good ever came of walking about the countryside like a pair of gipsies.

The opinion of a surgeon was sought, and the limb determined to be sound, though badly sprained. Our apothecary, Mr. Green, supplied a sleeping draught, and Cook a hot poultice—and by nine o'clock last evening the poor sufferer had taken a bit of broth in her bedchamber and consigned the worst of ill-fated Sunday jaunts to oblivion.

I wondered, as I doused my light, whether Orlando had reported the whole to Lord Harold—and what that worthy's strictures might have been, on the fate of heedless women left to fend for themselves in the wild. But perhaps his lordship had been too pressed by business—or the preoccupation of his heart—to attend very much to his servant's adventures.

"JANE!" MY MOTHER CALLED UP THE STAIRS EARLY this morning, "only look what has come for you by special messenger! Make haste, my love! Make haste!"

I was barely dressed, but hurried downstairs with one slipper in my hand and my hair quite undone. "What is it, Mamma?"

"Two parcels," she said, "and a letter. I do not recognise the seal."

The missive could hardly be from Lord Harold, for that gentleman's crest should never escape my mother's eagle eye. I crossed to the parlour table, where the parcels sat wrapped in brown paper and tied with quantities of string. I reached for the letter, and broke the dark green wax.

"It is from Sophia Challoner," I said. "She writes that she expects a large party of guests arrived this morning at Netley Lodge, and intends to hold an evening reception for them—coffee and cards, with music and refreshment—at the Lodge on Wednesday. She invites my attendance, and begs me to wear . . . *this.*"

I tore open the larger of the two parcels and found my fingers caught in the stiff folds of black bombazine—my gown of mourning, freshly-made from the *modiste,* with the cunning design of opened lapels, split bodice buttoned down the centre, and delicate bows tied beneath the right breast. The high white ruff *à la reine Elizabeth,* with Vandyke pleating, had not been forgot.

I lifted the costume from its tissue wrappings and stared at it in silence.

Beneath it lay a dove-grey paisley shawl, figured in black and gold. The second parcel, I presumed, must be the Equestrian Hat.

Abruptly I sat down in a hard-backed wooden chair, as though its uncompromising support was necessary at such an hour.

"Good Lord, Jane—what can she mean by it?" my mother enquired wonderingly. "For your acquaintance is surely very trifling, is it not? And the obligation is entirely on *your* side, for without Mrs. Challoner's aid, you should have died in a ditch!"

"It is extraordinary," I returned with difficulty, "and excessively good of Mrs. Challoner—but I cannot possibly accept so costly a gift."

"The cut of the gown is very fine." My mother ran her fingertips over the bodice. "And though it looks to be in the first stare of fashion, it is entirely within the bounds of what is proper for mourning. I should dearly like to see you wear it, Jane!"

"Impossible." I smoothed the folds of bombazine and reached for the tissue wrappings.

"But what else are you likely to choose, my dear, for such an evening party?" my mother observed mildly. "Not that this is *exactly* a gown for evening—but it is certainly the finest bit of mourning you possess. Do you mean to decline Mrs. Challoner's invitation? It would be a paltry gesture, in the face of such excessive goodwill."

That mild observation gave me pause. Did I intend to ignore Netley Lodge in future, and cut off all relations with its mistress? Did I believe that Lord Harold pursued a chimera of his own invention, and that the lady was blameless? And where, then, did I place the maid Flora's intelligence regarding strange men in cloaks and mumbled witchcraft? Did I think to leave Lord Harold and his *potent weapon* entirely to themselves? Or did I owe Sophia Challoner some effort at friendship—she who was so clearly bereft of acquaintance in her native land?

The gown, I discovered, was still clenched in my hands. My mother eyed me with interest.

"It could do no harm, surely, to open the second parcel?"

I removed the paper with trembling fingers, and held the hat aloft.

"Oh, Jane," my mother mourned. "It is beyond everything we have seen in Southampton this winter! Do not tell me you must deny yourself *that* also!"

I stared at her, wordless.

"I am persuaded that our dear departed Lizzy would not have wished it," she said firmly.

I FORCED MYSELF TO SIT DOWN AFTER BREAKFAST AND compose a note to Sophia Challoner thanking her for the excessive kindness she had bestowed upon me, but declaring that it was not in my power to undertake so great an obligation...

I tore the sheet in twain, selected a fresh, and commenced anew.

I informed Sophia Challoner that I was deeply obliged for the impulsive gift of friendship and mark of esteem she had offered me, but could not accept either...

My third attempt hovered between gratitude and hauteur, and ended by sounding churlish, as each of the previous attempts had done.

I stared into the fire, and considered of the lady's circumstances. She was possessed of a competence, an elegant household, a quantity of servants, and seemingly not a care in the world—but for the shadow that crossed her countenance when the memory of certain painful events recurred. She lacked nothing, in fact, but the most necessary articles on earth: love and friendship. From me she sought the latter; and to hurl her generous heart back in her face seemed the height of ill-breeding. That I hesitated to accept a gift for which I clearly longed, was a testament to pride: the pride of straitened gentility and dependent mortification. I was aware, moreover, that I had encouraged Mrs. Challoner's friendship under false pretenses—and my heart smote me as an ungrateful and scheming wretch.

I drew forward a fourth sheet of paper and dipped my pen into the ink.

My dear Sophia—

You have made me extraordinarily happy, and placed me under an obligation that years of dedicated friendship cannot repay. I shall endeavour to deserve your faith and trust, however, by appearing in this lovely costume at Netley Lodge on Wednesday evening, and by offering my deepest gratitude for the kindness you have bestowed upon—

J. Austen

I WALKED MY LETTER TO THE POST QUITE ALONE THIS morning, Martha being far too unwell to rise from her bed. All the usual activity of a Monday went on around me: nursemaids with small children tugging at their arms; carters unloading their goods before the doors of shops that had been closed in respect of the Sabbath; and the hurried arrivals of mail coach and London stage at the principal inns. A glimpse of the public conveyance recalled the boys, Edward and George, to memory. They must be resigned now to a schoolboy existence until the Christmas holidays should release them; it would be a poor visit home this year. I must endeavour to write a letter soon, informing them of the burning of the seventy-four. They might recount the lurid tale throughout the ranks of their forms, and earn considerable distinction from having looked into the vanished ship.

The brightness of the autumn day, and the peace it brought my burdened mind, was so powerful a tonic that I could not bear to return immediately to Castle Square; and so from the offices of the Royal Mail I turned towards the water, and took myself along East Street to the premises of Hall's Circulating Library.

This was a smallish establishment, three steps up from the paving, with ranks of books displayed on shelves that ran from floor to ceiling, and the added provision of comfortable chairs where a few gentlemen, in want of their clubs, were disposed to linger over the current numbers of the London papers. For such ladies as cared to look into an improving work or frivolous novel, a subscription of one pound, four shillings per annum permitted the loan of books; I had inscribed my name on Mr. Hall's lists upon first arriving in Southampton. Now I glanced through *Hours of Idleness,* by a young poet named Byron; picked up a new volume of Mr. Scott's, entitled *Marmion;* and sank down into one of the library's chairs to commence the reading of it.

I had not been sitting thus for longer than a few minutes, and had determined that I should like to take the book away with me, when a gentleman whose visage was entirely hidden by a fold of newsprint suddenly thrust the sheets together, rose to his feet, and adjusted his coat of dark blue.

"Miss Austen!" he exclaimed as he reached for his hat. "I should've guessed you were a reader. What work have you got there?"

"The most recent issue of Sir Walter Scott's pen," I replied. "How do you do, Mr. Ord?"

"Well enough, thanks. You've recovered from that knock on your head, I hope?"

I raised a gloved hand involuntarily to my brow. "Perfectly. Are you enjoying Southampton? Do you make a very long stay on these shores, or do you intend to return to America soon?"

He smiled at me easily, and replied that if his own wishes were consulted, he should remain in England forever—but that duty, his studies in Maryland, etcetera, conspired to demand his return home. He waited politely while I secured my book, and then conducted me in a gentleman-like fashion to the street, where he declared himself at liberty to escort me to Castle Square.

"You do not go to Netley Lodge this morning?" I enquired benignly.

"Mrs. Challoner expects a large party of guests. I don't like to be in the way, you know. Can't wear out my welcome."

"You were not acquainted with Mrs. Challoner, I understand, before arriving in England?"

Mr. Ord shook his head. "I've been moving about the Continent on a kind of Grand Tour for the past six months, handing one letter of introduction after another to people I've never met before—and to a soul they've been no end obliging. But Mrs. Challoner beats the rest of them all hollow. She's what you English like to call an Incomparable."

It was a word for the greatest beauty of the day—for a Diamond of the First Water—and I smiled to hear it on the lips of an American. "It is no wonder, then, that you cannot bear to embark for Maryland!"

He appeared to hesitate. "I've a matter of business I must conclude first. On behalf of my guardian."

"I see. You were so unfortunate as to lose your parents?"

"When I was very young," he said easily. "I was born here in Hampshire, you know—it's my native turf. But my mother, being a widow, followed her brother to Spain—my uncle James was in the employ of the Royal Navy."

"Indeed? He was an officer?"

"Able Seaman," Mr. Ord replied, "deputed to serve the King of Spain. It was there my family became acquainted with Mrs. Challoner's late husband—who, though a wine merchant in Oporto, took care that none of the British subjects in the Peninsula fell beyond his ken."

The statement was so extraordinary, that I nearly laughed in the young man's face—but a glance revealed that he spoke in all earnestness, and clearly believed the tale he told. That a fellow of such obvious gentility, good breeding, and education should be happy to admit that his uncle was a common sailor, was surprising enough; but that he could, in the same breath, claim that the sailor had been ordered to serve the King of Spain was beyond belief.

"And in America?" I asked hesitantly. "Your family, I must suppose, prospered there?"

"My mother, unfortunately, died but two years after our arrival."

"I am sorry to hear it."

"The climate did not agree with her. I was but six years old when she was taken off—and I spent the remainder of my youth under the guardianship of a very great family, the Carrolls of Baltimore, who are distant connexions of my mother's."

—who married, it must be assumed, to disoblige her family. Uncle James was undoubtedly Mrs. Ord's brother by marriage, not birth, as it seemed unlikely that a great family—even in America—would produce so low a member as an Able Seaman.

"How fortunate for you," I managed. "And it is the Carrolls who determined you ought to tour the Continent? And provided you with letters of introduction?"

Mr. Ord bowed. "Mr. Charles Carroll of Carrollton is never done exerting himself on my behalf. I may safely say that I owe that gentleman—and his family—everything."

It was a strange story, and one I felt nearly certain must be nine parts fabrication. Had this ingenuous young man, with the fair blond looks of a Greek god, invented the outline of his history on the spot? Was this my reward for too-inquisitive manners? But why, if phantasy were his object, should Mr. Ord choose a *seaman* for an uncle? Why not turn his father into the son of a lord? An attempt at fiction should have appeared more regular, more predictable, in its elements. The tale was just odd enough to seem... natural.

"I hope that we shall meet again before you quit these shores," I told Mr. Ord as I halted before my gate.

He raised his hat and smiled engagingly. "At Mrs. Challoner's, perhaps."

Chapter 17

A Coven of Conspirators

31 October 1808, cont.

~

I HAD READ NEARLY HALF OF *MARMION*, AND HAD reached the passage where Constance, the perjured nun—who is travelling in her lover's train disguised as a page—is betrayed to her convent and walled up alive in penance for her sins. So engrossing was Sir Walter's tale that I barely discerned Phebe's voice, announcing Lord Harold Trowbridge.

It appeared, from our maidservant's expression, that she had ceased to find anything very extraordinary in the Rogue's descent upon Castle Square. As she stood in the doorway, however, she threw me a speaking glance in respect of my crumpled black gown, and the ineffectual arrangement of hair that had sufficed for a morning at home. I thrust *Marmion* hastily behind a cushion, dabbed at my chignon with vague hands, and rose to greet his lordship.

"Miss Austen—I hope I find you well?"

He bowed, his countenance expressionless, and Phebe hastily closed the parlour door on our *tête-à-tête.* The news that I was closeted with Lord Harold, I thought despairingly, should be in my mother's ears within the instant.

"I am quite well. Pray sit down."

"I cannot stay—I have come only to enquire whether you know aught of my man Orlando's movements this morning."

"Orlando?" I repeated in bewilderment. "I last saw him at the Water Gate Quay yesterday evening. That would have been at—oh, half-past five o'clock."

"I am aware that he was so good as to convey you and Miss Lloyd from the Abbey to Southampton, following a mishap among the ruins—for Orlando left a note in our rooms at the Dolphin Inn, relating the entire history. Of Orlando himself, however, I have seen nothing since my return from Netley Lodge last night. I dined alone; and when I retired, he still had not appeared. Naturally I grew anxious."

As Lord Harold usually dined at the fashionable hour of seven o'clock, I understood from this that he had spent a good deal of the day in Mrs. Challoner's company. Before I could reply, however, the parlour door opened to admit my mother—who came forward with an expression of welcome, her arms outstretched.

"My dear Lord Harold! What a pleasure it always is to find you in Castle Square, to be sure!"

"Mrs. Austen—your humble servant." He bowed correctly. "I hope I find you well?"

"Very well, indeed! Though it has been more

than two years since we have met, I flatter myself that I have not enjoyed more than an hour's discomfort from ill-health in the interval!"

As the good lady had spent more than half the attested period in her rooms, complaining of a wealth of injuries to body and soul, I found this blithe testament difficult to support; but forbore to argue.

"And how well you are looking, I declare! Always the man of Fashion! Though I observe that you are in mourning like ourselves. My condolences on the passing of your mother."

"Thank you, ma'am." Lord Harold's expression was wooden. That he longed to see my parent returned to her needlework in an adjoining parlour was evident; but propriety insisted otherwise.

"May I offer you a cordial, my lord? A glass of brandy, perhaps?" my mother cried. "I am sure that Jane would benefit from a little ratafia, for she is undoubtedly looking peaked, from the effects of too much excitement and grief—she was quite devoted to our late Mrs. Austen, you know, and is so *unselfish* in her dedication to those she loves, that I declare she has quite gone into the grave with her! Can you perhaps conspire with me, my lord, to return our dear Jane to the bloom of health? We were so very grateful that you offered her an airing in your chaise—exactly suited to restoring the roses to a girl's cheeks!"

As I had long since left my girlhood behind, along with the roses to which my mother referred, this last was injurious to my dignity.

"Mamma," I said with studied patience, "would you be so good as to fetch a glass of brandy for Lord Harold?"

"I should be infinitely obliged," he concurred.

"Oh—certainly! And perhaps just a spot of ratafia for the ladies—"

She sped from the room, and in her wake I closed the door firmly. Frank, to my certain knowledge, had drained the last of the brandy before his removal to the Isle of Wight; and my mother should be forced to send Phebe to a local tavern in search of another.

"Orlando gave no indication of his direction in the note he left yesterday?" I enquired of Lord Harold.

"Not a word." He took a restless turn before the fire, his expression troubled. "We had no need of messages, for the progress of our campaign was understood. At my arrival in Southampton last week, I let my man know that I was capable of valeting myself, and that his exertions were better devoted to work of a more subtle nature. Having spent most of Sunday secreted in the subterranean passage, Orlando was to follow Mr. Ord at his departure from Netley Lodge, and observe where the young man went—to whom he spoke—and all that he did in Southampton."

"Mr. Ord!"

"Yes, Mr. Ord!" his lordship spat contemptuously. "There can be no one else so well-placed to communicate Mrs. Challoner's commands to a host of subordinates throughout the South. Ord was in Sophia's company when I appeared, unwanted and ill-received, at her door—and he remained there until I quitted the Lodge two hours later. I have no notion of *when* that insufferable puppy was at length torn from his lady's leading-strings, but I am certain that Orlando will have followed him. And Orlando has vanished."

"Vanished!"

"Do not make a practice, I beg, of repeating my every word in tones of shock and admiration. There are ladies, to be sure, who regard such a ploy as the highest form of flattery—but you are not one of them."

"I met Mr. Ord a few hours since, at Hall's Circulating Library. He was so good as to escort me home."

"And were his gloves stained with blood?"

"They appeared clean enough. His countenance, I may attest, was devoid of the desperate agitation that should characterise one who has kidnapped a blameless valet. But Mr. Ord is a perplexing fellow—his appearance is angelic, yet his performance on horseback is suggestive of the very Devil; he looks the gentleman, and yet professes to spring from no higher a station than Able Seaman."

"I beg your pardon?"

"He claims to be the child of a widowed woman named Ord, long deceased, and to have been supported in infancy by her brother, also named Ord, whose rank in the Royal Navy was confined to Able."

"I cannot credit such a tale! He looks—and conducts himself—as a man of Fashion!"

"I am perfectly of your opinion, my lord."

"The presumptious young dog has received an *education*, Jane! He has done the Grand Tour—which comes at considerable expence, from so remote a locale as Baltimore!"

"Well do I know it. And yet he related this humble history this morning, without the slightest hint of self-consciousness. He was born in Hampshire, and removed first to Spain, and then, at the age of four, to Maryland. His air of gentility we must impute to his mother's patron, a certain Charles Carroll—"

"—of Carrollton?" Lord Harold interrupted.

"I believe that is what Mr. Ord said."

"Good God!" the Rogue exclaimed. "Jane! Do you not comprehend what this means?"

"No, my lord. I do not."

"Charles Carroll was the sole Catholic gentleman of the Colonies among the signers of the Declaration of Independence! Charles Carroll's uncle was Archbishop John Carroll—a Jesuit, and the first head of the Catholic Church in America. I met the fellow some once or twice while he lurked in England—a great favorite of Mrs. Fitzherbert's. She regarded him, I believe, in the nature of a confessor, and sought his absolution for her alliance with the Prince."

"And did the Archbishop condone her moral abandon?"

"That must remain a secret of Maria Fitzherbert's heart. I have it on excellent authority that she continues to attend Mass—and must do so with a clear conscience. Nonetheless, dear Jane, the Carrolls and their powerful friends, at home and abroad, represent the very heart of the Recusant Ascendancy. If Mr. Ord is in the confidence of Sophia Challoner—as we know him to be—then the whole affair assumes an entirely different complexion."

"—Because the crime of treason is then aligned with the cause of Catholic Emancipation?" I suggested.

Lord Harold gripped the mantel and stared into the fire. "Exactly so. The interests of France, and the interests of a powerful body of the Opposition, must be united against the aims of the Crown—and, indeed, if our assumptions of Napoleon's plans are valid—against the survival of the Kingdom itself. If it is true, and the truth is published—then the Whig Party is done for, Jane."

Lord Harold's agile mind, formed for politics, had leapt immediately in a direction I should never have taken alone. The Whig Party, and the Prince of Wales, had long espoused Catholic Emancipation, against the King's firm support of the Church of England. The Whigs, therefore, must stand or die by the cause. If the Recusant Ascendancy—which included such powerful figures as the Duke of Norfolk, a member of the Carlton House set and crony to the Prince of Wales—were accused of treason, even by implication, then a kind of warfare should erupt on the streets of London that might make the Gordon Riots of 1780 look like child's play. The Prince's future must surely turn upon the outcome.

I thought of Mr. Ord—of the genial young man who had carried my volume of *Marmion* from East Street—and shook my head. "The construction is possible, my lord, but quite improbable. If deception were his aim, why should Mr. Ord impart only facts that must *incriminate* him? There was no guile, no stratagem in his looks; he was the soul of innocence. Indeed, he ever is. I cannot believe him so accomplished an actor—so hardened a criminal—as to utterly disguise the violence of his passions. Is it possible, my lord, that your fears turn upon a misapprehension?"

"That is certainly your preferred interpretation!" he returned with acerbity. "You believe me guilty in general, Jane, of assuming what is false—I appear in your eyes as a doddering old fool, beguiled by emotions beyond the reach of reason. What spell has Sophia worked upon you, that you credit her lies more readily than the counsel of a confirmed friend?

Do you doubt me—nay, do you doubt *yourself,* Jane—so much?"

This last was uttered in almost an undertone, with a conviction I had never remarked in Lord Harold's accent before. I stared at him; the grey eyes were piercing, as though he would see into my soul. He had asked, *Do you doubt yourself?*—but he had meant: *Do you doubt your power over me?*

"Spell, indeed," I said slowly. "Did you know that Mrs. Challoner is credited for a witch? I had the story of her serving girl, in the ruins yesterday."

He scowled. "Young Flora? The mere child, with the wide blue eyes? What can she know of witchcraft?"

"She has seen strange lights bobbing on the Abbey ramparts in the middle of the night, and heard muttered conjurings in a tongue she cannot recognise. Perfumed smoke burns in the parlour at certain hours, and a man in a long black cloak—whom Mrs. Challoner calls *mon seigneur*—is admitted to the coven. Mr. Ord is a member, too."

His gaze narrowed. "Perfumed smoke? Mutterings in a foreign tongue? Could the language be Latin, Jane?"

"—and the conjurings, nothing more than a Catholic Mass? I suppose it is possible, my lord."

"The man in the black cloak should then appear as a priest."

"—who is addressed by his title of monsignor. Mrs. Challoner is certainly a Recusant; she informed me of the fact over shortbread and marzipan."

"But is it solely a Mass the three would entertain?" Lord Harold muttered, "or are they so careless as to hatch French plots in the very Lodge itself?"

"We have no proof that *plots* are even under consideration!" I protested.

"You forget, Jane," Lord Harold returned harshly. "*A man in a dark cloak* was seen racing from the burning seventy-four. Murder was done, and hopes ruined. This is an ugly business, and it shall turn more brutal still before it is quelled. You ignore that at your peril."

I could make no immediate reply. I *had* forgot the murdered Mr. Dixon, and the testimony of Jeremiah the Lascar. I had wished to forget them—to clutch at the notion of a group of Catholics, worshiping in private, without political aim of any kind.

"Would they risk conspiracy before the servants?" Lord Harold mused.

"Yesterday, certainly, when the staff were absent at divine service," I replied.

"But why not continue to meet at the Abbey?"

"It is in general a lonely place—but on Sunday, must form a picture of sacred contemplation. Any number of pleasure-seekers might tour the ruins, of a Sunday in autumn when the weather is fine."

"That is true," he said thoughtfully. "And so we have them, the members of the coven: Sophia, Ord, and a man in a black cloak whom she calls *mon seigneur,* or monsignor. Who can he be, I wonder?"

I hesitated. "I suppose it is possible—although I have no proof—"

"When has proof ever stood in your way?" Lord Harold enquired ironically.

"The man might be a Portuguese, conversant in French, who goes by the name of Silva," I replied. "He was taken off the Peninsula by my brother's ship, in the first week of September, and disembarked at Portsmouth. Frank declares that he intended, so he said, to find out no less a personage than Mrs. Fitzherbert, at her home in Brighton. He bore a letter of introduction to her."

Lord Harold's looks were shuttered. "And do you know who is to come to Netley Lodge this very morning? Shall I tell you whom Sophia Challoner entertains—and shall present to us both on Wednesday evening?"

"Do not say that it is Mrs. Fitzherbert!"

He turned in some agitation before the fire. "Naturally. The first Catholic lady in the land. The friend of Mr. Ord's patrons, and, it would seem, of Sophia Challoner as well. The affair wanted only to implicate the heir to the throne, to augur total success! With Mrs. Fitzherbert thrown into the brew, we risk a scandal that defies description! Would that I knew what to do!" he said savagely.

"But, my lord—it cannot be possible that Mrs. Fitzherbert should willingly endanger the career of the Prince of Wales! Whatever she may be—however ridiculed her morals—she remains entirely dedicated to his interests."

"But if she were deceived?—If she believed she acted for his *good*? Oh, that I knew how it was!"

I could offer no aid that might ease his mind; I maintained a troubled silence.

His lordship took up his hat with an abstracted expression.

"I will bid you good day," he said. "I require further particulars, and it is possible I shall post to London tonight."

"What of Orlando, my lord?"

"Orlando must fend for himself." He settled his black stovepipe upon his head; the broad brim curving over his brow gave him a rakish air the London papers were determined to celebrate. "I shall attempt to consult Devonshire—his powers are fading, but still he will know what is best to do."[1]

"Shall I see you at Mrs. Challoner's reception, my lord?"

"I shamed her into extending me an invitation," he replied with a curling lip, "and I shall move Heaven and Earth to be there. Grant me this favour, Jane!"

"If it is in my power."

"Wear the gold crucifix you discovered in the passage about your neck on Wednesday night." His eyes glinted. "I should like to see it claimed."

He had succeeded in gaining the lowest step of his carriage when my mother reappeared, quite out of breath, with Phebe in tow. The maid bore a tray with a freshly-opened brandy bottle, a decanter of ratafia, and three glasses; and my mother's countenance, as she observed his lordship's departure, was the apogee of outraged mortification.

[1] Lord Harold refers to the Duke of Devonshire, regarded at this time as the grey eminence of the Whigs.—*Editor's note.*

Chapter 18

The Dead Spaces of the Earth

Tuesday, 1 November 1808

~

I AWOKE THIS MORNING WITH THE IDEA OF A BOAT IN my dreams: a dory, easily manned by a single oarsman, that had borne me swiftly across Southampton Water Sunday evening, then turned back in the direction of the monks' passage. Orlando must have left it hidden among the rocks of the shingle that night while he sat his patient vigil in the tunnel.

Orlando had vanished. But what of his vessel?

Lord Harold might declare that his valet should fend for himself—he might devote his hours to composing letters of statecraft and policy, intended for the eyes of a duke—but I could not be so sanguine. I owed Orlando a debt of obligation, for having saved Martha Lloyd a most troublesome journey; and I did not like to think of him in danger and alone, as he had been so much of his difficult life.

I breakfasted early, then wrapping myself up well against a sharp wind off the water, I went in search of Mr. Hawkins.

"STRANGE TALK THERE DO BE ABOUT THE FOLK AT Netley," said the Bosun's Mate darkly. "Old Ned Bastable swears as he saw balls o' light hovering over t'a Abbey two nights since, and the cottagers of Hound will tell you, after a tankard of ale, that the mistress can fly through West Woods, and speak with animals in a strange tongue."

"Young Flora has been spreading wild tales," I observed.

"Mrs. Challoner turned Flora away," Jeb Hawkins returned. "Said as she failed to give satisfaction. But Flora will tell any who listen that the lady is right strange. Says she looks through a body in a way that gives a Christian chills; and that there's doings at the Lodge as will end in blood, one o' these days. Is that why you and his lordship are forever going to Netley? Keeping a weather eye on the place?"

"Mrs. Challoner is not a witch, Mr. Hawkins," I said firmly. "It may be that she is nothing more than what she claims: a widow lately removed from the conflict in the Peninsula, and entirely without acquaintance in this part of the world. It is also possible that matters are otherwise. But you would do well to say nothing to anyone in Hound."

The old seaman eyed me unsmilingly; he would determine his own course as ever he had done. He threw his back into the oars, and said, with seeming irrelevance, "I like the cut o' his lordship's jib. If he's watching that woman, I reckon there's cause. Are we bound for the passage? Or the landing near the Lodge?"

"The shingle," I answered, "below the tunnel mouth."

He lifted a hoary brow, but said no more; and the remainder of our voyage passed in silence.

The sun was weak this November morning—the Feast of All Saints. A chill breeze slapped the waves into white-curled chargers, and the Bosun's Mate fought hard against a stiff current. I clutched at the edges of my black pelisse with mittened hands and thought of Lord Harold. Was he in Whitehall already, consulting at the Admiralty? Or had he sought his counsel in the gentlemen's haunts of Pall Mall—in the card room at Brooks's Club? Grouse season was at an end, but partridges were in full hue and cry: the majority of the Whig Great were still likely to be fixed in their country estates and shooting boxes. Parliament should not open until just before Christmas, when the foxes were breeding and all sport was at an end. He might find that his acquaintance—the men he most wished to secure—were thin on the ground in London at this season. He might, in sum, be delayed beyond his power—

The dory scraped across the shallows; Mr. Hawkins, without a word, jumped into the frigid sea and hauled the boat up onto the shingle. He assisted me carefully to land, and stood waiting for direction.

I cast about me; to all appearances, the place was barren of life. A grouping of boulders—cast by Nature, or dragged into position by monks five centuries dead—screened the tunnel mouth from the notice of the inquisitive. I made first for these, peering behind them to ascertain that no small vessel lay upended there. Then I paced in the opposite direction, peering diligently through the waving grasses at the shingle's edge, until the strand itself petered out to nothing. I turned back, to find Jeb Hawkins calmly lighting his pipe.

"Where's his lordship this morning?" he asked.

"He has posted to Town."

Mr. Hawkins glanced speculatively at the sky. "Might you tell me what you're looking for?"

"Lord Harold's man, Orlan—*Mr. Smythe*—has disappeared. He and his dory were last seen in this place, and I thought that if I could find the boat—"

"Boats drift with the tide," the Bosun's Mate observed. "A boat might fetch up anywhere."

"That is true," I replied dispiritedly. In this chill and empty place, the idea of searching at random for the valet seemed ludicrous in the extreme.

Mr. Hawkins gestured with his pipe stem. "Could he'uv gone up into that there passage?"

A chill flickered at my spine. Naturally he could have gone into the passage; it was his express purpose in coming here, to spy upon the party we suspected of treason. But Mr. Hawkins knew nothing of that, and I did not like to adventure into the passage alone.

"Will you help me to open the hatch?" I asked faintly.

He knocked the bowl of his pipe against his boot, and let the ashes drift onto the sand.

"Gather yer skirts," he told me, "and I'll give ye a hoist."

MR. HAWKINS, BEING A WISE SEAMAN, KEPT A BUNDLE of tapers in his boat. Though the daylight was now broad, the tunnel was darkest pitch; and so he fetched me several of the paper twists, and lit the first with his own flint.

Then he lit another, and said: "Shall you lead the way, miss? Or shall I?"

I was too relieved at the notion of company, for the demurrals of pride. "If you do not dislike it—"

He merely grunted, and stepped forward with bent back. I gratefully followed.

The tunnel floor was much scuffed, as though an army had passed through; and I found this surprising, for Orlando was a stealthy creature and a careful one. Mr. Hawkins, never having seen the interior of the passage, could not be expected to comment. The way steadily ascended, and darkness filled in the gap behind; it was as though the tunnel mouth was closed to us, and no return should ever be possible. But I said nothing of this desperate fancy to my companion. He should have hawked and spit his disdain at my feet.

"There's a branching in the way just ahead," he muttered. Even Mr. Hawkins had enough respect for the dead spaces of the earth to speak soft and low. "Left, or right?"

He swung round as he said this, and the light of his taper moved in a golden arc beyond his head. In that instant, I saw—I knew not what: a figure tall, motionless, watchful as Death. The tunnel wall was at its back, and pressed against it thus, the spectre might have avoided detection. But now I had espied it: and before I could so much as cry aloud, the figure hurtled past the Bosun's Mate, its right hand making a vicious strike for the taper. The fragile thing spun out of Mr. Hawkins's grasp and sputtered on the tunnel floor. In the swift current of air occasioned by the figure's flight, my own flame flickered and went out.

I felt his movement—the breeze of hurried passage—and heard the panic tearing at his lungs. As the figure darted past me, I clutched at the air—and closed on the stuff of a cloak.

Brutal hands gripped my shoulders and thrust me hard against the tunnel wall. I cried out as my head struck the stones; light exploded before my eyes, and I slid downwards to rest on the tunnel floor.

"Oi!" Jeb Hawkins shouted in rage towards the passage mouth. "Oi! You there!" He broke into pursuit, his stumbling gait that of an old, bent man in a darkened place; but in a moment, I was alone.

Gingerly, I felt with my fingers at the back of my skull. No blood—no broken skin—just a slight lump, to pair with the one I had earned on horseback. I pushed myself upright, and found that a slight dizziness passed quickly away. With care, I might make my way towards the tunnel mouth.

But what should await me there? The menacing figure, and brave Mr. Hawkins insensible at his feet?

Ought I to turn, instead, to the trapdoor set into the Abbey floor, and the freedom of the ruins above?

But what if the cloaked man—*mon seigneur*—had just quitted the place, and his conspirators remained?

Stiff with uncertainty, I could move neither forward nor back.

And then a voice shouted from the passage mouth. "Miss Austen?"

"Jeb!" I cried. "Are you unharmed?"

"Naught to do with me—but the skiff's gone! The damned blackguard scarpered in 'er!"

The outrage in Mr. Hawkins's words must have been comical, had our situation been less unhappy.

I descended to the shingle. "Do you mean to say that your boat has been stolen?"

The Bosun's Mate did not reply; he was employed in cursing with a fluency that attested to forty-odd years in His Majesty's service. My ears burned with every ejaculation, though I am sure my brother Frank should have heard them unmoved.

I waited until his fury was spent, and then said briskly, "We must walk along the shingle until we reach the landing area below Netley Lodge, and take the path that leads past the ruins. It is three miles from the Abbey to Southampton—a trifling walk. I have often achieved it."

The old seaman stared. "Do you not know that I've the gout in my leg? I can never walk all of three mile!"

It was true that our dealings with one another were generally afloat; I had formed no notion of his general spryness.

"Shall I go in search of aid?" I enquired. "Your friend, perhaps—Ned Bastable—who lives in Hound? Might he possess a cart . . . or . . . a conveyance of some kind?"

By way of answer, Mr. Hawkins lifted his bosun's whistle from the chain where it rested around his neck, and commenced to blow.

"There's vessels enough on the Water," he gasped between exertions, "to carry us safe home. It's not marooning what troubles me, miss! It's the loss of my boat! Mark my words—someone'll have to pay!"

He said this with such awful purpose that I understood, of a sudden, that my meagre purse should presently be petitioned to supply the want of Jeb

Hawkins's livelihood; and I wished all the more devoutly that I had heeded Lord Harold's advice, and left Orlando to fend for himself. Perhaps the valet had simply tired of labouring in his lordship's service, and had seized his chance to take swift passage elsewhere in the world—

"Ahoy there!" Jeb Hawkins cried, and waved his arms frantically. The whistle dropped to his chest. "It's the Portsmouth hoy, miss—travels each day up the Water, bearing folk from one town to the other. Ahoy there! On the water! We've need of aid!"

As I watched, the smart sailing vessel far out in the middle of the Solent seemed to hesitate, and then—as I joined Mr. Hawkins in waving my arms—slowly came about and turned towards us.

"The draught's too great to permit it to come in close," Mr. Hawkins told me regretfully. "You'll have to kilt yer skirts, miss, about yer knees."

I gathered the black cloth in my hands without argument, and consigned my poor boots to the deep.

The shock of cold was as nothing to the tug of the current, and for an instant, I was terrified of being borne under, and of drowning in three feet of water from the weight of my clothes. But Mr. Hawkins reached a steadying hand to my elbow, and urged me forward. I bit my lip to avoid crying out, and kept my gaze trained on the hoy as it steadily approached. A sailor, red-faced and bearded, leaned forward from the bow.

"Ye blow a fair whistle," he said. "That's a navy man's tune."

"Aye, and I've the right to play it," Mr. Hawkins returned testily. "I'm Jeb Hawkins, as once tanned yer backside on the *Queen Anne,* Davy Thomas—and how you can forget it—"

"Jeb Hawkins!" the sailor cried, and held out his hand. "How came you to be run aground?"

"My skiff was stolen, and the lady here incommoded."

The cold seawater surging about my knees was so frigid at that moment, my teeth were clattering in my head, and I could barely acknowledge the sailor's look of appraisal.

"Stolen?" he repeated. "And you marooned an' all?"

"Davy Thomas!" shouted the captain from the cockpit, "stop yer palaverin' and say what's to-do!"

"A lady and the Bosun's Mate as have had their boat stolen, Cap'n, sir," Thomas replied with alacrity. "They be marooned!"

"A lady?" enquired a third—and far more cultured voice. "Then for God's sake, man—swing her aboard!"

I raised my eyes to the centre of the vessel, where a quartet of passengers was seated. A young woman with round blue eyes that stared at me in horrified astonishment, a nursemaid in a dowdy cap, a child of less than two—and a man in the dress uniform of the Royal Navy.

"*Fly?*" I cried in astonishment—and dropped my skirts in the water.

Chapter 19

The Greased Monkey

1 November 1808, cont.

~

"WHATEVER ARE WE TO TELL MAMMA, JANE?" MY brother exclaimed as Mr. Hawkins and I settled ourselves amidships, snug in a pair of blankets afforded us by the hoy's captain. Frank's wife, Mary, was divided between wringing my gown of seawater, and murmuring vague phrases of sympathy. "She shall be forced to lock you in your bedchamber, if you do not display more sense."

"What has sense to do with it, Fly? We did not *intend* to be marooned!"

"Nor did you intend to fall off your horse—but the injury was as severe."

"I cannot think your decision to land in so lonely a place was wise," Mary ventured doubtfully. "What possessed you to choose that isolated stretch of shingle?"

A glance at Mr. Hawkins confirmed that he had no intention of rescuing me from my predicament; the old seaman was sunk in black anger at the loss of his skiff.

"I have lately acquired a taste for sketching," I told them lamely. "I thought to capture the prospect of... of Hythe, just opposite, by setting up my easel in that exact spot."

As there was nothing very extraordinary in the stretch of shore across the Water, my brother should well look perplexed.

"Mr. Hawkins was so kind as to oblige me, by putting me off at the desired point; but once we had landed, and walked a little way to determine the most advantageous position—we returned to find that the boat, along with my nuncheon, paintbox, and sketching things, had been seized by an unknown!"

"That is worrisome in the extreme," Frank said heavily.

I stared at him. "What can you mean? It is decidedly vexing—and I regret the loss of Mr. Hawkins's boat, not to mention Cassandra's paintbox—"

"Jane, have you heard nothing of the news out of Portsmouth?"

"I have not."

He glanced at his wife, whose eyes filled with tears.

"We suffered an extraordinary attack in the early hours of morning. All of Portsmouth is in disarray."

"The naval yard?" I demanded. "Was another ship fired?"

"Much worse, I fear," he said glumly. "The prison hulks, moored off Spithead, were liberated by a means no one may comprehend. With my own eyes, Jane, I saw the riot of French ranks—hundreds of the inmates, swarming over the decks. The crews of two hulks at least were murdered as they stood. Captain Blackstone is believed dead, though his body has not yet been recovered—it is thought that it was heaved overboard when the hulks were fired—"

"Good God! To consider such a scene!"

"It was dreadful," Mary muttered in a choked voice. "Beyond the power of words to describe. We saw the flames throughout the night, and Frank would not stay, but must hurry to the aid of those who fought the fires. He was gone well past dawn, Jane, and I could not sleep for fearing—"

He laid his hand over hers, and she bowed her head to his shoulder. "I determined to carry Mary and the child to Southampton this morning, to remain in Mamma's care until Portsmouth is deemed safe."

"Are the prospects so very bad, Frank?"

"Do not ask me to describe what I saw last night," my brother said harshly. "It defied even my worst experience of battle. In war, one expects devastation—one meets it with a certain fortitude—but to affix the horrors of engagement upon a well-loved scene, familiar through years of association—"

Years, indeed. It was at the Royal Naval College in Portsmouth that Frank had learned his love of the sea, at the tender age of twelve. He had been hauling or dropping anchor in those waters all his life.

"But did no one witness the fiend who sparked so grave a crime?" I enquired.

"That is the question that must consume us all! I should have said an army was required to liberate those hulks—"

"Not a bit of it," spat Jeb Hawkins. "At dead o' night, when the crews are settin' skeleton watch? All that's needful is one greased monkey lithe enough to climb up through the chains—slit a throat or two on the quiet, like—and pilfer the guard's keys. Then you've an entire hulk what's crying for blood and freedom, and the monkey's off about his business on the next scow down the line."

My brother frowned, and might have hurled a biting retort—for in his eyes, the pride and vigilance of the Royal Navy *required* an enemy legion, to suffer such an ignominious action. I grasped his wrist, however, to forestall dispute.

"What of the prisoners now?" I enquired. "Have any been recovered?"

He shook his head. "Too many slipped unnoticed into the darkness, Jane. We feared for the fate of several ships of the line, moored likewise in Spithead, and subject to the ravages of fire, to spare much effort in pursuing the French. It is a heavy business, to protect a fighting vessel from its own stores of gunpowder. We are lucky that none of them exploded last night, and in an instant set off all the others!"

If you *commanded the direction of Enemy forces... where next should you aim your imps of Hell?*

It was as Lord Harold had predicted. So much of chaos, and of death, in the wee hours; a strike unlooked-for, despite the Navy's vigilance. The liberation of the hulks should bring in its train a creeping fear, that not even His Majesty's strongest ports could be defended against an enemy as clever as it was insidious.

Did his lordship know already what had occurred? Word should have been sent along the Navy signal lines, from Portsmouth to the Admiralty, as soon as the dawn had broken. That the evil had occurred in Lord Harold's absence—when Orlando should unaccountably be silenced—when Mrs. Challoner entertained a party of friends in seeming innocence, and balls of light flared at midnight from the Abbey walls—

Had Sophia or her gallant Mr. Ord signalled the attack from the ruined heights?

"Hundreds of the French, still at large," I murmured, and thought of the black-cloaked figure who had fled the Abbey passage not an hour ago.

"That is what Frank meant," Mary added, "when he declared the theft of Mr. Hawkins's boat to be worrisome in the extreme."

"The skiff was stolen, no doubt, by a freed prisoner, who lurked along the shingle, and observed all that you did," my brother declared. "He thanked God and the Emperor when you appeared in his view, Jane, complete with vessel and nuncheon!"

"—Which is halfway across the Channel now, and may he drown before he ever sees Calais!" Hawkins spat once more into the bilge, drew his pipe from his nankeen pocket—and saw that the tobacco was wet with seawater. He subsided into morose silence.

I ENDURED MY MOTHER'S STRICTURES REGARDING the idiotishness of girls left too long upon the shelf; promised her I should never again quit the house of an early morning without informing her of my direction; and refused to pen a note to Mrs. Challoner denying myself the honour of attending her evening party.

"What can it be to you, Jane, to give up this small pleasure?" my mother demanded in exasperation. "It is not as though you bear the woman any great affection; and now your brother is come, you might plead the necessity of a family engagement. Frank thinks of taking Mary to the theatre in French Street while he is ashore—for, you know, his time is not his own, and he may be ordered back to sea at any moment. Cannot you remain quietly at home with the baby and Martha Lloyd tomorrow, and allow your brother to enjoy an evening with his wife?"

It was a simple enough request. I apprehended how selfish I must seem—how lost to everything but my own petty concerns. Being prevented from sharing so much as a word of the truth—that the attack on Portsmouth *required* me to exert vigilance in the only quarter I might suspect—I was left with but the appearance of disappointed hopes, and a mulish insistence that I could not fail Mrs. Challoner.

"Cannot Frank and Mary be persuaded to the theatre this evening instead? For I should gladly look after little Mary Jane tonight. But *tomorrow,* Mamma, is quite out of the question—"

"Mary is resting at present, and cannot say whether she shall summon even enough strength to descend for dinner. You know that she is a very poor sailor, particularly in so small a vessel as the hoy. And with Martha not yet able to set her foot to the floor—"

"Frank," I called to my brother as he appeared at the foot of the stairs, "would you care to take a turn along the Water Gate Quay? We might learn what news there is of Portsmouth on the wharves, and stop at the butcher's in our way, for the procuring of Cook's joint."

"That is a capital idea!" my brother cried. "Do not trouble yourself, Mamma, with fetching your purse—for I shall supply the joint this evening, in gratitude for all your kindness to my poor Mary."

• • •

I FORMED A DESPERATE RESOLUTION AS WE WALKED through Butcher's Row, and came out along the High, and turned our faces towards the sea. My brother is a fellow of considerable understanding, when dealing with matters nautical; but his notions of chivalry and the proper station of women are charmingly Gothick. He might ignore the vital nature of what I should tell him, and fix instead upon the impropriety of Lord Harold's every action.

"Should you not like to see the theatre this evening, Fly? For who knows when you shall be called back to the *St. Alban's.* Never put off until tomorrow the chance that might be seized today."

"Very true," he said with a look of humour in his eye; "and you might serve me admirably this evening, without the slightest disarrangement of your plans for tomorrow. What is this Mrs. Challoner, Jane, that she commands such attention? I will allow her to be a very dashing young woman—but I should not have thought her quite in your style."

"Frank," I said abruptly, "I must take you into my confidence on a matter of gravest import—but first, you must assure me that no word of what I tell you will pass to Mary, or, God forbid—to Mamma."

His sandy brows came down at this. "I know that you should never fall into error, Jane, by your own inclination—and so must assume that no wrongdoing is involved in your tale."

"None on my part. You are aware of my acquaintance with a gentleman by the name of Lord Harold Trowbridge?"

"Cass mentioned something of him, once," he said in an altered tone. "The fellow is a blackguard, I collect, who treated you most shabbily. Has he descended upon Southampton?"

"He is one of the Government's most trusted advisors, Frank, and privy to the councils of war. He has spent the better part of the past year on the Peninsula, communicating the movements of the French. Indeed, I believe your Admiralty consigns a principal part of its Secret Funds to Lord Harold."

"What do *you* know of the Secret Funds?" he demanded testily.

And so, as we strolled the length of the High with a leg of mutton tied up in waxed paper, I related the baffling particulars of the past week: the sudden meeting aboard the *Windlass,* Lord Harold's suspicions of Sophia Challoner, the oddities of Mr. Ord, and the cloaked figure I had encountered this morning in the depths of the subterranean passage. When I had done, Frank gazed at me with no little awe.

"You *are* a dark horse, Jane! But if your Lord Harold has had the use of a naval vessel—and no less a brig than *Windlass*—then his currency is good as gold. I know Captain Strong, and though he is but a Master and Commander, and young at that, I am certain he should never engage in any havey-cavey business along the privateering line. I may add that no less a Tory than Castlereagh professes to hold his lordship in high regard—and Castlereagh, in my books, can never err."[1]

[1] Frank Austen refers to Robert Stewart, Viscount Castlereagh (1769–1822), secretary for war in the Percival government. Castlereagh reorganized the army, creating a disposable force of 30,000 for use at short notice, with dedicated sea transport. He was one of Sir Arthur Wellesley's oldest friends, and valued Wellesley's advice on matters military. He is famed for having fought a duel with his fellow minister, Foreign Secretary Robert Canning; he committed suicide in 1822, a year after succeeding his father to the title of Marquess of Londonderry.—*Editor's note.*

I murmured assent to the wisdom of Tory ministers.

"But I should not have suspected *you,* Jane, of skullduggery by night or day—though I have always said that you possess the Devil's own pluck! And the *stories* you have fobbed off on Mamma—all with a view to making her believe his lordship is smitten with you—!"

"I did not have to work very hard at *that,*" I retorted, somewhat nettled. "Mamma is ready to find evidence of love in the slightest male attention."

Frank disregarded this aside; his moment of levity had passed. "Lord Harold truly believes Mrs. Challoner to have ordered the murder of old Dixon—the firing of the seventy-four—and the liberation of the prison hulks? I should be terrified to enter her drawing-room tomorrow; and I wonder at his lordship securing the services of a gentlewoman in pursuit of his spy, when he might have had a brigade of marines secured around Netley Lodge, merely for the asking!"

We had come up with the Dolphin Inn as he spoke, and almost without thinking, my feet slowed. I gazed towards the bow-fronted windows of the Assembly Room, and wondered which of the many glinting panes above disguised Lord Harold's bedchamber. Had he returned from London? "A brigade of marines should never serve, Frank. Mrs. Challoner demands subtlety and care."

"I apprehend. No mere cutting-out expedition, no shot across the bows, what? Don't wish the birds to fly before we've clipped their feathers?"

My gaze fell from the Dolphin's front to its side yard, where a group of ostlers loitered. They were the usual Southampton sort: roughly-dressed and fractured in their speech; sailors, some of them, turned onto land by dint of wounds. One of them lacked an arm; another had lost his leg below the knee, and supplied the want of a limb with an elegantly-carved peg. My brother no longer noticed such injuries; he witnessed them too often, once his deck was cleared for battle. The men of a ship of the line were torn asunder with a careless rapidity that defied belief in any God.

An oddity among the familiar grouping claimed my attention: the figure of a girl in a Prussian-blue cloak, a simple poke bonnet tied beneath her chin. She stood as though in suspense, being unwilling to venture the roughness of the stable yard's men, but determined to gain admittance. Her gaze was trained on the windows of the inn above, and it was clear at a glance that she sought someone within. The slightness of her frame suggested extreme youth; and when she darted a furtive look over her shoulder, as though fearful of being watched, I gasped aloud.

"Flora Bastable! The maid dismissed from Netley Lodge! I should know those eyes anywhere—the exact colour of gentians, Frank, on a summer morn. But what can have brought her a full three miles from her home in Hound?"

"What the Devil do you care for a maidservant's business, Jane?" he demanded impatiently.

At that moment, a chaise turned into the yard, blocking the girl from my view. When the way had cleared, she had vanished. Was it I who had driven her to flight? Had she sped deeper into the yard—or beyond it, to the alleyways and passages that led to the town's walls?

And whom had she sought within? Her late mistress's enemy—*Lord Harold*?

"She certainly did not come here idly," I mused, "and I read fear in her looks. Frank—say that you will help me! If the theatre is your object, persuade Mary that she is well enough to sit in French Street tonight; and insist upon my going to Netley Lodge tomorrow evening, despite Mamma's protestations."

My brother placed his hands upon my shoulders. "I dislike the notion of you walking into such a den of vipers, Jane."

"I dislike it myself. But I dislike the murder of good men—and the burning of ships—even more."

"When you put it thus, my dear—I have no choice." He drew my arm through his, and led me towards the Water.

Chapter 20

Message from an Unknown

Wednesday, 2 November 1808

~

AT SIX O'CLOCK THIS EVENING, MY BROTHER WALKED to Roger's Coachyard to secure a hack chaise for my journey to Netley Lodge. Mary settled on my bed to watch me dress for Sophia Challoner's party. I had laid my new black gown over a chair, and spread the paisley shawl across its folds.

"It is a lovely gown, Jane." She fingered it wistfully. "And the hat is too cunning for words! Mrs. Challoner must hold you in excessive regard, to send you such a gift!"

"Possibly," I returned, "but I believe it is the power of giving that she most truly enjoys. She informed me that she had not two groats to rub together when she married her late husband; and that spending her fortune is now the chief pleasure of her life."

"Then you do her a kindness in accepting of her generosity. Has she no children?"

"None at all."

"Poor creature! A fortune should be nothing, if one were all alone in the world."

As I was unlikely ever to have a child myself, I found I could not agree with Mary; the spending of a fortune, in the absence of more demanding preoccupations, might be engaging in the extreme. "Mrs. Challoner should disagree with you. She places the virtues of solitude—or freedom, as she prefers to call it—above all else."

"She sounds an odd sort of lady. Do you admire her?"

I hesitated. What did I feel for Sophia Challoner, beyond a persistent doubt as to her motives?

"I admire her bravery, certainly. She fears neither man nor woman; handles her mettlesome horses herself; presides over an elegant establishment alone, with utter disregard for the opinions of others; and went so far as to view the battle of Vimeiro at close hand. She snaps her fingers at propriety and cuts a considerable dash. She is the sort of woman that may never enter a room without a dozen heads turning; indeed, she seems to thrive upon notice as others must upon air. But I do not think she possesses an easy soul, Mary. She is in search of something—sensation, the regard of others, a purpose to her restless life. I do not begin to understand her; but *admire* her? Yes—if you would mean the sort of admiration one reserves for a wild thing of great beauty."

"I have never heard you speak thus about anyone," Mary said in a small voice. "You are so . . . so *relentless,* Jane, in the expression of your opinions. You may reduce a paragon to shivering shreds, with the well-placed application of a word."

I turned and stared at her. "Do I seem to you so vicious, Mary? So wantonly careless of the feelings of others?"

She coloured immediately. "Not vicious, Jane. Not *exactly.* But I am always thankful that the regard of a sister prevents you from speaking so frankly as you might, your opinion of *me.*"

My whole heart went out to her: the soft, round face under the cloud of curls; the wondering eyes of a child. Great strength of mind and purpose was concealed beneath her china-doll looks; and her goodness was unshakeable. But it was true I had disparaged Mary Gibson greatly when Frank first lost his heart to her: a mere girl of Ramsgate, with no more wit than fortune or influence. It was easy to dismiss Mary in her girlhood—but I could never regard the Captain's wife so lightly now.

"Will you oblige me, my dear—though I hesitate to ask it: will you help me to do up my hair as it should be done, to grace this remarkable hat?"

She jumped down from the bed with her face alight. She had left several younger sisters, some of them barely out in Society, when she quitted Kent a few years ago; and I knew she missed the joys of preparing for Assemblies and balls—all the chatter of a ladies' dressing room.

She held the Equestrian Hat aloft, her narrowed gaze surveying me in the mirror.

"You must let down the front section of your hair, Jane, for it is far too severe, and part it in the middle, I think. We shall curl the wings in bunches at the temple, and the brim of the hat shall dip *just so.* Have you, by any chance, a set of hair tongs?"

As she wove the heated iron through my hair, I gripped the gold crucifix tightly in my palm. There would be time enough to clasp it about my throat, once I had crossed the River Itchen.

IT SEEMED THAT MRS. CHALLONER HAD FOUND AN hour to commission her gown—and then had commanded several days and nights of Madame Clarisse's time. She was breathtaking in her evening dress, of rich white Italian sarcenet; it was embroidered in gold thread with grapevines and leaves that ran across the low bodice and the edge of the cap sleeves. Scrollwork in gold ornamented the hem, which was a full foot shorter than the under-petticoat and train; gold buttons fastened the dress behind. Her hair was combed sleekly back along the right side of her head, and blossomed in curls over her left ear; a circlet of gold and diamonds ornamented her neck, and another the upper part of her arm. With her brilliant complexion and liquid dark eyes, she appeared a triumphant goddess—a victorious archangel, who might equally reward a youth for excellence at sport, or watch him broken under the wheels of a chariot.

She was charmingly grouped as I entered the room, in a low chair by the fire, with Mr. Ord standing above her and a little girl of nine or ten on a hassock at her feet. The child wore a simple white gown of muslin, tied with a pale green sash; she was turning over the beads of a bracelet, and talking amiably of the afternoon's delights. I should mention that the drawing-room of Netley Lodge provided a perfect backdrop to this elegant domestic scene: it was filled with curious treasures, brought from Oporto by Mrs. Challoner, and displayed about the room with artless taste. A brilliant bird, quite dead and stuffed, was posed in a gilt cage in one corner; Spanish scimitars hung from the walls; a drapery of embroidered stuff, in the Portuguese manner, was flung across a sopha; and heavy paintings in oils—dark as the Inquisition—stared down from the walls.

"Miss Austen!" Sophia cried, and rose with alacrity to embrace me. I was startled at the effusion of her welcome, but returned her warmth unquestioningly. "How lovely you look in that gown!"

Her eyes moved lightly over my figure—lingered an instant upon the golden crucifix at my throat, but without any peculiar regard—and took in the effect of the paisley shawl with obvious pleasure.

"I must order a gown just like it, immediately—only not, I think, in black. Then we may be seen to be two girls together, sharing confidences, as we ride about the country in my charming phaeton! Maria—may I have the honour of introducing Miss Austen to your acquaintance?"

At that moment, a lady was entering the drawing-room, in a magnificent gown of deep pink drawn up over a white satin slip; it was fastened at the knee with a cluster of silver roses and green foil, and allowed to drape on the opposite side to just above the bottom of the petticoat. Had she been less stately in her person, the gown might have been ravishing; but as it was, she appeared rather like an overlarge sweetmeat trundled through the room on a rolling cart. Her ample white bosom surged above the tight diamond lacing of her bodice; and a necklace of amethyst trembled in her décolletage.

"Miss Austen—Mrs. Fitzherbert. Maria, this is

Miss Austen—my sole friend in Southampton, and a very great adventuress on horseback."

"A pleasure," said Maria Fitzherbert. She inclined her head. I curtseyed quite low—for one is so rarely in the presence of a royal mistress, particularly one who believes herself a *wife,* that I was determined no lack of civility should characterise our meeting.

She smiled at me; said a word or two respecting "dear Sophia, and her bruising experience in Oporto," made it known that she regarded me as an object of gratitude for having taken "dear Sophia" under my wing—and moved, in her ponderous fashion, towards the window seat. There she took up her workbag and commenced to unfurl a quantity of fringe.

I had heard from my cousin Eliza de Feuillide, who knew a little of the lady, that Maria Fitzherbert was the most placid and domestic of creatures; that she loved nothing so much as a comfortable coze in the countryside, particularly at her house on the Steine in Brighton; that the Prince's predilection for loud company and late hours was the saddest of trials; and that, if left to herself, she would summon no more than three friends of an evening, to make up her table at whist. She must be more than fifty, I presumed, and the sylph-like beauty she had commanded at eighteen—the year of her first marriage, to the heir of Lulworth Castle in Dorset—was now utterly fled. Mr. Weld had been six-and-twenty years her senior, and he had survived his wedding night but three months. She was no luckier in her second union, to Mr. Thomas Fitzherbert of Swynnerton Park and London; for he died but four years after their marriage, along with her infant son. She had been nine-and-twenty when at last the Prince prevailed against her scruples, and persuaded her to be his consort. Now the golden hair was turned to grey; her flawless complexion flaccid. But the Prince was said to prefer portly women.

Mr. Ord crossed the room, apparently to admire Mrs. Fitzherbert's fringe—his attitude all politeness—but a tug on the tails of his black coat from the little girl in the green sash brought him whirling around, at the ready to tickle her. She shrieked with delight, and hid herself behind the column of Sophia Challoner's dress; Mr. Ord, however, forbore to pursue her there.

"Minney," said Mrs. Fitzherbert quietly, "it is time you were returned to Miss LaSalles; come, kiss my cheek and make your adieux."

The child affected to pout, and cast down her eyes; but she was a dutiful creature, and did not hesitate to peck the matron's cheek and skip out of the room in search of her governess.

"That is little Mary Seymour," Sophia informed me in a low voice. "You will have heard of her troubled case, I am certain."

I had read of Minney Seymour, as she was known, in all the London papers. She was the seventh child of Lord Hugh and Lady Horatia Seymour, the latter a consumptive who had placed the infant in Mrs. Fitzherbert's care before going abroad for a cure. Poor Lady Seymour, whose husband was a Vice-Admiral of the Royal Navy, had returned to England when her daughter was two—only to die of consumption a few weeks later. Her husband, serving on the West Indies station, had survived her but a matter of months. The child had remained with Mrs. Fitzherbert, much doted upon by the lady and her royal consort—until the Seymour family demanded her return when Minney was four. The furor that then ensued was indescribable.

The Prince claimed immediately to have had conversations with the dying mother, in which she made over the care of her child to Mrs. Fitzherbert; he used his influence with every member of the Seymour clan; made over a fortune for the girl's use, once she should be of age—and when the case was brought to the House of Lords two years since, His Royal Highness shamelessly manipulated the votes of his cronies to require a judgement in Mrs. Fitzherbert's favour. Some part of the Seymour family was said to be outraged: not least that the child was to be raised by a Catholic, and subject to the polluted atmosphere of the Prince of Wales.

But having seen the blooming girl and her adoptive mother, I could not think Minney Seymour so very unhappy. The child had never, one must remember, known her true parents—and could hardly be expected to rush from all the comforts of a royal household in Brighton, to the arms of her unknown relations.

"I am very glad that you are come," Sophia said in my ear. "Would you oblige me—before the rest of the guests are assembled—in walking into my dressing room for a little conversation? For I should dearly like to consult you."

"Of course," I said in surprise.

With a glittering smile at Mr. Ord, who now stood in a becoming attitude near Mrs. Fitzherbert's seat, she swept out of the room and led me swiftly up the stairs. I could not imagine the source of such urgency—had she commissioned a gown of whose style she was in doubt, and required a second opinion?

"Ah, *Conte,*" she said as she achieved the head of

the stairs, "they are all waiting for you. How distinguished you look, in the Order of the Regent!"

The man to whom she spoke was tall and black-haired, with the olive skin of Iberia; a thin, whipcord figure exquisitely dressed, with a sword swinging at his side. A broad scarlet riband crossed his breast, and from it hung what appeared to be a gold and enamel medal: the Order of the Regent, she had called it, by which she signified the vanished Regent of Portugal now resident in Brazil.

Hand on his sword-hilt, he clicked his heels together and bowed deeply. "You are the brightest flower in the English garden," he said with considerable effort.

"Your command of our tongue certainly increases." Sophia's tone was playful. "Miss Austen, may I have the honour of presenting the Conte da Silva-Moreira to your acquaintance?"

Silva-Moreira. *Silva. A common enough handle, by all accounts, in that part of the world,* Frank had said. Sophia had spoken in English, rather than her accustomed Portuguese—and again I heard my brother: *He may have been an Iberian—but I'll swear the fellow spoke nothing but French!*

"The Conte is a very old friend of myself and Mrs. Fitzherbert, with whom he has been staying in Brighton since his removal from Oporto. Conte, Miss Austen."

I made my courtesy, and the black-haired Count clicked his heels again. He bent over my hand, his lips grazing my glove, and his eyes swept my figure indolently. Then his gaze returned, arrested, to the pulse at my throat.

Under the weight of his look, I felt the crucifix burning there, as though each throb of my heart burnished it the brighter. My hand nearly strayed to cover it, but the Count's dark eyes flicked up to mine—and the spell was broken.

"Miss Austen?" he said. "There is an English sea captain by that name."

"There are two, Conte—both my brothers. Have you happened to meet with one of them?" *On the* St. Alban's, *perhaps, off Vimeiro?*

"I have not had that pleasure. I merely heard of Captain Austen from . . . friends." His eyes strayed once more to my throat. "That is a most beautiful crucifix you wear, madam. May I examine it?"

He employed the tone of a man who is never refused anything; his fingers were already reaching towards my neck.

A great, tall man wrapped up in a black cloak, Flora had said, *nose as sharp as a blade, and eyes that glittered dark like a serpent's.* Was it he? The man Sophia Challoner called *mon seigneur*? The man I had blundered against in the dark of the subterranean passage, only yesterday? The man who had stolen Mr. Hawkins's boat?

He had been staying at Netley Lodge, after all, since Monday.

"How did you come by this?" he demanded sharply.

"It was pressed upon me by a friend."

"Curious! On the obverse, it bears the family seal of my house!"

"Indeed? I cannot imagine how that could be so."

"Can you not?"

"If you will excuse us, Conte," said Sophia firmly, "we shall not be a moment."

She clasped my hand and led me towards her

dressing room. I felt the Count's eyes follow me the length of the corridor, and shuddered.

"He is an imposing figure of a man, Sophia—too imposing, perhaps."

"He *ought* to be. He was reared to rule estates as vast as a kingdom, and may command a quarter part of the wealth of Portugal, my dear. For all his power and fortune, Ernesto knows but little of the world, however; only the gravest necessity would drive him from his native land—and into the arms of the English Crown. But such is the goad of war."

"—Into the arms of the Crown?" I repeated, perplexed.

"Indeed. The Conte has sought the aid of Maria Fitzherbert not merely from the ancient friendship between her family and his—but because of her influence with the Prince, and by extension, the Whig Party! Without the support of some part of the Government—without assurances that English troops will not desert the Peninsula, and consign its peoples to the French—the Conte's future will be bleak, indeed. He remains here in Southampton only a day—long enough to engage a ship for his eventual return to Oporto. Tomorrow he posts to London, to meet with the Prince at Carlton House."

She offered the recital as though it were of no great moment; from her air she had not an idea of the speech's effect upon myself. That Sophia Challoner should disparage the French—that she should welcome to her household a man determined to win the English to the cause of war in the Peninsula—was so at variance with my ideas of the lady, that I was entirely confounded.

"That is why I extended an invitation to this soiree to Lord Harold Trowbridge—that insolent rake we encountered in Mrs. Lacey's pastry shop on Saturday," she continued easily. "He had the presumption to call here the following day, and could not be got rid of for full two hours! I detest the man—but I know him to wield great influence in Whitehall, and I thought it necessary for the Conte to make his acquaintance. Maria might do much with the Prince; but Lord Harold is vital to the persuasion of the Whig Great."

"Is he?" I said wonderingly. "I did not know that one could be a... what did you call him? a *rakehell*? ... and yet command the respect of members of the Government."

Sophia threw back her head and laughed. "Oh, my poor, dear Jane!" she cried. "Have your brothers never taught you the way of the world?"

The droll look of a cynic sat well on her beautiful countenance—but I could not credit the change. She had shown a depth of passion—a hatred in respect of Lord Harold—that could hardly be so easily done away with, merely for the sake of *policy*. I suspected duplicity, on one hand or the other; but looked diffident, as though her words had shamed me.

"I will not teaze you any longer." She smoothed an errant wisp of hair, her eyes on her own reflection. "Lord Harold may go to the Devil—provided he serve my interests first. But that is *not* why I carried you away with me, Jane. Pray attend to *this*."

Now she would bring forth a selection from her wardrobe—or offer a ravishing jewel for my delectation, I thought. But instead, she opened the drawer of her dressing table, and drew forth a letter, its seal already broken.

"What do you make of that?"

I opened the page slowly, afraid of I knew not

what—that it was penned in Lord Harold's hand? That it contained a declaration of ardent love? But I could not recognise the fist. The note was dated Monday—the thirty-first of October.

Mrs. Challoner:

If you wish to hear something to your advantage, be at the Abbey ruins at dusk on Thursday. I know your secret; ignore this at your peril.

There was no signature.

"How very odd," I said softly.

"That is a note that smacks of blackmail, Jane. It appeared on my doorstep Monday morning."

"But what does it mean?" I enquired with a puzzled frown. "And from whence did it come?"

"If I were forced to offer a guess—I should say that my late serving-maid, Flora, had penned it; though I confess I cannot speak to her hand."

The writing was fluid and without hesitation, though from the appearance of several blots, it appeared to have been written on an unstable surface—the back of a jolting cart, perhaps? Flora had certainly suggested, in our conversation amidst the ruins, that she might pursue such a course; but I would not disclose so much to Sophia Challoner. She did not need to know that I had met with the girl on Sunday, while overlooking the Lodge.

"But why should your maid attempt extortion? What can this girl profess to know of your affairs?"

She shrugged. "Nothing I should not publish to all the world. She is gravely mistaken if she believes me likely to pay for her silence. I must assume she suffers a grievance, for having been turned off without a character—but in truth, Jane, she was a wretched servant."

"I am sure of it—your opinion could not err in such matters," I returned with complaisance. "But how shall you answer such a letter, Sophia?"

"I shall meet the scheming wench tomorrow at dusk. Should you like to bear me company?"

"Take Mr. Ord," I advised. "You do not know, after all, whom you may encounter—and a gentleman of parts should be of infinite use, in so lonely a place, and at such an hour."

A clatter in the hallway below—and my companion turned hastily from her mirror. "That will be Lord Harold, or I miss my mark. Come, Jane—let me make you better acquainted with the most despicable man in the Kingdom!"

Chapter 21

A Deadly Challenge

2 November 1808, cont.

~

THEY PLAYED AT FARO ON MRS. CHALLONER'S ENAMELLED table, with the faces of the thirteen cards painted on its surface: Sophia as dealer, Lord Harold the bettor. As she drew each card from her box, he wagered a sum as to its face; and as she displayed it, he must react with neither pleasure nor pain—but rather as a man in acceptance of his Fate. The game was well-suited to their varying tempers—Lord Harold should keep a mental register of every card that fell, and might, with time, wager successfully as to the nature of those that remained—while Mrs. Challoner stood in the guise of Fortune's handmaiden: powerless to affect the hand she dealt, but determinant of success or failure all the same.

He had appeared this evening at Netley Lodge

with his usual careless grace; claimed acquaintance with Maria Fitzherbert in a cool but affectionate tone that was returned with polite indifference; bowed correctly to the Conte da Silva-Moreira, who would have drawn him apart immediately if he could—but that Lord Harold was determined, I saw, to take notice of me.

"Ah, and it is—Miss Austen, I think? Of Mrs. Lacey's pastry shop? You are in excellent looks this evening, ma'am. I confess that it has been a long while since I have seen such a daring hat."

He pressed my hand to his lips, raised a satiric brow, and allowed his attention to be claimed by others—but the rallying tone, and the attempt at intimacy, had not been lost upon Sophia Challoner. She came to me not five minutes later and said, in an undertone, "Do you not believe me, now, Jane, when I say that the fellow is lost to all claims of respectability? He shall be offering you *carte blanche* next, if you are not on your guard."[1]

All conversation was soon at an end, however, for Sophia Challoner opened her instrument, and commenced to play a dashing air while Mr. Ord sang. The American possessed a rich, full voice that paired admirably with the pianoforte—and I thought how well Sophia and her swain appeared together: the dark head and the bright, the cultivated beauty and the fresh-faced youth. Were they, despite the disparity in their ages, equal in attachment? I witnessed no peculiar mark of regard—no look of adoration or lingering touch. It was a puzzlement. I almost wished them

[1] A gentleman's *carte blanche* was his promissory note—offered to a woman he supported as a mistress, guaranteeing complete funding at her discretion.—*Editor's note.*

to be lovers, so that they might not be joined by conspiracy alone.

"Her performance is admirable," said Lord Harold in my ear, "but I cannot approve her taste. What do you think, Jane?"

He had moved between my chair and the wall. Beyond me stood the Conte da Silva, his gaze trained on the fair proficient, while Mrs. Fitzherbert had retired to her fringe in the window seat, and must be well beyond the range of hearing.

"I think that you run the risk, my lord, of alerting Mrs. Challoner's senses. She mistrusts your notice of me, and is determined to thwart it."

"Sophia—jealous? All the better!" he murmured provocatively. "I enjoy considering you the object of that woman's envy, Jane. You deserve a little envy. Your dress becomes you as nothing has these four years, at least."

"My lord—"

I felt too exposed in the room, under the gaze of those assembled; but I apprehended that it was exactly this degree of risk his lordship enjoyed.

"Are you not desirous of learning my progress in London?"

"I cannot believe there is wisdom in such a subject."

"Jane, Jane—you were never faint of heart! But I make you uncomfortable. And Sophia detects a disturbance in her ranks; she shall end her song presently. I have time enough for this: Beyond the power of imagining—to the shock and dismay of her intimate friends—*Mrs. Fitzherbert has lost the Prince's favour.* He now pursues another: the Lady Hertford, whose husband rules the Seymour clan. It would seem that in pleading Lord Hertford's indulgence, in the matter of Minney Seymour, His Royal Highness fell in love with Hertford's wife. Poor Maria has won a daughter—but lost her Prince."

His speech was done, as well as his provocation; but he had left me much to consider. If Mrs. Fitzherbert had been spurned once again—if, in the autumn of her life, she were abandoned a second time by the man to whom she had sacrificed every notion of honour and reputation—might she not have cause for vengeance? Our assumptions of her fidelity to the Prince must be routed. And that meant—

—That she might lend her entire support to a Catholic plot, without the slightest qualm.

I studied the pink and guileless countenance of the middle-aged woman bent over her fringe, and felt both doubt and immense pity. What must it be, to be born with the burden of beauty, and pursued to the ends of the earth by the Great—only so long as one remained young?

IT WAS AFTER SOPHIA'S SONG HAD ENDED THAT I FELL prey to her rapacity for whist-players, a table being made up of Mr. Ord, Mrs. Fitzherbert, the Conte da Silva, and myself. I am no lover of cards, and detest the waste of an evening spent in such a pursuit, when the hours might better pass in conversation or music—but I understood that Sophia Challoner pursued a double purpose, in arranging her drawing-room thus: she might satisfy Mrs. Fitzherbert's desire for placid amusement, and engross Lord Harold entirely to herself, the better to further the Conte da Silva's interest with that gentleman.

"Do you play at faro, sir?" she had enquired with mocking sweetness.

"You know that I do. Would you consent to deal me a hand?"

They had then established themselves at the cunning table near the fire; and I found that my eyes strayed too often from my own cards, to observe the battle of wits they waged, to offer my partner Mr. Ord much success. This was entirely as it should be, for Mrs. Fitzherbert and the Conte were allowed to carry all before them—a result they appeared to enjoy.

"Have you lived all your life in Southampton, Miss Austen?" Maria Fitzherbert enquired as she set down her trump.

"But a year and a half, ma'am—though Hampshire has always been my county. I was born in the town of Steventon, some miles to the north."

"Then I have spent several years in your part of the world!" she cried, with the first evidence of animation I had seen. "I stayed on numerous occasions at Kempshott Park."

"And how did you find the neighbourhood of Basingstoke?"

"Decidedly agreeable. It is a good market town, and as a staging post for London, must offer every convenience to one of itinerant habits. It is nearly twenty years since I was staying there—but I recall that the local hunt was rather fine, and the society in general not unpleasing."

The Prince of Wales had leased Kempshott Park for some years in the late 1780s, or the early 1790s; I had been too young a girl to recollect much of the household, but my elder brother, James, had been wont to ride to hounds with the Prince's party. I doubted, however, that Mrs. Fitzherbert had seen anything of James. That she could refer with equanimity, to a place she had occupied under the most dubious of circumstances, confirmed my belief that she was impervious to the weight of scandal.

"I knew the house in Lord Dorchester's time," I returned, "and attended many a ball there, in my youth. It is a lovely place."

"I was very happy at Kempshott." Her eyes lifted thoughtfully—not to meet my own, but to regard Mr. Ord, who was bent over his cards. Her gaze rested on his golden head, and an involuntary sigh escaped her.

"Youth, and its memories, are precious—are they not, Miss Austen?"

Did she think of the Prince, and the beauty of his youth? Prince Florizel, he had been called—one of the most engaging young gentlemen of the last age. Half the ladies of the *ton* had harboured a *tendre* for him—but at six-and-forty years of age, he was very much dissipated, now.

Mr. Ord chanced to look up—chanced to meet the benevolent countenance trained upon him—and smiled at Mrs. Fitzherbert. "You are forever young in the eyes of those who admire you, madam."

Something tugged at my heart—some look or word whose meaning I could not decipher—and then the moment passed. A cry broke from the faro table beside us, and Lord Harold thrust back his chair in triumph.

He stood over Sophia Challoner, his narrowed eyes gleaming. An expression of fury and challenge darkened the lady's face, and for an instant I almost believed she might tip the table and its contents—cards, bills, a dish of sugared almonds—onto the floor at his feet. Her parted lips trembled as though to hurl abuse at his head; but Lord Harold straightened, and stepped away from the table.

"My God, Sophia, how you hate to lose!"

"You saw the cards. Admit it! You cheated in my house! As you once cheated Raoul of life!"

The colour drained from Lord Harold's countenance. "Madam," he said stiffly, "in deference to your sex I may not answer that charge; but were you a man, I should toss my glove in your face!"

Mr. Ord rose from his seat. "Then toss it in mine, sir! I stand behind Mrs. Challoner's words!"

"Do you, pup?" He bared his teeth in a painful grin; and I saw the mastery pride held over him. He would not hesitate to challenge the American—to meet him with pistols at dawn—and the outcome must be desperate. Lord Harold's reputation as a marksman was fearful; but I had seen Mr. Ord spur his black mount, and guessed at the passions his gentle exterior must hide. I found that I had risen as well, and stood swaying by the whist table; the Conte da Silva was very still, his black eyes glittering as they moved from one man to the other.

Mr. Ord pulled off his glove.

"James—*no!*" cried Mrs. Fitzherbert. *"I beg of you—"*

He stepped forward, and slapped Lord Harold across the face.

Chapter 22

Conversation by Lanthorn Light

2 November 1808, cont.

~

"NAME YOUR SECONDS, SIR."

Mr. Ord stared at Lord Harold, his fair skin flushed. "I have none. I am a stranger in this country."

"I shall stand as his second," said Sophia Challoner, and rose from her seat. "You do me the gravest injustice, Lord Harold, in supposing that I am incapable of defending a matter of honour."

"I shall not raise a pistol against a woman," he returned, tight-lipped. "Find a substitute, Ord."

"May I offer myself as second?" enquired the Conte da Silva politely. "I had hoped to meet you on more amicable terms, my lord—but circumstances . . ."

"Nothing you might undertake on behalf of a friend, Conte, shall influence my opinion of your worth; nay, it shall only increase it." Lord Harold bowed. "My second shall wait upon you here tomorrow afternoon. Good evening."

Without another word or look, he deserted the room; and as swiftly quitted the house. I thought, in that instant, that I should faint dead away with anguish; but the sight of Sophia Challoner's blazing looks forced me to adopt an attitude of insouciance. It should never do to betray a dangerous sensibility.

"James! *James!*" Maria Fitzherbert cried, and stumbled towards Mr. Ord. "You must not meet Lord Harold! He has the very worst reputation as a marksman! You must fly from this place tonight, do you hear?"

"Forgive me, madam—but you speak of what you do not understand," he responded gently.

Mrs. Fitzherbert sank down upon the hassock little Minney had once employed, and put her face in her hands. I apprehended only then, that her acquaintance with Mr. Ord must be of far longer standing than I had previously thought.

Sophia Challoner went to her, the fire fading from her countenance. "Oh, my dear—I should have considered. I should have thought! It is all my fault!—Reckless, foolish Sophia, to spur the flanks of such a man! And now I have involved my friends in my disgrace!"

"Go to him, Sophia," Maria Fitzherbert said faintly. "Go to him, and offer an apology. It is the only possible course—"

"You will not consider such a thing!" Mr. Ord said severely. "The Conte da Silva and I know what we have to do. Begging your pardon, Mrs. Fitzherbert—Mrs. Challoner—but I think it's time we all retired. There's a deal of work to be faced in the morning."

Sophia raised her head and gazed at me miserably. "My poor Miss Austen! What a tragedy we have played for you tonight—and all on account of my ungovernable temper! Lord Harold is right: I *do* hate to lose at cards. But I hate even more to yield to his lordship—and I have done nothing else, to my shame, since making his acquaintance. Shall I summon your carriage?"

"Pray do." I crossed the room to her, and offered my hand. "And do not hesitate to inform me, Sophia, should you require the least assistance in coming days. I should be honoured to aid you in any way I can, to thwart the policies of *such* a man."

THE AUTUMN MOON WAS JUST PAST THE FULL, MAKING travel at an advanced hour far less hazardous than it might have been in utter darkness. I had merely three miles to cover in my hack chaise—but the interior was more spartan than Lord Harold's conveyance, and I was jolted against the stiff side-panels more than once on my way through West Woods to the Itchen ferry. The Abbey ruins rose up silent and ghostly in the silver light, a stark outline as I passed; no spectral fires lit the shattered ramparts this evening. I considered the singularity of human experience. I had contemplated the romantic possibilities of touring a ruin under moonlight, at the dead hour of night; and never dreamt the chance should fall in my way. Now, confronted by the chilly prospect, I shuddered.

We rumbled through Weston at a steady pace, for the coachman was eager to be home in his bed, and I was no less impatient to regain Castle Square. The hour was close to midnight, and the ferryman must be asleep at his post; for as we rolled down Weston hill to the river, I espied a second carriage, waiting on the desolate shore. My driver pulled up, and quitted the box to hold his horses' heads—and a low murmur of conversation ensued beyond my window.

I raised the glass and peered out. Neither ferry nor ferryman was in sight; but a lanthorn glowed on the opposite shore, and the neighbouring chaise was Lord Harold Trowbridge's. In another instant the gentleman himself had approached the window and extended his hand. I grasped it in my own. The current of life in his fingertips was so strong that I trembled.

"Jane," he whispered. "Well met, my dear. Are you comfortable in that bandbox?"

"Not at all," I replied. "Are you comfortable in your soul? Do you really mean to kill that poor boy, who has no more idea of a duel than he has of the interior of White's?"

"Better that he should learn, then, from a proficient. I do not take kindly to being slapped with a glove—but it is not the first time I have suffered the insult. I shall inflict nothing worse than a flesh wound; his heart shall be saved for another meeting."

"Who shall act as your second, my lord?"

"Orlando, of course. I can summon no one else on such short notice."

"Orlando?" I cried. "Has he then returned? What were his adventures? How does he appear?"

"Like a man reborn," Lord Harold replied. "A common sailor discovered him in Portsmouth, lying unconscious near Sally Port. There was a great deal of trouble last night in Portsmouth, as no doubt you are aware—"

"But how did Orlando come to be there?"

"His story is a strange one. You will recall that he did not return to the Dolphin Inn, Sunday evening."

"And you were anxious."

"After leaving you and Miss Lloyd at the Water Gate Quay, he returned to Netley—though not, this time, to the Abbey. He waited in darkness for Mr. Ord, and witnessed him quit the Lodge well after the dinner hour—at perhaps nine o'clock."

"I recall that you set Orlando on to follow him."

"Though Ord was on horseback, he went at a walk, and thus Orlando was able to keep pace. The American travelled *not* in the direction of Itchen ferry, as one might expect—but to the northeast, and the village of Hound."

"And what did he there?" I whispered.

"He pulled up his mount before the cottage of a family called Bastable, though the hour was exceedingly late and all such simple folk are early to bed. He knocked—gained admittance at once—and disappeared within."

"That is decidedly strange!"

"I agree," said Lord Harold coolly, "for even did we believe him capable of a liaison with Sophia's late serving-maid, we must assume her to claim a populous family, not excepting a querulous old grandparent, which must decidedly diminish the charms of *amour*."

"Mrs. Challoner believes Flora Bastable to be an agent of blackmail," I said thoughtfully. "She received an unsigned missive, alleging privileged knowledge, and suggesting a meeting to the advantage of both."

"Blackmail?" Lord Harold repeated with quickened interest. "Is it possible that Ord was sent as intermediary?"

"Possible," I said doubtfully, "but I cannot say whether the note I read tonight was received so early as Sunday."

"That was the day the girl Flora was turned away from her employment, was it not?"

"For an injudicious fit of strong hysterics—the natural result of having witnessed a bout of witchcraft, or a Catholic Mass."

"I recollect a commotion in the servants' wing near the close of my call at Netley Lodge: the sound of tears and lamentation, and the hurried departure of a girl in the direction of Hound. Perhaps Sophia regretted of her haste, and despatched Ord later as supplicant for Flora's return."

"Such solicitude is hardly in keeping with Mrs. Challoner's character! We must declare it a puzzle, and have done. But tell me of Orlando!"

"As he waited in suspense in the underbrush of Hound, a man came upon him from behind, and delivered such a blow to the head as to knock him insensible."

"No!"

"Orlando was bound hand and foot, and spent the better part of the night and day subsequent in the Abbey tunnel. He awoke to find himself bobbing down the Solent in his own skiff, with a Portuguese gentleman in a long black cloak and hat plying the oars—bound for Portsmouth. His captor having achieved Spithead, Orlando was tossed summarily into the water, and left for dead."

"Good Lord! The cloaked figure from the subterranean passage!"

"*Mon seigneur,*" Lord Harold agreed. "He must have worked at Ord's orders, and mounted watch upon his confederate's back when the American ventured to Hound."

"—and served poor Orlando with such vicious treatment! No wonder you feel no compunction in challenging Ord to a duel! But, my lord—" I paused in puzzlement. "I had thought the cloaked figure to be the Conte da Silva. And we know him to have arrived at Mrs. Challoner's on *Monday*."

"Do we?" Lord Harold countered.

"Flora, the serving-maid, did observe a tall man in a black cloak to enter the house on Sunday," I said slowly, "the man we presumed to be a priest. But perhaps it was the Conte."

"However that may be—Orlando is an adept at freeing himself from tight corners, and had the better of his captor. He slipped his ankle bonds and swam so far as Sally Port, where he dragged himself up onto the breakwater. From that position he witnessed the liberation of the prison hulks."

"With *mon seigneur*—the liberator?" I breathed.

"Would that Orlando knew the man's name—or had seen his countenance! But he was struck on the head by a flying splinter from one of the fired boats, and nearly drowned. When the seaman roused him at dawn yesterday, Orlando had swallowed a quantity of the sea, lost a good deal of blood, was chilled to the bone—and was taken at once to tell his story to the Master of the Yard."

"An unenviable position, in the circumstances."

"Yes," his lordship agreed grimly. "Orlando was nearly hanged for the second time in his young life. It seems the Royal Navy was convinced they had a spy on their hands: a foreigner out of Oporto, who could neither produce his employer nor explain his presence near Sally Port. He cooled his heels a full day before they sought my advice at the Dolphin Inn."

"Poor fellow! I saw the marks of his struggle on the passage floor," I mused. "They were everywhere in evidence."

His lordship's profile was suddenly arrested. "You returned to the tunnel, Jane? Quite alone?"

"Yesterday morning. I was under Mr. Hawkins's especial care. We ventured within, but were surprised by a man in a black cloak, who dashed out our tapers, hurled me flat against the wall, and stole Mr. Hawkins's boat!"

"Left to your own devices," he murmured, "you shall get yourself killed, one day. What if it should have been Orlando's assailant?"

"I must assume that it was. But why should he return to the Abbey?"

His lordship shrugged. "To hide from the naval authorities presently in search of him? Or... to retrieve something precious he once dropped there?"

Lord Harold reached for the gold crucifix at my neck and held it up to the lanthorn light. "The gold is warmed by the pulse at your throat," he said softly.

I could not speak—and for a second time that evening, felt as though I might swoon.

"Did anyone at the Lodge deign to notice this?" he asked.

"The Conte da Silva," I replied with difficulty. "He all but accused me of stealing it—and claimed that the seal of his house is stamped on the obverse."

Lord Harold turned the cross in his fingers and peered at it more closely. The brim of his hat grazed mine; I closed my eyes, and drank in the scent of tobacco that clung to his greatcoat.

"There is an emblem of arms, certainly—the

head of a wolf, with teeth bared, and two sabres crossed. *Curious.* And yet: he did not claim it as his? Merely *of his house,* he said?"

I nodded. "He chose not to interrogate me too closely; and if he knew me for the woman encountered in the tunnel, he did not betray his fear."

"Perhaps he considered of his risk—or perhaps ... perhaps he intended to shield another. Someone, as he said, *of his house*..." Lord Harold dropped the chain. "Tell me, Jane: what was the scene, when you quitted the Lodge?"

"Mrs. Fitzherbert was utterly overcome—almost fainting with despair—and urging Sophia Challoner to seek your pardon. She wishes Mrs. Challoner to retract her accusation against you; but I do not believe that Mr. Ord will allow it—tho' they are on such terms as for the lady to call him *James.*"

"So Maria would shield the boy?" In the light of the side lamps, I saw him frown. "I confess I do not understand the business at all, Jane. What interest binds that party? Such a disparate group of souls—so ill-matched, to all appearances, and yet united by an unspoken trust."

"It has the look of conspiracy; and Mrs. Fitzherbert is in the thick of it."

"The blackmail note," he demanded suddenly. "It prescribed a meeting, you say?"

"At the Abbey ruins—tomorrow at dusk."

"Then I shall be there."

"If you live so long."

"*Jane,*" he returned patiently. "There shall be no duel until Friday morning at the earliest. You can have no idea of the details to be arranged—wills to be witnessed, doctors procured, the ground to be laid out, and the hour of meeting to be struck—and my pistols fetched from my flat in London. All conducted in the gravest secrecy, so that the Southampton constables are not alerted."

"Wretched business! I might inform upon you myself, and save a good deal of trouble."

A faint gleam of teeth as he smiled at me through the darkness. "If I killed Ord, I should have to flee to the Continent—duelling is illegal in England, as you well know. Flight is not at *all* in my line, Jane. The cub's life is safe with me."

"But what of yours, my lord? Are you safe with him?"

I stared at the man in the moonlight: insouciant, self-confident, as careless of age as he must be of public opinion. James Ord, in all the flush of youth and heedlessness, might cut off his thread in an instant, and sail for America with the tide. I felt a great fear rise up in my heart: for what should my world be, after all, without Lord Harold in it?

He covered my hand with his palm. "Do not excite yourself, my dear. All shall be well."

The lights of the ferry loomed out of darkness; the flat-bottomed vessel bumped against the dock.

"Pray take the lady's carriage first," Lord Harold called out to the ferryman. "The moon is high; and when the lady in question is Miss Austen, it does not signify how long I wait."

Chapter 23

Pistols for Two

Thursday, 3 November 1808

~

I AWOKE WELL AFTER TEN O'CLOCK THIS MORNING, and made a slow toilette in the stillness of the Castle Square house. The rest of my family having breakfasted and gone about their various errands, I was alone with my thoughts—and they were all of Netley Lodge, and the duel that was to come. Would it indeed occur on the morrow, at dawn? And should I have the courage to face it?

At least I might go suitably attired in black.

I descended to the breakfast room and applied to Cook for some late coffee and rolls—she threw me a harassed look, being already embroiled, as she said, in preparations for "the Cap'n's dinner." I fetched the victuals myself, but found I had little appetite for them. Ought I to go to the magistrate for

Southampton—Mr. Percival Pethering—and inform him of the affair of honour that should presently take place? He might then prevent it, by arriving at the duelling ground with a company of constables—but he could not stand watch upon the duellists forever. As long as Lord Harold and Mr. Ord remained in the same country, they should be determined to draw blood.

My brothers, I am sure, would assert that I refined too much upon a trifle. I allowed my fancy to run away with me, and form an idea first of Lord Harold—and then of Mr. Ord—torn and bleeding upon the ground. In a spirit of anger at the foolishness of men, I crumbled my roll between my fingers and ignored my scalding coffee. I could not sit idly by while Lord Harold sent to London for his pistols. I must inform Mr. Pethering—but if my intelligence was to be of any use, I must know the choice of duelling ground.

I rose and fetched my pelisse and Equestrian Hat. In a matter of moments, I had quitted the house in the direction of the High.

"MISS AUSTEN." THE INNKEEPER'S STOOPED FIGURE was thin as a whippet's, his bald head shining with exertion. He had come through the saloon to the Dolphin's entry on purpose to greet me, and stood drying his hands on his apron. "You are in excellent looks, ma'am, if I may be so bold—and how is the Captain? Keeping stout, I hope?"

"My brother is very well, Mr. Fortescue, I thank you. He has lately been much at sea."

"I don't doubt it! Off the Peninsula, with all the rest of 'em? A grand old party it must be, when

Boney's back is turned. And how may I serve you this morning?"

"An acquaintance of mine is lodging in the Dolphin at present," I said, blushing furiously, "and I should like to enquire whether he is presently within."

"Indeed?" the innkeeper said curiously. "May I have the gentleman's name, ma'am?"

"Lord Harold Trowbridge."

Fortescue's expression darkened. "I'm afraid you're the second party this morning as has asked for his lordship; and I've been told to turn away all visitors, as the gentleman is engaged. Howsomever, the young woman chose to wait; and his lordship's man has agreed to see to *her*."

For a fleeting moment I had an idea of Sophia Challoner, driven forth by terrors like my own, to beg Lord Harold's forgiveness—but the innkeeper should never have called Mrs. Challoner a "young woman." That appellation was used for females of the serving class; or those who were not quite respectable.

"If you've a mind to speak with the valet," Fortescue concluded, "you're welcome to take a turn in my parlour. Good day."

He nodded stiffly, and moved off; leaving me to wonder what had inspired such disapproval. Far from being quelled in my ambitions, however, I was cheered by his recital. If Lord Harold was indisposed to receive visitors, so much the better. I might learn more from an application to Orlando.

I walked through the parlour doorway, and stopped short in surprise.

"Flora!"

The girl gripped her reticule tightly in gloved

hands. She was dressed as I had observed her on Tuesday, in the Prussian-blue cloak and poke bonnet. Her countenance bore the same furtive expression of fear or deceit.

"Miss Austen?" She rose, bobbed a curtsey, and sank down once more onto the settee.

"Are you waiting for Orlando?"

Her pretty eyes narrowed. "What do you know of him, miss? Or my business?"

"Nothing good," I returned abruptly, and sat down in the chair opposite her. "You have got yourself into some kind of trouble, my dear—and I cannot think it worth your while. Mrs. Challoner knows that you wrote that letter; and she is excessively angry. She means to call your bluff this evening; and she is bringing Mr. Ord."

"What letter?" The girl's reply was high and clear; it should drift out into the hall, and to any prying ears disposed to listen.

"I suggest you lower your voice. The letter you sent to Mrs. Challoner. She showed it to me last evening, at Netley Lodge. *I know your secret; ignore this at your peril.* Isn't that what you wrote, Flora?"

"It's a lie," she muttered, her eyes now on her lap. Her neck and face had flushed a dull, angry red.

"You told me yourself that you intended to profit by your knowledge. *When the mistress considers of the stories I might tell, she'll make it worth my while.*"

"But she didn't, did she?" The girl looked up; the blue eyes flashed. "She turned me away without a character, easy as tipping her hand. My mother's that anxious about the little ones, and how they're to be fed, now I've lost my place—it's driven her right wild. But I never wrote no letter."

"Very well. If that is your story—"

"I never wrote no letter," she insisted with a look of defiance, "because I never *learned* my letters—and where I'd be like to get a bit of paper and a pen—"

A sound from the doorway drew both our heads around, and with an expression of relief in her voice, Flora said, "You've come at last. Thought I'd have to wait all day, I did."

"Forgive me, Miss Austen." Orlando glanced at the girl, and his brows lifted in disdain. "I had no notion you were waiting upon his lordship. If you would be so good as to pass through to the stable yard, I am certain he will be delighted to see you."

"Flora is before me," I said equably.

"Flora," the valet returned, "will have to content herself with *me*."

A giggle escaped the maid's lips.

"Miss Austen—if you will be so good—"

He turned on his heel as though Flora had ceased to exist; and I was reminded again of the various skills required of a gentleman's valet: dogsbody, defender, spy. Orlando had mastered them all.

I rose, and with one final speaking glance at the girl, quitted the room.

HE WAS STANDING IN HIS SHIRTSLEEVES AT THE FAR end of the yard, his body canted sideways, his right hand extended. In his long white fingers was a gleaming silver pistol with ebony mounts. A large black and white target of concentric circles had been painted upon a board, which was established near the broad coach-house doors.

Two of the Dolphin footmen, in breeches and powdered wigs, stood behind Lord Harold, their countenances deliberately devoid of expression. The stable lads had gathered at the gates, which were closed to carriage traffic; from time to time, when a ball sang home and the target's wooden face splintered agreeably, a cheer went up from this serried rank.

"Lord Harold, Miss Austen," Orlando said quietly. He bowed, and melted back into the safety of the inn; I hesitated on the edge of the yard, unwilling to disturb his lordship's activity.

One of the footmen took the spent pistol from Lord Harold's hand, and commenced reloading it with powder, wad, and ball; the other offered the second weapon, and as he reached for it, the Rogue's eye fell upon me. His expression did not alter. He turned back to the target and steadied his aim. No trembling in the wrist, no hesitation as he pulled the trigger—but perhaps it should be different when he stared at the face of a man.

Seven more times the ritual was repeated; and then, when the target's black centre had been cloven in two by the pounding of lead balls, his lordship blew the smoke from the pistol's mouth and said: "Come here, Miss Austen."

I stepped forward, my mouth suddenly dry. He was so much more like the man whose acquaintance I had made years before—inscrutable, remote, dispassionate—than the one I had lately known, that I was afraid of him.

"My lord?"

He lifted the freshly-loaded pistol from the footman's grasp and placed it in my gloved palm. The barrel was warm with firing; the grip smooth as an egg. I nearly dropped the thing, and was glad when I did not; for such foolishness must disgrace me.

"Wrap your other palm around the butt just so, and extend your arms."

He stood behind me, his hands at my shoulders. "Steady. You must turn your body side-on to the target, Jane—otherwise your opposite will tear open your heart."

I drew a ragged breath and did as he bade. His cheek brushed my own.

"*Steady,*" he muttered. "More blood is spilled from sheer lack of nerve than from wanton malice; for it is a poor coward who cannot aim true, and prick his opponent as he chuses. Where do you intend to strike? Which part of the rings?"

"At the height of a man's shoulder," I said, "there, in the outer black."

"Then align the pistol mouth and gaze without fear the length of the barrel. Fire at will—a gentle squeeze upon the trigger, no more."

I felt my heartbeat suspended—and in a moment of clarity saw nothing but the edge of black where my ring turned white. My forefinger moved. An explosion of sound, a jolt up to my shoulder, and I stepped backwards, amazed.

A cheer went up from the assembled ostlers. The target showed a gaping hole at its furthest extent—well beyond the tight cluster of circles Lord Harold had made. I felt no small pride in my accomplishment; but I was newly aware of the difficulty inherent in aiming and controlling such a weapon. Years of practise must be required to command the sort of skill Lord Harold exhibited; and the knowledge of his precision forced a little of the fear from my soul.

"Did you come to me this morning on an errand of persuasion?" His looks were intent. "Did you think to put an end to this affair by stratagems and pleading?"

I shook my head, and handed him the weapon. I had made my decision—I would not go in search of Percival Pethering. "When is your meeting?"

"Tomorrow at dawn."

"And where shall you do it? Porter's Mead?"

He smiled thinly. "The ground there is flat enough—but too close to the magistrate for comfort."

"I should like to witness the duel."

"But you must wear *black,* Jane—and I confess I find the colour . . . disheartening."

"I shall sport any shade you command, my lord," I answered clearly, "provided you will allow me to be present."

"To save my life?" he enquired ironically, "or James Ord's?"

Chapter 24

Last Rites

Friday, 4 November 1808

~

THE SECONDS—ORLANDO AND THE CONTE DA SILVA met yesterday evening at the George Inn to lay out the rules of engagement.

The principals in the affair—Lord Harold and Mr. Ord—were both of them at Netley Abbey, the former securely hidden behind a tumbled cairn of rock, and the latter at Mrs. Challoner's side. As dusk fell and the hour of meeting came and went, no blackmailer appeared. *Perhaps,* Lord Harold wrote last night from the Dolphin, *the girl was frightened off by the appearance of the American.*

Orlando and the Conte fared better in their purpose. The duel was to be tried at dawn—perhaps forty minutes after six o'clock—and the ground they chose, a place called Butlock Common, northeast of Netley Lodge.

Orlando has paced off the distance, Lord Harold wrote, *and assures me that the place is lonely enough. No one shall disturb us. I shall not think less of you, Jane, if you refuse to venture forth. It is a tedious distance at such an hour—but know, my dear, that whether you are present in the flesh or not, I shall carry an idea of you in my mind. Adieu—*

I thought of hack chaises, and the difficulty in procuring one at five o'clock in the morning; I thought of lead balls and how they splintered wood—or flesh—despite acute precision; and then I went in search of my brother.

BUTLOCK COMMON IS A SMALL, OPEN FIELD THAT serves as grazing land for the livestock of Hound. A lane runs along the eastern edge, and here in the crepuscular murk Frank pulled up our hired gig and said, "I wonder, Jane, if your man intends to meet this morning. It's all of four bells, and not a carriage in sight!"

Shivering in my pale blue muslin—a shade unlikely to offend Lord Harold's sensibilities—I peered through the darkness. A few candles glowed in the windows of a distant hamlet, faint stars against the mantle of sleeping countryside. Someone in a barn somewhere should be milking a cow, without the faintest notion that nearby, men were assembling to shoot each other.

"Honour!" I said bitterly. "How I detest it!"

"Pshaw, Jane—that's a hum." My brother went to the horse's head; next to a ship, he loved best to have the management of a nag. "Without honour, society can have no just foundation; without honour, we should live as savages."

"Murdering one another at random, you mean?"

He stared at me wordlessly.

At that moment, the sound of hoofbeats and iron wheels resounded upon the road. From the south, in the direction of the sea, came an open phaeton and a pair I should guess to be grey geldings; from the north, and the direction of the Itchen ferry, a heavy coach with its side lamps doused.

"Perhaps they shall run headlong into one another," Frank observed cheerfully, "and settle the dispute by overturning. Do you mean to observe from the gig, Jane? Or shall I tie up the horse and give you my arm?"

How, I wondered, could Fly speak as though we were in attendance upon a mere race-meeting? As though nothing greater than a prize-fight were to be won? I rose from my seat and descended without his assistance, suddenly wild to have the madness done. As I set foot upon the ground, the Trowbridge equipage pulled up not ten feet from our position. Orlando jumped down from his footman's perch and opened his master's door.

He stepped out: a sharp silhouette in the rising dawn. Though he had commanded me to abandon mourning, he went, as ever, in black—the coat double-breasted, and buttoned high to the cravate, which was tied in the Jesuit style: a simple band folded once over the coat collar.

"My lord knows his business," Frank murmured. "In that coat he has given Ord a double set of buttons, and no division in front, to confuse the fellow should he attempt to aim for the heart. By Jove! But he is cool."

"Jane," Lord Harold said, and bowed low over my hand.

Frank's brow came down at his lordship's use of my given name—but he forbore to comment. The Rogue looked up, and said, "Will you do me the honour of introducing me to your friend?"

"My brother, sir. Lord Harold Trowbridge—Captain Francis Austen, of His Majesty's ship *St. Alban's.*"

"You were in Oporto, I think," his lordship said.

"Off the coast of Merceira only. I cannot claim to have set foot on the Peninsula. May I wish you every hope of good fortune, my lord?"

They clasped hands, and then with one serious, parting look for me, Lord Harold moved to stand by his second, Orlando.

A horse's whinny brought my head around, and there, in the gloaming, was Mrs. Challoner. She held the phaeton's reins, and her mettlesome greys pawed the ground. Mr. Ord sat to the lady's right; and behind the equipage, on horseback, rode the gentleman's second—the Conte da Silva. Mrs. Fitzherbert, it seemed, had not deigned to witness an event whose mere idea had caused such profound misery.

"Miss Austen!" Sophia cried aloud in amazement. "How come you to be here?"

"I begged her attendance," Lord Harold said swiftly. "Miss Austen is, after all, a witness to Wednesday's challenge—perhaps the only disinterested one. She has brought her brother, an officer of the Navy whose integrity must be unimpeachable, to set the marks."

Frank started—he had not understood he was to be employed in the affair—and looked to me for explanation. "Do we await a doctor? Or are we to proceed without? The light will soon be too full for action, and the parties shall risk discovery."

Mr. Ord rose from his place and bowed. He looked pale, but resolute. "I have no objection to proceeding."

"Nor have I," Lord Harold returned.

"We expect Dr. Jarvey from Southampton at every moment," Sophia Challoner broke in, "but you may set the marks, Captain, in expectation of his appearance."

"Very well." Frank's jaw was rigid, his eyes hard and unsmiling. "I should judge the proper alignment to be north-south, along the greater edge of the common, running parallel to the lane. Any glare from the rising sun shall thus be equally borne by the duellists. I shall set the first mark on the furthest southern extent of the flat part of the ground—and for the second mark, pace off thirty yards to the north. The gentlemen shall draw straws for their positions."

I apprehended, of a sudden, that my brother had witnessed such affairs before. As second—or principal? Defender—or accused? Fly stepped forward, and we turned as one to observe his progress.

For the first time that morning, our eyes fell full upon Butlock Common. Slanting yellow light from the east picked out the withered grass stems, silvered with frost; and in the very centre of the field, a pile of rubbish lay abandoned as if for firing.

Frank stopped and raised his hand to his brow. He peered into the sun—the slight slope of high ground, his quarterdeck, and the entire common his sea.

"My lord," he said—and in that instant, I could not tell whether he addressed the man waiting quietly by his coach, or the God of Heaven above. But I, too, had seen the cloak of Prussian blue, and the simple poke bonnet tossed in the grass like an empty basket. I did not need the confirmation of Frank's horrified gaze to apprehend the truth.

"It is a *girl,* Jane."

And then—as though the lifeless thing were his own Mary—he rushed to her side.

DR. JARVEY MADE SHORT WORK OF HIS EXAMINATION, though he had been an age in arriving.

"The cords of the neck have been cleanly severed, and the corpse drained of blood. Life will have been extinct in a matter of seconds."

James Ord, his countenance pale as death, walked slowly forward and fell on his knees near Flora Bastable. Had Orlando glimpsed the truth, a few nights past, when he saw the American enter the girl's cottage? Had Ord loved Flora, despite the difference in their stations?

Ord raised his hand as though he might caress the dead cheek—and then, to my surprise, he made the sign of the cross over the body, and began to murmur in a tongue that could only be Latin.

After an instant, both Sophia Challoner and the Conte da Silva knelt together behind him.

"Last Rites," murmured Lord Harold. "But the girl is not Catholic, and Ord is no priest."

The American did not falter in his speech until he had done. Then he rose, and turning first to assist Sophia Challoner to her feet, said abruptly to Lord Harold: "You are over-hasty, sir. Tho' I am no priest, I have long been a student of the Catholic faith, and intend to enter the Society of Jesus in time."

I stared at the young man—the blond Adonis—

and exclaimed: "You, intended for the Church! I cannot credit it! No Jesuit would challenge a gentleman to a duel!"

He smiled at me wryly. "Do you believe us incapable of defending our honour, ma'am? Or perhaps—that we possess none?"

We were all of us silent a moment in confusion, but Lord Harold surveyed James Ord's face with interest. "You were raised, I understand, among the Carrolls of Maryland? Archbishop Carroll—also a member of the Society—is your patron in the Church, I collect?"

"He is, my lord. I have been acquainted with His Grace almost from infancy, my family having emigrated to America in the Archbishop's ship."

"And are you also acquainted, I wonder, with the Conte da Silva's brother?" Lord Harold enquired silkily. "Monsignor Fernando da Silva-Moreira, of the Society of Jesus—late of Oporto?"[1]

The Conte da Silva started forward, his hand on his sword hilt. "What do you pretend to know of my brother?"

"Too little, alas. I know that he was educated at Liège, and that he has wandered throughout Europe in the years since the Jesuit order's suppression. I am reasonably certain that he came to these shores aboard His Majesty's ship *St. Alban's*, and that he has lately been staying in Brighton with Mrs. Fitzherbert—as you have done yourself, Conte. I suspect

[1] The term "monsignor" now refers to a specific rank of seniority within the church hierarchy, and is only rarely applied to members of the Jesuit order—specifically, when a Jesuit is designated a monsignor by the local bishop. In Austen's day, however, monsignor—or monseigneur, as it was variously spelled—was an honorific or term of respect applied to persons of rank throughout Europe, whether ordained or not.—*Editor's note.*

that he has come to rest in Southampton—and that he haunts the ruins of Netley Abbey in a long black cloak."[2]

The Conte drew breath as though he would hurl Lord Harold's claims in his face, but Sophia Challoner intervened. "His lordship knows everything that moves in England, Ernesto," she said softly. "That is why you require his influence. Do not be a fool."

I recalled with a shudder the looming black form in the tunnel's depths, and glanced at Orlando. He had suffered much at that creature's hands. The valet's countenance was pale and set; his eyes were fixed not on his master or the Portuguese Count, but on the lifeless form of Flora Bastable.

I had very nearly forgot her.

"This is all very well," Dr. Jarvey declared, "but I would beg you to canvass your mutual acquaintance at another time! We must attend to a corpse! This unfortunate girl was your serving-maid, Mrs. Challoner?"

"I turned her off," the lady retorted, "almost a week since."

Dr. Jarvey stared down at all that was left of Flora Bastable. Her gentian blue eyes were fixed, unblinking, on the morning sky. "She is very young, is she not? Too young to wander the country alone at night.

[2] Founded by Basque nobleman Ignatius of Loyola in 1540, the Society of Jesus came to be regarded as an army devoted to the Papacy, and thus as a threat to temporal kingdoms and power. It was expelled from Portugal, Spain, and their overseas possessions between the years of 1759 and 1768; it was also outlawed in France. In 1773, Pope Clement XIV suppressed the order under pressure from the Bourbons, and many Jesuits fled Europe to join their brethren in the American colonies. By 1814, however, Pius VII had revoked the brief of suppression and restored the Society of Jesus.—*Editor's note.*

One must question how she came here—*exactly* here, on your intended dueling ground. . . ."

"What are you suggesting, Doctor?" Mr. Ord enquired. The American's eyes glittered dangerously in the waxing sunlight.

"My dear sir—the girl was most certainly murdered, and murdered *here.* Her blood has soaked into the earth. It is as though she were left in this spot for a purpose. I must ask again: *why?*"

"Don't you mean—*which of us?*" Lord Harold observed.

It must be true. Only a select party had known of Mr. Ord's challenge, and the isolated spot in which it should be carried out: the company presently assembled on Butlock Common—and Maria Fitzherbert, who awaited the duel's outcome in suspense at the Lodge.

"That is absurd," Sophia Challoner said tautly. "The girl lived in Hound, but a half-mile distant. She might have wandered here for any number of reasons. A legion could have killed her."

"But in dying as she did," Lord Harold countered, "she fulfilled a peculiar purpose. She forced the suspension of this duel for an indefinite period—and one at least of our acquaintance shall be heartily glad."

The lady threw back her head and laughed—a harsh, ringing sound in the silence that surrounded the lifeless girl's body. "Did you fear to meet Mr. Ord so much, my lord?"

"Not nearly as much as Mrs. Fitzherbert feared his meeting *me,*" the Rogue returned. "I wonder which of us should consider *murder* a means of preserving a life?"

Mrs. Challoner raised her whip as though she

might cut him across the face—but the Conte da Silva grasped her wrist tightly in gloved fingers.

"You are overwrought, my dear," he said in his studied way. "You must return, now, to the Lodge."

I saw the wild rage surge into her countenance—saw her hand strain against her captor's—and then her gaze fell before the Count's implacable black eyes.

"Yes, Ernesto. . . . You are right. I believe I *am*. . . overly sensible to the scene. Pray—would you be so good as to give James your horse, and manage the phaeton for me?"

"I should be charmed, my dear."

The Conte released her whip hand with utmost gentleness, and helped her into the carriage; and never, until that moment, had I disliked Sophia Challoner so acutely. The murdered girl, with her grotesquely ravaged throat, might have been a fox thrown to the local hunt for all the concern her late mistress spared her. Indignation rose up in my breast, and I might have uttered ill-advised words—but Lord Harold spoke before me.

"How did the maid come to lose her place in your service, Sophia?"

"That is none of your concern," she retorted. "Hold your tongue, my lord, lest you be visited with a second challenge!"

"There shall be an inquest," Dr. Jarvey interposed, his hand at the horses' heads. "We shall all of us be called."

Without deigning to answer, the Conte da Silva lifted the reins, and immediately, the matched greys stepped forward. The doctor fell back, his gaze following the pair. Their action was sublime—almost as sublime as the insouciance of the lady who rode behind them, the black feather of her Cossack Hat bobbing merrily in the wind occasioned by the equipage's passage.

"My lord," said Mr. Ord as he mounted the Conte's horse, "I believe we should declare this matter between us at an end."

"It is no great sacrifice on my part."

"You have my full apology for the hastiness of temper with which I visited you; I accept complete responsibility for the consequences." Ord raised his black hat, and bowed; then he kicked the gelding into a canter and caught up with the diminishing phaeton.

"That is a waste of a fine seat," observed Dr. Jarvey regretfully, as he stared after the self-destined priest.

"What—do you think a Jesuit will have no cause to ride? I imagine nothing that young man does is wasted—except, perhaps, the hours he has devoted to Sophia Challoner." Lord Harold gazed down at the serving-maid's corpse. "I shall go in search of the girl's people in Hound. Orlando is acquainted with the cottage."

"I shall accompany you." Dr. Jarvey knelt down, and drew the edges of the Prussian-blue cloak about Flora Bastable's frame. In places, blood had stained the cloth purple. All her young life, clotted in the wool. "We might carry her home in my hack"—the doctor had travelled to the ground in a hired conveyance, like ourselves—"if the driver does not protest."

"Take mine," Frank said abruptly. "I drove it myself, and can have no objection."

"Excellent thought." Lord Harold extended his hand, as though we parted from nothing graver than a rout at his brother Wilborough's in London.

"Captain Austen—be so good as to take charge of the doctor's chaise, and convey your sister back to Castle Square. Pray accept my deepest apologies for the considerable inconvenience to which you have been put this morning."

"Not at all," Frank replied. "You will supply us with the inquest's direction?"

"Provided I am at liberty so long," the Rogue said.

Chapter 25

The Rogue's Toss

Saturday, 5 November 1808

~

THE INQUEST INTO THE DEATH OF FLORA BASTABLE was to be held at two o'clock today at the Coach & Horses Inn.

"Another murder, Jane!" my mother cried. "And why must *you* go traipsing about the town in search of sensation, merely because a serving-girl has got her throat slit? You had much better remain at home, in expectation of a call from Lord Harold. I am amply supplied with brandy at present."

I had said nothing of the duel, or my early-morning jaunt yesterday in Frank's company to Butlock Common; and the three-quarters of an hour required for our return trip along the Netley roads had so restored our sensibilities that we might face our relations without the slightest evidence of deceit.

At our return to Castle Square, at half-past seven o'clock, nobody else in the house was even stirring—but for Phebe in the kitchen. I found to my consternation that my hands would not cease shaking, and my brother's countenance was unwontedly grave. Frank and I fortified ourselves silently with fresh coffee and bread, and greeted the others in their descent from the bedchambers with the virtuous air belonging to all early risers.

Neither my mother's protests, therefore, nor Martha's anxiety, nor my fear of public display could prevent me from attending the coroner's panel.

"The maid was in service at Netley Lodge, Mamma," I told her mildly, "and her death must cause considerable discomfort in Mrs. Challoner's breast. I should not consider myself a true friend, did I fail to lend support at such an hour."

My mother declared that if I was determined to make a cake of myself, then she utterly washed her hands of me. My brother Frank said instantly, however, that he would bear me company—and dear Mary confessed herself glad of his decision, in a gentle aside she imparted in the upstairs hall.

"Frank is so restless when he is turned ashore, Jane, that I declare I can do nothing with him! Better that he should enjoy an hour of freedom about the town, and interest himself in all the doings of Southampton, than rebuke poor little Mary Jane for her irrepressible spirits."

I thoroughly agreed. At a quarter to the hour, therefore, I left Mamma prostrate in her bedchamber, smelling salts at hand, while I tied my bonnet strings unsteadily in the hall. I had not slept for most of the night, nor had I eaten more than a square of bread all day; I was in dreadful looks. I had considered of Lord Harold's parting remark—*provided I am at liberty so long*—and concluded that he expected to be charged with murder. I understood the painful course his thoughts had taken. He did not like to admit to an affair of honour, which the law must frown upon; he refused to implicate Mr. Ord in a matter of bloodshed; and he hoped to shield me, my brother, and Dr. Jarvey, who had attended the meeting in good faith. Therefore, he was left with but a single course: to inform the authorities that he had discovered the girl's corpse himself, in an isolated field, at half-past six o'clock in the morning. It was an unenviable position; but one from which Lord Harold was unlikely to shrink. Ever the gambler—and man of honour—he should surely cast his fate upon the toss of a die.

"But *why*?" I demanded of my reflection. "Why must he bear the weight of so heinous a crime, and not Sophia Challoner?"

"Are you ready, Jane?"

Frank wore his full dress uniform, complete with cockade, to lend the proceedings an air of dignity.

"You should not attempt to bear me company," I warned him. "You will hear vile things said about everybody. It is the general rule of inquests, to contribute everything to rumour, and nothing to justice."

"You make it sound worse than the Royal Navy," he observed mildly.

THE SMALL DINING PARLOUR IN THE COACH & Horses was usually bespoken for dinner by wealthy merchants in the India trade, who put up at the inn while en route from London to Southampton. It was chock-a-block with local faces by five minutes before two: seamen reddened with exposure to the elements, retired officers of the Royal Navy, a few tradesmen I recognised from shops along the High. Frank bowed left and right to his large acquaintance, but kept a weather eye on me. My brother's countenance was composed and unsmiling: much, I suspected, as he might enter into battle.

Of Sophia Challoner there was no sign, nor of Mr. Ord; the entire Netley party had dignified the inquest by their absence.

Lord Harold was seated near the front of the room, his valet at his side, but both were so sober in their mien, that neither turned his head to notice our entrance. The press of folk was so great, I did not like to force my way forward. Frank cast about for seats to the rear, and several men claimed the honour of offering theirs to me. One of them was Jeb Hawkins.

The Bosun's Mate pulled his forelock in my brother's direction, and received a sturdy clap on the shoulder; they had long been acquainted, and knew each other's worth. "This is a rum business, miss, and no mistake! Poor old Ned Bastable! His granddaughter served out like that—I've never seen Ned so shaken, not even when the French took his right leg with a ball!"

I grasped his rough hand in my gloved one. "It gives me strength to see you here, Mr. Hawkins."

He harrumphed, and cast his eyes to the floor.

At that moment, the coroner thrust his way to the front of the room and took up a position behind a broad deal table, much scarred from the rings of tankards.

"That'll be Crowse," whispered the Bosun's Mate

knowledgeably. "Not a bad sort, though hardly out of leading-strings."

A hammer fell, a bailiff cried, and all in the assembly rose. "The coroner summons Mr. Percival Pethering to the box!"

Frank snorted in derision beside me.

Percival Pethering was a magistrate of Southampton—a pale and languid article, foppishly dressed. His great height and extreme thinness made of his figure a perpetual question mark. Stringy grey hair curled over his forehead, and his teeth—which were very bad—protruded like a nag's of uncertain breeding. He seated himself at the coroner's right hand, and took a pinch of snuff from a box he kept tucked into his coat.

The mixture must have been excessively strong: he sneezed, dusting powder over the leaves of paper on which the coroner's scribe kept his notations.

"Mr. Pethering?"

"At your service, Mr. Crowse." The magistrate pressed a handkerchief to his nose.

"You are magistrate of Southampton, I believe?"

"And hold my commission at the pleasure of Lord Abercrombie, Lord Lieutenant of Hampshire."

"Indeed. And you have been in the commission of the peace how long?"

"Full fourteen years this past July seventeenth."

"Very well. Pray tell the jury here impaneled, Mr. Pethering, how you came to learn of this sad case."

The magistrate grimaced at the twelve men arranged awkwardly on two of the publican's sturdy benches, and tucked his handkerchief into his sleeve. "A sad case, indeed. One might even say a *gruesome,* not to mention a *shocking* business, had one less experience of the cruelty of the world in general than I have, and the depravity of the Great—"

"The facts, Mr. Pethering," the coroner interrupted impatiently.

"Certainly, Mr. Crowse. I had just sat down to my breakfast yesterday—no later than seven o'clock, as is my custom—when a messenger arrived from the village of Hound, crying out that murder had been done, and I must come at once."

A murmur of excited comment rippled like a breeze through the assembly, and Mr. Crowse let his hammer fall. "*Murder* is a word grossly prejudicial to this proceeding, sir. Pray let us hear no more of it until the panel has delivered its verdict."

"Very well. I undertook to accompany the man—valet to Lord Harold Trowbridge—to the cottage of old Ned Bastable in Hound. There I found Dr. Hugh Jarvey, physician of this city, and Lord Harold—a gentleman of London presently putting up at the Dolphin—who had discovered the corpus of a young girl on Butlock Common earlier that morning."

"And what did you then?" Mr. Crowse enquired.

"I examined the corpus, as requested by Dr. Jarvey, and agreed that the maid—Flora Bastable, by name, old Ned's granddaughter—had died of a mortal wound to the throat. I informed the coroner that an inquest should be necessary, and arranged for the conveyance of the girl's body here to the Coach & Horses."

"Thank you, sir—that will be all."

Mr. Pethering stepped down. "The coroner calls Lord Harold Trowbridge!"

I discerned his figure immediately: straight and elegant, arrayed in black, striding calmly down the central aisle. His countenance was cool and impassive as ever; he looked neither to right nor left. Mr. Crowse, the coroner, might have been the only other person in the room.

"Pray take a chair, my lord," Crowse said brusquely, "and place your right hand on the Bible."

He swore to God that he should speak only the truth, and gazed out clearly over the ranks of townspeople arrayed to hear him. He espied my brother Frank, and the corners of his mouth lifted; his eyes settled on my face. I am sure I looked ghastly—too pale above my black gown, my features pinched and aged. For an instant I read his disquiet in his looks, and then the grey gaze moved on.

"You have stated that you are Lord Harold Trowbridge, of No. 51 South Audley Street, London?"

"I am."

"Will you inform the panel of the business that brings you to this city, my lord?"

"Certainly. I have a considerable fortune invested in shares of the Honourable East India Company, and have been in daily expectation of the arrival of a particular ship out of Bombay—the *Rose of Hindoostan.*" His lordship drew off his black gloves.

Mr. Crowse raised an eyebrow. "I observe, my lord, that you are presently in mourning?"

"My mother, the Dowager Duchess of Wilborough, lately passed from this life."

"Pray accept my condolences. She was interred, I believe, only a few days since? Surely your man of business might deal with an Indiaman at such a time, rather than yourself?"

"I employ no man of business, Mr. Crowse; and I fail to comprehend what my affairs have to do with the subject of your inquest."

"Very well, my lord. Will you tell the members of

the panel here convened, how you came to be at Butlock Common yesterday morning?"

I held my breath. Would he admit to the affair of honour?

"I had arranged to meet an old friend of mine—Dr. Jarvey, of East Street—in order to take a ramble about the countryside," he said tranquilly.

My heart sank. Lord Harold meant to bear the full brunt of suspicion.

"A ramble?" the coroner repeated in surprise.

"Yes. We are both of us fond of walking."

"You are presently lodging at the Dolphin, are you not, my lord?"

"I am."

"And Dr. Jarvey, as you say, resides in East Street?"

"He does."

"Then would you be so good as to explain why you chose to meet over four miles from the town, in an isolated field, where a corpse happened to be lying?"

"We had a great desire to view the tumuli at Netley Common, nearly two miles distant, and thought that Butlock Common should make an excellent starting point. One might wander through Prior's Coppice along the way; it is a lovely little wood at this time of year."

"I see." Mr. Crowse looked unconvinced. "You arrived well before Dr. Jarvey?"

"Perhaps a quarter of an hour, all told. It was yet dark as I approached the common."

"And what then occurred?"

"I stepped out of my chaise for a breath of air—took a turn upon the meadow that borders the lane—and found to my great distress that a young woman had been left for dead upon the ground."

"Did you recognise the girl?"

"I did. She was serving-maid to an acquaintance of mine, one Mrs. Challoner of Netley Lodge."

"You had seen her in your visits to the Lodge, I collect?"

Lord Harold shrugged. "One maid is very like another. I recalled, however, that one of them was quite young—and had startling blue eyes. The corpse was similar in these respects."

"You do not recollect meeting the young woman elsewhere?" Mr. Crowse enquired in a silken tone.

Lord Harold hesitated a fraction before answering. "I do not."

"Very well. What did you next, after discovering the corpse?"

"I ascertained that the young woman was dead; and then returned to my carriage to await the arrival of Dr. Jarvey, as I thought him likely to know best what should be done."

Mr. Crowse appeared on the point of posing a final question—considered better of it—and said, "You may step down, my lord."

Lord Harold quitted the chair.

Dr. Jarvey was then called to the stand. He informed the coroner's panel that he had arrived at Butlock Common yesterday at perhaps half-past six o'clock in the morning, where he had examined the body of a woman discovered upon the ground.

"Her throat had been cut by a sharp blade, severing the principal blood vessels and the windpipe. I should judge the instrument of her death to have been a razor, or perhaps a narrow-bladed knife; the corpus was barely cool, and given the chill of the weather yesterday, I should judge that life had been extinct no more than an hour prior to my arrival."

"Can you tell the jury, Doctor, why you travelled alone to Butlock Common so early in the morning, and in a hired hack—rather than availing yourself of his lordship's chaise?"

"A doctor's hours are not his own," Dr. Jarvey answered equably. "I cannot be certain, in arranging for activities of this kind, that I may not be called out at the very hour appointed for the meeting, in attendance upon a patient who is gravely ill. I generally chuse to meet my friends, rather than inconvenience them through delay. Therefore, if I am prevented from appearing on the hour, they may pursue their pleasures in solitude."

Mr. Crowse, the coroner, looked very hard at Dr. Jarvey as he concluded his diffident speech; then he turned to the twelve men of the panel and said, "I must now require you to rise, and accompany me into the side closet, so that you might observe the corpse as is your duty, and testify that life is extinct."[1]

With varying degrees of alacrity, the panel shuffled from their benches and through the doorway indicated by Mr. Crowse, who waited until the last man had exited the room before closing the door behind the entire party.

A tedious interval ensued, during which Frank shifted in his chair and folded his arms belligerently across his chest. He was uneasy with the degree of duplicity in the proceedings, though I doubted he had perceived its logical end.

The closet door opened, and the men—sober of countenance but in general composed—regained their seats. Mr. Crowse ignored the craning of heads

[1] It was common practice in Austen's day for the coroner's panel to view the corpse at an inquest.—*Editor's note.*

from the assembly as several tried to glimpse what lay beyond the closet door.

"The coroner calls Mrs. Hodgkin!"

A plump, kindly-faced matron in a bottle-green gown with outmoded panniers made her way to the box. She curtseyed, then seated herself stiffly on the edge of the chair.

"You are Elsie Hodgkin?"

"I am. Housekeeper at the Dolphin Inn since I were eighteen year old, and I'm nigh on eight-and-forty this Christmas, as I don't mind saying straight out."

"Very well," replied Mr. Crowse. "Please inform the men of the panel what you know of Deceased."

"She were a lot better acquainted with that there Lord Harold than he's admitting," Elsie Hodgkin said immediately. "Two or three times the girl's come asking for his lordship at the Dolphin, and once she spent an hour or more waiting on his pleasure in our parlour."

Lord Harold held himself, if possible, more erect in his chair; I had an idea of how his expression should appear—eyes narrowed, every feature stilled.

"Indeed? Have you any notion of the girl's business?"

"She seemed respectable enough," the housekeeper said, "but I'm not the sort to send a girl that age into a gentleman's room for any amount of pleading."

"Did you observe Lord Harold to meet with Deceased?"

Elsie Hodgkin's small eyes shifted shrewdly in her face. "Sent that man of his down, he did, to have a word; and I'm that busy, I cannot rightly say whether his lordship followed the valet or not."

"Do you recall the last time you saw Flora Bastable in the Dolphin?"

"The day before her death," Mrs. Hodgkin said with relish. "Waited in the parlour, Flora did, while his lordship fired those pistols in the yard, as though he hadn't left the poor young thing cooling her heels above an hour."

A murmur of comment stirred the assembly, and I espied a few heads turn in his lordship's direction.

"Were you aware that Lord Harold quitted the inn quite early yesterday morning?"

"He were gone before I was out of my bed," she said flatly, "and quiet about it, as though he hoped a body wouldn't notice. Furtive and stealthy, like."

"Thank you, Mrs. Hodgkin. You may step down. The coroner calls Miss Rose Bastable!"

A frightened young face under a mobcap—a pair of hands twisting in a white apron—and Rose Bastable took her place at Crowse's right hand. She stared at him fearfully, a sob escaping her lips.

"Now, Rose," the coroner said gently, "you have lost your sister in the cruelest manner, and that is a dreadful thing. Be a good girl, and tell us what you know."

"Just that Flora went to that monster, and he were the death of her! I told her not to go—I told her she didn't ought to meet with strange gentlemen like a coming straw damsel; but she thought to make her fortune, Flora did—and it were her ruin!"

A sigh escaped me—brutal and despairing. What in God's name had Flora Bastable wanted with Lord Harold, in all those visits to the Dolphin?

And then it came to me. Flora Bastable had never learned her letters. *She required someone to write her notes of blackmail to Mrs. Challoner.* But why Lord Harold?

"Your sister's name was Flora Bastable?" Mr. Crowse continued.

Rose nodded from the depths of a crumpled cambric handkerchief. "Sixteen she would've been, this January. She were in service at Netley Lodge as housemaid."

"A boarder?"

"Aye—but Sunday night she come home, dismissed for failing to satisfy. Mrs. Challoner's a strange woman, and Flora had some tales to tell. She thought the lady might pay for her silence—but the idea weren't Flora's own. She'd had it from his lordship."

"How can you be certain?" Mr. Crowse enquired, leaning forward avidly.

"After dinner that night, Flora told me private-like as how she had a call to pay in Southampton, on a high-and-mighty lord from Town, and that she thought to make her fortune by it. 'We'll never have to fetch and carry again, Rose,' she said, 'when I've struck my bargain.' "

Several ejaculations from the crowd met this declaration.

"Miss Bastable, did you accompany your sister to her meeting with Lord Harold?"

She shook her head.

"Was your sister . . . a *good* girl, Miss Bastable?"

"She were an angel," Rose declared pathetically, "and certainly not the sort to act as she shouldn't, if she were properly looked after. But some devils will stop at nothing, sir! I begged her not to go back, when the note come from his lordship Thursday!"

I straightened in my chair. Had he written to the child? That must look very bad—

Mr. Crowse was frowning at the weeping Rose. "Pray collect yourself, Miss Bastable. Your sister received a note from Lord Harold Trowbridge?"

"That she did, sir. I read it myself. Asked her, bold as brass, to wait upon his pleasure at Butlock Common just after cock-crow yesterday."

The public reaction to this intelligence was of an alarming turn. One man actually rose from his seat and cried, "The scoundrel! Hanging's too good for 'im!"

I whispered agitatedly in Frank's ear. "The note must be the grossest fabrication! Lord Harold, to my knowledge, had no notion of Flora Bastable's direction—any more than I did myself!"

"Did your sister keep this letter?" Mr. Crowse demanded of Rose.

"I saw her throw it on the fire. She was afraid, I suppose, that if my mother saw it, she would be forbidden to go."

"Would that her mother had," the coroner said heavily. "She might be yet alive today."

At this, the wilting Rose—who was hardly more than a child herself—cast her face into her hands and wailed aloud. One could not help but feel the deepest pity; and Mr. Crowse, with an air of benevolence quite unsuited to his relative youth, commanded that the proceeding should be adjourned for a period, to allow the young woman to collect her faculties.

Every person in the Coach & Horses, I am sure, must regard such an interlude as unbearable in its suspense. We rose, and watched the panel of twelve directed to an antechamber, where they should be safe from any untoward suasion of gossip or commentary. More than one cast a look of indignation at Lord Harold before quitting the room.

"Jane," my brother whispered anxiously, "I do not like the complexion of this affair. Lord Harold could well hang!"

"We must speak to him, Frank."

I forced my way against the current of Southampton folk intent upon procuring a tankard of ale from the publican before the proceedings should recommence—and saw that a wide berth had been left about the position of Lord Harold and his man.

The former rose, and bowed to me courteously.

"Have you gone mad?" I demanded. "Are you determined to place your neck in a noose? Sophia Challoner is not worth such circumspection!"

"No, my dear," he said with acid precision, "but she has managed my fate with admirable skill. Whoever killed that girl—and I cannot doubt it was one of the Netley party—the outcome must be the same. The duel is prevented, Mr. Ord is safe—and Sophia's chief enemy, Harold Trowbridge, is consigned to oblivion!"

"And so her despatching of French agents may proceed unimpeded," I said thoughtfully. "It is a masterful stroke, to be sure. But, my lord—"

"Orlando—pray go in search of refreshment, there's a good fellow. I am perishing of thirst."

The valet turned without a word and thrust his small frame into the surging knot of humanity.

"My lord—"

"While I cool my heels in the Southampton gaol," he continued in a goaded tone, "yet another port town shall be set alight. The thought is such as to inspire rage—and yet, my friends, what else may I do, but heel to the present course? I cannot escape the charge of murder, by claiming an attempted duel: the latter merely establishes my credentials as a bloodthirsty rogue. You see how they have routed me, with this business of the girl's visits to the Dolphin—"

"You must not allow it, my lord," Frank said hotly. "Your notions of honour—of shielding the innocent—do you the greatest credit, to be sure; but the impulse towards discretion is ill-placed in the present circumstance."

"*My lord,*" I said urgently. "Did you never speak to Flora Bastable when she sought you at the inn?"

"I had no notion that she did so. I must consider the housekeeper's testimony a complete hum."

"But I certainly saw her there—on two occasions at least, and once with Orlando. That was the very day before the duel."

His eyes, which had been roving fitfully about the room as though in search of some means of escape, came to rest suddenly upon my own.

My brother snorted. "What does that signify, Jane? The valet did his duty, and sent the girl about her business! Lord Harold had better have the fellow sworn, and admit his evidence to the coroner—and then we might tell all the world how little his lordship knew of the maid!"

"What of the letter her sister claims that Flora received of you?" I persisted. "The missive summoning her to Butlock Common?"

"I sent no such letter. What are you suggesting, Jane?"

"That the note was a ruse! Flora told me herself: she never learned her letters. She could neither write nor read."

"And so she must exhibit the paper to one who

could tell her what it said—and thus the summons to Butlock, and the name of the man who signed it, must be recalled with clarity later." Lord Harold's voice was grim.

"—Once the girl was dead. Such coldness and calculation! It is beyond my ability to credit! But which of the Netley party penned that note?"

Lord Harold, however, was gazing beyond me now, at the doorway of the inquest chamber. The sound of commotion behind suggested that the panel was on the point of reconvening—but it was not *this* that had drawn his attention.

I turned, and glimpsed a blond head above a black cloak. A countenance serene as a god's. And a look of resolution about the set mouth.

Mr. Ord, it seemed, had determined to speak his part.

Chapter 26

The Confession

5 November 1808, cont.

~

AS THE YOUNG MAN APPROACHED THE CORONER, Lord Harold held up his hand, as though to forestall disaster.

"Stay, Mr. Ord. Do you apprehend what you are about? The consequences of any admission—to yourself and others—must be grave."

"Would you like me to keep silent," the American drawled, "when suspicion of murder rests on your head? I consider myself as good a judge of conscience as any man. Mr. Crowse, I cannot swear your oath, as I am a Catholic; but I pledge to you, on this Bible I hold, that I shall speak the truth."

"Very well." The coroner gazed doubtfully from Lord Harold to Mr. Ord, then motioned the latter towards a chair. "State your name and your direction, my good sir—and then be seated."

The American complied—supplying the words "student at the College of Georgetown" for occupation—and took the witness chair. The room had begun to fill once more with the curious, and I hastened to take my seat between Frank and the Bosun's Mate—who now smelled strongly of spirits, I am sorry to say. Lord Harold, his expression set, resumed his position at the head of the room; but the valet's chair beside him, I noted, remained empty.

"Mr. Ord, you have pled the indulgence of this inquest in hearing your evidence," Mr. Crowse began briskly. "Pray inform the panel of any matter that you believe may bear upon the death of Flora Bastable."

"I am happy to do so. It is merely this: that on the morning in question, I was present at the discovery of the girl's body at Butlock Common. I was there to fulfill a challenge I had offered Lord Harold Trowbridge, and which he agreed to defend. Dr. Jarvey appeared solely as witness."

Like a rising wind, the stir of public comment rippled through the chamber. Heads turned in excitement: an affair of honour must always draw sensation.

"Are you suggesting, sir," Mr. Crowse said sternly, "that a duel was in contemplation?"

"I am."

"—Though such affairs run counter to the laws of England?"

"Indeed."

Mr. Crowse glanced soberly about the room. "I must consider whether this places the entirety of the previous testimony in question! Charges of perjury, on the part of gentlemen sworn before God and this panel, must be weighed! The matter increases in gravity, Mr. Ord. However—be so good as to describe your recollection of events."

"I and my party—"

"You were not alone?" Crowse interrupted. "How many people were assembled at this dawn meeting, pray?"

"It is customary, in such affairs, to appoint a second—or perhaps two—to act on the challenger's behalf."

"You will forgive me if I profess an ignorance of the habits of hot-headed gentlemen," the coroner returned austerely. "You were accompanied by two others, I collect, who have chosen to remain unnoticed by this panel?"

Mr. Ord inclined his head. "My party arrived at Butlock Common just as the sun was rising. Lord Harold and his party, which numbered four in all"—Mr. Crowse expelled a sigh of annoyance—"had already arrived, in two separate conveyances. Dr. Jarvey was not yet upon the scene. As the sun rose, we observed what appeared to be a pile of discarded clothing lying in the centre of the common. We approached, and I saw to my horror that it was in fact Flora Bastable. Her position and injuries are entirely as have been described."

"You knew the girl?" Crowse demanded in surprise.

"In the course of my stay in Southampton, I have frequently been a guest at Netley Lodge. The girl was employed there as serving-maid."

"A position, I understand, which she lost but a few days prior to her death."

"That is true."

"Can you account for the maid's dismissal, Mr. Ord?"

For the first time, the American hesitated. He was willing enough to offer frankness when the truth touched upon himself—but the direction of the coroner's questions must surely implicate Sophia Challoner.

"I believe the maid was subject to fits," he answered at last, "and moreover, was regarded as . . . unreliable."

"Unreliable?"

"I do not wish to speak ill of the dead, Mr. Crowse."

"Flora Bastable has been murdered, sir. You must offer this panel what intelligence you possess."

"Very well. Her mistress and I, in walking for exercise in the direction of Netley Abbey, on several occasions surprised Flora Bastable with a man."

"A man?" At this, the coroner turned and stared suggestively at Lord Harold. "Can you put a name to the person she met?"

"I can, sir. He is valet to Lord Harold Trowbridge—a fellow known as Orlando."

Frank stiffened in his chair. "Good Lord, Jane!" he exclaimed softly. "The tale is better than anything mounted in the theatre in French Street!"

"He never means that Mr. Smythe?" demanded the Bosun's Mate.

Lord Harold half-rose from his position near the front of the room, and glanced over his shoulder. His gaze sought out the figure of his valet: but he was unlikely to find the man. Having escaped the threat of a noose on one occasion, Orlando had no taste to dance attendance upon another. He had been sent in search of refreshment a quarter-hour since; and I knew now he had seized his chance—and fled Southampton.

Much was suddenly explained: Flora's visits to the Dolphin Inn; her recourse to the Abbey ruins after the fit of hysterics; even Orlando's familiarity with the direction of the girl's cottage. Had he fallen into a dalliance with the maid while standing guard upon the subterranean passage? I suppose it must be natural enough. They were both of them in positions of servitude; Flora was pretty, and Orlando, perhaps, as restless as any man of seven-and-twenty.

"It's never true!" cried Rose Bastable hotly. She sprang from her seat and thrust an accusing finger in Mr. Ord's direction. "You saw her dead, and now you'll see her good name ruined! It was *you* as came to our cottage, knocking at the door in your fine clothes and asking to speak with Flora! Fie upon you!"

Mr. Crowse took up his gavel and struck it several times. "Pray contain yourself, Rose Bastable. You impede sworn testimony! Mr. Ord: were you on such terms with Deceased as to call at her home?"

"I did so only once," the American replied evenly, "on the day the girl was dismissed from her position."

"That would have been—"

"Sunday, the thirtieth of October, *six* days ago."

Mr. Crowse peered at Ord. "And why did you seek out the maid?"

"I felt some concern regarding her fate. She had left the Lodge in considerable distress. I told her that her mistress was sometimes hasty in her temper, and that matters might be improved with the passage of a few days. I then gave her a few shillings, and quitted the place. I should judge I did not remain in the cottage above a quarter-hour."

And in that period, Orlando had been abducted

and conveyed to Portsmouth by an unknown: Monsignor Fernando da Silva? I craned forward, the better to observe Mr. Ord's face. It shone, as ever, with sincerity. Did he speak the truth? Or did he spin a subtle web designed to ensnare us all?

"Mr. Ord, do you intend to quit the vicinity of Southampton in the near future?"

"I do not, sir."

"Very well. You may step down. The coroner calls one Orlando, valet to Lord Harold Trowbridge!"

The words fell heavily into silence. Mr. Crowse waited, his eyes roaming the room. Heads turned; speculation rose; and still the valet did not appear.

"By your leave, Mr. Crowse," Lord Harold said quietly, "I shall go in search of my man in the public room."

He rose and strode towards the doorway, his countenance inscrutable as ever; but I read in the steadiness of his gravity the depth of his concern. He was absent perhaps seven minutes, all told; and when he returned, he was alone.

"Well, my lord?"

"My valet appears to have quitted the inn."

"That is very singular behaviour!"

"I confess I cannot account for it. We might enquire after him at the Dolphin."

"And keep this assembly waiting on the man's pleasure? I think not, my lord." The coroner stared meditatively at his clerk, whose pen hovered in midair, awaiting direction. "I have no choice but to suspend this proceeding, until such time as *all* the testimony regarding the death of Flora Bastable has been heard. Inquest adjourned!"

• • •

"JANE," LORD HAROLD SAID HURRIEDLY AS WE MET near the door, "I must not stay. Captain Austen, my thanks for your support of your sister this afternoon. It has been a trying few hours."

"But less troubling than it might have been—thanks to the American," Frank replied.

"You believe so? I cannot be sanguine." The Rogue thrust himself into his greatcoat, his expression abstracted. "They strike first at me—then at my valet—but it is all diversion! There is devilry in train, and the wretched girl was deliberately silenced. She knew what was towards—but her knowledge died with her. Captain, I must ask of you a great favour—"

"If it is within my power—"

"Will you take a horse from the inn's stables, and ride like the wind to Portsmouth? I wish a message despatched by your Admiralty telegraph. Inform the First Lord that Trowbridge believes the Enemy will strike tonight. All yards must be placed on alert—and the Channel ports closely guarded. Will you do so much?"

"Gladly, my lord, once I have seen my sister safe in Castle Square."

"I am perfectly capable of effecting the walk in solitude," I retorted drily. "Whither are you bound, Lord Harold?"

"I hardly know." He raised bleak grey eyes to my own. "I must go after Orlando. I am responsible for the man, and he is more than valet; I count him among my friends. His flight is natural in one afraid—but it must look damnably like guilt to those unacquainted with his character. If you were in fear for your life, Jane—and possessed no private equipage, no gentleman's claim upon society, and very little coin—how should *you* proceed? What course must I set?"

"That depends," I said slowly, "upon your object, my lord. Do you mean to find Orlando, and subject him to the law—or allow him to go free?"

Chapter 27

The Usefulness of Brothers

5 November 1808, cont.

~

"AND SO YOUR RAKEHELL CORINTHIAN, LORD DEVIL-May-Care, has come to grief at last!" my mother declared as I seated myself at the dinner table. The inquest had demanded the whole of the afternoon, and it being already half-past four o'clock, the ladies of the household were assembled in honour of my parent's early dinner hour. "You were very close this morning, Jane, as to the nature of your interest in the coroner's panel; but I know it all!"

"Has word of the proceedings sped through town?" I enquired, as she handed me a dish of potatoes.

"Folk are all but shouting it from the very walls! I had the story of Madame Clarisse, whose establishment I had occasion to visit, once you were gone out to the Coach & Horses. She learned it of her drover, who had chanced to look into the Coach's public room for a tankard of ale."

"I have an idea that the drover's story derives more from his ale, than from anything approaching the truth."

Mary tittered from her position across the board.

"He knew enough to say that a young girl—no more than a child—was left for dead in the middle of a field, and not a body within miles but Lord Harold!" my mother returned indignantly. "There is nothing I abominate more than a man who has a straw damsel in keeping—unless it is one who sees fit to cut throats! I may only thank God—as I told Martha this morning—that your name was never joined to his! How your father should have blanched at a public scandal being visited upon his household! Not that we are such strangers to the magistracy—my poor sister, Mrs. Leigh-Perrot, having taught us what to expect of justice—but I cannot think that murder is at all the same as pilfering a card of lace."[1]

"That is because you are a woman of excellent understanding, Mamma—and so must equally discern how unlikely it should be for Lord Harold to have anything to do with that unfortunate maid's murder."

"I see nothing of the sort!" she cried. "He has sported with your interest in the most abominable manner imaginable, Jane—and as there is not the

[1] Jane Leigh-Perrot, the wife of Mrs. Austen's brother, James Leigh-Perrot, was accused of shoplifting by a Bath merchant in 1799. She was held in Ilchester gaol for seven months, tried for a capital crime, and, had she been convicted, faced transportation to Australia or public execution—all for a card of lace. She was acquitted but remained subject to rumors of kleptomania ever after.—*Editor's note.*

least likelihood of your getting him now, I hope he may hang! That will teach him how a gentleman ought to behave. You intend to wear the willow for him?"

I stared at her archly. "Mamma! You have been indulging in dissipation! When we thought you prostrate upon your bed, you have only been reading novels! Where else can you have learned such a despicable cant expression?"

"Madame Clarisse is forever using it," she replied unexpectedly, "and if one cannot learn the latest expressions, along with the latest fashions, from one's *modiste*—then for what does one pay her?"

"True enough. We all want excellent value for our coin. But I see no cause to mourn Lord Harold's loss: I know him to be quite innocent, and must trust to Providence. Others among Madame Clarisse's acquaintance must sigh in vain for love. Mary, I trust you received Frank's note from the Coach & Horses? He is gone to Portsmouth on a matter of business."

"Orders, I reckon," she said darkly. "They will be sending him to Portugal again, and the *St. Alban's* in want of coppering for her bottom. It's a positive disgrace!"

I SOUGHT RELIEF AFTER DINNER IN THE PAGES OF SIR Walter Scott, for my thoughts were in a whirl and I feared the onset of a head-ache. I had hardly opened *Marmion,* however, when a tug at the bell brought Phebe from the kitchen. A murmur of conversation in the hall: the sound of a woman's voice, rich and low. Instantly I set my book aside and moved to the door.

"Sophia!" I said in surprise. "I had not looked for

the pleasure of seeing you in Castle Square today! Pray come in and sit by the fire!"

"I may stay only long enough to take my leave of you, Jane." She drew off her gloves with fretful, impatient movements. "You are well, I trust? James told me you were in attendance at the inquest today."

"It seemed the least I could do for that unfortunate girl." I led Mrs. Challoner into the parlour and closed the door behind us. "Are you leaving Southampton, then?"

"Ernesto—the Conte da Silva—quits Netley for London tonight, and I shall be with him. You are to wish me joy, Jane. The Conte has begged my hand in marriage."

For a lady charged with so weighty a communication, she lacked the appearance of happiness. I stared at her, all amazed. "The Conte? He is a formidable personage—and—decidedly handsome..."

"—And possessed of a title, vast wealth, and estates considerable enough that I might be prevented from ever feeling want," she concluded briskly. "Though somewhat dull and ponderous at times, he is a man of integrity and worth, Jane. I do not love him—but I shall be able to respect him; and he shall never impinge upon that freedom I once talked so much of."

"But, Sophia—" I sank into a chair. "You cannot require so much security, surely? There is nothing you presently lack. You command an independence—a home—a *life*..."

"I command them in England, Jane—and I declare I detest the entire Kingdom! Portugal is my home, and Portugal is at war. I cannot return there without protection—and the Conte will ensure that I am safe."

"I see."

"I cannot pretend to regret anything I shall leave behind," she continued, "except you, my dear friend."

Did the sum of our intercourse deserve the name of friendship? I knew that the term was too great a benediction; I had approached Mrs. Challoner from motives of deceit, and had acted by design throughout. She cannot have understood so much—but her trust in me was ill-bestowed.

"I wish you safe, Sophia, and very happy," I told her.

"Would that I could see you the same! But I have a favour to ask, Jane, before I go."

"Anything in my power."

"I cannot leave without knowing that Mr. Ord is well looked after." She gazed at me clear-eyed and forthright. "He is a dear friend, far from home, and unacquainted with our ways. He requires safe passage on *some* ship or other bound for the Atlantic station—but in all the flurry of my own departure, I scarcely know where to begin!"

"The coroner requested that he remain in Southampton for the nonce," I told her with a slight air of puzzlement.

"Pshaw! Mr. Ord has done nothing wrong, and thus cannot be considered subject to the coroner's trifling ways!" she declared warmly. "That is why I have sought you out in this application—discretion is essential. I will not have the poor boy subjected to the nonsense of a murder enquiry. When I cast about for a means of brooking delay—I recollected, of a sudden, your excellent brother!"

Frank. Of course she would consider of Frank.

"He is a naval Captain," she continued, "and

must be aware of all the ships that are bound for the Americas. Can you not engage his interest on behalf of our friend, and solicit passage in some naval vessel—without too great a publicity?"

I felt myself flush hot, and then cold, as the full comprehension of what she asked broke upon me. Sophia Challoner had so far mistaken my position as to believe me capable of aiding Mr. Ord to escape English law! Was she so desperate? Did she consider me naïve?

"—By dawn, if possible?" she added.

Was the American that vulnerable to a charge of murder, that he must flee with the tide?

I gripped the arms of my chair and said only, "My brother is from home at present, in Portsmouth. His orders have come from the Admiralty, it seems; he was forced to a desperate haste. I suppose it is even possible he shall embark in the *St. Alban's* without our meeting again."

Her countenance fell, and her restless gaze shifted about the room. It occurred to me then that if I turned her away, she should find a more certain method of spiriting Mr. Ord from the country—and that I should have no share in the knowledge. Hastily I said, "I consider that eventuality unlikely, however, for his wife is presently in our care, and he should never abandon her without a word. I expect him returned this evening. I might speak to him then on Mr. Ord's behalf."

Mrs. Challoner expelled a soft breath, as though she heard my amendment with relief. "Excellent Jane! I knew you could not refuse to help me. I knew you understood the worth—the goodness—the *sanctity* of that boy! It is a duty to shield him from the eyes of the impertinent—from the invasion of the Law! A duty of friendship, as well as honour—"

She broke off, as though she had been betrayed into saying what she ought not, and cast her eyes upon the floor. I expected her to rise at that moment, and hold out her hand—or, perhaps, condescend to kiss my cheek, at which point I must convey her from the room—but after a space she continued.

"I ought to have said that Mr. Ord travels with a companion. Passage for two will therefore be required."

"A companion?" My surprise was real—my mind, instantly in search of a possible candidate. The intimates of Netley were in general accounted for. Unless—surely it could not be—*Maria Fitzherbert*?

"A companion—a superior—an instructor of the highest order, and one I may soon claim as a brother," Mrs. Challoner said. She lifted her eyes to mine. "Monsignor Fernando da Silva-Moreira, of the Society of Jesus, who is bound for America in his student's train."

"*Monsignor?*" I repeated.

"You may recall Lord Harold Trowbridge pronouncing his name. Monsignor is the Conte da Silva's brother, and a Jesuit these five-and-twenty years at least," she replied. "An excellent man, though vastly persecuted as are all his brethren in this violent age. He first fled France, at the Revolution, and took up residence in his native Portugal; but the present circumstances of battle made his position there impossible. It was to conduct Monsignor da Silva to Maryland that Mr. Ord came to Oporto—and found himself subject to English liberation."

I thought of the black-cloaked figure; of the encounter in the tunnel; of Mr. Dixon with his throat cut, and Orlando abducted to Portsmouth. It was the Conte's brother, who spoke nothing but French, who had dined with Frank in his cabin on the *St. Alban's;* the Conte's brother who had met with Mrs. Challoner in the Abbey ruins. I was to be the means, through Frank, of despatching a French agent to safety—or, if I alerted Lord Harold, of betraying a friend.

"Where is this Jesuit—this brother of the Conte's—presently situated?" I enquired in a faltering accent. "I have not had the pleasure of meeting him at your house."

She shrugged indolently. "The Monsignor detests England. The Society of Jesus has suffered too much at Protestant hands—I need not outline the executions and martyrdoms to which they and all Catholics have been subjected—and his predilection for the French tongue makes him doubly subject to suspicion. He took a room at the George, and scarcely ventured forth without a long black cloak, as though fearful that a priest should be attacked in the streets. Indeed, I may say that he quitted his rooms only to enter a hack bound for Netley—so that he might say Mass each day, and enjoy Mr. Ord's company. The two have much to discuss, for the Monsignor intends to join Mr. Ord's college in Georgetown—and Mr. Ord, the Monsignor's Society, when his years of study should be complete."

"And can you accept that kind of destiny for your young friend? Do you think the cloister a fitting end for so charming a man?"

"I know that in God, James Ord has found peace—and I would not deny that gift to anyone."

"Has it proved so elusive in your life, Sophia?"

"I have known the want of peace since I was five

years old! Bitterness and rage soured my father, and blighted my early years; but I vowed to differ from my parent in this: I vowed to practice forgiveness." Her brilliant eyes shone with inner warmth that was entirely engaging; she laughed aloud. "And I do not believe I have utterly failed, Jane! I made a life—if only for a fortnight—in England; I made at least one English friend"—this, with a smile for me—"and I have even managed to forgive so desperate a character as Lord Harold!"

"Indeed?" I exclaimed, with surprise. "But I thought you hated him!"

"I do," she replied serenely, "but I forgive him, from my heart, for being what he cannot help—the most detestable man in England." She rose, and held out her hand. "I must leave you now. There is a quantity of packing, and the servants to be directed. I owe you a debt I shall be a lifetime repaying."

Her expression of gratitude and faith was so sincere as to smite my traitorous heart. If forgiveness was her chosen art, I hoped she might spare a little of it for me, when all was known.

I unclasped the gold crucifix, and pressed it into her palm. "Take this, Sophia. It belongs to your Monsignor."

She looked at it curiously. "But how did you come by it, Jane?"

"I found it... among the ruins of Netley Abbey once, when I had gone there to paint."

I grasped her hand, and walked with her to the door—and saw her phaeton safely turned towards Samuel Street.

Then I sat at the writing desk, chose a sheet of fine paper and a well-mended pen, and set down the substance of Mrs. Challoner's conversation. It required but a few moments. When I had done, I raised my head and listened. The house was quiet: Martha, her ankle on the mend, had retired to her bedchamber; Mary was bathing her daughter in the kitchen, under the benevolent eye of Phebe. My mother might already be snoring over her needlework, though it was but six o'clock.

I donned my pelisse, and went in search of Lord Harold.

Chapter 28

Setting the Snare

5 November 1808, cont.

~

"GOOD EVENING TO YE, MISS AUSTEN," FORTESCUE the publican said truculently when I appeared at the Dolphin. "Are ye wanting his lordship?"

"Indeed I am—but I know him to be much involved today, and should not presume to trouble him. Would you be so good as to convey this note on my behalf? The communication it contains is of an urgent nature."

The publican eyed my missive apprehensively. "You'll have heard the news of the inquest?"

"I was present throughout, as was my brother, Captain Frank Austen. I know that you have long held the Captain in esteem, Mr. Fortescue, and you should be happy to learn that my brother regards Lord Harold as worthy of the highest confidence."

Fortescue's pale blue eyes shifted uneasily. "Folk do be saying as how that valet—the foreigner—is guilty of murder."

"Or perhaps of nothing worse than fleeing in fear of his life. Will you carry my letter to his lordship?"

The publican studied my countenance, and the doubt lifted from his own. "His lordship's just ordered dinner, ma'am. If you care to wait, I shall enquire whether he is receiving visitors."

I certainly cared to wait, and retired to the side parlour in which I had last seen Flora Bastable. It was lit this evening by a quartet of candles in pewter sconces; the early November dark had already fallen. Townsfolk hurried home along the chill pavings beyond the window, with their collars buttoned high and paper parcels tucked under their arms. I thought of the long, dreary winter—of soldiers slogging through mud and gore on the Peninsula, of Frank buffeted by brutal seas; of George and Edward shivering in the dormitories of Winchester College. A greater sense of oppression than I had lately known settled upon my soul, as though all the light in life was bound for London in the baggage-coach of Sophia Challoner.

"Pray to follow me, miss," said Fortescue from the door.

He led me up two flights of the broad front stairs; Lord Harold should never be placed directly above the public rooms, where the noise and odour must penetrate the bedchamber. The Rogue had been situated instead at the rear of the edifice, well removed from the clatter of the stable yard, in a comfortable suite that encompassed a private parlour. This door

Fortescue threw open with a flourish, and announced, "Miss Austen, m'lord!"

It was a simple space, quite out of keeping with what I imagined to be his lordship's usual style: a round deal table; four chairs; a dresser with a few serving pieces upon it; a poker and tongs propped near the hearth. A pug dog, done in Staffordshire, sat upon the mantel—Mrs. Hodgkin's bit of whimsy, I conjectured. Lord Harold was established at the table, with a quantity of papers spread out before him. He was working in his shirtsleeves, his coat discarded upon a chair. Left to his own devices, without a valet, he must be inclined to the informal. A pair of spectacles perched on his nose, bringing age and wisdom of a sudden to his visage.

"*Jane.* Have you dined?"

"Thank you, sir—I have."

"A little wine, perhaps? Claret—Madeira—"

"Port, this evening," I said thoughtfully.

Lord Harold smiled. "A bottle of your best Port, Fortescue, and two glasses."

"Very good, sir," the publican replied with greater cordiality than before, and closed the door behind him. I began to remove my bonnet, acutely conscious—as I had been only once before, in his lordship's carriage—of the intimacy that surrounds a man and woman confined in a small space.

"Is your mother aware that you visit strange gentlemen in their rooms?" his lordship demanded abruptly.

"As Mr. Fortescue apprehends that much, we may presume the fact will circulate through the town by the morrow."

"Then I commend you for bravery."

"Have you discovered Orlando?"

"—No, though I searched every road out of this wretched place," he answered bitterly. "I have been in the saddle nearly two hours, Jane, and intend to remount as soon as I have dined; but I have little hope of finding him. He has gone to ground somewhere, like a wounded fox."

"Or to *sea,* perhaps?"

He removed the spectacles and stared at me.

"That is how I should flee Southampton, my lord. The sea, after all, betrays no footprint of man or beast."

At that moment, Fortescue reappeared at his lordship's door, burdened with a tray. A weary figure stood behind him, in a greatcoat splashed with mud.

"Frank!" I cried. "Returned from Portsmouth, and not a moment too soon!"

"Found the Captain in the stable yard, I did," Fortescue explained, "and understood straightaway that it's his sister he'll be wanting. I've brought extra rations for the Captain, and no need to offer thanks."

Lord Harold rose, and clapped my brother on the shoulder. "Come in by the fire, man—you're perishing of cold."

"I encountered rain seven miles from Portsmouth, and a long, wet road of it we made," Frank said, and shook his sopping hat over the hearth. "However, a bit of weather does not signify. I delivered your message to the Admiralty telegraph, my lord—and waited only for a reply. Here it is." He extended a letter sealed with wax. "I have no notion of the contents."

Lord Harold broke it open immediately, and surveyed the close-written lines.

"Here's rabbit stew," Fortescue continued, "a bit of baked fish; warm bread; a wedge of cheese; and a quantity of peas. *And* the London papers, what's fresh off the mail! *And* the Port, for the lady!"

"Well done, Fortescue," his lordship murmured.

"Any friend of the Austens cannot ask for too much, and that's a fact." He beamed at Frank, glared severely at his lordship, and backed his way out of the room with his empty tray dangling.

"My status has received an elevation," Lord Harold observed drily. "I forgot that Southampton is your home, and not a mere way-station, as it so often proves for me. You have been acquainted with Fortescue for some time, I collect?"

"Everyone knows Mr. Fortescue," I replied, unwilling to relate the sad history of the Seagrave family, and the end it had found in the Dolphin. I could not revisit the place, however, without recalling that desperate period in our first Southampton winter, and the hard truths it had taught me of the naval profession.[1] "And, too, we have our Assemblies here in the winter months—the ballroom is not indifferent."

"And filled with every random officer so fortunate as to gain a bit of shore-leave! Dare you venture into such a place? I have an idea you are besieged!"

Frank dragged a chair from the table near the fire, and proceeded to divest himself of boots and coat. "I confess I am equally surprised to discover my sister here, my lord, at such an hour of the evening. What drew you out of Castle Square, Jane?"

"A matter of some urgency; but I would beg you both to take your meal while I relate the whole."

Lord Harold furnished me with a glass of wine, which I gratefully accepted; and as the minutes wore

[1] Jane is recalling here the history recounted in *Jane and the Prisoner of Wool House* (Bantam Books, *2001*).—*Editor's note.*

away in that comfortable room, and the good Port fired my veins, I told them of Sophia Challoner, and the Conte's offer of marriage; of her petition for passage on a western-bound ship, and the mysterious companion Mr. Ord should carry with him.

Lord Harold listened, and drove a knife into his cheese, and drank some of the wine with an expression of absorption, as though he heard my words less clearly than the thoughts that ran through his brain.

When I had done, my brother whistled soft and low. "So the Jesuit and Ord must flee by dawn, is it? And I am to be the tool of their flight?"

"And Mrs. Challoner is bound for London," Lord Harold mused. "They are all of them concerned to distance themselves from Southampton—and in that, I read a warning, Captain. There will be trouble in Southampton tomorrow."

"Then we must prevent it, my lord."

"But *how*?" He thrust away his meal, half-eaten. "If we arrest Ord and the Jesuit tonight, we merely alert the Enemy of our vigilance. The attack itself will come from another quarter."

"One of the French prisoners, freed from the prison hulks at Spithead?" I enquired.

"Very likely. But how do they intend to communicate? When shall the signal be given? Would that I might set Orlando upon their heels— We should then watch the rogues in secret, and follow where they led!"

"We might still do so much," I returned. "Do you know of a ship out of Portsmouth, Frank, bound for the Americas?"

He frowned in consideration of my words, and then his brow cleared. "By Jove—the *Adelphi* is readying for Halifax! Captain Mead intends to haul anchor at about four o'clock, when the tide shall be on the flow."

"Halifax is never Baltimore—but in a moment of crisis, any landing will serve," I said calmly. "Let us write to Sophia that her friends may have passage. Ord and the Jesuit shall consider themselves *safe.* We might then wait before the Vine, where Ord lodges, and as he quits the place—"

"—follow him," Lord Harold concluded softly. "I will warrant he makes direct for Netley Abbey, and the turret stair, where a lanthorn light shall serve as signal."

My brother rose and yawned wearily. "Jane, I should be much obliged if you were to inform Mary that I may not find my bed for some hours yet. Say that a matter of business detains me; and think of your friends, established for King and Country in a frigid coach, while you settle into your quilts, my girl!"

"You must be joking. Do you really believe I intend to leave you?" I demanded.

"But, my dear," Lord Harold protested, "your brother is correct. You had much better turn for home, and await the issue of events."

I crossed to the writing desk placed against the far wall, and extracted a piece of paper and a pen. "Finish your dinner, sirs, while I write to my sister. I shall not be a moment."

A MESSENGER GALLOPED FROM THE YARD WITH MY brother's note for Mrs. Challoner, informing her that Captain Frank Austen extended his compliments, and would be delighted to secure the passage of her friends aboard the *Adelphi,* commanded by one Captain John Mead, and bound for Halifax at the four o'clock tide. Fortescue sent a kitchen boy to Castle Square with my letter to Mary. The fitful rain had passed, but the night was cold; I secured the advantage of hot coals for Lord Harold's braziers, that we might not suffer from frostbite during our lengthy vigil.

Amble, his lordship's coachman, sat upon the box with his breath steaming in the air; but his master shook his head, and despatched his man back to the stable yard.

"I do not like to make a show of the Wilborough arms about the streets. We shall travel tonight in one of Fortescue's conveyances—and I shall drive it myself."

It was an open gig, and the braziers, however comforting, should soon lose their effect in the chill wind streaming over the box; but I forbore to comment, or protest that the Wilborough arms should mean little to either a Jesuit or an American. His lordship knew his business.

We had assembled before the stable, and my brother was about to lift me into the gig, when a man sped in haste through the gates of the yard. "Lord Harold Trowbridge! Is Lord Harold within?"

The voice, though charged with excitement, was yet further burdened with the mangling of vowels that heralded a foreigner. In the flickering light of the torches, I studied the man: brown-skinned, wide-eyed, with a forelock of gleaming hair. Perhaps it was the play of flame and shadow that recalled his name; a face glimpsed through conflagration.

"Jeremiah the Lascar!" I said aloud.

Chapter 29

What the Lascar Saw

5 November 1808, cont.

~

"Is that Dixon's Lascar?" Frank asked me in surprise. "I have seen him some once or twice, at the Itchen Dockyard."

"But what has brought him here?" I whispered.

Lord Harold stepped forward. "Good evening, my good man. I must beg to defer our conversation until tomorrow. I and my friends are about to quit this place on a matter of pressing business."

"My business is also urgent, m'lord," Jeremiah said. "You will remember that when most honoured Dixon was killed, you said I am to come to you with informations? And you so kindly honoured me with your card, and the direction of this inn?"

"I remember." Lord Harold glanced about; the curious eyes of the ostlers were trained upon our party. "Lower your voice, man. There are ears everywhere, and some of them unfriendly."

"Well I know it. But I come to you now, and not to the fool of a magistrate, who cannot catch a hare when it pilfers his garden."

"You have learned something to the purpose?" Lord Harold enquired.

"I have seen the very man! The villain in a cloak who slit old Dixon's throat!"

"Where, for the love of God?"

"At the Itchen dock. He crept in by cover of darkness, not half an hour since, and made off with a skiff. There were several small boats, you see, undamaged by the fires; and it is a small matter to drag a skiff over the lock and launch it in the river."

"And this he did?"

The Lascar nodded. "When he had gone, and I was sure to be safe, I looked out over the lock itself. He went downriver, in the direction of Southampton Water."

"And thence to the sea," Frank muttered in frustration.

"You're certain it was the same man?" Lord Harold demanded. "The one you espied from your rooftop last week, when the seventy-four was fired?"

"Certain as I breathe, sir." Jeremiah shuddered. "Thanks be to Vishnu that he did not observe me—that he did not know I was alone in the yard—for certain sure he'd have treated me to a taste of his knife."

Lord Harold clapped the fellow on the back and reached for his wallet. "Our thanks, Jeremiah. Pray accept my first payment towards the restoration of the yard. And walk with care tonight: there are others who carry knives. Into the gig, my friends! We waste the hour!"

• • •

It was clear to us all that Mr. Ord was now immaterial; it was his companion in the dark cloak we desperately sought, and his decision to move by water must be instructive. He had long made a habit of lurking in one spot: the subterranean passage beneath Netley Abbey.

We abandoned all notion of holding vigil near the Vine Inn, and made directly for the Itchen ferry, and the road towards the ruins.

"If he intends to embark for the Americas," Lord Harold said grimly, "then we must assume that the firing of a lanthorn signal is his purpose tonight. He shall make by water for the Abbey tunnel, and achieve the turret stair undetected. Once the signal is given, he will be joining Ord—and bent upon the Portsmouth road."

"We must not allow the devil to light his lamps," Frank said, "for then the attack shall be set in train!"

"Pray God we are not too late!"

Lord Harold lashed the horses with his whip, and subsided into silence, while the gig—poorly sprung and exposed to the night air—rattled hell-bent for the River Itchen. There we were in luck; the ferry stood ready and waiting on the Southampton side; and after a tedious interval when I thought I should scream aloud with impatience, the barge bumped against the nether shore. My brother sprang immediately to the bank.

We surged up the hill, and clattered through Weston—a sleepy hamlet sparked by a few fires—and then, as we achieved West Woods, Lord Harold slowed the team to a walk.

"We must go quietly now, and secure the gig at

the far edge of this copse," he murmured. "Jane—will you remain with the horses, while we walk the final half-mile?"

"Never, sir."

Frank snorted aloud. "Jane and horseflesh do not suit, my lord. It is useless to persuade her."

The trees thinned; the darkness that encroached in the heavy wood, lightened ahead; and there, against the night sky, loomed the tumbled ruin of rock.

"No moon," Lord Harold muttered. "We divide the advantage thus: his movements are hidden; but so are ours."

He halted the gig, and Frank jumped down. In a trice, the horses were hobbled and a rock placed behind the wheels. Lord Harold drew a flat wooden case from the rear of the equipage: his matched set of duelling pistols. One he secured in his coat; the other he handed silently to Frank; and so we set off.

Did the stolen skiff nose against the cliff's foot below? Or had the Jesuit beached it already, and entered the subterranean passage? Would he move with ease, confident that his plans were undetected?

We came upon the Abbey from the rear; the turret stair, blasted and exposed to the elements, rose up on the forward side. The ground was everywhere uneven, and I dreaded lest I should stumble in the course of that last treacherous walk; but the thought had no sooner entered my mind, than Lord Harold's hand was extended, and silently gripped my own. And so we went on, Frank to the fore and our breathing almost suspended, so desperately did we guard our progress, until my brother stopped short and held out his hand.

"Look!"

Light had blazed forth from the blasted walls above us, shining vivid as a beacon through the surrounding dark. No candle-flame that might flicker and burn out, but a lanthorn fueled by whale-oil. It burned straight and true, and might draw one eye, or many, trained upon it from the Dibden shore.

We stared in horror, and then Lord Harold began to run.

He had seen, as a darker shape against the night sky, the figure of a man—distorted, perhaps, by shadow and cloak, but unmistakable in its movements.

My brother and I followed in an instant, but my stays prevented me from achieving the necessary exertion, and I soon fell back. My eyes were fixed, however, upon the turret's heights—and I saw that the Enemy in the cloak had been alerted to the sound of pursuit—footsteps rang on stone—he whirled about wildly, but escape was closed to him: Lord Harold had gained the ramparts.

I saw him outlined in the glare of the signal lamp. His right arm rose, and levelled the pistol; he uttered a harsh command; and then the lanthorn shattered under the impact of the lead ball. In the sudden eclipse of darkness, I thought that Lord Harold staggered—that he sank sharply against the wall where two figures grappled as one—and that the cloaked figure then hurled himself at the turret stair.

A second shot rang out before me: Frank must have achieved the turret—but what, oh, Heaven, was the issue of the mad engagement?

And why did the huddled form on the walls not rise, and give pursuit?

With a sob tearing at my throat—ignorant of pain or breathlessness—I ran as though the hounds of Hell were upon my heels. Through the blasted kitchen garden and past the tunnel's mouth—through the buttery and refectory and the south transept of the church—and there, at the foot of the stair, stood my brother, a spent pistol in his hand.

Darkness welled in the ruins at night; I strained to discern the tumbled form at Frank's feet. It was the cloaked and lifeless figure of a man. He had fallen from the stair's height, and landed upon his face.

Frank knelt and turned him to the sky.

"Orlando," I whispered.

Chapter 30

The Rogue Is Sped

5 November 1808, cont.

~

WITH THE BRISK INHUMANITY OF ONE ACCUSTOMED to death, Frank dragged the valet aside and bolted up the turret stair. I saw Orlando's staring eyes—shuddered to the depths of my soul—and followed my brother.

A few moments only were required to gain the walls' height: and there was Lord Harold, his left hand clapped to his shoulder, weaving unsteadily towards us.

"My lord!" Frank cried. "You are wounded! But how—?"

"A knife," he said with difficulty. "It has lodged in the bone. I cannot pull it out—"

My brother grasped his waist, or I am sure Lord Harold should have fallen. Frank tore at the knot of his own cravate, and handed it to me. "Wad it into a square, Jane. My lord, you must press it against the wound, if you have the strength."

I stuffed the wad under the cold fingers of his left hand, and felt the clean steel of a blade protruding from his coat—he had snapped off the haft in struggling to extract it himself.

"Lean upon me," Frank ordered. "We shall attempt the stair. Jane—follow us. I would not have you before, if we should stumble and fall."

The slow descent commenced. Inevitably my brother jostled his man, and Lord Harold groaned—but cut off the sound with a sharp clamping of teeth. It seemed an age before the ground floor of the Abbey was achieved. When I stood at last near my brother, with the body of Orlando huddled at the stair's foot, I saw that Lord Harold had fainted.

"His hand had slipped—the wad is somewhere on the floor. Pray find it, Jane—he is losing a deal of blood!"

I groped for the linen, and found to my horror that it was soaked through. Frank half-carried, half-dragged his lordship through the Abbey and laid him on the earth.

"Press the wad hard against the shoulder," he commanded, "and do not release it for anything. You must stem the flow of blood, Jane, or he's done for. I shall run for the gig—we shall never manage him so far as the woods."

He was gone before I had time to draw breath: and that swiftly I was left alone, in the shattered ruins of Netley, with the man I loved near dying. Careless of the blood, I sank down beside him and pressed both my hands against the sodden linen, muttering a desperate plea to any God that might still linger in that hallowed place.

FRANK WHIPPED THE HORSES INTO A FRENZY AND WE rattled downhill to the Lodge in a style Sophia Challoner might have approved. Few lights shone in the windows of the comfortable stone house; no torches burned in the courtyard. Was it possible that but a servant remained, and all the fires were doused? Hysteria rose in my breast. Without help, Lord Harold should surely die.

Frank drew up before the door, secured the reins, and sprang down from his seat. Never had I so admired the decision and authority of my brother, as now; I understood what he must be, striding his quarterdeck with a French frigate off the bow. Lord Harold rested insensible upon my lap; I could not move for the weight. Frank pounded at the door and cried *Halloo!* The noise roused the man in my arms, and he opened his eyes.

I could barely see his face through the darkness. "Lie still," I said. "Guard your strength. You will need it."

"Jane—" he whispered. "On the wall . . . Orlando. Not . . . the Jesuit—"

"I know. *Hush.*"

"The knife"—his fingers feebly sought his wound—"he killed that girl, and Dixon—"

The massive oak door swung open to reveal José Luis, the Portuguese steward, a candle raised in one hand.

Behind him stood Maria Fitzherbert.

"Thank God!" I cried out in relief.

"Your pardon, ma'am, for the imposition," my

brother said hurriedly—he had never, after all, made Mrs. Fitzherbert's acquaintance, and was not the sort to recognise a royal mistress—"but we have a wounded man in grave need of assistance."

"Lord Harold Trowbridge," I added urgently. "He requires a surgeon."

"Help his lordship into the house, Zé," Mrs. Fitzherbert ordered in her tranquil voice. "I shall see to the boiling water."

IN THE HOURS THAT FOLLOWED I ACQUIRED A FUND OF respect for Maria Fitzherbert. Despite the weakness she had lately shown at the prospect of a duel, tonight no horror or pain could disturb her, no sight of gore cause her to blanch. While Frank took a horse from the stables and flew like the wind to a surgeon in Hound, she saw his lordship laid on a sopha in the drawing-room, regardless of the blood, and tore open his shirt herself.

"This is very grave," she observed calmly. "Poor man—he is not as young as he was.... Miss Austen, there is a closet in the hall near the kitchen. You will find a quantity of linen stored there. Pray bring a dozen napkins, and commence tearing them into strips. We can do little until the blade is drawn."

I did as she bade, and fetched water from the steward. Lord Harold had fainted again in quitting the gig, but he stirred a little under Mrs. Fitzherbert's hands.

"This is not the first time, you understand, that I have ministered to a gentleman's wounds," she observed. "The Prince once affected to mortify himself, early in our acquaintance, when I was adamant against the connexion—he slashed himself with a letter knife, and I was summoned to his bedside at midnight by the news that he was dying. Not even the most determined of lovers should drive steel into bone, however. Who did this thing?"

"His valet. A man by the name of Orlando."

"Ah, yes—the murderer of that poor girl." She said this as though there had never been the slightest doubt; and I suppose, in being an intimate at the Lodge, she should hesitate to believe any of her friends the culprit. "James—Mr. Ord—told me how it was, at the inquest. The valet ran, I think?"

"His lordship has been grossly deceived. It is probable that Orlando has been in the service of the French—that he is responsible for violent actions among the dockyards—"

She raised one brow. "But I thought it was Sophia that Lord Harold suspected? She chuckled over the notion a good deal."

"Sophia was aware of his suspicion?"

"There is very little that escapes that lady's notice. She told me not long ago that the French had placed a cuckoo in Lord Harold's nest: the valet had better have hanged in Oporto. What has become of him?"

"We left him for dead, among the Abbey ruins."

Lord Harold's eyes flicked open at this, and he stared full into Maria Fitzherbert's face. "I tried, Maria . . . tried to prevent . . . Ord speaking . . ."

"Hush, Harry," she murmured.

"He is safe, now. *Portsmouth.* Forgive inquest . . . wronged you . . ."

She pressed her fingers against his lips, and shook her head. He passed once more into unconsciousness. His pallor was dreadful, and his limbs cold. A bubble of fear rose in my breast, and I bit my finger to thwart a sob.

"You love him very much, do you not?" she said. "A pity. He was always a desperate character. I have known him quite a long time, you see."

She wrung out a linen wad in a basin of hot water; it flushed a dangerous red.

"Desperate, perhaps—but honourable withal."

"Exactly so," she agreed calmly. "His lordship's voice was among the loudest that counseled the Prince to throw me off—he could not condone illegal marriage, and indeed, I could not condone it myself—but I never held his opinions against him. They could not prevent our being friends. Lord Harold is ever the gentleman in his address; mere politics could not turn him a cad."

Sophia Challoner should certainly have protested at this. I remembered how she had viewed him: as a man who employed a blackmailer for valet, and profited from the spoils. Certainly Orlando had penned the threatening letter for Flora Bastable—and had learned what he could of Sophia from the girl—but with *Lord Harold's knowledge*? Was it for this the Rogue begged forgiveness?

"Mrs. Fitzherbert—if Mrs. Challoner was not a spy, and her frankness with regard to her own affairs is everywhere celebrated—what possible cause could her maid find for blackmail?"

The Prince's wife sank back against her seat, and stared at me limpidly. "Did you believe it was Sophia she thought to touch, with that frippery tale of secrets? You may rest easy, my dear. The maid's object—and the valet's, if it comes to that—was always *me*."

A pounding at the front door forestalled what she might have said. It was Frank, with the surgeon.

• • •

We were banished from the room while they worked over him. As the door closed upon the scene, I caught a glimpse of the surgeon and his tool: an iron tong, akin to the sort used for pulling teeth, poised above the blade in Lord Harold's shoulder. Then I heard a gruff voice—"Hold him, now—hold him steady—" and the agonised groan of a man in mortal pain.

Mrs. Fitzherbert placed her arm about my shoulders and murmured, "Brandy, I think."

She drew me aside into the dining parlour, where a decanter stood upon a sideboard. "It is well you found the Lodge inhabited this evening. We intend to quit this place on the morrow."

I drank little of the liquid she gave me, and summoned what composure I could. My thoughts might fly to the man on the sopha, but my tongue could yet utter commonplaces. "Mrs. Challoner left for London in good spirits, I hope?"

"She stayed only for the receipt of the note you sent. The knowledge that James—Mr. Ord—was secure in his passage, was everything to her; and the Conte da Silva was equally happy to learn that Monsignor should achieve the Americas without further delay. We are all of us in your debt."

"My brother's, perhaps—but not mine." Guilt, powerful guilt, over the false pretences under which I had pursued Sophia Challoner's friendship surged again in my heart.

"Indeed, I may say that I only remained at Netley another night—extraordinary conduct, in the absence of the Lodge's mistress—to be certain that Mr. Ord was sped on his way."

It seemed, then, as the lady stood before the gilt mirror in Sophia Challoner's dining-room, that she desired to impart a confidence; but the drawing-room door burst open, and Frank reappeared.

"The wound is stitched, but continues seeping," he informed us brusquely; "the surgeon believes there is not much time."

"You mean—?" I set down my glass of brandy unsteadily. "But cannot we send for Dr. Jarvey? Or take him directly in the gig to East Street now?"

"No, Jane. He is too weak; if the wound does not kill him, movement will." Frank's gaze was merciless. "He is asking for you. *Both* of you."

I gazed at Maria Fitzherbert, but she declined to take precedence. I may say that I ran to him.

He was propped a little on a pillow, and his eyes—though heavy-lidded—were yet alert. A clean bandage stretched from collarbone to ribs; but a dark aureole of blood had already blossomed there. He held out his hand, and I seized it in my fingers. Maria Fitzherbert sank down in a chair.

"Maria," he said.

"Yes, Harry?"

"Your son is . . . safe . . . no word of the truth—"

"How long have you known?" she demanded quietly.

He shook his head. "Guessed. He has the look . . . of the Prince—twenty years ago . . ."

Twenty years ago, when Maria Fitzherbert had been happy at Kempshott Park. Understanding fell upon me like a dash of cold water.

She rose abruptly and walked away from us, to stand by the window seat where I had observed her working fringe—as placid, I had thought then, as a cow. What sacrifices this woman had endured! Two husbands and a son in the grave—all the scorching calumny of public comment over her liaison with the

Prince—the loss of reputation—and then the most painful ordeal: the royal child sent out into the world, there raised by virtual strangers.

"Remembered how you admired Archbishop Carroll," Lord Harold said wearily. "Found out that Ord's family emigrated on the same ship to the Americas that Carroll took. Your work of course. Understood then. Does Ord know?"

She shook her head.

He clutched at my fingers—a spasm, perhaps, for the touch relaxed almost instantly. *"Jane."*

"My lord."

He smiled faintly, a curving of the lips; but the face was so haggard, and beaded with sweat. "You cry, dear? Waste. Should've married you years ago."

I kissed his cold hand—my throat was too constricted for speech, and my heart beating wildly. "You must *try,* Lord Harold. You must rally!"

His grey eyes opened wide, and he gazed clearly at my face. "Promise me . . . you will *write.* Heroine—"

"What is writing compared to life, my lord?"

"All we have. Fool, Jane. *Fool.*"

"No, my love—"

But he was already gone.

Editor's Afterword

The present volume of Jane Austen's detective memoirs is distinct from the six manuscripts I have previously edited in that it concludes abruptly—without the sort of coda she often wrote, to assure her readers of the pleasant future in store for those whose lives she had followed. We know from her novels that Austen enjoyed happy endings; but one clearly eluded her here, as it so often did in matters of the heart.

The story that unfolds in *Jane and the Ghosts of Netley* is one that I find particularly absorbing, because I have long been a student of the illegal marriage between Maria Fitzherbert, Catholic commoner, and George, Prince of Wales (later George IV of England). In editing the present manuscript, Saul David's *Prince of Pleasure: The Prince of Wales and the Making of the Regency* (Great Britain: Little, Brown, 1998) was extremely helpful. David outlines the history of James Ord, Fitzherbert's putative son, and his rearing among the Catholic gentry of Maryland. Ord did become a member of the Jesuit order, and later confronted his friends with questions regarding his parentage that were only partially answered. Mrs. Fitzherbert, though she never publicly admitted her parentage of Ord, declined categorically to sign a document testifying that her marriage to the Prince had been without issue. She is believed to have borne the Prince a daughter as well, one Maryanne Smythe, who was passed off as a niece and eventually reared in Mrs. Fitzherbert's household.

For those interested in religious issues of the period, *Catholics in Britain and Ireland, 1558–1829,* by Michael A. Mullett (New York: St. Martin's Press, 1998), is instructive. For a history of the English and French in Portugal, I can recommend no finer work than Michael Glover's *The Peninsular War, 1807–1814* (London: David and Charles, 1974).

Stephanie Barron
Golden, Colorado
March 2002

About the Author

STEPHANIE BARRON, a lifelong admirer of Jane Austen's work, is the author of six previous Jane Austen mysteries. She lives in Colorado, where she is at work on the eighth Jane Austen mystery, *Jane and His Lordship's Legacy.*

If you enjoyed **Jane and the Ghosts of Netley**, you won't want to miss any of Stephanie Barron's tantalizing mysteries. Look for them at your favorite bookseller's.

And read on for an exciting early look at the next mystery featuring Jane Austen!

Jane and His Lordship's Legacy

Being a Jane Austen Mystery

by

Stephanie Barron

Chapter 1

All We Have

Tuesday, 4 July 1809
Chawton, Hampshire

~

I CAME INTO MY KINGDOM TODAY AT HALF-PAST three—or so much of one as shall ever be granted me on this earth. Four square brick walls, five chimneys, a simple doorway fronting on the Winchester road and a clutch of outbuildings behind: such is Chawton Cottage.

"Lord, Jane," my mother breathed as she surveyed the unadorned façade of her future abode from the vantage of our hired pony trap, "I should not call it *charming*, to be sure—but beggars cannot be choosers, you know, and we must admit ourselves infinitely obliged to your excellent brother. Observe, a new cesspit has been dug, and the privy painted! I declare, is nothing forgot that might contribute to our comfort?"

I did not reply, for though the raw mud near the new plumbing works looked dismal enough, my mother could not hesitate to approve the generosity Edward has shown. A man of considerable property, as the heir of our distant cousins the Knights, my brother chooses to reside at his principal estate of Godmersham, in Kent—but has given us the use of his late bailiff's cottage here in Hampshire. If a former alehouse, fronting the juncture of two highways overrun by coaching traffic, with rough-hewn beams, low-ceilinged rooms, and cramped stairs, may be considered a luxury, then we are bound to be grateful to Edward; he has saved four women the expence of lodgings, and for a household of strict economy and perpetual dependence, that cost must be a saving indeed.

There are some among our acquaintance who would hint that, in possessing the freehold of every house in Chawton village, my brother might have done more for his widowed mother, and done it years since; but I will not join my strictures to theirs.[1] My heart rises to smell the good earth again, and rejoices to think that my mornings will never more be shattered by the bustle of a town, and all the noise of commerce crying at the gate! There is nothing, when one is broken-hearted, like the healing balm of the country!

[1] The manor of Chawton, which included the Great House and the whole of the village, was deeded to Jane's third brother Edward in 1797 as part of his inheritance from distant cousins, Mr. and Mrs. Thomas Knight of Kent, a childless couple who adopted Edward as their heir. Edward enjoyed the freehold of more than thirty cottages and gardens in Chawton, as well as the Great House, farm, and Chawton Park. The entire estate, including the village holdings, was gradually sold off in the twentieth century by Knight family heirs.—*Editor's note.*

"I shall plant potatoes," my mother declared briskly, "and if we are fortunate, we shall gather them by late September. The cottage's aspect might be softened, Jane. It requires only a flowering vine, I think, to grow romantickly across the door."

"—and to complete the picturesque, ought to be sagging in its casements. It is too much to hope for a shattered roof or a tower crumbling into ruin; we must contrive to be satisfied with a building that is only ample, sturdy, and in good repair, Mamma."

The house's position at the fork of Chawton's two principal roads *must* be adjudged an evil—but outweighing this are the broad meadows to north and east, the stout wood fence and hornbeam hedge enclosing the grounds, and the delightful promise of birdsong from the thriving fields. Mr. Seward, the late bailiff, maintained a shrubbery and an orchard, but Mrs. Seward cannot have loved her flowers; the borders must and shall be worked. Syringas, and peonies, and the simpler blooms of mignonette—all these we shall have, and Sweet William too.

While the carter jumped down to secure his horse, I studied the distant view of the privy and banished the idea of a water closet, recently installed in brother Henry's London house; such ostentation has no place in a country village. It is not for *Jane* to repine. I had found no love or joy in the habitation of cities—I had rather witnessed, in first Bath and then Southampton, the gradual erosion of nearly every cherished dream I held in life. It was time I made a trial of rural delights; it was they that had formed my earliest vision of happiness.

"The man will want something for his pains," my mother urged in an audible hiss as the carter helped her to descend. "See that he shifts the baggage before he deserts us entirely. And do not go spoiling him with Edward's coin! I am gone to inspect the privy."

She moved slowly in the direction of my brother's improvements, her gait marked by the stiffness of rheumatism. I stepped down to the rutted surface of the road and prepared to be—content.

WE HAD SET OUT FROM CASTLE SQUARE IN APRIL, bidding farewell forever to the glare and stink of a town. We made for Godmersham, where we tarried nearly two months in the pleasant Kentish spring, tho' the place and all who live in it are remarkably changed from what they once were. Elizabeth is dead now nearly a year and my sister Cassandra resident in the household, supplying the want of a mother; she is careworn but steady in her attachment to the little children, and a prop to Fanny, who at the tender age of fifteen must now fill Eliza's place. Tho' the chuckling of the Stour was as sweet as I remembered, and the temple on the hill beckoned with serenity, I could not stomach the climb to its heights, nor rest an interval between its columns. In happier times I had sat in that very place with my brother's wife beside me—and once, looked up from my pen to find the tall figure of a silver-haired man climbing the grassy slope—

Edward has not yet learned to endure Eliza's passing. Indeed, he has come to see in it a deliberate blow of Divine Judgment: that having loved his wife too well, and delighting in the gift of every luxury and indulgence her fair form desired, he incurred the wrath of Providence—Who despised Edward's attachment to things of this world so much, that He tore from my brother's bosom the one creature he cherished most.

"Were it not for the children," Neddy said bitterly as we sat together before a dying grate in the stillness of Eliza's drawing room, "I should have gone into the grave with her, Jane. I should not have hesitated at self-murder."

"—Tho' the very act should damn you to Hell?"

"It is Hell I endure at present."

I could not assure him that I understood too well his sentiments; could not add my misery to his own, as he sat glaring at the waste of all that constituted his happiness. Edward knew nothing of the Gentleman Rogue, beyond a passing acquaintance with one who had called briefly at Godmersham several years before, and had long since been forgot. I could not explain that I, too, must submit to all the agony of bereavement—with the added burden of suffering in silence. Never having been Lord Harold Trowbridge's acknowledged love, I must be obscured and forgot in the world he deserted so abruptly last November.

As I studied my brother's countenance—grave, where it had once been gay; worn, where it had formerly appeared the portrait of inveterate youth—I concluded that there was at least this relief in public grief: one was not forced to shield the feelings of others. The Bereaved might be all that is selfish in their parade of unhappiness. Whereas I was continually chafing under the daily proofs of inconsideration, imperviousness, high animal spirits and insensibility that surrounded me, when every hope of happiness for myself was at an end.

When the Rogue expired of a knife wound on the fifth of November, some ten months ago, it was as though a black pit opened at my feet and I trembled on the brink of it for some days together without being conscious of what I said or did. I know from others that the body was fetched back to London in the Duke of Wilborough's carriage; that Wilborough House, so lately draped in black for the passing of the Rogue's mother, remained in crepe for this second son; that nearly five hundred men followed the cortege first to the Abbey church at Westminster and then, on horseback, to the interment in the Wilborough tomb. It was said that no less than seven ladies of Fashion fainted dead away at the awful news, and three fell into decline. All this my mother read aloud from the London papers, offering comment and opinion of her own.

> *Murdered by his manservant, so they say, a foreigner his lordship took up with on the Peninsula. I'll wager that fellow knew a thing or two of Lord Harold's unsavoury affairs! It is a nasty end, Jane, but no more than he deserved. I always said he was a most unsuitable tendre for a young lady such as yourself, and quite elderly into the bargain; but nobody listens to me, I am always overruled. Still, it is a pity you did not get him when you could—you might have been the Relict of a lord! And now all his riches will go to Wilborough's son—who will find no very good use for them, I'll wager. A rakehell and a gamester, so they say. The Heir has taken a page from his uncle's book, and will undoubtedly prove as disreputable a character. We must impute it to Her Grace's French blood, and habits of parading onstage . . .*

Four days after the murder I took up my pen to compose a few paragraphs of explanation and regret that ought to have been dispatched without delay to his lordship's niece, Desdemona, Countess of Swithin. That lady, despite her lofty position in Society and the cares attendant upon her duties as a mother, has been narrowly concerned—as much as woman could be—in Lord Harold's affairs, and loved him more dearly, I suspect, than her own father. It seemed imperative that the Countess be in full possession of the facts of his lordship's death—of the bravery with which he embraced it, and his determination not to submit to a form of treachery that might imperil His Majesty's government—so that no scandalous falsehood put about by his enemies among the *ton* should shake her faith in his worth. From what I knew of Desdemona, I doubted that anything could.

Her answer was brief, correct and exceedingly cold. I knew not whether she regarded my letter of commiseration in the light of an impertinence; or whether she charged me with having precipitated her uncle's death. Perhaps she merely judged his attentions to a woman so clearly beneath his touch as deplorable. I cannot say. But her ladyship's brevity cut me to the quick. I have had nothing from her since.

Only Martha Lloyd, who in Cassandra's absence has become as dear as a sister to me, understood a little of the pain I suffered. Tho' she referred to my grief as a chronic indisposition, she was quick to order me to bed, and leave me in silence with a pot of tea during the long gray winter afternoons. My brother Frank, who had witnessed the Rogue's death in company with myself, was a considerable comfort. Tho' he no longer shared our lodgings, his occasional visits afforded the opportunity to unbend—to speak openly of what we both knew and mourned in his lordship's passing. Even in Frank's silence I felt sympathy, and in his accounts of his naval activities—he oversaw the landing in January of the remnant of Sir John Moore's Peninsular army, a tattered band of harried soldiers deprived too soon of the leadership of that extraordinary man—I felt some connexion to the greater world Lord Harold had known and ruled. We are forced to go on living, however little we relish the interminable days.

In April, Frank quitted home waters for the China Station and we devoted ourselves to the activity of household removal. My mother's querulous demands and persistent anxieties regarding the packing provided diversion enough; so, too, did the necessary farewells to naval acquaintance, the last visits to the little theatre in French Street, and a final Assembly endured at the Dolphin Inn. I even danced on that occasion with a black-eyed foreign gentleman too shy to enquire my name. But I had no joy in any of these things. The coming of spring mocked me with a promise of life I no longer shared. At the moment of our descent upon Edward's house in Kent, I had determined I should never feel hopeful again.

There is no remedy for the loss inflicted by death except remembrance. And so I tried to recollect what his lordship's dying words had been.

Promise me . . . you will write . . .
What is writing compared to life, my lord?
All we have, Jane.

He was wont to speak the truth, no matter how harsh its effect. It was one of the qualities for which I esteemed him: his unblinking gaze at the brutality of existence. But I could not keep my promise. What are words and paragraphs in comparison of what might have been? A cold solace when love is forever denied. I had written nothing in the long months that followed his headlong flight from this world but stilted letters to Cassandra, remarkable for their brittleness of tone and the forced lightness of their jokes.

Now, as I stood in the dusky heat of a Hampshire July, lark song rising about me, I felt the first faint stirrings of life. Feeble, yes—and a hairsbreadth from guttering out; but stirrings all the same. I unknotted my bonnet strings and bared my head to the sun. Lord Harold's gaze—that earnest, steadfast look—wavered before my eyes; I blinked it away. *Perhaps here,* I thought, as I opened the door of the cottage and stepped inside its whitewashed walls, *perhaps here I might begin again.*